After a successful career in advertising, working as a media buyer, Rod Reynolds took City University's two-year MA in crime writing, where he started *The Dark Inside*, his first Charlie Yates mystery. This was followed by the second book in the series, *Black Night Falling*, in 2016. He lives in London with his wife and two daughters.

Follow Rod @Rod_WR

Further praise for *Cold Desert Sky*:

'[Reynolds] has created another exquisitely authentic masterpiece, his 1940s America coming alive with its richly drawn setting, terse and believable dialogue, and powerful characterization, and it draws on the best elements of American noir . . . A first-class, evocative thriller . . . This is page-turning, highly engaging entertainment . . . If you haven't read Rod Reynolds yet, you are missing some of the best crime fiction you may ever read. Simply outstanding.' *Orenda Books*

'An evocative tale full of mid-twentieth-century American hard-boiled traditions – terse dialogue, violent gangsters, a near self-destructive hero . . . The involvement and influence of Lizzie are fascinating counterpoints to a masculine era. Reynolds scratches at the US underbelly, skewers glitz and fantasy.' *New Zealand Listen*

'A solid chunk of American   i-
tions . . . This i   e,

cool banter and a lone wolf investigator, washed up, on the edge and looking for redemption. All the glitz and the glamour, the clean, shiny surfaces of the post-war era, are just a veneer for masking the grime; this is the underbelly of the American dream ... Reynolds is pitch-perfect on place and time.' *Nudge Books*

'A thing of beauty ... an extraordinarily compelling, genuinely absorbing and totally immersive piece of storytelling that will stay with you long after you turn the final page ... Excellent.' *Liz Loves Books*

'Reynolds is a master at creating authentic crime fiction steeped in American noir ... His descriptions are evocative and atmospheric, his dialogue sharp and spot on ... A fast-paced read.' *Off The Shelf*

'One top-class novel. It has everything you need from a gangster-themed thriller ... Gritty writing, kick-ass dialogue, and scene-setting so authentic you can smell the cheap aftershave and the stench of the cigarettes as you move from one dodgy bar to the next ... It's cinematic in scope ... and purely golden entertainment.' *Book Trail*

'Beautiful ... There is such fluidity to Rod Reynolds' style.' Joy Kluver

'Since his debut novel, *The Dark Inside*, Rod Reynolds has emerged as one of the UK's most talented new crime authors ... If you're a fan of James Ellroy, this one would be worth checking out.' *Crime Fiction Lover*

Cold Desert Sky

ROD REYNOLDS

FABER & FABER

First published in 2018
by Faber & Faber Limited
Bloomsbury House
74–77 Great Russell Street
London WC1B 3DA
This paperback edition first published in 2019

Printed and bound by CPI Group (UK) Ltd, Croydon, CR0 4YY

A CIP record for this book
is available from the British Library

ISBN 978-0-571-33472-8

2 4 6 8 10 9 7 5 3 1

For Dawn and Michelle

CHAPTER ONE

No one wanted to say it to me, that the girls were dead. But I knew.

Maybe the desperation showed on my face. No one wants to disappoint a zealot when he's coming at you, demanding answers and looking for a sign that his search isn't futile. The ninth day since they went missing, and every street rat and lowlife I could collar told me just enough to get me off their back: *no clue/they probably split town/I'll ask around*. Walked out thinking they'd soaped me and that I didn't know how this would end, the same as ever – two broken bodies in a funeral home or some godforsaken alley in this bullshit City of Angels.

Sunlight came at me between two buildings; late afternoon, already low in the sky – winter's touch on an otherwise bright day. I bought a newspaper from a vendor, leaned against the wall and pretended to skim the headlines, front and back. I'd already been through it for real that morning, found no mention of them. Now it was just cover to scope the diner across the street. The joint was a corner dive on North La Brea, name of Wilt's, nothing going for it save for the pretty broad dressed in Mexican getup out front, peddling the brisket special and looking like she'd sooner be someplace else.

Most everything I'd done so far was conducted in the hours of darkness; this was the first daylight meet I'd risked. Not my choice, but short notice was Whitey's condition when we'd arranged it that morning. Whitey Lufkins – a lifetime losing gambler who stemmed his losses turning snitch for anyone with enough green. I knew him from my stint at the *LA Times* when he was a bottom-rung stop for every legman looking for street talk. Now that same street talk held that he was in over his head with his bookmaker – and his readiness to meet suggested it was true. He didn't know it'd be me on the other side of the table, though; caution came first. Whitey thought he was seeing a private dick on the missing girls' trail; I had to ask Lizzie to make the calls to set it up, and she played the dispassionate secretary without much call for pretence.

I was early but I spotted Whitey through the window, already inside. I stayed where I was, waiting and watching, looking for anything out of place. It was automatic now, had been since we returned to LA three weeks before.

I'd felt it as soon as we set foot back in the county, and Lizzie the same. It'd taken less than a day to confirm that Bugsy Siegel was searching for us. Buck Acheson, my editor at the *Pacific Journal*, was the one to break the news; a rushed call from a payphone on Wilshire the day we got back, Buck saying he'd picked up on it a week before, while Lizzie and I were still upstate. His voice, his words – he played it all as low key as he could in the circumstance, but his sign off was resounding: '*I'm pleased you're back and your job's still yours if you want it, but Charlie, it's best if you stay away from the offices for now.*' Buck wasn't one to worry for himself, so the meaning was clear: don't make it easy for him to find me.

The city that used to be mine, and now I couldn't move for looking over my shoulder.

I let five minutes go by. Whitey fidgeted with his cup and checked his watch twice. Two men left the diner but no one else went in. About half the tables were occupied, more seated along the counter. No one that worried me on first glance, but who the hell knew any more? After Hot Springs. After Texarkana—

Whitey checked his watch again, looked ready to bail. I cracked my knuckles and crossed the street, went inside. He was facing the door, saw me as soon as I did. He had a pallor about him, where the name came from, but worse than I remembered and accentuated now by pockmarks on his cheeks. He made to get up then stopped himself halfway, caught in two minds. I slid in opposite him.

'Charlie?'

'Have a seat.'

He glanced around as if looking for his real guest, then slid down the backrest, realisation dawning. 'You a gumshoe now, or am I a mark?'

'How've you been, Whitey?'

'Better than you, what I hear.'

I sat back, a glance over his shoulder, wrong-footed by the remark. 'And what's that?'

'You don't need me to tell you. It's on your face.'

'Make like I'm dumb.'

'You must be. Being in town when he's looking for you.'

I shrugged. 'I'm not a hard man to find.'

'You ought to reconsider that.'

I traced a line across the table. 'I didn't come here to talk about Bugsy Siegel.'

3

'No?' He showed real surprise. 'Hard to believe you got bigger troubles.'

'How's your luck with the horses?'

He set his cup down on the Formica. 'Some days are better than others.'

I took my money clip out – two tens and a twenty wrapped around a wad of ones to pad the roll. 'I'm looking for information on a couple women. Hollywood-dreamer types.'

He made a point of not looking at the cash, a stool pigeon in a fraying suit clinging to the remnants of his pride. 'I don't know Hollywood from dirt.'

'They were fresh off the bus. They were living in a boarding house in Leimert Park. Nancy Hill and Julie Desjardins.'

He half-smiled. 'Julie Desjardins from Kansas – sure. Real names?'

'I don't know.'

'These are the missing dames your woman called me about?'

I nodded. 'They've been gone more than a week.'

'Were they turning tricks?'

My arms tensed.

'What?' he said. 'How else would I hear anything about a couple starlets?'

I closed my eyes and flattened my free hand on the table again. The question was a fair one. 'The names mean anything to you or not?'

'Not. But you must've figured that, so my guess is you want me to ask around.'

I peeled a ten off.

He shook his head, held up two fingers. I breathed out through my nose and peeled the other one off.

4

He rolled them tight and pocketed them. 'What are they to you anyway?'

It was Lizzie's question to me, word for word. I gave him the easy answer. 'It's for a story.'

'Still working that side of the street. On whose dime?'

I didn't like the question and on reflex I checked the window. A Packard with blue trim cruised by. The vendor across the way hawked his papers. Nothing to see. Whitey picked up on it.

'Would you quit it?' He was snapping his fingers to get my attention back. 'Harder to come by a paycheck these days is all; one of you's got green to spend, I want to know who else does.' He pocketed my money. 'You have photographs of them?'

I shook my head, not sure what made me lie. Something about wanting to protect innocents from the likes of him. If that's what they were.

'How do you know they didn't just pack up for home?' he said.

'You ever hear of any that did?'

He stuck his bottom lip out, thinking. 'Give me something to go on at least.'

I drummed the tabletop absently, weighing what to share. 'December third was the last time their landlady saw them. Alice told her they were—'

'Who's Alice?'

I looked away. My wife's murdered sister; one of the trio of dead that seldom left my thoughts. Blood on my conscience. 'Nancy. Slip of the tongue.'

He kept staring at me, his face a question, but I ignored it. It irritated me that Alice's name meant nothing to him – even knowing there was no reason it should.

'Nancy told their landlady they were headed for an audition at TPK Studios. They never made it. I can't find any trace of them since.' Not the full story, but enough for him.

He thought for a moment. 'They owe the landlady?'

'Two weeks' worth.'

He nodded along as I said it. 'Sounds to me like they didn't get the gig and they ran out on the rent.'

I opened my hands. 'Maybe. Doesn't mean they left the city, though. I'd still like to know.' It came off weak even as I said it, such optimism long since dissipated.

He pushed his cup aside. 'I'll see what I can do. How do I contact you?'

'You'll hear from me.'

He stood up and straightened his jacket, taking his time and surveying the diner and the people along the counter. Then he looked down at me, setting his finger on the table. 'You're right to be scared, you know.' He tapped it as he spoke. 'Do yourself a solid and don't be calling him Bugsy no more. He favours Benjamin.'

As he walked away, a sick feeling came over me. It was the way he said it, the regret in his voice. The question about who I was working for suddenly haunted me; it'd spiked me because I was worried he was looking for dirt on me to sell. It came to me the other way now, exactly as he'd said it: he wanted to know who else he could tap for coin – if I wasn't around.

A black coupe pulled up outside – slow, as if it'd been waiting nearby. On the street, Whitey glanced at it and kept walking, head down, and I realised for sure what was happening. I closed my eyes and damned myself, wished it all away, couldn't figure how I'd slipped up. I looked again and saw two heavies climb out, one I recognised as a Gilardino brother, long-time Siegel foot soldiers.

I ran to the payphone on the wall, shoved a dime in and dialled Buck Acheson's number.

The other hood waited on the kerb while Gilardino came through the door, drawing sideways looks from the counter staff, eyes to the floor when they recognised him. He started towards me.

Acheson answered. 'Buck – get hold of Lizzie, tell her to run right now.'

'Charlie? What's . . .' He cottoned. 'Hell, he's found you—'

CHAPTER TWO

I rode in the back, Gilardino next to me, the other man taking the wheel. Neither had showed a weapon, but they didn't need to – they wouldn't be on the street without one. I squeezed my right hand in my left and tried to keep my breathing steady. I pictured Lizzie at the motel now, someone from the manager's office fetching her for Acheson's call, her grabbing the bags and disappearing.

'Where're we going?'

The driver ignored me and flicked the radio on. We travelled north until we came to Sunset, made a left onto Hollywood Boulevard and kept going, passing the colonial-style mansions and Angelo's Liquor, palm trees overhead. At the Bank of America billboard, heavy traffic reduced our speed to a crawl, spooling out the tension in my guts; the music on the radio sounded so loud and so raw it seemed to come from inside my head.

Eventually we turned onto a side street and came to a stop outside the rear of a property that must have fronted the Boulevard. Gilardino climbed out and beckoned me. The driver hit the horn and after a few seconds, the back door of the place opened, a man I couldn't make out standing in the shadows. The driver stayed behind the wheel, eyeing me in the rearview.

I stepped out of the car and looked around, bad flutters in

8

my chest. It was a hundred yards back to the main street. Gilardino must have read my thoughts because he put a hand on my shoulder, making me flinch. He steered me towards the doorway.

The man inside pointed with his thumb. 'Go inside, Yates.' His accent was from New York – sounded like Queens or Brooklyn.

As I came closer, I could make out his face – Moe Rosenberg. Siegel's right-hand man.

I stopped dead, scuffing loose concrete underfoot. I couldn't tear my eyes away from his face, a thundering sound in my ears, everything rushing towards me even as I froze.

Gilardino pushed me from behind and I started moving again, stilted movements made on reflex. I could hear my own voice screaming in my ears, telling me to run, to do anything to sidestep this, that if I went through the door I was dead and so was Lizzie.

'I didn't kill William Tindall.' Siegel's representative in Hot Springs; it was all I could think to say, knowing they were wasted words.

Rosenberg nodded. 'I know. We'll talk about it inside.'

I heard the car take off behind me. Gilardino hustled me through the doorway and I stepped into the darkness and hesitated while my eyes adjusted. I looked at Rosenberg – thin hair on top, just a few strands combed back over his pate; sunken eyes, a roll of skin creeping over his shirt collar.

We were in a short corridor, a naked bulb overhead giving off little light. Rosenberg walked in front, to what looked like the door to a meat locker. He rapped on it; there was the sound of a heavy bolt sliding and then it opened. I could smell cigar smoke waft out. Rosenberg went in and I followed, Gilardino backstopping me. Nowhere to run.

As I stepped over the threshold, someone smashed their fist into my stomach.

Someone pulled my hair to straighten me up. Now I saw Bugsy Siegel to my right, just as he punched me again, harder, driving the air out of me. I tried to cover up, but they took my arms.

He laid his shots in – right, left, right, left. Siegel was a blur, clenched teeth, his necktie flying wildly.

He hit me one more time. They let go of my arms and I fell to my knees, spluttering spit and bile. He kicked me prone and kicked me in the side, then stood back, panting.

I lay still, the tiled floor cold against my cheek, clutching my stomach and gasping for air.

Rosenberg said something I didn't catch to the others.

Someone pulled me up and pushed me against the wall. Gilardino. The other two stood in front of me. Rosenberg had a cigar in his hand now and I focused on the tip, glowing orange in the murk.

Siegel pointed his finger in my face, still breathing hard. 'The trouble you've caused me.'

He slapped me, a heavy ring breaking the skin on my cheek. I lurched sideways and had to brace myself on a table. He stepped away, shaking his hand like he'd hurt his wrist. Pain ran up and down my abdomen from his blows; I steeled myself for more and swore to myself that I'd buy Lizzie as much time as possible to get away.

'Sit him down.'

Gilardino dragged a wooden chair against the wall and I

lowered myself onto it. I eased my head back against the bricks, still trying to get some air into my lungs.

Siegel threw a glass of water over my face. 'I want you listening.'

It ran down my throat and neck and onto my collar. I drew my sleeve over my eyes and looked at Siegel. He was wearing a black-and-white checked jacket over a white shirt and patterned necktie. He had hooded eyes and his hair was pomaded back but with strands out of place over his forehead now.

'Hot Springs is worth a mil-nine per annum to my organisation,' Siegel said. 'Bill Tindall had that place ticking over more than a decade.'

'I didn't kill him.'

'You said that already. It don't excuse it.'

I touched my cheek, felt the laceration. The room was cramped and had no windows. There were three small restaurant tables pressed together along the length of the left-hand wall, a heavy ashtray and an open bottle of wine on one. There was another door opposite, closed. 'What do you want?' I said.

'I want you nailed to a fucking tree with your throat cut.'

Just try to breathe. 'It was Teddy Coughlin sold Tindall out. He was working against him. Against you—'

'That cocksucker is not your concern.'

A bargain I'd made with Coughlin, not to rat him if he left us in peace – up in smoke as easy as that. To no avail.

Rosenberg drew on his cigar. Siegel went to one of the tables and took up a half-filled wine glass. He watched me over the rim as he took a gulp. The room was silent while he did, then he put it down, rushed over and gripped my face, pushed it to the side and against the wall, his finger in my eye. 'Don't you eyeball me, Yates. I can't stand the fucking sight of you.'

He pressed harder, leaning his weight in, my neck feeling it was about to snap, his finger against my teeth. I let out a cry of pain.

He broke off and looked at Gilardino. 'Kill him.'

Gilardino pulled a pistol and put it to my head. I flinched away—

No gunshot came.

I opened my eyes, Gilardino still standing there, the barrel an inch from my skull.

Siegel waved him off and put his hand in his pocket. 'You remember how you feel right now.' He stared at me from under those heavy lids, head tilted forward, his mouth ajar. 'That's how far you are from dying here on out. No matter where you are, you ain't more than a second from a bullet. My say-so.'

I righted myself slowly in the chair and stretched my neck. Through the frenzy in my mind, I realised he was saying he wasn't going to kill me then.

He shook his head in disgust and turned to Rosenberg. 'I'm gonna choke him myself, I gotta stand here any more. Lay it out, then turf him.' He looked at me. 'I have to bring you back to this room again, you won't see out the minute, you understand?'

Before I could find my voice, Gilardino slid the bolt and opened the door and Siegel breezed. When the door slammed shut again, it felt like I took my first breath in minutes.

Rosenberg set his cigar down in the ashtray and filled a wine glass with water. He stepped over and handed it to me, Gilardino looming next to me.

'Ben's given to theatrics but don't let that fool you,' Rosenberg said. 'He won't hesitate, you give him reason.'

I set the water on the floor, a rattle as it touched the tiles – tremors in my hands still. 'You've made your point. What do you want?'

He paused over the ashtray. 'Don't sass mouth me. Don't get brave on account of Ben leaving.'

I broke his stare, sickened that he'd called my number so easily.

He opened an envelope I hadn't noticed on the table and took out a large photograph, held it up. It was a headshot of a young man, smiling at something in the middle distance off camera – a professional job. He had slicked hair, trimmed short, with strong features and a cleft chin. This town, a shot like that, had to be an actor. He passed it to me. 'You know him?'

I shook my head, looking at it. Rumours of Siegel's involvement with the studios were well known – off-ledger financing at last resort rates, sway over labour contracts, muscle for strong-arming the unions. None of it proven, all of it likely.

'His name's Trent Bayless. His working name, anyway. He's been in pictures for Universal and Jack Warner – strictly B-stuff so far, topped out as third-lead, but he's got the goods to move up.'

I looked up from the photo, waiting for the payoff.

'He's also a queer with a bent for muscle-boys and a lax attitude to privacy.'

An extortion racket, Bayless the target. I couldn't see my part yet, but it was likely the only reason I was still alive. 'What's this got to do with me?'

'Which outfit you work for now?'

'I don't.'

Gilardino shot him a look and straightaway I knew the lie was a mistake.

Rosenberg cast his eyes down and passed his hand over his mouth. 'Which outfit?'

But I didn't need the full picture to realise he needed me, and the thought buoyed me. The pain eased off just a little. 'Blackmail – that's what this is?'

'This is you working off what you owe.'

Which outfit? – I got hip to his question. 'You want me to be your mouthpiece.' I shook my head. 'You've got the wrong man. My newspaper will never run a smear story.'

'Then you better convince him to pay.'

I stared at him, not understanding.

'This is your gig,' he said. 'You talk to him, explain what needs to get done.'

I focused on his face, squinting in the gloom. 'You want me to front your shakedown racket?'

'Ben wants ten grand from Bayless, by Wednesday. Otherwise you run the story.'

'That's three days.'

He reached into the envelope and stopped. 'You want I show you the pictures we got? He'll pay in three hours.'

I shook my head, disgusted that I'd already slipped into negotiating for more time, as though it were any other goddamn deadline.

He held it up. 'Copies are in here, same with his address. We want him to pay, so lean on him hard. Don't swoon for any sob stories – he's got a sugar daddy in the county that keeps him in champagne, so he can raise the gelt.' He dropped it in my lap. 'But if he won't pay, you write the story. You make it good and you make it stick.'

There was a note of urgency in the way he said it that

seemed out of place. But already my thoughts had run ahead, to the only way this could wind up for me. 'And then what?'

'It's barely started yet, concentrate on the job at hand.'

'There are more, though. To follow, I mean.'

He held out his cigar, as if thinking whether to answer, then let go of the breath he was holding. 'We wouldn't go to this trouble just for ten grand, no.'

Confirmed what I thought: a pawn at their disposal. Dead when they were through with me. Three days to get out from under it.

He motioned for me to get up, Gilardino at my arm. 'We're through. Vincent'll see you out. Come back here at midday on Wednesday and bring good news. Do I have to spell out what happens if you screw around?'

'No.'

'Then all I'll say is if you fuck this up, won't be just you sees a bullet – but it'll be you goes last.'

CHAPTER THREE

Lizzie cracked the motel room door when I knocked. When she saw it was me, she threw it wide and wrapped her arms around my neck. I gathered her close and held her. She started to sob gently. After a moment, she said, 'We can't go on living this way.'

It'd taken four hours to get to her after Rosenberg let me go. We'd put the escape plan in place the day Acheson told me about Siegel – telling ourselves we'd never have to use it. No more pretending that we could get on with our lives as normal. There wasn't much to it – as soon as Lizzie got a call to run, she was to find a new motel, take a room and then call her cousin in Phoenix, telling her alone where she was. The thinking being if no one in LA knew her whereabouts, then Siegel couldn't squeeze me or anyone else to get to her.

Gilardino had manhandled me back out the same way he brought me in and tossed me into the parking lot. Still trembling, I'd followed the street up to Hollywood Boulevard, circling around the block until I came to the front of the property. Turned out to be an Italian joint name of Ciglio's; it was a known mobster haunt, I should have figured it sooner.

From there I'd taken three different cabs across the city, making sure they weren't following me. It wouldn't have made sense after the scam they'd laid out, but my fear of leading them to Lizzie overruled logic. Only when dusk fell and I was certain I had no tail had I made the call, finally making it to Lizzie's motel in Inglewood after nine.

Lizzie broke the embrace first. 'Was it Siegel?'

I nodded and she sat down on the bed, her face in her hands. I dropped Rosenberg's envelope on the table and took a seat next to her, put my arm around her waist. I took the room in – off-white walls, hard-wearing carpet, swirls of colour to hide the stains. A window looked out over the street, the hulking North American Aviation plant looming in the distance. The two bags we lived out of were set on the patched-up sofa, and the folder I was looking for, the one holding my notes on the disappearances, was there too.

She dropped her hands and looked at me. 'I've been going out of my mind. What happened?'

'The man I went to meet ratted me out.'

She held my gaze, waiting for me to continue. I told her all of it, ending up with the blackmail racket on Trent Bayless. By the end she was shaking.

'This is madness, Charlie. I can't— We can't go on like this.' She stood up and walked halfway to the window. 'What are we supposed to do?'

I pushed my hair off my forehead. 'I don't know yet. My only thought was to get to you.'

'I could wring that man's neck. If he were here right now . . . My god, I never thought I could speak that way and mean it.'

'I need to pay a visit to this Bayless. Try to warn him off.'

She looked uncertain. 'What about the police? Are you sure we shouldn't involve them?'

'We settled this, I thought? Siegel owns the cops. Besides,

what could I say? As far as it looks to the law, as of right now, I'm the shakedown artist.'

She put her hands on her hips. 'What if we were to leave?'

I glanced at my folder of notes on the sofa, not meaning to, but my first thought in response. 'We can't.'

She'd seen me look and she traced the line of my gaze to where the folder lay. 'Why not?' Daring me to say it.

'I can't give up on them.'

'It's been over a week and you've got no leads, Charlie. What more is there to do?'

'Those girls didn't just vanish.'

'No. They either left the city, or—' She stopped herself, not wanting to say what we both already knew.

She came over to me and put her hand on my cheek, probing the cut there gingerly. 'You can't change the past.' It was trite and she knew as much, closing her eyes, frustrated at not finding the words. 'If wishing could make it so, I've done enough of that for both of us. You can't hold yourself to blame.'

'That's not why I'm doing this.' I looked up at her.

'You're only fooling yourself if you believe that.'

I took her hand from my face and held it, the conversation a retread of one we'd had a dozen times already, nothing new to be said and yet a resolution more urgent now. After a moment she slipped her fingers from mine and pointed to the envelope on the table. 'What's that? Photographs?'

'Yes.'

She shook her head, disgusted. 'Such cowards. To not even do their own dirty work.'

I took the envelope before she could pick it up, as if letting her touch it was to taint her. I opened the top and looked inside for Bayless' address. As I thumbed the contents, I couldn't help but glimpse the grainy black-and-white shots inside and it made me feel complicit. There was a piece of paper folded over at the bottom; I fished it out and saw that it was what I was looking for – an address near Echo Park. I looked at my watch.

'Do you think you should see a doctor?' she said.

I shook my head. 'They just worked me over. I'll be fine.'

'Have you eaten?'

'I'm not hungry.'

I stood up and opened our bags, looking for a clean set of clothes.

'What are you doing?' she said.

'I need to fetch the car from where I left it this afternoon.'

'Now?' She looked at the slip of paper in my hand, recognised it for an address. 'Please don't say you're thinking of going to see this man now.'

'They gave me three days, is all.'

She fell silent but I recognised the expression, knew she had more to say.

'Speak your mind,' I said.

She opened her mouth and closed it again. Then she said, 'If your mind's made up then you should go, there's no sense drawing this out. But I want to come with you.'

I stopped what I was doing and looked up from the bag. 'Come with me? Out of the question.'

'I can't sit here on my own again wondering. Please. I'm safer with you, and you could use my help.'

I took a shirt out of the bag and made for the bathroom to clean up.

'I can help you soften the blow,' she called after me. 'Think about the message you're going there to deliver; it's like you said earlier, he could think you're the one threatening him.'

Lizzie came to the doorway.

I ran the faucet and splashed water on my face. 'I can live with him thinking I'm against him. I can't live with you being in danger.'

'Tell me where I'm not in danger now.'

'Right here.' I dabbed my face, leaving a watery bloodstain on the threadbare towel. 'Tonight you're safe here. I'll be back before you know it.'

She looked at me in the mirror. 'Every time you walk out that door, I wonder if I'll see you again. This is killing me. Do you know what I was doing earlier when Mr Acheson called?'

I held her gaze in the reflection.

'I was writing down addresses for all the hospitals in the city – to carry with me. So I'd have somewhere to look for you if we got separated and I got the call to run. That's how I spend my days now.'

I turned around and took her face in my hands and touched my forehead to hers. 'I'm sorry.'

'I'm not saying you're at fault.'

'Close the curtains, lock the door. I'll be back in a couple hours.'

'And then?'

I kissed her on the lips. 'We'll figure this out for good.'

CHAPTER FOUR

Trent Bayless' address was a two-storey Victorian at the top of a low hill in Angelino Heights, just east of Echo Park Lake. The timbers of the lower half of the house were stained a dark green, the upper storey clad in matching shingles. A single gangly palm rose from behind the house, painted silver by the moonlight.

There were lights on in the upper rooms, shrouded by drapes. I sat outside for a time before I went to his door, brooding over what I would say. There was a temptation, small as it was, to tell him to pay. I felt bad for the kid, but his problems were his own. Except that they weren't, they were wrapped up in mine now; and if I helped Siegel and Rosenberg extract so much as a cent out of him, then I was an accomplice. My conscience wouldn't accept that.

So the way I saw it, he had to run. The consequences of that were bad for me, but they meant to kill me anyway, somewhere down the line, so whether he paid or not, it was just a question of how long I had. Better to have Bayless out of the way and all the risk on my shoulders.

I rapped on the door three times. After a moment the porch light above me came on and then Bayless opened up. The photograph was a good likeness – even with his hair out of place, there was no mistaking him. He had on a purple dressing gown that was an inch short in the sleeves. He cinched the neck against the cool night breeze.

'Yes?'

'My name's Yates, I need to talk to you, Mr Bayless.'

'About what? Do you know what time it is?'

'I'm sorry, but this won't wait. Ben Siegel sent me.'

He recognised the name, but his face didn't register any trepidation at hearing it. 'I'm not acquainted with Mr Siegel, I think there's some mistake.'

I held up the envelope. 'He's acquainted with you. Can we talk inside a minute?'

Bayless glanced around the street behind me, looking embarrassed at my being there. 'I'm not in the habit of inviting callers in at this hour. I'd like you to leave.'

'I can't until we speak. And this isn't a conversation you want to have on your doorstep.'

He shifted his weight, showing nervousness for the first time. 'I think I'll decide that. What is this about?'

'Siegel's about to shake you down. There are photographs in here. Can we go inside?' His face drained of colour and it gnawed at me enough I had to look away.

'I'm not one of Siegel's men,' I said. 'I'm here to try to help you. Come on, open up.'

He stepped back from the doorway, the actor in him reaching for composure, the tension in his movements betraying the truth.

I crossed the threshold and waited for him to lead me into a small parlour, one of the walls covered with behind-the-scenes shots from movie sets: Van Nuys airport doubling for somewhere in Arabia, identifiable by its Art Deco radio tower; two lovers on a Parisian street, the photographer's angle revealing it as a set on a back lot. I couldn't see Bayless in any of them.

'I'll get to the point. Siegel has compromising photos of you.'

I set the envelope down on the glass coffee table in the centre of the room. 'I haven't examined them.'

He looked at it and away again just as quickly.

'He wants ten thousand from you by Wednesday, otherwise he's going to expose you.'

'What?' His eyes flicked around the room. 'This is . . . I have nothing to—'

'Save it. If that was true, he wouldn't have sent me.'

'You grubby little man.'

'I'm not here to turn the screw. But you have to understand this is serious.'

He picked up the envelope and opened it. He pulled the contents halfway out and looked through the first few images, bug eyes locked on them. 'This can't . . .'

'Is there someplace you can go to, outside of Los Angeles? Out of California, if possible.'

He lowered himself onto a leather Chesterfield on the other side of the table, the envelope next to him, its contents face down, halfway spilling out. 'Leave California?'

'That's your best move.'

'My best move? My life is here. I'm an actor, where would I go?' He threw his hands up, stopping himself. 'Christ, what am I thinking discussing this with you?'

'I want to help. I'm only here because Siegel would kill me if I didn't come. But I'm not telling you to do as he says, I'm telling you to run.'

He gripped his head in his hands. 'What is— Who are you? What's your part in this?'

'I'm a reporter – the messenger. I have no part. Siegel wants me to—'

'A reporter?' He looked up, sliding forward in his seat. 'This has nothing to do with Benny Siegel, does it? You're a hack for a scandal rag.'

'I write for the *Pacific Journal*. Go look me up. I don't want anything to do with this but Siegel's got me over a barrel.'

'What sort of a barrel?' His eyes strayed to the pictures next to him.

'That's not important.'

'That's a hell of a line to take. You stand there and tell me I'm being blackmailed and I should run, but you won't take your own advice. If there's truth to any of this.'

'I can't run. Besides, if it wasn't me he'd only send someone else.'

'How noble of you to come then.'

'The photographs are right there. You think I took them? Get serious. That is days or weeks of surveillance work. You want to get hot at someone, maybe you should think about who put Siegel on to you in the first place.'

He bristled, his gaze losing focus, and I wondered if it was because he had a culprit in mind.

'This is too much. Where the hell am I supposed to find ten thousand dollars?'

Rosenberg's line about a sugar daddy was too vulgar to broach. 'You'd think of paying?'

'What choice do I have? I have to consider it, don't I?'

I spread my hands. 'In my experience, if you pay once, they'll come knocking again.'

'Well, that would keep you in a job, at least.'

I looked away, enough truth in the slight that it landed. I made to go. 'I've told you what I think. I know this is a lot to take in and I'm sorry for your troubles, truly.'

'And now he pities me. Take it down the road, pal.'

I went out into the hallway.

He called after me. 'Did you even try to talk Siegel out of this?'

I stopped by the front door, noticing the framed shots of Los Angeles lining the wall and up the staircase. He appeared in the doorway. 'Of course I did, but they had a gun to my head.' But as I said it, I tried to think back to that room, think if I did even try to refuse. As futile as it would have been.

'You're a real hero, aren't you?'

The spite in his words provoked thoughts of Nancy Hill and Julie Desjardins. Of all the killings I should have prevented – Ginny Kolkhorst, Jeanette Runnels, Bess Prescott. And Alice Anderson. The one I should have saved. The guilt that walked everywhere with me, like a shadow.

Even now, by staying in the city I was exposing my wife to danger, trying to make things right for myself. A selfish man with selfish motivations, forever trying to outrun himself. And now a kid actor in another man's dressing gown calling me out from the moral high ground. I turned the door handle, wanting the night to swallow me up.

'Wait.'

An unseen clock ticked, filling the silence.

'Please.'

I ran my hand over my mouth and turned to face him again.

'I don't . . . What the hell am I supposed to do?' He sat down on the staircase. 'Look at me, I'm so unglued I'm asking you for help.'

I bowed my head, hands on my hips, trying to think of something to say. 'Maybe I could speak to Siegel's men, try to buy you some more time.'

'What use is that? If I had a year I couldn't raise that amount.'

'Then we're back to where we started. You take off.'

He shook his head as if that would make it all go away. Then he focused on me again. 'Tell me why you aren't running. If that's the smart move.'

I watched him, saw the hope in his eyes that I had some remedy. 'I told you, I don't have that option. There are matters I have to take care of. Here, in the city.'

'So you're working your debt off, is that it?' He spoke over me before I could deny it. 'Then you can speak to Siegel, maybe I can do something for him too. Instead of the money?'

I felt Siegel's finger in my eye, against my teeth; the tightness in my chest that came with the certainty that he'd kill me when this was through. 'That's the last thing you want. Being in his debt.'

'No. This is the last thing I want.' He glanced towards the parlour doorway, where the photographs still lay.

'I'll talk to Siegel, see if I can get him to lay off, but for Christ's sake don't get your hopes up. Take my advice and start packing.'

I turned and opened the door, the fear in his eyes too much of a mirror of my own.

CHAPTER FIVE

The next morning I skipped out early, avoiding the conversation I'd promised Lizzie, the questions I had no answers for. She sat up in bed as I opened the door, watching me go but saying nothing. With a look, letting me know she recognised what I was doing.

I tried to set aside Bayless for a few hours while I worked on the missing women – but the shakedown nagged at the back of my mind, like a splinter in my brain. I reasoned that the one upside of Siegel catching up with me was that I could move more freely now, at least for a day or two, and I meant to make the most of whatever time I had.

I left the car in the shadow of City Hall and walked a half-block down to the *LA Times*. The building hadn't changed in the years since I'd left. The lobby was still closer to that of a smart hotel than any newspaper office I'd worked at; the giant globe centrepiece held sway, circled by Ballin's ten-foot-high Streamline Moderne murals on the walls above. I'd always interpreted their purpose as a reminder we were following in the footsteps of giants. Seemed grandiose now. The surroundings felt familiar and yet not – as if known to me only from the recounted memories of another man. I pictured myself walking through that lobby, a time when my cares ran as far as careerism, or whatever story I was chasing at the time. It seemed an inconsequential life now – but at the same time possessed of an innocence that left me feeling diminished by the comparison.

The employee roster was nothing like as familiar. Of the dozen or so men I might've considered friends, all had moved on in the years since I'd walked beats for the *Times*. Of the remaining names that I recognised, my best shot for an audience was Hector King, a copy editor I'd worked with fitfully. The girl at the front desk called his line and directed me to a bank of seating to wait.

He kept me waiting fifteen minutes – the forced inaction grinding my gears. When he appeared, I had to remind myself I'd showed up with no appointment and had no call to be mad at him.

I met him halfway across the floor and we shook hands in front of the globe. 'Thanks for seeing me.'

'I'd heard you were back in town. You're with Buck Acheson's outfit, right?'

'Right.'

'They working you too hard? We've got a couple openings here – mailroom, secretarial pool . . .' His smile grew as he trailed off.

'I like the beach too much.' I dredged up a wink – jovial Charlie on the clock.

'Well, if you're happy slumming it out there, to what do I owe the pleasure?' He made no signal to move or sit down.

'I'm working the story of a couple missing girls. Aspiring starlets, left their boarding house for an audition ten days ago and never came back.'

'What's your angle?' Even by the way he said it, I could tell he was wondering if I had a story worth hijacking.

'From the Heartland to Hollywood, that kind of thing.'

'Who are they?'

'Nancy Hill and Julie Desjardins.' I reached for the photograph in my pocket—

There was nothing there. I patted down my other pockets, trying not to look frantic, found nothing. My brain skipped through the possibilities – dropped in the motel room, the car, the street—

'Everything okay, Yates?'

I felt inside my pocket one more time. 'I had a photograph. Guess I misplaced it.' It didn't matter for right then – there was no reason he'd know two new faces in a city with a million and half already here. But it felt like one more strand to the girls had been severed.

'What's this got to do with the *Times*?'

My thoughts were a jumble. I saw him tap his foot and it was enough to make me collect myself. 'The story needs a happy ending. Right now I'm nowhere close.'

'I don't think I follow.'

'I've been working this more than a week and I can't turn up any kind of line on them. They—'

'What makes you think they didn't go back to where they came from?'

'I spoke with Nancy Hill's mother in Iowa, she hasn't heard from her since the day she left home. She didn't even know she'd wound up in LA.' The conversation burned in my memory – a crackling long-distance circuit, Luanne Hill distraught; a stranger breaking the first news she'd heard in weeks of her runaway daughter – that she'd disappeared in a city a thousand miles away. Telling me about the pink dress she was wearing the last day she'd seen her; about the pot roast she'd made for dinner, left to go cold on the table when she didn't come home that night. Begging me to give her something more in return. To do something.

'Only one of them?'

'What do you mean?'

'You only spoke with one of the families?'

'I can't track down anything on Desjardins. Guessing it's a stage name, and Hill's mother didn't recognise the description as anyone known to her or her daughter.'

'Doesn't sound like much of a story.'

The newsman's response. The tragedy of the situation lost on a man who saw it only in terms of whether it was good for enough copy. 'That's why it needs a happy ending. I'm looking for a favour. You've got legmen all over the city – give them the names, get them to ask around. Not in place of whatever they're working on, just an extra question whenever they're on the street. I've tasked our men with the same, but there's only four of us – you've got ten times that.'

'Twenty times. We've grown since you left.'

'Even better. I know it's a needle in a haystack deal, but it's worth trying.'

He looked at me, considering it, and I waited to see what it would cost me.

'Sure.'

I said nothing, still expecting his demands.

'I don't deal with all of the boys, so I can't get everyone on it, but I'll speak to as many as I can, as and when the opportunity arises. I wouldn't expect good news, though.'

He held his hand out and I thanked him and shook it. I held

his grip a beat too long, thrown by his lack of a quid pro quo. It occurred to me that I needed his interest to prove to myself that there was something worth chasing.

'There anything else you needed?'

I let go of his hand. 'I kinda figured you'd want something in return.'

'They're missing kids, Charlie. Let's see if we can't find them before we worry about the spoils.'

*

I ran back to the car and tore it apart looking for the photograph. The floor, the seats, the glove compartment – no dice. I tried to place the last time I'd held it, but couldn't remember for certain. Was it in my pocket when I'd lied to Whitey Lufkins about not having one the day before?

Then a new thought: the back room at Ciglio's, Siegel pounding on me. If it'd slipped out then. I tried to picture the room in my mind, thinking if it could have been down on the floor – but with the beating, in the dark, the tables, the memory was indistinct. I stood next to the open car door, traffic speeding by me, everything out of focus.

It was a minute or two before I regained enough sense to start moving, put the nervous energy to work.

I blitzed through downtown, doubling back to Main Street and working my way along it as far as Jefferson – two or three miles at least. I quizzed anyone I saw that might have an ear to the street: a pair of bar-hoppers still chasing a night that had left them behind, a beat cop with a drinker's face, doormen at the Rosebury and the Chartham. It was too early; for the most part the streets were quiet. The kind I needed, those most at home once darkness fell, wouldn't show their faces until later in the day. Still, it was all I could think to do. I dropped names and descriptions but got blank looks and shakes of the head time and again. In my heart I knew the photograph wouldn't have made the difference, but still it felt like I'd done half a job – the latest in a string of failures, the consequences unknown.

When I'd exhausted my options downtown, I drove Sunset Boulevard all the way to the Strip. On the way I passed the backstreet they'd taken me down to Ciglio's. It loomed in my mind; the smell of Rosenberg's cigar and the feel of cold tile against my cheek. Siegel's threat against my life. Still, I felt a pull to go back there. Not just to search for the photograph, but from a sense of unfinished business. A delusional idea that if I went on my own terms, the shoe would be on the other foot.

I hit the Strip and parked across the street from the Mocambo. The striped awning over the entrance brought to mind memories of the drinking clubs in Hot Springs, and I looked away when I realised it.

I set about redoubling my efforts. I stopped in every diner, restaurant, bar and club – even pounding on the doors of the ones that weren't open. I gave out their names but also went further, asking about fresh girls on the scene, girls looking for work, new waitresses – anything I could think of might spark a connection.

It was wasted shoe leather. Best I came away with was a mention of a girl, *maybe* sounded like my description of Julie Desjardins, working at a movie theatre on Fairfax, and a carhop with a story about a Nancy looking to score reefer from him – which he swore he knew zip about when he realised I wasn't buying. He clammed up after that, said he couldn't remember what she looked like. Neither led me anywhere, but loose as it was, I made a note to swing by Fairfax soon as I could.

*

Noon.

I was sweating in my suit by the time I got back to the car. I dabbed my forehead with my sleeve and started the engine, then took Sunset east to Gower Gulch, making the turn at the Columbia drugstore. The cowboys that gave the Gulch its name milled around outside it, ready to roll in Stetsons and bandanas, looking to catch on as extras in this week's Western. Dreamers hoping to make it big following in Gene Autry's footsteps.

TPK Studios was easy to find, even among the plethora of them along the block. A globe on one corner of the roof was topped with a model radio mast, the company name spelled out in vertical letters along its length; it towered above even the power lines along the street. I parked by the main gate and checked the time again and hunkered down to wait for the guard shift to change, watching who came and went.

Just past one, the man in the small hut stepped out with his lunch pail and Joseph Bersinger clapped him on the shoulder as he passed to take his place. I climbed out and made my way over. Bersinger had worked at the studio going on fifteen years, starting out as a prop hand before winding up in a security gig that afforded him time enough to study the runners at Santa Anita every day. Buck Acheson put me on to him – a long-time source he'd picked up via one of his legmen when he ran the *Times*.

He saw me coming and closed his paper just as he'd got it open. 'It's only lunchtime and you look like you had a long day already.'

'I roll out of bed looking this way every day.'

He cracked a smile. 'How's Buck?'

I weaved my hand. 'Keeping afloat.' In truth, I hadn't seen Buck in person since we came back to the city. 'It's a small outfit, I think he gets bored.'

'He should retire while he's got time. Take up golf.'

'Never happen.'

'I know it. They'll carry him out of there in a box.'

I nodded along, itching to wrap up the small talk. 'Listen, what we spoke about before—'

'I got nothing like good news for you.' He righted himself on his stool. 'I spoke to one of the casting agents gives me the time of day and there were definitely no auditions scheduled for December third. *Red River Ride* was four days over and nowhere near finished, so most everyone in the place was at the back lot in Burbank pitching in. I wanted to be certain, though, so I double-checked the logs for that day and there was no Nancy and no Julie anywhere on the list. Anyone comes through this gate should be on there; even if they're a last-minute deal, they're supposed be added as a matter of course. Studio regs.'

I rubbed my temple with my thumb.

'Now, does that mean they always are?' he said. 'Of course it doesn't. They pay these fellas peanuts to sit here and expect them to be as conscientious about the rules as I am. And what's besides is, not everyone comes onto the lot comes through here.'

Another line of enquiry closing off in front of my eyes. 'How else would they get in?'

He opened his hand to the building behind him. 'Any number of ways. But the one I'm thinking of is when the high-ups bring girls in through the side entrance on Melrose. It's one of them things no one talks about, but everyone knows goes on.'

I twisted my mouth and looked off towards the street. I'd built a picture of the two girls as innocents, but whatever the truth of what happened to them, talk of reefer-rovers and private casting calls was a reminder they were strangers to me. It was unsettling, making me question the assumptions I'd made about their disappearance. Wonder whether I'd built a castle in the sand for my own selfish ends – one that'd already washed away, and I was the only one couldn't see it.

He put his hand back by his side. 'But I go back to what I said about everyone being on set that day. I'd be surprised.'

'Any luck with convincing someone inside to talk to me?'

He shook his head. 'And it's not like I can press it.'

'I don't expect you to, that's my job. What about the casting agent you mentioned just now? Would he give me five minutes?'

He folded his newspaper, smoothing the crease. 'You have to understand, if the names aren't on the logs, it's because they were never here. That's what it's supposed to signify. No one's going to tell you otherwise.'

'Even if I knew whether they made it here that day – just being able to narrow their movements down some would make a big difference.'

'I don't know what else to tell you. I'm sorry.'

I fiddled with the door handle to his kiosk, a distraction to fill the silence while I thought on it. 'What normally happens to the girls get brought in sub rosa? Afterwards, I mean?'

He puffed his cheeks. 'I don't know, Charlie, I'm playing up rumours here. They get cast, they don't get cast – what difference does it make?'

'No, I mean right after. Do they ever come out the main gate?'

'Who knows? Unlikely.'

I took a dollar bill from my fold and passed it to him, thanked him for his trouble. The dots wouldn't join, but there was no reason they should. The information on their movements had come from the landlady at their boarding house – but there was any number of ways it could be wrong. Maybe she was mistaken about the studio they were headed to that day – easy enough to do. And that was assuming they'd told her the truth; what if they'd been spinning her a line for their own purposes?

CHAPTER SIX

The boarding house was in a planned neighbourhood in Leimert Park and I made the dash over there in no time. A grey stucco building in Spanish Revival style, it was fronted by four decorative arches, partially concealing a long veranda along the ground floor and balconies outside the upstairs rooms. It was set back from the sidewalk behind a neat patch of yard, purple bougainvillea adding a splash of colour to the front of the property. Two women were just visible behind the upper right archway as I walked up the path.

The landlady, Mrs Betsy Snyder, answered the door. Her face was blank a moment when she saw me, until recognition set in. 'Mr Yates – we spoke before.'

'I'm sorry to call unannounced, ma'am. I was in the neighbourhood and wondered if you'd answer a few more questions?'

'What sort of questions?'

'About Miss Hill and Miss Desjardins.'

She blanked again a moment, as if she couldn't think why I'd be asking after them. Her countenance threw me. 'Would you like to come inside?'

I thanked her and followed her into a simple dining room with two tables and seating for a dozen. She gestured for me to sit. 'May I offer you something to drink?'

'No thank you, ma'am.'

She remained standing, holding onto the back of a chair, so I stayed on my feet. 'May I ask what is this about?' she said.

'I've been trying to get a fix on Miss Hill and Miss Desjardins' movements before they disappeared. Last time you mentioned they told you they were expected at TPK for an audition that morning, but I've been to the studio and there's no record of them having made it there.'

She pulled a puzzled face. 'Mr Yates, you have me at a loss. What do you mean disappeared?'

The line almost floored me. 'Mrs Snyder, do you recall the conversation we had previously? You told me your two boarders had disappeared and—'

'Of course I recall it, that's what I said – *disappeared*. But I didn't mean . . .'

I waited but she didn't finish. 'You didn't mean what, ma'am?'

She took her hands off the chair and sat down now. 'To imply anything. *Disappeared* – it's just a word. One day they were here, then they were gone. Thankfully it doesn't happen often, but they're not the first fly-by-nights I've encountered.'

I looked at her, plucking at my shirt cuff to mask my surprise, trying to remember how our prior conversation had unfolded. 'But . . . when we spoke, you expressed concern for their welfare. You said you were sure they weren't the type to skip out and you thought they might be in trouble.'

She waved it off. 'I suppose I still expected that they'd come back at the time. I don't like to think the worst of people.'

I couldn't think what to say. The impression I'd taken away was of a woman deeply concerned; I remembered being dragged under by a sense of dread as she'd talked, the feeling that the next cycle in an unending loop had begun. And now—

'What about their effects? You told me they left everything behind.'

She shifted her gaze from me to the cabinet filled with white crockery against the wall. 'They did, but they didn't amount to much in the first place. A few items of clothing, some costume jewellery – nothing of any significant value.'

'What about their personal things? Were they gone too?'

'I couldn't say – I'm not in the habit of making an inventory of my boarders' rooms.'

I didn't know whether to believe her. A silence settled as the foundations of everything fell away under me. There was a noise from the hallway outside and Mrs Snyder snapped her head around to look over. A faint scraping, then the sound of footfalls on the staircase. She moved to the door and opened it, glanced around.

After waiting a few seconds, she left the door open and sat down again, looking rattled. 'I told you they owed me two weeks' lodging, didn't I? In the context, a few dresses would be no great loss.'

I tapped my finger lightly against my leg. 'You did.'

'I've involved the police, of course, but I don't expect to ever see a cent of it.'

I took a step towards the door, Lizzie and Ben Siegel crashing my thoughts on the flood of doubt. Thinking that Lizzie was right all along and we should have run the minute we had the chance. It felt as if I were waking from a bad dream to a worse reality.

'I've taken enough of your time. I'll see myself out.'

She followed me to the front door. 'I'm sorry if I gave you the wrong idea last time, Mr Yates.'

I stepped out into the sunlight and put my hat on, unease washing over me. I jogged across the road to the car and ducked inside, picturing the streets around there; trying to think where the nearest payphone booth was, meaning to call Lizzie and tell her she was right and to start packing.

Then I lifted my head and noticed a scrap of paper under the windshield wiper – a note, one corner lifting in the breeze. I climbed out again and pulled it free, looking around me as I did so. It was a single line in a neat cursive script:

Please come to O'Doull's on Crenshaw & 39th as soon as you read this

*

The name had me expecting a bar, but O'Doull's turned out to be a small coffee shop sandwiched between a post office and an insurance outfit, situated on a short commercial strip running parallel to the main boulevard.

I walked in hinky, waiting for someone's eyes to meet mine. Ten tables, each of them occupied. No one reacted at first, and I started to get mad at the games, but then a young woman with a wilting curl-job made eye contact and held it. I recognised her and made my way over.

I sat down and set the scrap of paper in front of her. 'Was this your doing?'

She nodded.

'Charlie Yates. What's your name, miss?'

'Angela Crawford. I'm a boarder at—'

'Mrs Snyder's place. I saw you on the balcony before.'

'Yes, sir, that was me.'

I waited for her to elaborate, noticing her accent – East Coast. A waitress came over and neither of us spoke while she poured me a black coffee from her pot.

When she was gone, Crawford took the message slip in her hand, turning it. 'You're looking for Nancy and Julie, aren't you?'

'That's right. Do you know where they are?' It was a dumb question, getting ahead of myself.

'No. We've heard nothing since they disappeared.'

'But you were friendly with them?'

'Sure, friendly enough. We're all trying to make it the same way.'

'Meaning what? The movies?'

'What else is there?'

Another time I might've said, but my interest was only in whatever she had to say for herself. 'What was it you wanted to talk to me about?'

'May I ask why you came to the house again today?'

Again. I didn't like the idea of her taking note of my movements. 'Miss, I'm not about to sit here and play twenty questions. If you know something about where those girls are at, I'd be obliged if you'd spill it.'

She chewed her cheek, trying not to show I'd upset her.

I glanced to the side and breathed out, furious at myself for snapping. 'Pay me no mind, ma'am. I'm going crazy looking for them and I'm getting nowhere. If you can help, I'm all ears.'

She looked at me a moment and then down, righting the fork on the place setting in front of her. 'Mrs Snyder said you're a journalist, is that right?'

'Yes.'

'Another man came asking about Nancy and Julie. Did she tell you that?'

I shook my head, putting my coffee down, alert now.

'Why are you looking for them?'

I started to say it was for a story, but instinct told me to tell the truth. 'I'm concerned about their wellbeing.'

'Me too. Bridget thinks they might be in Mexico. She says—'

'Who's Bridget?'

'We're roommates. At Mrs Snyder's. You would've seen her on the balcony earlier. She says the Mexicans take white girls across the border to keep as maids.'

An old story I'd heard as a kid, still going strong in the minds of California newcomers; Anglo parents told it to their daughters to scare them away from pachucos. But it made me think about the rumours of starlets being lured over the border with promises of movie work, then finding themselves forced into skin flicks. 'Do you have any basis for thinking that? Did you know them to associate with any Mexican men?'

She frowned, shaking her head. 'No. No. I think Bridgy is just guessing but do you think she could be right?'

'I think it would be hard to get an American citizen over the border against their will. What about other men – friends, a sweetheart, anyone they were dating?'

She shook her head. 'There's no one I knew of.'

'Did you talk about that sort of thing? Boys?'

'No one in real life.'

'Movie stars you mean?'

She nodded, looking down and smiling. 'We all daydreamed about who we'd marry when we made it big.'

I leaned forward over the table. 'Miss, who was the other man came asking about them?'

She feathered her collarbone. 'He said he was a detective with the LAPD, that Mrs Snyder had called them in.'

That didn't chime right. Detective bureau involvement didn't fly for two girls skipping out on a couple weeks' rent. 'Go on. Did you get his name?'

'Yes, it was Belfour, he showed me a badge. Do you know him?'

'No. I don't work with the LAPD much.'

'He asked about you.' She put her hand to her mouth after she said it, as though she'd shocked herself by letting slip.

I spoke slow so as not to let my voice waver. 'Asked what?'

'Who you were, why you'd come around, what your involvement with them was. I don't know all of it for sure, he mainly spoke with Mrs Snyder.'

I remembered the noise in the hallway, the sound of someone rushing upstairs, Mrs Snyder being jumpy. 'You were eavesdropping on their conversation. Same as you did to me just now.'

She reddened. 'That was Bridgy. And she wasn't snooping, she was just watching out for me.'

'While you put that on my car?' I pointed to the note.

She nodded. 'Mrs Snyder wouldn't like me talking to you.'

'For what reason?'

'I can't say for sure. She's been acting strange since that man came around. My guess is she's scared the police will blame her. She's the nervous type.'

I wondered if that explained Snyder's change in attitude. If she was a square John who got nervous around the law – or

43

there was more to it. 'Do you think there's something she's not letting on?'

She frowned. 'I don't know. Like what?'

The conversation was fracturing and my head swam. I couldn't be sure if she was building up to something or she was just enjoying the chance to gossip. 'Speculation doesn't serve anyone's interests. May we talk about the detective again a moment – did he speak to you on your own?'

'Some.'

'What did he ask?'

'What I told you before. About Nancy and Julie, where they could be, if they'd talked about running off, anything like that.' She flicked her thumbnail against the one on her little finger. 'If we'd spoken to you.'

Her mannerisms sent off all kinds of signals – suspicion foremost, but also a willingness to give voice to something unspoken. 'Miss, did this detective unsettle you in some way?'

She studied the tabletop. 'My uncle Patrick is a policeman in Fells Point in Baltimore. Not a detective, he walks a beat.'

I watched her, saying nothing. Jitters in the pit of my stomach.

'The man that came by ... he didn't remind me of Uncle Patrick and his friends.'

Play devil's advocate. 'Los Angeles is a very different town to Baltimore.'

'I know, but ... I just had this feeling that— This feeling that he wasn't a real policeman.' Her face dropped when she said it, as if saying it aloud had increased the burden rather than taking it away.

Questions crowded my thoughts. Lizzie knew about my

search, but aside from her, the only people knew I was looking for the girls were those I'd spoken to in the course of the investigation. 'Can you describe what he looked like?'

She gestured with her hands. 'Thin.' She looked at the ceiling, remembering. 'About as tall as you, but he had sandy-coloured hair. But he was really thin, like he hadn't eaten – not how most cops look. That's another thing made me wonder.'

It didn't bring anyone to mind. I couldn't find a way to make sense of it.

I reached into my pocket for some coins to pay for the coffee. 'Thank you for telling me. I know this can't have been easy.'

She sat back in her chair. 'How long will you keep looking for them, Mr Yates?'

I set a quarter on the table. 'As long as I'm able.'

*

There was a payphone across the side street on the corner of Crenshaw. I called LAPD headquarters and asked if they could put me in touch with Detective Belfour. After a few minutes holding, they redirected me to the South Bureau. The operator there told me Detective Belfour wasn't available at this time, and she didn't know when he would be.

I walked back to the car feeling as though someone was at my heels.

CHAPTER SEVEN

Lizzie peeked from behind the curtain when I pulled up outside our motel room.

Seeing it was me, she opened the door and stood behind it, something tentative in her manner.

I kissed her and took my tie off, then checked around the room, hoping against hope that was where I'd left the photograph of the girls.

'What's wrong, Charlie?'

'I misplaced something. I'm—'

'Is this what you're looking for?'

I turned to see Lizzie holding the photograph towards me. It showed the two girls hanging from either side of a palm tree trunk, posing with one leg bent at the knee, making a mirror image. Both of them laughing. Nancy's head thrown back, Julie with a snaggletooth on the left side of her mouth. At a guess, both of them in their early twenties.

'You found it? Where was it?'

Her free arm was across her stomach, her elbow propped on it. 'I took it from your jacket.'

'What? Why?'

'I had to find a way to get through to you. And even that didn't work.'

'This is—' I reached across and took it from her fingers, staring at her, the silence between us like a brick wall. 'I spent all morning canvassing people with no picture to show. What were you thinking?'

'I could ask the same of you. Think about what you just said.'

'You're trying to hinder me, is that it?'

'No, never. I wanted to do something to give you pause – to stop and think. But nothing is working. You're obsessed, Charlie, and you're ignoring the danger we're in.'

'How can you stand there and say that to me?'

'You've been gone all day. All day, not a word. Even after what I told you last night.'

'I'm— Goddammit, Lizzie, I'm trying to figure this out. I need your help, not some try at silent protest.'

'I am helping. I've been walking around for hours showing this photograph to people. I told you I couldn't face sitting here wondering again.'

'You did what?'

She took a step closer to me. 'Exactly what you would have done. If nothing else, to prove I wasn't acting out of spite.'

I held my hands out. 'You accuse me of ignoring the danger and you're out there parading yourself for Siegel to find.'

'What does it matter now? They found you, they've made their threats. Why would they even care to look for me?'

My own thoughts from that morning, somehow sounding deluded coming from the mouth of another. I took a breath and put my hands on her shoulders. 'This isn't a game. They—'

She shrugged me off. 'Don't patronise me. I've lived through every second of this with you, I know damn well how serious this is.'

Alice's memory lingered in the space between us. My sense

that an unvoiced accusation was close to the surface: that she was tired of me acting as if I carried a heavier burden of grief than she did over the loss of her own sister.

I screwed my eyes closed, trying not to raise my voice. 'If they don't know where you are, they can't harm you. That's the one thought keeping me going right now.'

'They found you before, Charlie. They let you go without so much as taking your telephone number. They can get to us anytime they like if we stay in the city, you must see that.' She walked to the table and planted both hands on it with her back to me. 'What you mean to say is that you don't care if they kill you so long as they can't touch me.' She gave me a hard look in the mirror. 'You can't know how terrifying it is for me to realise that.'

I put my hands on my hips and looked at the wall, flailing for something to say as it dawned on me she'd recognised something I hadn't yet seen in myself. 'I'm trying to protect you.'

'You're being reckless on account of something you can't fix.'

I went over and stabbed the tabletop. 'If they're alive, I can find them.'

She lifted my finger off the table and interlinked it with hers. 'You can't bring Alice back. Any of them.'

'That's not—'

'Please don't deny it. I know how it weighs on you.'

I turned away, feeling my eyes film with tears. The silence an indictment of my guilt, the memories beating their way to the front of my mind. 'I can't stop thinking . . . if I'd just been quicker and asked the right questions sooner . . .' I rubbed my eyes with the heel of my hand and then slapped the wall. 'Goddammit.'

She put her arms around my neck, and I felt a fool as my tears started. The images wouldn't leave my mind. I untangled myself from her and moved away, ashamed of my weakness.

'She was my sister. I've had all the same thoughts and I still do.'

'Not the same thoughts. Even now I think about killing them – Richard Davis and Harlan Layfield and all their type. I'm angry all the time and it means nothing because when I had the chance I couldn't bring myself to.'

'That's the difference between you and them.'

'Inaction.'

'Stop this.' She lifted my chin to look her in the eye. 'Charlie, stop this. You're not to blame and eventually you'll come to see that. But we've got to deal with what's in front of us.' She ran her thumb over the tearstain on my cheek and we stood like that without speaking, traffic noise outside and the chatter from some other room's radio an undercurrent to the quiet.

After a minute she said, 'You never told me what happened with Mr Bayless last night.'

My thoughts were so wrecked it took me a second to place the name. 'He said he can't pay. He was in shock, I think. I can't blame him.'

'That poor man.'

'I told him he should run.' I said it softly, indicating I recognised the irony.

'Do you think that's wise?'

'I didn't know what else to do. I felt like a heel even going there but I had to warn him at least.'

'Of course. Do you think he'll listen?'

'I wouldn't bet on it. He was more worried about where he'd get work if he left. He thinks he can talk his way out of it.'

'How?'

I told her about his idea of working off the debt. 'There's something else as well. There's a man been asking questions about me. He says he's a cop but I'm not sure.'

She closed her eyes in a manner that suggested she couldn't take much more.

I told her the rest – about going back to Mrs Snyder's and Angela Crawford's story and the call to the LAPD.

Her face turned quizzical at the last part. 'I don't follow. So this man is a real police officer?'

'Not necessarily. Anyone could get a tin badge and be using his name.'

'Why would— Who would have reason to ask after you?'

'I don't know. My first thought was someone at the studio doesn't like me asking questions.'

She shot me a look, uncertain.

'You think movie studios are above hiring private eyes?' I said.

'You're suggesting the studio is somehow involved?'

'No, I'm just trying to find a way to make sense of it. Who has means and motive.'

She stood up and flattened her skirt, then crossed the room and checked the bolt on the door, re-locking it. 'Charlie, I have to tell you, traipsing around all day brought home the futility of what you're trying to do. I don't mean to criticise you or your dedication, but I lost count of how many people I showed that photograph to and I didn't get a single hint that any of them was interested, let alone could help. This city's too big.'

She paused, a loaded silence while she composed herself. 'We need to decide, right now, what we do about Siegel. I can't see a choice other than to take off again.'

'You said to me, "*What happens when we've got nowhere left to run to?*" Those were your words on Pismo Beach.'

She pressed her lips together. 'You needn't throw them in my face. When I said that it was in the context of just being forced to flee my home for a second time. Now I don't even have a home.' She stared at me, not an accusation but letting the words hit their mark. 'Tell me what you'd suggest instead.'

I turned around, feeling light-headed. 'I'm going to talk to Siegel. Plead Bayless' case. I don't know, maybe I can work out a deal with him.'

She moved to stand in front of the door. 'That's crazy. My god, you said yourself—'

'It's worth a shot. If it does no good, we could still leave to-morrow.'

'You're still trying to buy time, aren't you? To search for those girls.'

'For them. For Bayless. For all of us.'

She shook her head and looked away and I saw her glance at our bags, still packed.

'Will you be here when I come back?' I said.

'Don't be ridiculous.'

'I wouldn't blame you if you wanted to go. I could follow—'

'I won't leave this city without you. But I'll be damned if I'm going to stand by and let you get yourself killed because you're too stubborn for anything else.' She walked over and picked up one of the bags, then unlocked the door. 'I'll wait in the car while you speak to him. If it goes wrong, we leave straightaway.'

CHAPTER EIGHT

Two miniature spotlights strafed the facade of Ciglio's, sweeping across the gold lettering of the restaurant's name. I cruised by it and parked the car on a side street a block away. I left the key in the ignition and climbed out. 'If I'm not back in an hour—'

'Just see that you do come back.' Lizzie blew me a kiss and slid behind the wheel.

I tracked back along Hollywood Boulevard, awash with cars, lights and the early evening dinner crowd. The Boulevard had been dressed for Christmas – bells, stars and candy canes strung on wires across the roadway, fake Christmas trees topping the streetlights. I couldn't remember if it was like that before, or if I just hadn't noticed.

I went into the restaurant and straightaway the maitre d' was on me, asking for my reservation. A face that didn't fit.

'I'm not here to eat. I'm looking for Mr Siegel.'

His expression ran to impassive at the name. 'Mr Siegel isn't joining us tonight.'

Stock answer. I drew close. 'What about the back room?'

'Sir, you'll have to come back when you have a reservation.' He gestured to the door, feigning disinterest, but I'd caught him glance at a heavy sitting at a table near the back.

'What do you say I go take a look myself.' I moved past him and started towards the kitchen.

He came after me and the man near the back stood up as I approached. He stepped in front of my path. 'We have a problem here?'

'No problem. Tell Siegel Charlie Yates wants to see him.' Eyes were on us now, the diners at the surrounding tables turning to look. I went to barge past the man, but he corralled me with his arms. I tried to brush him off. I heard a fork drop somewhere, clanking against a china plate.

He started to muscle me back towards the door, pinning my arms to my sides, me struggling against him. 'Get off me—'

'Keep your voice down.'

'SIEGEL – GET OUT HERE.'

There were two of them on me now, suited, wrestling me towards the street but trying not to make a scene, so I kept resisting, knowing if they got me outside all bets were off. 'SIEGEL.'

I heard a new voice and suddenly everything stopped. They let me go; I gulped a breath and saw Moe Rosenberg standing behind them. Hand by his side, he pointed with one finger. 'Walk.'

He turned and went the way he'd pointed, towards the kitchen. I stepped between the two hoods and trailed after him, every head in the place following me. The pianist started playing again.

Rosenberg pushed through a swing door into a white tiled kitchen with a half-dozen chefs at work. He went through another door to the side and then we were back in the room they'd beaten me in. It was empty apart from us.

'What the hell do you think you're doing?' he said.

'I need to talk to Siegel.'

'If he'd seen what you just pulled you'd be dead already.'

'Enough with the threats—'

'I'm telling you straight. He'd have dragged you out the back and done you himself. You got no clue how bad he hates you.'

I stabbed a finger in his chest. 'Then it's a goddamn shame he needs me so much, isn't it?'

He took a step back, glanced at his shoes, looked up with dead eyes. 'He needs you like he needs crabs. It's only me talked him down this long.'

'Am I supposed to be grateful?'

'Why are you here, Yates?'

'I'll talk to the organ grinder, not the monkey.'

He spat in my face.

The shock made me recoil. I put my hand to my cheek, wiped the saliva away, trembling, scared worse than a punch.

He scratched the corner of his eye with his forefinger. 'Every time you open your mouth you make me regret keeping you alive. What do you want?'

I stared at him, wanting to turn tail, his show of power having its effect. I wiped again with my sleeve, trying to still my tremors. 'I saw Trent Bayless. He's not worth your trouble, lay off him.'

He was shaking his head even before I finished. 'No.'

'He's a kid. You said the money's what you care about, he can't raise it. Shake down someone else, there are easier targets to knock off.'

'As easy as that? The kid's a fruit with a line to some deep pockets. He made his bed.'

'What will ruining him achieve? It leaves you back at square one. There must be a hundred bigwigs you can squeeze who'll cough up the green.'

'You're smarter than that. You concentrate on your part and we'll take care of the rest.' He unfolded a white napkin from a table and tossed it to me. 'I told you not to swoon for any sob stories.'

'You son of a bitch.'

'He pays by Wednesday.'

He stepped to the door leading to the rear exit and slid the bolt. 'Don't come back here again without an invite. I won't blab about you showing up, but word will get back to Ben anyway.'

*

I hit the street feeling like a piece of dirt under another man's sole. I steadied myself against a streetlight, wondering if I'd expected any other outcome.

A dirty adrenaline propelled me. I crossed the street and ran back to the Boulevard and found a payphone. I dialled the operator and asked to be connected to Bayless' line. He answered, slurring his words.

'It's Charlie Yates.'

'Mr Messenger. I'd say it's a pleasure to hear from you, but . . .'

'I just talked with Siegel's men. They won't budge.'

'You did what? I never asked for you to do me any favours.'

'I'm trying to help. But what I said the other night – it's over. Now's the time to take off.'

'Goddamn you. And what happens then? You move on to your next poor chump and I'm left looking over my shoulder.'

I thought about Lizzie, wanted to tell him I was leaving too, right then. But I couldn't make it ring true in my head. 'I won't write the story. I don't know what they'll do then but it won't be safe for either of us.'

He snorted. 'They'll kill us both is what.'

I had no retort.

He said nothing for a moment and it sounded like he took a drink. Then, 'You're spineless. Tell yourself what you will, but you'll bend whichever way they want in the end. I'll take care of myself. Don't try to contact me again.' He hung up.

I let the receiver hang by my side, feeling as though I'd been cut loose from the city around me.

I moved off slowly, working out what to say to Lizzie, angling for another twenty-four hours, a last-ditch effort to find Hill and Desjardins. I passed a movie theatre, a line of teenagers out front, and remembered the tip about a girl resembling Desjardins working a joint on Fairfax – one last straw to grasp at. I made it to the end of the block and turned onto the side street where I'd left the car.

I stopped and looked, double-checking the street sign. Lizzie and the car were gone.

CHAPTER NINE

I ran the length of the block. It let out on Franklin and I stood at the intersection looking up and down it, a stream of red and white lights moving in opposite directions, no sign of Lizzie. Never feeling so alone in all my life.

I retraced my steps to where we'd parked and stood in the middle of the road, wanting to scream.

I remembered the way she'd looked at the bags in the motel and I bit down on the notion that she'd changed her mind and decided to run without me. Then another thought overtook it: that they'd found her.

I started to walk back towards the Boulevard, picking up speed, heading towards Ciglio's, anger burying my fear. When I made the turn, I could see the gold letters again, shining as the spotlight moved over them, a party of smiling and laughing diners making their way inside. I broke into a run.

A car horn sounded, then again. I heard someone shout my name.

I turned to see Lizzie cutting across two lanes of traffic, the manoeuvre drawing honks from angry motorists. She pulled up alongside me. 'Charlie—'

She threw open the passenger door and waved me inside. I jumped in and she pulled away again.

'What happened?'

'There was a man watching you.' She was breathless. 'When

you went into the restaurant. I tried to follow but I lost him and—'

'Wait, start over.'

'I turned the car around when you left and brought it to the corner, to be closer.' She flushed. 'I thought ... in case we needed to get away. When you walked up to the restaurant I saw a man across the street get out and watch you go. He was leaning on the roof of his car. I wasn't certain at first, but his eyes were locked on you. When you went inside, he looked around and, I don't know how, but he noticed me looking. I got out and started over to him, to ask him who he was, but he climbed back into his car and drove off. He went that way.' She pointed west, the same way we were travelling. 'He slipped around a tow truck and I lost him at the light.'

I stared at her, wondering at the change in my wife in the time I'd known her. Then thinking that only the stakes had changed, not the woman. 'I can't believe you'd take a risk like that. Are you all right?'

She nodded her head too violently, fired up. 'Yes. I'm cross that I lost him.'

'Did you get the plate?'

'I didn't get a chance. It was a Dodge, grey or blue I think. I'm not sure what else.'

'You did good.' I peered through the traffic ahead. 'What did he look like?'

She creased her eyes. 'He was gaunt. It happened so fast, I barely saw, but that stood out. I think he had fair hair, but with the lights ...' She shook her head, frustrated.

I kept watching the road ahead, Hollywood Boulevard teeming with cars, plenty of them Dodges but nothing to distinguish one from the rest. 'The girl said Belfour was skinny with sandy hair.'

'What does he want with you, Charlie?'

I shook my head, no answer to give.

We slowed to a standstill, Lizzie's face lit red by the tail lights in front. A band was playing in one of the joints outside, an up-tempo number, the drums and the trumpet discordant above the traffic noise.

'What happened with Siegel?'

I had to drag my thoughts away from this new unknown. 'He wasn't there.'

'What are you thinking?'

'I want to know why we're being followed.'

'What about your private detective theory?' There was impatience in her tone. 'I thought you had your explanation?'

'If that's the case, the only reason for the studios to have eyes on me is that there's something they don't want me to know about those girls.'

She held her tongue a beat too long, obvious she didn't buy it. 'How do you know it's not one of Siegel's men?'

'I don't.' I chewed on that, thinking it would make sense for him to have someone watchdogging me. 'But why follow me to the boarding house?'

We started moving again. 'To know what you're up to.'

'Would one of Siegel's men take off when you approached him? That was right on their own turf.'

She blew out a breath, out of answers.

We crossed another intersection and I looked at the street sign, picturing LA's sprawl in my mind. 'Make the next left. Let's settle this one way or the other.'

We pulled up outside the LAPD South Bureau, a mile or so east of Leimert Park and Mrs Snyder's boarding house. Lizzie didn't want to wait in the car, so we went inside together. She walked in at a march, as if we were late for the last train out of town.

A young sergeant was manning the desk, his hair trimmed in a fresh crew cut. He was hunched over some papers, pen in hand, but he looked up when we drew close. He strained to keep his eyes off Lizzie. 'Help you, sir?'

'I'm looking for Detective Belfour.'

He stole another look at Lizzie. 'What do you want him for?'

'He called me about my case a few days back. He'll know me.'

'What's your name?'

I thought about giving an alias, figured it made no difference. 'Charlie Yates.'

He looked down at something in front of him, then picked up a telephone. He waited, then said, 'Can you get a hold of Marty Belfour? Civilian here for him.'

He waited again, eyes on the file cards in front of him, glancing at Lizzie through his eyebrows. Then he nodded, said, 'Thanks.' He looked up. 'Detective Belfour isn't on shift right now. I can't say when he'll be back.'

'When is he expected?'

'What I said, I don't know. All the other detectives are busy, so why don't you leave me your bona fides and I'll have him look you up.'

'You happen to know what he looks like?'

He folded his arms, his shirt cuff snagging on his badge. 'What's it to you?'

I was scrambling for an answer when Lizzie hooked a thumb in my direction. 'He knows I'm sweet on cops. He likes to keep me away from the handsome ones.' She winked at him. She accentuated the Texas in her accent.

He looked from me to her with a straight face, but his cheeks reddened some. 'All the dicks look the same to me. Marty's no oil painting and he could stand to lose a few pounds. Stick with the boys in uniform.' He let his gaze rest only on her now.

But Lizzie had already turned to me, the pretence gone from her face and her eyes wide.

*

I left the cop with a false address and we fast-walked back to the car in silence, Lizzie making for the driver's side again until she saw me holding the passenger door open for her. I closed it after her and slid behind the wheel.

'You were right, then. He's not who he's claiming.'

I checked over my shoulder and pulled into the street, shaking my head. 'This whole situation stinks.'

'Are you ruling out the notion it's one of Siegel's men?'

'No. I just . . . I can't see where it all joins.'

She put a hand on my cheek. 'You need to sleep.'

'There's no time. You go ahead and close your eyes if you need.'

'It's not one-way traffic. We could both benefit from some rest – even just for a short while.'

I felt all the hours weighing down on me, and only then did it dawn on me she must be feeling the same. 'You're right. Look, what if we find a new motel? One more night.'

She looked at me, finally nodding.

'There's just one thing I have to do first.'

*

I cruised down Fairfax until I found the place the tipster had pointed me to. The Regal was a broken-down movie theatre with its name in green neon letters across the front. There were bills outside for the new Jimmy Stewart flick, but it looked the kind of joint that trucked more in Z-grade fare.

Lizzie had lost her fight with exhaustion as we drove and was passed out against the passenger window, her lips ajar. She stirred as I parked and opened her eyes just as I stole a glance at her. She jerked when she woke, realising she'd fallen asleep.

'Where are we?'

'Last stop tonight, I promise. I'll be back in two minutes, rest up.'

I double-checked the photograph of the girls was in my pocket and opened the door before she could quibble.

It was between show times, so there was no line at the ticket booth. The window had a crack running its full length and the seller behind it looked desperate for the dregs of his shift to be over.

I pressed the photograph to the glass. 'Sir, I'm looking for these two girls. I heard the one on the left may be working here.'

He leaned closer to look.

'I'm not a cop, she's not in any trouble.'

He flicked his eyes to me and back to the image, no expression. 'This one looks a little like Virginia.' He pointed through the glass to Julie Desjardins. 'She's one of the cigarette girls.'

A spark ran through me. 'Is she here?'

He shook his head, collar gapping where the top button was undone behind his necktie.

'What days does she work?'

He scratched his neck, acting like he was having to think about it. 'I'm not sure.'

I took the photo away so he had to look at me. 'Is there someone else to ask?'

'I'm not allowed to leave the booth.'

'I got a mouth, leave it to me.' I gestured inside with my head.

He'd scratched the skin on his neck red. 'There's only me left tonight, mister, why don't you try another day?'

I glanced over at the entrance, all the doors propped open, looking to see if anyone was at the concession stand. I couldn't make it out so I started to make my way inside. I heard a shout behind me, muted by glass. 'Hey, you need a ticket . . .'

I shot through the entrance, but the concession stand was unmanned and there was no one else in the lobby. I heard another shout behind me, still muted. I threw open the door to the screen and walked to the front.

The white glow of the projection lit the auditorium. I counted no more than a dozen moviegoers; no cigarette girls or employees of any kind. I turned to leave again, felt something hit my back. I looked down and there was popcorn scattered around my feet – thrown by some jerk in the seats.

When I stepped back into the lobby, the ticket seller was

standing in the open doorway of his kiosk. 'You can't be in there. I have to call the cops if you won't buy a ticket.' There were tremors in his voice and that told me I could squeeze him. After all the dead ends, I wasn't walking out empty-handed.

'Why are you holding out on me? All I'm interested in is the girl's wellbeing.'

'I'm not.'

'When do you expect her back?'

'I don't know.'

I walked up to him, pointing. 'Yes you do.'

'I swear—'

'When was the last time you saw her?'

He backed into the kiosk and slammed the door.

I stormed over and hammered on it. 'Tell me, goddamn—'

'Charlie?'

Lizzie's voice stopped me cold. She was standing to my left. She glanced over to the ticket seller, pressed into the corner of his booth, as far from me as he could get.

'She works here,' I said. 'Julie D. He just picked her out, now he's playing dumb.'

She looked at him again. 'I think perhaps you ought to take a moment.'

'This is my first warm lead.'

'We can come back.'

'We don't know that. What if—'

'We can come back.'

My wife held my gaze across the deserted lobby, the smell of popcorn and cheap hotdogs pervasive. Everything was red, I noticed then – the carpet, the walls, the lampshades. Even the uniform the ticket seller was wearing, and his dumb pillbox hat.

I stepped back from the kiosk and went to Lizzie. She turned and walked away before I got to her.

We crossed the street, Lizzie a half-step in front of me so I couldn't see her face. I opened the car door for her and she got in without a word.

I climbed behind the wheel stewing.

'What's gotten into you, Charlie?'

'He was sitting on something. To come that close and then have the rug pulled out from under me—'

'Causing a scene won't help matters.'

'Who's causing a scene? We were the only ones there.'

'He was a kid and he was terrified. He was fixing to climb the walls to get away from you.'

I took a breath, let it out slow. 'You know how important this is.'

'I do, and I know why. But I'm afraid of what it's doing to you. Seeing you like that . . .' She shook her head and turned away to look out her window.

'Speak your mind.'

She shook her head again, still not looking at me.

'You're worried this is how I used to be,' I said. 'At the end, with Jane.'

She didn't look, didn't speak. I could see the blurred reflection of my face next to hers in the window.

The man I'd been before. The temper that'd cost me my wife and my job, derailed my life and left me in a hotel lobby in Texarkana begging to resurrect a marriage that was already dead. It wasn't even a year since.

'I didn't say that. But I've never seen you act this way.'

'I'm stretched, Liz. We both are.'

'I understand that and it's why you need to keep a cool head now more than ever. He was shouting about calling in the police. The last thing we can afford is you winding up in a cell for the night.'

'He was just running his mouth.'

'You don't know how intimidating you are. If you could've seen yourself in there . . .'

I squeezed the steering wheel, tempering my voice. 'I know when someone's lying.'

She stared at me across the bench seat, the green lettering of the Regal sign reflecting in her eyes. 'If we get through all this, I want the man I married to be there on the other side. Not some hot-head bully.'

'Is that what you think of me?'

'No, it isn't.' She reached out to cover my hand on the wheel. 'But don't lose sight of what makes you better than Siegel and his kind.'

*

We stashed ourselves in a budget flop on Wilshire Boulevard, paying cash up front for a no-questions-asked bed for the night. I tried to grab a few hours' sleep, but it wouldn't come.

At first it was Lizzie's words that kept me awake. The consequences of my temper were all too fresh in the memory, and when I thought back over that time with Jane, there wasn't a specific point when the bottom fell out. My jeep crash was the start of it, for certain, but it wasn't as though everything finished that day; it had been a gradual slide into anger and recrimination, finally coming to a head when I trashed our apartment and she ran out of the door terrified. After the first time, it became easier – a kind of mental permission slip signed and accepted – and I'd wrecked the place with increasing fury and diminishing release on three subsequent occasions. Thinking, each time, that it didn't matter because I couldn't hate myself any more – and each time having the truth rammed home when the aftermath brought a new depth of self-loathing.

What worried me was that if I hadn't recognised the descent before, how would I know if it was happening again? Or if it had already started?

After an hour or more fretting those same questions, the present reasserted itself. I could barely hold a thought long enough to interrogate it, so many images and fears circling me. Rosenberg spitting in my face was more vicious than most, and with it in my mind, the feel of his saliva on my skin was as real as when he'd done it.

At some point, I started thinking about our first meeting, his final threat ringing out – how I'd see a bullet, but I'd see it last. The implication was clear – and so was the danger to my wife, and maybe others. I'd come away from that room certain that they needed me more than they'd let on; it was that notion led me to think I could skate on not writing the piece exposing Bayless. But what if I was wrong? What if Lizzie paid the price for it?

Then something else Rosenberg had said came back to me – a throwaway line from earlier that evening: *'We'll take care of our part.'* What was he referring to? Maybe setting up the next target, maybe not. The implication that I was caught up in a bigger scheme.

I slipped out of bed and went to the window to crack the curtain. The traffic on Wilshire was light – too late for the party crowd, too early for the morning shift. Streetlamps ran as far as I could see in either direction, a blue liquor store sign still lit over the way. Too much relied on me staying, but I wondered if Lizzie could be safe anywhere in the city. I was sick to my stomach of running scared. Wondered if I had a counter-punch left in me.

*

By six, the sky was roiling with grey clouds, bands of rain coming off the Pacific and sweeping over the city. I made a crouched dash to the payphone down the block and called Buck Acheson on his home line. The man rarely slept anyway; he'd forgive the early call.

'Christ, Charlie, you've had me worried sick. Are you still in one piece?'

He was silent as I laid out to him what'd happened since my aborted call from the diner two days before. The only time he interjected was when I told him about them wanting me to use the *Journal* to run the smear on Trent Bayless.

'Over my dead body.'

'I said the same. Don't worry, I didn't call for that. It's about Siegel himself.'

'How do you mean?'

'You have any idea where I can find him at? I need to go around his lapdog, Rosenberg. And I need something to use against him.'

'Charlie, I'm the last man to question you, but don't you think you're in over your head this time? Maybe you ought to speak to the authorities. There's—'

'Who would I speak to? You know how many cops Siegel's got in his pocket – LAPD and County.'

'Well, who's this Detective Belfour? I was hoping it was you who'd involved him.'

Hearing his name made me miss a beat. 'Say that again?'

'Detective Belfour – you know him? He left a message at the offices trying to reach you.'

I took a breath, struggling to make sense of his words.

Buck mistook the hesitation for something else. 'Don't worry, the secretaries told him you were out on the street, of course. They know better than to say anything more.'

'Did he say what he wanted?'

'Just left a number. I don't have it with me, but call in and someone will furnish you with it.'

'I'll do that.' The Santa Monica public bus roared past, spraying surface water, the noise drowning out the connection. I turned away until it passed. 'Go back to Siegel – where can I find him?'

'He keeps a place in the city, but I'm assuming you know that much from the papers.'

'Can you get me the address?'

'Shouldn't be hard, but, Charlie—'

'Don't say it.'

He exhaled slowly. 'I try not to concern myself with thugs like Siegel, but everything I hear is that he is a man of unpredictable nature – in the worst way.'

'Buck, I'm short on options.'

He was silent a beat, leaving the desperation in my voice echoing in my ears. Then he cleared his throat. 'If you really want to walk that road, leave it with me.'

'Thank you, I appreciate it. I'll call back later.'

I hung up and tried the *Journal*, reaching one of the night-shift crew working overtime. He left me holding while he tossed the secretaries' desks for the number, came back and told me he'd found it.

I took my pen out. 'Shoot.'

I thanked him and cut the call, re-dialling the number he'd given me. No one picked up. To confirm my suspicions, I called the operator and asked her to connect me to the LAPD South Bureau. The switchboard girl there picked up right away, but when I read out the telephone number he'd left for me, she came back puzzled. 'Sir, that's not a line connected to this exchange.'

I put the receiver back in its cradle and checked my watch, thinking. Iowa was two hours ahead, already past eight there. It was more than a week since I'd spoken to Nancy Hill's mother; a hundred to one shot she'd returned home safe since. A desperation play but worth a coin. I picked up and dialled one more time, waiting while the operators made the connections to Luanne Hill's party line and announced me.

'Mr Yates? Do you have her?'

'No, I'm sorry, ma'am. I was calling to see if she'd returned on her own.'

'Oh.' I heard her swallow, her breathing turning ragged. 'No. I've heard nothing at all. It's— I can't stand being so alone. And the farm, it's already going to ruin but it's just too much for me, and every morning I pray to god that . . .' Her voice broke up.

She hadn't mentioned her husband when we spoke before and I'd taken the notion he never made it home. 'Is Mr Hill . . .?'

She sniffed, stopping herself. 'Missing. He was with General Patton's army in France.'

It was chastening to be reminded mine wasn't the only life had been turned upside down in short order.

'We're still hopeful,' she said, 'but now with Nancy as well . . .'

I looked at the telephone, thinking I'd done more harm than good by calling. 'I understand. I'm sorry to have raised your hopes.'

She sighed, shaky. 'Forgive me, Mr Yates, I appreciate all you're doing.'

'Ma'am, the woman I mentioned to you before, Julie Desjardins – she may have also gone by Virginia, does that sound any bells?'

She thought for a beat. 'None at all. I don't know a Virginia. Or a Julie.'

Belfour was still on my mind. I suddenly wondered—'What about the name Belfour? A tall man, slim-to-gaunt, sandy hair.'

'No. That doesn't sound like anyone I can think of. Who are these people, Mr Yates?'

I felt deflated without cause. 'Just names that have come up in the course of my enquiries. I've taken enough of your time, ma'am, I'll—'

'Mr Yates, you won't forget about her, will you? Please. She's my only child.'

A lump in my throat like a golf ball. 'I'll do everything I can.'

*

I went down the street and bought two coffees and took them back to Lizzie. She was up and dressed when I walked into the motel room. Her makeup was immaculate and her blue tea

71

dress looked freshly pressed, and I wondered at how a woman living out of a bag could keep it together so well. Still, that she'd been cheating sleep told in the redness of her eyes.

She took the coffee I offered her. 'The man calling himself Detective Belfour has been trying to reach me,' I said. I told her about the messages and the telephone number.

She perched on the edge of the bed and blew into her cup. 'Do you mean to speak to him?'

'I already tried calling, no one answered. It's early.'

She took a sip and looked down. 'Are you sure it's wise?'

'I don't see what choice I have.'

She looked at me over the rim of her cup, then blinked in a way that seemed to indicate acceptance. 'I think we should go back to the Regal this morning. If there's any stones left un-turned, we should address them. I think it would help with the rest of the decisions we have to make.'

The way she said it told me she was wavering on her call to run – strengthening my own resolve. I set my cup on the bed-side table. 'Let's go.'

*

We were outside the Regal by nine. The matinee showing was an hour off, so I figured someone had to turn up to open the doors before long. I asked Lizzie to keep watch on the place while I went around the block to a payphone, to try Belfour's office again.

This time, a man snatched up the phone after one ring. 'Yes?'

'This is Charlie Yates calling for Detective Belfour.'

'Mr Yates, I'm glad you telephoned. I think it's time we were introduced.'

CHAPTER TEN

I raced back to the car, but Lizzie was already standing by the doors to the movie theatre, talking to the same ticket seller from the night before. He looked a man transformed in Lizzie's company – at ease and a little embarrassed. She caught my eye but then focused on him again, so I let them talk alone a moment, circling around so I could see his face, watching as it shifted from contrition to apprehension. I wondered what Lizzie had drawn out of him. Then she flicked her wrist to wave me over.

Give the kid credit, he didn't shrink when I joined them. 'Charlie, this is Philip,' Lizzie said. 'You've met. Philip, why don't you go ahead and tell Charlie what you just told me?'

'Your wife told me about what's going on.'

Lizzie nodded, coaxing him. 'It's all right. Tell him about the girl you know as Virginia.'

'She quit coming to work.'

'When was this?' I asked.

'A couple weeks ago.'

'Did she tell you she was quitting?'

He shook his head. 'No, she just didn't show up one day. I thought maybe you were a cop or the like and she was in trouble for ditching out.'

'Did she give you any hint she was thinking of leaving town, anything like that?'

73

'No, sir, nothing like that. She told everyone she was only working here until she won a contract with one of the studios, but she'd been saying that as long as she'd been here. I thought she'd just show up again one day.'

'How long did she work here?'

He blinked, looking off to the side. 'Six weeks or thereabouts.'

Lizzie jumped in. 'Philip, do you know exactly when the last time she showed up for work was?'

He shook his head. Then another thought: 'I can take a look at the rota.'

Lizzie smiled and her approval set him to action. He unlocked the main doors and went inside to the ticket kiosk. He studied a sheet of paper and then came to the window. 'Here. December second.'

The day before their appointment at TPK. 'Do you recall Virginia talking about going for an audition around that time?'

He nodded, looking blank. 'She was always talking about them.'

Lizzie shot me a look, reading my mind: *something he's holding back*.

'Did she mention TPK Studios specifically? I need you to think real hard.'

He squinted, tapping a dime against the metal tray under the issuing window.

'You can tell us,' Lizzie said. 'Remember, you're not in any trouble and neither is Virginia.'

He wrapped his fist around the dime. 'Sure. She talked about going for a call at TPK. I asked her what part she was auditioning for and she said it wasn't an audition exactly.'

Lizzie fixed me with a stare, concern in her eyes and looking for direction.

'Did she elaborate on what she meant by that?' I said.

He shook his head.

'Did she say who her appointment was with?'

Another shake. 'The names wouldn't mean anything to me anyway.'

I looked him over, trying to figure if there was anything more he was keeping back, but all I saw was a nervous kid. At most, I figured he was sweet on her, but I couldn't imagine it'd gone further than that. 'Philip, what surname did Virginia go by?'

'Lake.'

Lizzie and I shared another look – too close to Veronica Lake to be real. 'Did she ever show you any identification?'

'No.' He looked at the ground. 'I know that wasn't her real name, but I guess I thought, what did it matter?'

'It's understandable, Philip, forget it.'

'She used to—' He let go of the dime, watching it slide into the tray. 'She would always do strange things like that. Calling herself Virginia Lake.'

I went to speak but Lizzie put her hand on my chest. 'What else, Philip?'

He squinted one eye, pursing his lips. 'One time she kissed a guy during the show. Just sat right on his lap and started making out with him.'

'Someone she knew?' My ears perked up at the mention of a sweetheart.

'No.' He shook his head. 'A customer. *The Secret Heart* – that was the movie. I wanted to tell her she couldn't go around acting that way.'

'Did you?'

He shook his head. 'She wouldn't take any notice of me.'

'She make a habit of doing that?'

'I only saw it the one time.'

I pictured a young woman who could steamroll this kid. 'One more question and we'll be on our way: did she ever talk about a friend, name of Nancy Hill?' I took the photograph out and showed it to him again, pointing to her.

He showed no reaction. 'Sorry.'

'That's okay, you did just fine,' Lizzie said.

'I feel bad I didn't say anything yesterday,' he said, looking at Lizzie. 'I guess I got nervous.' He never glanced my way.

Lizzie gave him a weak grin and handed him a scrap of paper. 'If you hear from her – anything at all – call this number and leave a message for Charlie.'

'Yes, ma'am. I hope you find her.'

*

Back in the car, as I went to put the photograph away, Lizzie touched my wrist and gently took it from me. She held it in her lap, studying it. 'What do you make of that?'

I was thinking about what Joseph Bersinger had told me at the TPK gate, about producers bringing girls onto the lot on the QT. I finessed it for Lizzie's ears. 'I'm worried they went to the studio under false pretences.'

'Meaning what?'

'There were no auditions slated for that day and according to the gate logs they were never there—'

'What if they set out for the studio but never made it?'

I tilted my head. 'It's a possibility, but I can't think of a reason they'd tell the same lie about TPK to two different people, which means they thought it was a genuine deal – when everything I've heard makes it sound more like something off the books.'

'What do you mean by *off the books*?'

I spoke falteringly, choosing my words. 'I mean someone might have invited them there with the intention of taking advantage of them. Everyone was supposed to be at the back lot wrapping up a shoot, their names aren't on the gate logs – it stinks.'

She looked up from the picture. 'Does that go on?'

'Hollywood's not halfway as glitzy as they'd have you believe.'

'That's disgusting.' She studied the photograph again, as if reassessing it.

'Set it aside for a moment. Whatever the girls' reason for going there, it doesn't explain why they've vanished.'

'What if they were so sickened they upped and left? Maybe the movies weren't so appealing after that.'

'Where would they have gone if not home?'

Lizzie handed the photograph back to me and a silence fell between us. I didn't look at it, but didn't put it away immediately either.

'I spoke with him,' I said. 'Belfour.'

She angled towards me in her seat. 'Who is he?'

'I don't know. He wants to meet. He said it's about Siegel and he'll explain matters in person.'

She looked at me. 'Did you agree to it?'

'What choice do we have?'

She looked away, not saying the obvious. 'When?'

'One hour, downtown.'

*

We arrived at the meet point fifteen minutes early. I stood on the corner of Ninth and Broadway, two blocks from what the *Times* called the busiest intersection in the city, guessing Belfour wanted the anonymity a crowd bestows. Throngs of pedestrians streamed around me, and I watched faces, even though I didn't know what Belfour looked like beyond sandy-haired and gaunt. Lizzie was down the street, set behind the wheel of our car – a precaution in case things went south. I resisted the temptation to glance to where she sat.

A streetcar rumbled past, drawing my eyes. Then I felt a hand on my arm and whipped around.

'Take a walk with me, would you, Yates?'

The man was tall with square shoulders and brown hair. I backed off a step. 'Who are you?'

'My boss is in the car.' He inclined his head to a late-model grey Dodge a short way down Ninth, and I saw the outline of a man on the passenger side. 'He sent me to fetch you.'

He started walking towards it and I followed a few paces behind. As I drew close, the man inside came into focus and I saw the hair and the thin face that Lizzie had described. The first man opened the back door and held it for me, watching the street with an alertness that unnerved me. Belfour called from inside, 'Make yourself comfortable, Mr Yates.'

I lowered myself onto the seat. Belfour was swivelled around, had his hand out to shake. 'It's good to meet in person at last.' He had an easy expression that did nothing to soften the sharp angles of his face. More than gaunt, he was skeletal.

The first man climbed behind the wheel and started the engine.

'Where are we going?' I said.

'Nowhere, just a drive. The best place to talk in this city is in a car.'

We pulled away and slipped into the traffic stream, following Broadway towards the Bullock's department store.

'Who are you?' I said.

'We'll get to that. First thing I'd like to know what's going on between you and Benjamin Siegel.'

'We're tennis partners. Who are you?'

He cracked a grin, but only for my benefit. 'We have a common interest, which you're smart enough to have worked out by now is Siegel. We—'

'Answer the damn question or I'm gone at the next light.'

He strung out an exhale. 'I didn't want to get off on this footing. You've been asking around after me, so you know I'm not who I've claimed to be. If I were to say I'm a law enforcement officer and I'm investigating Benjamin Siegel, would that suffice for now?'

'No one investigates Siegel, so my guess is this is actually some second-rate attempt to scare me.'

'You're only half-right. No one local.'

The grey car, the staid suits, the matching navy ties – it came together then. 'You're government men.'

He stalled, looking for another sidestep.

'Which agency?' I said.

'We'll come back to that. I'd like you to answer my question first.'

My strongest instinct told me not to answer him straight. For one thing, almost anything I said could incriminate me; for another, the man had lied his way to my door, and now expected the truth out of me. And yet I was floundering enough that anything that looked like the cavalry held appeal. 'Siegel wants me dead. I helped break up one of his rackets in Arkansas and he's holding a grudge.'

'Hot Springs.' His eyes glimmered. 'That was you.'

I pressed myself back against the seat, feeling overmatched.

'I was late coming to events down there,' he said, 'the details were sketchy. I thought it was the newsman that died in the fire turned everything upside down.'

Jimmy Robinson. The fire he started, still burning long after his death. A fire I'd poured gasoline on. 'Neither of us knew about Siegel's involvement. I would have handled matters a different way if I had.'

Those last words came unexpectedly, ones I'd never said even to myself before.

He was nodding his head, riveted to the point where I suspected him of mocking me. But he wasn't. 'Then why did you go to Ciglio's restaurant the other night? You must know it's one of his bases of operation.'

From the way he said it, I realised he didn't know about my first visit to Ciglio's – the beating and the fallout from it. I filed that discrepancy. 'You were following me. You ran when my wife saw you.'

He pulled at the skin under his chin. 'I meant to make my first approach to you that night, and then when I realised where you were going, to warn you. But, for obvious reasons, there are certain elements I can't allow to see me talking with you. The same for your wife.' He put his hand back in his lap. 'I'd been readying to make contact with you for a time.'

Now we get to it. 'On account of what?'

He closed his eyes, a long blink, but it felt rehearsed. 'You said Siegel wants you dead, and yet you walked into his restaurant and you're still alive. That's not a normal state of affairs where he's concerned. You ask me why I want you – that's the best answer I can think of. What's between the two of you?'

I thought about Trent Bayless, wondered if there was a line to safety here. 'If you're who I think you are, can you take a man into protective custody?'

He screwed his eyes up. 'Charlie, you can't talk about a price before I've even got a look at the goods you're selling.'

'I'm not talking about me.'

'Then who?'

I held his stare, saying nothing, and he almost looked embarrassed at trying to play it that way.

'Yes,' he said then. 'In a manner of speaking. But it's not a simple matter, nor is it one undertaken lightly.'

I gripped the seat leather. 'Siegel is attempting to blackmail an actor, name of Trent Bayless. He's squeezing him for ten grand.'

He inclined his head. 'What does he have on him?'

'Photographs.'

He leaned closer to me. 'You string everything out like this, we won't accomplish much.'

'Why do you need more than that?'

'If the man's a degenerate, taxpayers won't be crazy about sheltering him on their dime.'

'They show him with another man. Consenting adults, if that's what's worrying you.'

He scoffed. 'As if that makes it acceptable. Still ...' He glanced at the driver who nodded without being asked anything. I'd already lost track of where our route had taken us, but when I looked out, I realised we were still downtown, making a scattergun loop.

'What's your part in it?' he said. 'It's not you in the photographs, is it?'

I shot him a dirty look and then I told him about Siegel coercing me to front the racket and write the smear.

He whistled. 'That is interesting. And you mean for me to take this Bayless out of the picture? That's a big risk to you, isn't it? Why not just write the story?'

I paled as he said it, thinking I'd misjudged the man.

'Loosen up,' he said. 'I'm playing devil's advocate. But it's a steep price to go to for a queer. What's to stop Siegel clipping you when it all goes belly-up?'

'I think this is the thin end of the wedge. They have bigger paydays in mind.'

'And what? You think you're indispensable, is that it?'

'At least for now.'

'That's the craziest pitch I ever heard.' He closed his eyes, shaking his head. 'Look, I can stash your man away, but I need something in return.'

'I took that as read.'

'For my ends, it might be better if you wrote the story. I—'

'I won't do it—'

He held his hand up to cut me off. 'It might be better, but I'm not about to sit here and encourage you to engage in conspiracy to blackmail. How certain are you Siegel will keep you around?'

I got an idea of what he was driving at. 'You want me to feed you information on him.'

He nodded. 'I want you to help me build my case. A man who can walk in and out of the back room someplace like Ciglio's has unique value.'

I thought about all the things Siegel was responsible for and how much I wanted to attend his fall. There was a risk to me in agreeing, more in saying no. But it wasn't the risk to me I was thinking about. 'You never told me your name. Your real one.'

He reached into his pocket, produced a card that identified him as Special Agent Colt Tanner, alongside the four words I realised then I most wanted to see: Federal Bureau of Investigation. Then he pointed at the man driving. 'This is Agent Bryce. Now, do we have an agreement?'

'There's something else I need.'

He took an abrupt breath in. 'I said unique value, not unlimited. Don't push your luck.'

'This is a deal breaker.'

He looked out the window and when he turned back he was chewing his bottom lip. 'Go on.'

Anticipating Lizzie's reaction, I almost couldn't say the words. I scratched my throat. 'I want close protection for my wife too.'

CHAPTER ELEVEN

Tanner let me out along the block from where Lizzie was parked.

'It'll take me a few hours to set everything up.' He looked at his watch.

'How do I corroborate you are who you say you are?'

He looked at the driver as if unsure what I was asking. 'You saw my card.' He was reaching for it again as he said it.

I held my hand out to halt him. 'Identification can be faked.'

He hesitated, his hand in his pocket. 'Call the Los Angeles office, give them your name and ask for me. You'll reach one of my men, I'll authorise them to confirm it. Will that suffice?'

I nodded once.

'You still have the number I gave you earlier?'

'Yes.'

'Call me on that line at six o'clock this evening and I'll tell you where to take your wife. Then we'll go talk to Bayless. Are Siegel's men watching his place?'

'We?'

'I want it to go down without him kicking up a fuss. That requires a friendly face.'

'That's not what I am to him.'

'You're the closest thing to it. Now, are Siegel's men watching? They're not tailing you.'

I looked at him, trying not to show my annoyance. 'Just you, then.'

He screwed up one side of his face. 'Don't gripe. We took a look at you for the sole purpose of establishing if it was safe for us to meet. Goes without saying Siegel can't know about me or this arrangement. So, once again: Bayless' place?'

'I don't know. I've only been there once.'

He glanced at Agent Bryce and then back at me. 'We'll have to survey it then. Call me at six.'

Without another word they pulled away from the kerb and were gone.

It was a short distance to where Lizzie sat but it felt as if I walked through glue to get there. My mind was in tumult. When she saw me, she started the engine and slid over onto the passenger side. I climbed in and she stared at me expectantly.

'He's with the FBI. They're investigating Siegel.'

She watched me in profile. 'I'd have said that's a good thing, but you look like you're thinking a different way.'

'It's a complication.'

'How so? They can put a stop to this, can't they?'

'Bayless? Yes, but not how you mean. They're going to put him on ice until we can get out from under this.'

She thought about that a moment. 'I meant all of it – but I suppose if it were that easy to stop Siegel they would have done so by now.' She rubbed her forearm. 'Still, it seems unfair that Mr Bayless is the one ends up in jail.'

The words ran down my throat like stones. 'It's not jail, it's protection. It's the best thing for him – and us.'

'Us?'

'If they can't touch him, Siegel hasn't got that hold over us . . .'

She'd turned her body towards me, picking up on my

reticence, sensing there was something more. 'Charlie?'

I made a left at a light, realising then that I was driving without a destination. 'I've asked them to provide protection for you too.'

She stared a hole in the side of my head. 'Why would you do that?'

'To keep you safe.'

'But not you?'

'They want me to stay inside Siegel's operation so I can—'

'Goddammit, Charlie, after what I said to you before? You want to leave me in a room with strangers while you're on the street trying to get yourself killed?'

'Will you quit saying that? That's the last thing I want—'

'The worst hell for me is being left to wonder – how can I make you understand that? It's what I went through with Alice all over again, waiting for someone to show up at the door and tell me you're dead.'

I thumped my palm against the wheel. 'What would you have me do, Liz? You want to run, is that it? So we can climb the walls waiting for one of Siegel's men to show up at our door instead?'

She covered her face with her hands. When she spoke it was barely audible. 'I want this to be happening to someone else.'

There was nothing left to say. I kept driving, aimless at first, then suddenly knowing where to take us. I made another left to pick up Route 26, followed it all the way out to Santa Monica, then south to Venice.

At the beach, the boulevard was busy with people, the sun reflecting off the ocean in a glistening corridor of white light. I parked facing it and rolled down the windows, the breeze carrying salt spray and the smell of shrimps from the shacks a little further down the block.

'What are we doing here, Charlie?'

'Do you remember when I first brought you out here? How you felt?'

It was after Texarkana. In the brief period when it felt as though we'd made it through the worst hell the world could throw at us. And where I'd later asked her to be my wife.

'Yes,' she said.

'We can have that again. For keeps. Hold onto that thought.'

'You can't promise that.'

I took her hand. 'Please, if I know you're safe, they can't do anything that scares me. I'm asking you to give me that much.'

'That's unfair, Charlie. You can't ask that of me when you're not willing to do the same. After everything I've told you.'

'If Tanner's legitimate, this is our way out. I'll be with you, and when I'm not, they'll be watching my back.'

She closed her eyes, her jaw set tight.

'A couple weeks and it'll be over. Please.'

*

At six, I dropped a dime into the telephone and called Tanner's line. I'd called the Los Angeles office of the FBI an hour earlier and after I gave my name to the switchboard, I'd been routed to an agent called Caxton who confirmed Colt Tanner was a Special Agent attached to that office.

This time, the man himself answered right away.

'Yates?'

'It's me. Are you set?'

'I've arranged a place for tonight. It's temporary, I'll have to move him tomorrow, but it's a start.'

'And my wife?'

'I'll post Agent Bryce on her door tonight, and, again, I'll have someone else assigned by morning. Where is she?'

'With me.'

'And where is that?'

'Venice Beach.'

'The beach.' He paused, a clicking noise coming down the line – a pen tapping against teeth. 'Take her to the Breakers Motel – you know of it?'

'I can find it. But—' I looked at the ocean, uncertain. 'Earlier you made out like you had somewhere in mind. You sound like you're improvising.'

'I can't just snap my fingers and make things as you want.'

I gritted my teeth and thought about hanging up and driving away.

He sighed, must have read irritation in my silence. 'Look, everything has to be improvised when time is short, pay that no mind. The property is safe and there will be a Federal agent between your wife and the outside world at all times. On my word.'

I jangled the dimes in my pocket, the sound drowned out by the rolling waves down the beach.

'Go to the Breakers, Yates. We'll be there in thirty minutes to collect you. We checked on Bayless' place and it's clean, so we can go there directly.'

Safety for Lizzie. Safety for Bayless. A way out. 'Thirty minutes.'

We took a room at the motel and waited, small talk petering out early on, a nervous silence taking its place, neither of us wanting to address what came next. The room was like every motel we'd stayed in, even if the finishings weren't. Island scenes on the walls and a pastel paint scheme couldn't dull the sense of endless desperation that filtered through me.

When Tanner and Bryce arrived, I made the introductions and promised Lizzie I'd be back as soon as I could. I left her standing in the middle of the room with her arms crossed, looking as though she was revisiting her worst nightmares. Tanner posted Bryce in our car outside, with instructions not to crowd her.

*

We rode back into Los Angeles along Olympic Boulevard, passing through the outskirts and into the Miracle Mile development. 'How long have you been after Siegel?' I said.

'I can't comment on an ongoing investigation. You must know that, your background.'

'How close are you to getting him?'

He glanced at me, a disapproving look.

'The government thought they had him in 'forty-one,' I said. 'He skated then.'

'Before my time.'

'His button man, Abe Reles, was set to spill his guts on Siegel in open court. The DA's office had him under guard for months. The case collapsed when he made like a bird out of a sixth floor hotel room on Coney Island, right before it was due to start. He was in there by himself, supposedly. Local cops on the door, never saw a thing.'

'"*The canary who could sing but couldn't fly*". I remember the headline and I know the details.'

'Siegel got to him, even under—'

'I said I know the details. When I said it was before my time, I meant it would have worked out differently if it'd been my case. That would never have been allowed to happen. Your wife is safe.'

I touched my finger on the dash. 'I covered the story. I made it to the scene while they were still cleaning him off the sidewalk.'

He made eye contact, the briefest of looks. 'I know what we're up against, if that's your point.'

I watched him, his torso pitched forward towards the wheel, the skin so tight on his face it was almost like a mannequin's head.

'What is it you expect me to give you?' I said. 'I can read between the lines – you don't want to get him just for a shakedown scam.'

'If I could prove extortion under Federal statutes, I'd take it. Break it open from there. Wouldn't be my first choice although.'

'What would?'

'Racketeering is the Bureau's interest, but I want all of it. I want to know everyone's ever had a hand in his pocket. Use him to blow apart his own damn organisation.'

'You think you can make him talk?'

'With the right incentive.'

'Which is what?'

He glanced at me out the corner of his eye but ignored the question. 'What's your next engagement with Siegel?'

I told him about the meeting set for the following day. 'I'm supposed to have the money or the story.' I looked at him, expectant.

He nodded his head, keeping his eyes forward. 'Let's talk to Bayless.'

*

When we reached Bayless' address, Tanner made a loop of the block before stopping, checking again for Siegel's men. As we passed the house, I saw one of the windows on the ground floor had been boarded up. Tanner logged it too, pointing as we passed, but kept on driving, completing the circuit. Satisfied the house still wasn't being watched, he jumped out and rounded the front of the car, patting the hood twice as he went, as if to rally me. I climbed out and followed him up the path.

Approaching the door, I saw the threshold was stained red. I put a hand on Tanner's shoulder but he'd seen it too and was reaching for his weapon. I looked all around. There were lights on in the house. I took a step, heard the crunch of broken glass underfoot – a remnant from the window.

Tanner edged around the red stain and tried the door. It was locked. He banged on it and stepped back, his hand gripping the butt of his weapon. 'Get back, Yates.' He motioned for me to retreat without taking his eyes off the door.

There was the sound of movement inside. Unhurried. Tanner drew his weapon and gripped it with both hands, aimed at the ground.

Seconds dragged by. The sound of a car starting somewhere down the block.

Then the door opened. Trent Bayless saw Tanner first and looked dazed, then caught sight of the gun and scrambled backwards, stumbling. 'Oh Jesus—'

Tanner called over his shoulder. 'Yates?'

'It's him.' I dashed forward, put a hand on his trigger arm. 'It's him.'

Bayless had staggered back against the hallway wall. He saw me and looked lost.

Tanner edged inside. 'Mr Bayless, are you in the house alone?'

'What? Who are—'

'Mr Bayless, are you alone?'

'Yes, goddammit. Yes. Who the hell are you?'

Tanner looked along the hallway again and through the parlour doorway. He remained poised a moment more, the gun by his thigh, and I realised he was listening. No sound came from the house.

Finally he holstered his weapon and called back to me. 'Come inside and shut the door.'

I did as he asked, then looked at Bayless, still pressing himself against the wall. He had on a crumpled brown suit and sported a five o'clock shadow that was a day old at least. There was a smell of liquor in the air. 'What happened here?'

'Who is this?' He gestured to Tanner.

'Special Agent Colt Tanner.'

He looked incredulous. 'Am I expected to take that at face value? For all I know . . .'

Tanner whipped out his identification. 'Answer Mr Yates' question.'

Bayless looked from Tanner to me, as if seeking confirmation. He took a breath and it rattled in his chest like a faulty tailpipe. 'Mr Yates most probably knows better than I do.'

'Well, I'm asking you, chief. The doorstep?' Tanner said.

Bayless righted himself, colour coming back to his face. 'Paint. Pink paint. Mr Yates' friends getting their kicks. I did my best to clean it up.'

'They broke your window as well.'

Bayless nodded once. 'A house brick. It was the dead of night, I was asleep – damn near gave me a heart attack. The paint was everywhere when I went to look.'

'You didn't see who did it?' Tanner asked.

'I didn't try. It's not hard to fathom.'

Tanner glanced at me, reaching the same obvious conclusion. Intimidation measures.

'What are you doing here?' Bayless said.

I positioned myself next to Tanner. 'This man can help you.'

'You're a real jack-in-the-box, aren't you? I never asked for your help.'

Tanner unbuttoned his jacket. 'I'm your ticket out, that's all you need to think about. You've got five minutes to pack a bag. Take the minimum but make like you're never coming back here.'

Bayless looked from him to me and back again. 'Are you . . . having me arrested?'

'We don't ask you to pack a bag when we arrest you.'

'They're going to take care of you until we can get Siegel to lay off,' I said.

Bayless shook his head. 'I'm not going anywhere.'

'It's the only way,' I said.

Tanner walked a little way down the hall and stuck his head through the parlour doorway. 'Where are the photographs?'

Bayless' face soured. He was still looking at me when he said, 'I burned them.'

Tanner stepped back and shot him a look. 'You're not that stupid. Surely?'

'To hand them to the FBI? No.'

Tanner flicked his eyes to me, shaking his head. 'Bad start for your man, Yates.'

I motioned Bayless to the stairs. 'Just go get your things together, will you?'

'This is my home.'

Tanner was still watching. 'I can have you arrested if you'd prefer. Photographs or not.'

I looked Bayless full in the face. 'Please.'

Slowly, he gathered himself to his full height. He made his way along the hallway and up the stairs as though he was treading on broken glass.

Tanner strode inside the parlour. When I came in a second behind, he was scouring the room. 'You buy that?' he said. 'That he destroyed them?'

'Wouldn't you?' I heard footfalls above me – Bayless moving around upstairs.

Tanner rifled a pile of magazines and, finding nothing, moved over to the bookcase. 'I think they're still here somewhere.'

'Did you have to come on strong like that?'

He jerked his head around to look at me. 'You'd have me mail him an invitation instead?'

I said nothing as he kept moving around the room, inspecting

94

everything in plain view. Three or four minutes went by and it felt like an hour.

Then I heard Bayless coming down the stairs and I looked over. He was carrying a grip across his chest and had changed into a fresh shirt. From the bottom step, he said, 'Where are we going?'

Tanner straightened. 'It's imperative you pass me those photographs if you still have them. You're impeding a Federal investigation otherwise. You're certain they're no longer in your possession?'

Bayless held his stare, his jaw moving as though he were chewing a candy. Then he said, 'I burned them.'

Bayless kept looking at him, then sniffed. 'Let's go to the car.'

*

We rode in darkness, Tanner behind the wheel, Bayless in the back. I could feel Bayless' eyes on me but every time I glanced over my shoulder he was staring right ahead.

'Where are you taking me to?'

Tanner waved a hand. 'Somewhere safe. Be grateful to Mr Yates, he's gone out on a limb for you.'

I turned my gaze to the road.

'Thank you, Mr Messenger.' Bayless lit a cigarette. 'When will I be able to go back home?'

'That's unclear at this stage,' Tanner said.

'You're proposing to hold me indefinitely?'

Tanner eyed him in the mirror. 'You're free to take your leave any time you like.'

Bayless looked off to the side as though scolded.

'They'll have forgotten about you in a few days,' I said. 'They'll switch their attention to someone else.'

He blew smoke out the side of his mouth. 'That's a comfort.'

'I don't think you appreciate the seriousness of the situation you've gotten into, Mr Bayless. Be thankful you're not being arrested at this time.'

'I abided by what was expected of me. It's not as though I took those photographs.'

Tanner drew over to the side of the road, the quiet street we were following ending in a riot of lights at the intersection with Wilshire Boulevard ahead.

Tanner turned in his seat to address Bayless. 'Let us have the car a moment, please.'

Bayless looked at me and then at Tanner again.

'I need to speak with Mr Yates before I let him out,' Tanner said.

Bayless put his cigarette in his mouth and opened the door. He took a few paces along the sidewalk in front of us, skirting the pool of light from the headlamps.

'You can take the bus back to Venice from here,' Tanner said.

Some reason, I'd assumed he'd bring me along too. 'You don't trust me?'

'Trust plays no part. If you don't know, you can't talk.'

He watched my face as the implication of what he said hit home. The chance that Siegel could work me over. He didn't know I'd been through that wringer once already and was alive to the threat.

'I want you to keep the meeting tomorrow,' he said. I waited for something more, but nothing came.

'That's it? What the hell am I supposed to say?'

He watched Bayless on the street. 'Tell them he disappeared after you braced him. Who's to say any different?'

I scoffed, incredulous. 'What's to stop them putting a bullet in me?'

'You told me you think they have bigger plans for you – let's take advantage of it. If we know their next move, we can plan for it.'

I stared at him. 'What if I'm wrong?'

'They brought you in for a reason. If Bayless is off the board, they've accomplished nothing, so there's no sense in them dispensing with you – and meanwhile your wife is safe.'

I took a slow breath and bowed my head.

'Look, I can't deny there are risks, nor can I force you to take them. The decision is yours to make – but trust your gut. When you laid it out to me, the word you used was *indispensable*. We can take great strides here – with your help.'

But it wasn't my safety I was thinking about, nor the greater good. I just needed Lizzie protected. 'All right.'

He grimaced, nodding his appreciation. 'I need you to take note of every man in the place, everything that's said, every detail. Things you think have no value might be useful to us.'

'Where does this end?' I realised the irony that it was the same thing I'd asked of Rosenberg.

'Get through tomorrow. Make your own way back to the Breakers afterward, we'll debrief there. But be sure they don't put a man on your tail. Your wife's safety depends on it.'

'I've kept us alive this long.'

'I don't want you to get complacent now I'm involved.' He put his hand on my shoulder.

I recalled the black and white tiles of the floor, the gun next to my head. 'I can handle it.'

'Keep your wits about you. No one's kicking down the door if you find yourself in trouble.'

'You said you'd be watching.'

'Exactly that, but we can't see everything. That's why your part is so important.'

'If they kill me you'd have your case at least.'

He looked dismayed, then saw my crack for what it was. 'I'd rather go about it the long way round.' He leaned across me and yanked my door handle. 'Get some sleep.'

I got out and went around the front of the car onto the sidewalk. Bayless came over, trailing smoke. He stood in front of me, taking a drag and working up to something. 'You really spoke to Siegel?' he said.

'His right-hand man. They weren't for negotiating.'

He nodded, thoughtful. 'I asked a man at my studio to get a message to Siegel. To meet. I never heard back but that night . . . well, you saw what the answer was.'

'I didn't know anything about that. I'm sorry.'

His gaze roved over my face and then he looked away.

Mention of his studio made my mind jump to a different tack. It felt crass in the situation, but my desperation was stronger. 'Let me ask you something – do you know anyone at TPK Studios?'

He squinted. 'Why?'

'Humour me.'

'It's Hollywood. Everyone knows everyone – until you need something.'

'Two girls were invited onto the lot, on a day there were

no casting calls and most everyone was out on a shoot. What would they be going there for?'

He tilted his head. 'All I would say is I hope she wasn't your sister.'

'Figures. If I gave you their names, could you find out who they went there to visit with?'

'If it's what it sounds like, no one will ever remember their names.'

'They haven't been seen since.'

He blinked at that. Dipped his head to take a drag and blew it at the ground. 'That's not usually part of the arrangement.'

'That's why I'm concerned.'

'How do you know the two things are connected?'

I scratched my cheek, looking for an answer I still couldn't put into words. 'Instinct.'

He frowned. 'I've got enough trouble on my hands, Yates, I could do without any more.'

The car horn sounded, making both of us start on the dark street. I turned and Tanner was motioning for us to wrap it up from behind the wheel.

Bayless rubbed his neck, his eyes distant again. 'It's not even my goddamn house. That's what I feel worst about.'

'Julie Desjardins and Nancy Hill. December third. Please?'

I waited but his gaze was trained over my shoulder. He dropped his cigarette between us and stamped it out. 'Thanks for what you did.'

CHAPTER TWELVE

Lizzie stood behind me in the mirror as I dressed in silence the next morning. She reached around to flatten the collar on my suit jacket, leaving her hand on my lapel.

She pressed her forehead to my back.

I turned and wrapped my arms around her.

She let me hold her a moment, then planted her fingers on my chest and pushed back a fraction, to look me in the face. 'When we were young, our grandpa was fond of telling Alice and me, "*You can't hit second and come first in a fight.*"'

She flushed at volunteering it, nerves making her talkative.

I touched her face.

'Is there no way we can leave this in the FBI's hands?' she said.

'They want me to go. Their help comes with strings.' *Anything to keep her safe.*

I heard a car pull up outside, and both of us looked towards the window. The curtains were closed most of the way, only a narrow band of light coming into the room. I motioned for Lizzie to step back and crossed over to look.

A second agent had relieved Bryce by the time I'd returned the night before, but now he was back, leaning into the man's car. An animated discussion. Bryce looked up and saw me at the window. He said something else to the agent in the car, then started across the lot towards us.

I opened the door. 'What's going on?'

'May we talk inside, Mr Yates?'

I backed up to hold it open for him.

He rushed past me and set himself in front of the window, nodding to Lizzie. 'Ma'am.' He turned to me, his posture rigid. 'Sir, have you had contact from Mr Bayless in the last several hours?'

My guts knotted up. 'Not since I left him with Tanner last night. What happened?'

'Do you have any idea as to his whereabouts?'

'No. I don't even know where you had him.'

He parted the curtains to signal the agent in the car, shaking his head twice. Lizzie came to stand by my side.

'Bryce, what is going on?'

He turned back to me. 'Mr Bayless is unaccounted for right now.'

'You lost him? You couldn't keep him for a single goddamn night?'

'We're not at liberty to detain him against his will.'

'You're telling me he just walked out?'

'He asked to use a telephone. He intimated it was something on your behalf.'

The girls and TPK. Guilt cut through me like a knife.

'Given the circumstances, Special Agent Tanner advises for you to proceed with your appointment today. If Mr Bayless shows up, we'll endeavour to bring him in again.' He looked at Lizzie. 'Agent Hendricks will remain posted outside in the meanwhile, ma'am.'

I tried to keep up with my own thoughts. 'What about you?'

'Sir?'

'You need to stay here too. If they've taken Bayless . . .'

'Sir, we don't know that's the case.'

'It's a hell of a coincidence, wouldn't you say?'

'In my experience, it doesn't pay to jump to conclusions.'

'Look, either you stay here, or I do. Put that to your boss.'

Lizzie gripped my hand. 'Charlie? Do you mean to go through with this?'

'I couldn't live with myself if I didn't.'

'Why? What did you ask of him?'

'The girls.' I felt Bryce's eyes on me, like an accusation. 'I asked him to make a call, nothing more. I never meant . . .' I felt Lizzie's hand slip from mine. I jammed my head back against the wall. 'Goddammit.'

Bryce looked at his watch. 'Sir, it's almost eleven.'

I opened my eyes. 'Stay or go, Bryce?'

'Hendricks is a very capable agent, Mr Yates. Your wife couldn't be in safer hands.'

'I'm not questioning that. I want more than one man here.'

He looked at Lizzie, her back to us as she roughly fastened one of our bags.

'All right,' he said.

I nodded and went to her, kissed her goodbye on the cheek without saying another word. She kept her back to me but leaned into me and I could tell she didn't want Bryce to see her eyes were wet.

CHAPTER THIRTEEN

Ciglio's looked different in the daylight. Without the spot-lights, the gold letters came off as plain garish. Even the diners at the outside tables looked somehow cheap.

Inside, the piano man was still warming up – a staccato tink-ling that mimicked my pulse. Kitchen smells came at me – oil and garlic and cream, the scent of a heavy sauce, fetid to my senses in that moment. The maitre d' saw me right away, the same man as before, and out of the corner of my eye I registered someone at a far table glance up when he moved towards me. Looking properly, I saw it was Gilardino.

A signal went to the back and then Moe Rosenberg was at the kitchen doorway. Seeing him appear, the maitre d' returned to his lectern and his reservation list – clued in to what was going down, happy enough to bury his head. Rosenberg made no sign for me to approach, just waited on me, jangling a set of keys in his right hand. I took a breath and started walking towards him, all of it so subtle that the sprinkling of other patrons didn't even notice what was happening. As I passed him, Gilardino rose from his table, leaving a half-eaten plate of linguine and a white napkin covered in orange stains. He fell in step behind me.

Rosenberg turned and made his way down the dark corridor to the same back room. I followed him without a word, steeling myself to see Siegel again. Brooding on what to say. Praying my gamble was right.

The room was empty.

'Where's Siegel?'

'Ben's got bigger concerns than you. So do I, but, short straw right here, I guess.'

Relief washed over me. Behind it came a sense of disappointment.

The harsh crack of the back door bolt being thrown snapped me to attention. Gilardino pulled the door open and went down the corridor towards the rear entrance. Rosenberg waved one finger, nonchalant, signalling for me to go too. Suddenly the outside door was open and light flooded in, blinding me a moment.

They led me out into the rear lot that had been my first introduction to Ciglio's. The dented garbage cans and patched-up paintwork were more revealing of the nature of the place than the frontage. A custom Chrysler limousine was idling at the kerb, a man behind the wheel I didn't know. Gilardino opened the back door and pointed for me to get in. Rosenberg dropped down next to me, Gilardino riding shotgun.

We took off towards Sunset, then crossed it and continued down a cookie-cutter residential block lined with palms. We made two turns in quick succession and my sense of direction failed me, my mind a riot I was no longer in control of.

'You write the piece?' Rosenberg said.

'What do you think?'

'I think your mouth has balls enough to get you in trouble.'

He took a cigar from his pocket and put it to his lips.

'What's the rest of the scam?' I asked. 'You said to me—'

'Don't tell me what I said. You didn't write a word, did you?'

'My editor would never have gone along with it.' I felt disgust as soon as I said it, an abdication of responsibility I never meant to take. 'I would never have gone along with it,' I added, my voice sounding small.

The car turned sharply and Rosenberg waited it out before lighting his cigar. A fleck of half-burned tobacco settled on his necktie, blue-grey smoke diffusing around the cabin. 'You told him to run,' he said.

He let the words hang there, my pulse accelerating into the red. 'You told him to run, didn't you?'

I kept my eyes on the street, trying to figure where we were, fearing where we were headed. Wondering if Tanner had eyes on me still.

'That was a bad decision.' He flicked ash into the silver ashtray in his door.

We drove a short while longer, backstreets exclusively, time slipping. I didn't notice we were in an alleyway until we stopped outside what looked like a warehouse. Gilardino got out and opened Rosenberg's door for him. He gestured for me to do likewise, flashing his piece as he did.

A metal door in the warehouse wall had been opened from inside. Gilardino hustled me towards it, and the car was already leaving by the time I went in.

It was unlit inside, but I could tell the building was cavernous, the air cool and damp. It was a warehouse or loading bay of some kind, but empty. Our footfalls echoed off the brick walls, a brittle sound. Gilardino turned a lamp on and set it on the floor.

Not quite empty.

On the far side, a figure was slumped in a chair, back to me. My heart skipped, and then the guilt came on when my eyes adjusted enough to see it was a man – not Lizzie.

'Real bad decision.' Rosenberg started moving towards him, the man pitched sideways and unmoving.

I drew up behind the figure and knew it was Trent Bayless even before I saw his face. Rosenberg circled around him, a wide berth, and positioned himself right in front. Gilardino had slipped away into the shadows somewhere, but I heard him draw his gun.

Rosenberg summoned me with two fingers. I followed his path and could barely stand to look as Bayless came into full view. His face was a bloody mess; a dull sheen of blood caught in the lamplight. His hair was matted with clots of it. There were holes in his shirtfront where they'd burned him with cigarettes. His head was lolled to one side, and he looked ready to fall off the chair. The ropes around his wrists were barely holding him in place.

I saw his chest rise and fall, realised he was still alive, and couldn't look any more. 'You goddamn son of a bitch.'

'In every sense, you did this to him.'

A faint wheeze came from Bayless' throat.

'Let him go. He needs a doctor. Let me take him to a hospital—'

'He's past that, and you know it.'

'No.'

Rosenberg waved his hand again, not at me. Footsteps from the dark—

'NO—'

Gilardino appeared in the lamplight and shot Bayless in the temple. The chair toppled sideways and he fell the short distance to the floor, hitting shoulder first with a soft thud.

I gripped my head, my hands like a vice. Couldn't tear my eyes off the corpse in front of me.

Rosenberg stepped to my shoulder. 'He tried to set up a meeting with Ben. That your idea too?'

Took me two tries to get a word out. 'No.'

'You sure? Because that was what marked him out in the first place. Then you telling him to run came out this morning, once we got to talking, and that was the ballgame right there.'

I screwed my eyes shut. 'But he didn't run.'

'No, but it wasn't him we needed to punish.'

My jaw trembled, from guilt as much as anger.

'You understand?'

He took a photograph from his pocket and held it out to me between his thumb and fourth finger, cigar in the same hand. Before I could think, I slapped it away, the cigar skittering across the floor, embers sparking off the concrete, and the photograph spinning off to the side.

In a blur his hand came up and I braced for a punch, but I realised he was holding up his palm, telling Gilardino to hold off. I looked around, saw he was only a few feet behind me.

Rosenberg dropped his hand. 'You just can't keep out of your own way, can you?' He folded his arms. 'Pick it up.'

I stood there, motionless – not defiance but a fear that as soon as I bent over he'd shoot me. But he inclined his head towards where it lay, said again, 'Pick it up.'

I backed away a couple steps and crouched down to get it, hating myself every inch of the way, keeping both men in front of me and in sight as I did. The photograph was face down. I snatched it and stood up, held it out to give back to him. 'I don't want it.'

'That's not your choice to make.'

I lowered my eyes and turned it over. It was a shot taken from distance, and hard to make out in the gloom. I held it closer, squinting, and saw Lizzie standing at the window of the Breakers Motel.

It fell from my hand.

'Think about how you'll feel when it's her at your feet over there, and not a stranger.'

My eyes followed Rosenberg's finger, almost a surprise to see Bayless' corpse again – briefly forgotten in the shock. Fresh blood pooling under his head and creeping across the concrete.

'You screw around this time, and it's her next. And if you get some stupid idea like you're indispensable, think twice. I know what you're about, and once she's dead, there'll be no screw left to turn on you, so you'll go too.'

I kept staring at Bayless, my vision losing focus, seeing only red on grey shrouded in blackness; then looking straight into the lamp, the white light burning through my eyes and searing into my brain, knowing I deserved the pain and more, and that it was only a down payment on what was to come – for them, for me, for all of us. All of us apart from Lizzie. 'I'll never let you lay a finger on her.'

He watched me a moment and I could feel his eyes roving over my face. 'Do as I say and you won't have to worry about it.' He sounded almost conciliatory, as if the conviction in my voice unnerved him.

He nodded towards Gilardino. 'Vincent'll give you the next envelope. Three days to make them pay the money, but I want your piece written and ready to print inside of forty-eight hours. Bring it by Ciglio's so I can see it. Square it all with your editor now – he presents you a problem again, you take care of it. No excuses this time.'

CHAPTER FOURTEEN

Standing in the sunlight outside felt like a betrayal. Feeling its warmth on my skin, seeing the powder-blue sky, even being alive to take a breath – all of it facing the man who'd put a bullet in Bayless. Waiting on him to give me my next assignment.

The car that'd carried us to the warehouse was waiting when we came out. Gilardino popped the trunk and produced an envelope same as the last one. He handed it to me, but kept a grip on it when I reached to take it. 'Why'd you act up? Kid would still be alive but for you.'

I searched his eyes, saw there was no cynicism, no recognition of the hypocrisy in his words. 'You shot him, you goddamn animal.'

'I pulled the trigger, there's a difference. We're all pawns to them, you should realise that.'

'Justify it however you want.'

'You cross him again, Moe will kill you and your old lady, no question. But if Mr Siegel involves himself . . . hell, he might kill everyone you ever knew. There's a reason he picked up that nickname.'

I let go of the envelope, sensing his fear. 'Don't counsel me, you worthless son of a bitch. Do you even remember what it's like to not be scared every minute of your life?'

He pressed it to my chest. 'Do you?'

I held his stare, the gun under his suit coat seeming to radiate heat.

'You don't hide it well,' he said. 'Never seen a man such an obvious disappointment to himself.'

'It's the company I've kept all these years.'

'That what you tell yourself?'

I took the envelope from him and turned to go.

'Don't you want the lowdown?' he said, his tone taunting, knowing he'd got under my skin.

I stopped, desperate to get back to Lizzie but wrestling with what would put the next target in more danger, knowledge or ignorance. Wondering what course might have spared Bayless. A flash of self-pity hit me, wishing Harlan Layfield had never saved my life in Hot Springs so I'd never have known this bind. Alice Anderson's words, *There are worse things than dying.* Disgust hot on its heels – selfish, indulgent, weak.

I wheeled around again. 'Say your piece.'

But he was already opening the car's passenger door to climb in. 'It's all in the envelope. I was just curious to know how far they got their hooks into you.'

The car pulled away. I turned to go in the opposite direction, walking at speed until they were out of sight and then starting to run. But visions of Bayless made my legs buckle and I stumbled against the alley wall, trying to hold myself up and failing. Collapsing to the ground, feeling like I belonged there.

*

Took me five minutes to find a payphone. I called Tanner's office, pacing on the spot while it dialled, finally hanging up after thirty rings with no answer. I dropped another dime and called the office at the Breakers Motel, the dial tone taunting me, again no answer. I slammed the phone down, feeling like I was the last man left in the goddamn city.

I had to flag a cab to take me back to the car, left a block from Ciglio's. When it dropped me off, I jumped inside and tore off towards the beach, but a wreck in Beverly Hills brought traffic almost to a standstill. I hit the horn, yelling at no one, weighing if I should ditch the car to make a run for a payphone. I thumped the steering wheel.

Questions started to pierce my frustration. How had they found Lizzie and me? The list of people knew our whereabouts was short: Tanner, Bryce and Hendricks – the agent who'd kept watch overnight; I'd even kept Buck Acheson out of the loop. A darker thought: if they knew where Lizzie was, why not take her to use as leverage against me? Siegel's outfit had tried it before, when I was in Hot Springs – why not now? The only answer I could make stand up was that they'd spotted the agents outside and put it together that I was talking to the law. Was that what sealed Bayless' fate? Rosenberg said I was the one being punished – but he implied it was for telling Bayless to run. Now I wondered if he was hinting at this instead.

My head swirled with it all, and then a charge went off in my brain. Go back – the list: Tanner, Bryce, Hendricks. The men who knew where we were—

Impossible. But with everything I'd seen, there were no absolutes any more.

I leaned on the horn and didn't let go.

*

It was another hour before I made it back to the Breakers. I made the turn off the highway and raced across the lot. I braked hard, jumped out and left the car with the door flung open.

Bryce and Hendricks were where I'd left them, seated in their vehicle. Bryce jumped out when he saw me, looking alarmed. Seeing his face, I turned to our room – drapes drawn, door closed, and ran the last few steps. Bryce called after me. 'What happened?'

I ignored him, hammering on the door. After a moment, Lizzie opened up and ushered me inside.

Bryce came up behind me. 'Yates, what happened?'

I kept my eyes on him. I moved Lizzie inside gently, said to Bryce over my shoulder, 'Get Tanner here now.' He made to follow, but I closed the door on him.

I stood there, holding Lizzie and wondering what the hell to do. She sensed something had changed, pulling me into the embrace and saying nothing.

Bryce rapped on the door, 'Yates?' Neither of us moved.

Finally she looked up at me.

'They killed him,' I said.

She closed her eyes and buried her head in my chest, whispering something I couldn't catch.

I gave her a moment then told her the rest, sparing the details. She flinched when I mentioned the photograph of her, her shock obvious enough to make me hold back on the implications. But the look on her face told me she'd already arrived at them. Her eyes moved to the door. 'You don't think . . .'

'Who else knew where we were?'

'That's . . . how can that be? They're government men.'

Bryce knocked on the window now. 'Yates? Will you open the door please?'

'We shouldn't jump to conclusions,' she said.

I nodded, grinding my teeth, neither of us convinced. Feeling trapped in that room.

'What should we do? We can't stay here.'

'Maybe what you said all along.'

Bryce knocked once more. 'Special Agent Tanner will be here in ten minutes. Yates, can you hear me?'

I looked around, thinking. The only other way out was the bathroom window. I went to it, sized it up as just big enough to fit through. It led onto an empty lot covered in sand and a scattering of weeds. But leaving that way would mean ditching the car.

Lizzie put her hand on my arm. 'Charlie, wait a moment. You've had a terrible shock, maybe you're not seeing straight.'

'You had the same thought.'

'Maybe neither of us are.'

I closed my eyes, wishing I had time just to think. 'It doesn't add up.'

I looked at her again, desperate for her to see an angle I couldn't.

'If Siegel's men knew you were talking to the FBI, surely they wouldn't take a risk like that.'

There was sense in what she said. 'I need to talk to Tanner. Put him on the spot.'

'Somewhere public.'

I stared at her, my certainty undermined again.

'It can't hurt to be cautious,' she said. 'The coffee shop on the corner – you can have Bryce tell Tanner to meet us there.'

I kissed her on the forehead and went to the door, called out.

'Bryce? When Tanner shows up, have him go to the joint on the corner. Now get in your car and shut the doors and windows.'

'What?'

'You heard me. Get going.'

I peered around the drape, saw Bryce backing towards his car slowly, glancing at Hendricks, his face twisted in confusion. I pulled it back a little so he could see me. He kept going.

When he'd shut himself in, I gathered our bags and took Lizzie by the hand. 'Let's go.'

I opened the door and fast-walked to the car, shielding Lizzie with my body, watching Bryce and Hendricks. Neither man made a move.

The car door closest to us was the one I'd left open, but I led Lizzie to the far side, so the car was between us and them as we got in. The key was still in the ignition. I pulled around in a tight circle, watching Bryce in the rearview all the way out of the lot.

*

Tanner walked in looking dazed. I'd calmed down some, enough to feel a creeping uncertainty in my actions. We'd taken a table right in the middle of the coffee shop. I was thinking safety in a crowd, but listening to the conversations around me, hearing normal people with normal cares, brought on a perverse sense of relief; a reminder that the world went on undaunted.

Tanner came over and sat down heavily. 'Can you explain to me what the hell is going on?' He looked at Lizzie. 'Forgive me, ma'am.'

Lizzie cocked her head.

'I'd ask you the same thing,' I said.

'Where did they take you?'

'You weren't watching?'

'I didn't anticipate them moving you. We were aware they took you out the back way but we weren't able to follow covertly.'

'They killed Trent Bayless in a warehouse near Hancock Park.' I watched his face but he only glanced at the tables either side of us, as if I'd spoken too loud. 'I can take you there but my guess is the body's gone.'

He snapped back to look at me again. 'We need to discuss this in private. Every detail. Give me the address, I'll send some men right away.'

I didn't know it exactly, but gave him directions based on the cab journey I'd taken back. 'There's something else. They had a photograph of our room at the Breakers.'

'What?' He leaned forward over the table, his voice barely a hiss now. 'How is that possible?'

I watched him, felt Lizzie's eyes burrowing into him at the same time.

He glanced at her and then back at me again. 'What's with the look?'

'Who else knew where we were staying?'

'What do you mean?'

'You, Bryce, Hendricks. Who else?'

'Two more agents under my charge, that's all. Just what are you implying?'

'How would you explain it?'

He stabbed his finger at the middle of the table. 'You're way off track if you're suggesting the information somehow came from my men. A million miles off.'

He said it with enough fury to make me break his stare. 'I don't have any answers.'

'You damn sure do not.' He rubbed the side of his face, eyes screwed shut. 'Wait a minute, if they knew where to find you, how do you know they aren't still watching?' He jerked his head around to look through the window. 'You goddamn—' His eyes flicked to Lizzie and he checked himself, came back in a whisper. 'You jackass, if they're watching now, you've jeopardised my operation.'

All the blood ran from my face. He pushed his chair back sharply. 'I'll be at my office in thirty minutes. Call me there immediately. I'll have Bryce and Hendricks tail you, they'll let me know if you're being watched.'

He stood up and was gone.

*

We gave Tanner a two-minute lead, then left the diner as fast as we could without making a commotion. I scanned the street as we came outside, looking for waiting cars or men watching us, wondering if meeting with Tanner would've forced Siegel's hand and put us in immediate danger.

I bundled Lizzie into the car through the driver's door, not wanting to waste a second, only feeling a small measure of safety when we were moving again.

'What do we do now?'

I didn't answer at first, driving without a direction in mind other than back towards the city, the ocean quickly slipping away in the rearview. I caught sight of Bryce and Hendricks two cars back, made a late turn and jumped a red light – anything I could think of to shake a tail, halfway hoping to throw them off too. It felt like every damn motorist I saw was watching us.

I weaved through traffic until we hit a clear stretch of black-top. Bryce was still behind us. 'Did you buy that back there?'

She rubbed her forehead with trembling fingers. 'I don't know what to think. He got pretty hot at you.'

I nodded, switching lanes, thinking.

'He seemed more worried about his operation than anything else,' she said. 'If that's his priority ...'

'I don't doubt that it is.'

'Then what cause would he have to work against us?'

'One of his men then?' The idea grew more outlandish every time I spoke it aloud.

'I couldn't say. But they don't ... they don't seem the type.'

'The ones we've seen.'

She screwed her eyes shut, covered them with a hand. After a moment, she turned to me again. 'If you give evidence as to what you saw, surely Mr Tanner can make arrests?'

'That's my hope.'

'You sound doubtful.'

'A murder charge would mean giving the case to the LAPD.' I hit the left blinker and made a right turn. 'And besides, Siegel wasn't there to implicate.'

*

Thirty minutes after we left, I stood at a payphone in Culver City in the shadow of the Helms Bakery. The factory sign loomed over the street, giant letters shilling their Olympic Bread.

Bryce and Hendricks cruised up to the kerb behind where I'd parked. Bryce rolled his window down. 'You're clean, Yates. No one was on you.'

'You're certain? You managed to keep up.'

'That's why I'm sure – you weren't hard to tail.'

I nodded, trying not to show my disappointment. I expected him to pull away, but he gestured for me to make the call.

I dialled and Tanner answered immediately. 'Yes?'

'It's me.'

'Were you followed?'

'Bryce is here, he says not.' I looked at him as I said it.

'All right. I've dispatched men to the address you gave me.'

'I'll tell you everything that happened. Moe Rosenberg and Vincent Gilardino were there, Gilardino pulled the trigger. You can put me on the stand—'

'Yates, hold up, I can't take a statement over the telephone.'

'I'll come to your office then. They've got me running another shakedown – you've got to put a stop to this.'

He muttered 'Goddammit' away from the mouthpiece. 'Who's the target?'

'I didn't open the envelope yet.'

'Three days again?'

'Yes.'

'All right. Put Bryce on the line.'

I waved him over.

He took the receiver from me and listened. Lizzie watched, hard eyes flicking between me and him.

Bryce said, 'Yes, sir,' and hung up. 'He wants you to go directly to the field office. We'll follow after you again, as a precaution. When you get there, wait in your car until I give you the all-clear. If you don't see me, drive off and make contact again by telephone.' He scribbled something on a piece of paper and handed it to me. 'Get going.'

*

The address was a low-rise office building in Bunker Hill, the entrance nothing more than a scuffed brown doorway across the street from Grand Central Market. The smell of fresh fish and raw meat carried on the air from the rows of stalls, the din of commerce rising and falling like the last throes of a bad party.

As soon as I pulled over, Bryce cruised by and called 'Clear' through his window.

Even before we climbed out, a man who could've been Bryce's cousin opened the brown door and waved us inside. He led us up two flights of stairs to a small antechamber that gave way to a larger office. Inside, Tanner was waiting by a desk that was pressed up against the length of one wall. A second, smaller, desk sat opposite, and there were box files stacked all over the floor.

Tanner gestured to an empty chair. 'Take a seat.' He turned his attention to the man that had greeted us. 'Agent Caxton, will you make Mrs Yates comfortable.'

He held the door open for Lizzie to go back to the antechamber.

She looked at him and then took a seat next to me. 'I'm not easily offended, Mr Tanner.'

Tanner looked at me.

'Whatever we talk about in here affects both of us.'

He hesitated a minute, then signalled to Caxton to shut the door. 'So be it.' He retook his own seat and held his hand out. 'Where's the envelope?'

I held it by my side. 'Don't you want to ask me about Bayless?'

'Yes. But the clock's ticking on this.' He took it from me and tore it open.

'What about the warehouse?'

'My men found bloodstains, but the body's been removed. As expected.'

'Why didn't you send a man to accompany him to the goddamn payphone?'

He looked up from the envelope. 'We're stretched thin. Should I have sent the man who was busy standing sentry for you?'

'You can't turn this around on me—'

'No? Care to tell me what you were thinking sending him out on an errand?'

I felt my face redden and looked away.

He dropped a torn piece of envelope on the desk. 'Look, we had no reason to fear for his safety at that moment. My information indicated no imminent threat.' He reached inside, but stopped. 'He was going down the block to a payphone for Christ's sake.'

He looked down again and flicked through the contents, pulling out a handwritten page. The script was precise if not tidy. 'Well, this isn't Siegel's writing. Who handed this to you?'

'Gilardino.'

'Doubtful it'd be his doing. So Rosenberg then.' He said it to Caxton.

'You say that as if it's important,' I said.

Tanner waved it off, skim reading. 'Hell, they're escalating.' He handed the sheet to Caxton and rifled through the rest of the contents.

'Tanner?'

'They're going for Lyle Kosoff, the producer at MGM. Fifty thousand dollars.'

I recognised the name but knew nothing about the man beyond what made the press. 'What's the lever?'

He started to say something but then made a point of looking at Lizzie and handed me one of the pictures instead, face down. 'See for yourself. Safe to say that's not his wife.'

The snap was an action shot, the two bodies a blur, but the man's face was clear enough to be identifiable to anyone knew him. He appeared to be naked, as did the young black woman he'd hit the mattresses with. I handed it back.

Tanner took it and slipped it away, his eyes widening when he looked at the next shot. 'Generous with his affections.' He flashed it to Caxton and then passed it to me. It showed Kosoff tangled between two black women. 'For smart men, some of these hotshots act dumb as rocks.'

I startled at the sound of the office door opening suddenly. Bryce and Hendricks walked in, nodding to Tanner and taking up a place behind me.

I caught my breath and turned back to Tanner. 'What do you intend to do?'

He sat back in his chair, gripping the envelope. 'We'll need to start planning. He has too high a profile to whisk off the street like Bayless.'

'For all the good it did him.'

I regretted it as soon as I said it.

Tanner glared at me but let it pass. 'He has means, maybe he can be convinced to vamoose of his own accord until this blows over.'

I leaned forward in my seat, my throat dry. 'Rosenberg said he'd come for me if I didn't go through with it again.' I held his stare and gestured towards Lizzie with a flick of my eyes. He gave a slight nod, indicating he understood the danger was to her too.

He angled himself away from us, resting his arms on the desk. He crumpled the torn piece of envelope, thinking. 'In the first instance, Kosoff has to be informed.'

'You intend to alert him?'

He glanced at Caxton. 'Yates, I know you're not going to want to hear this, but it ought to come from you. For appearances' sake.'

'Whose appearances?'

'All parties.'

I fixed my eyes on the side of his face. 'Your first concern is still protecting your operation, isn't it?'

'We're making fair progress, I won't have that compromised unnecessarily.'

'Listen to what you're saying; a man died unnecessarily, doesn't that count for anything?'

'Precisely my point. I took a risk stepping out of the shadows, it didn't pay dividends.'

I shook my head in frustration. 'Go arrest Rosenberg and Gilardino, I'll testify against them in any court you want. The whole scheme goes under.'

He took a deep breath. 'Understand: I sincerely regret

what's come to pass, and I want them held to account for what happened to Mr Bayless – and they will be, god willing. But there are two problems with arresting them now. First, it doesn't get the Bureau to Siegel, and second it's your word against theirs. They'll have alibis lined up, no doubt, but more to the point, it leaves you as the only witness they'd need to eliminate to scuttle the case. The same situation as with Abe Reles – and you told me yourself you saw what they did to him.'

Reles: the button man who turned on Siegel to save himself – and ended up dead. I felt Lizzie's hand reach for mine in my lap, kept my eyes on Tanner. 'We're at their mercy already.'

'You would be *acutely* so.'

I leaned forward. 'A murder charge is no use to you because you'd have to give the case to the LAPD. You're putting your pride before a man's life.'

'Siegel owns half of the LAPD.'

'So find the half he doesn't. Do you understand what these men are capable of? I saw what they did to Trent Bayless, he couldn't even open his eyes to see the bullet coming.'

'You're saying he was tortured?'

'Severely.'

The two agents looked at each other, a note of alarm passing between them. 'For what purpose?'

'How should I know? Maybe because they're animals.'

He was shaking his head. 'That doesn't fit observed behaviour. They wanted to know something. Could he have told them about our involvement?'

I went cold at the suggestion, a possibility I hadn't considered. I glanced at the window, seeing nothing but the flat roof of the market hall over the street.

'Yates?'

'I don't know. Rosenberg knew about me telling him to run. Bayless told them that much.'

Tanner folded one arm across his chest and ran his hand over his face – more expressive now than when I'd first told him about Bayless' murder. 'So it's possible he could have told them anything.'

'Why would they let me out alive if they knew I was talking to you? Your own men checked us for tails, so it can't be a ruse.'

'Much as I despise Siegel, you learn the hard way not to underestimate him.'

I got to my feet and paced to the door and back, turning it over. 'Did we state our location in front of Bayless?'

Tanner's eyes narrowed. 'Not that I recall.'

'What about after you let me out? Did you talk about it in front of him?' I waved a finger between him and Bryce and back.

'Yates, please.'

'Then how do you propose they found us?'

He stood up. 'We talked about this already, and if you're about to start throwing stones again—'

'Sit down, I'm just thinking aloud.'

'He might have realised it had some value.'

Lizzie said it. All eyes turned to her.

'The information,' she said. 'Mr Bayless was trying to talk his way out of his predicament. Maybe he thought he could use it as a bargaining chip if he knew where we were.'

Tanner scratched his ear. 'That still wouldn't explain how he came to know it in the first place.'

I glanced around the office – papers on the desk, box files. 'You bring him up here? If he went snooping . . .'

Tanner waved it off – but said nothing.

'Look, where is Siegel now?' I said.

'Why do you ask?'

'Because I'm tired of playing catch-up.'

'You think you can talk to him? Is that it?'

I put my hands in my pockets, looking at him.

'Don't be foolish,' he said. 'Besides, he travels constantly. New York, Chicago, Florida, Nevada. And you know about Arkansas . . .'

I thought about Hot Springs and the damage I'd done to Siegel's operation there – the cause of the grudge. But now I needed one, I couldn't come up with a way to hurt him; no ammunition to force him to back off. But still, it had to be there. He had enemies and he crossed lines; there would be something. There always was. 'Forget it.'

'I'd counsel you to do the same.'

'Take my statement so we can be through here. Step outside with me so I can spare my wife the details.' I looked at Caxton. 'Would you fix the lady a cup of coffee?'

*

It'd taken more than two hours – Tanner checking and re-checking various details, Bryce sitting in and piping up with his own questions from time to time. At the end, I was left slumped in my seat feeling empty.

Tanner took me back into the main office. Lizzie looked up when we came in, a tiny fleck of red varnish on her blouse, the nail on her little finger still wet where she'd been biting it.

Tanner took out one of the photographs, and the slip of

paper with Kosoff's particulars. He placed them in a new envelope and handed it to me. 'Approach Mr Kosoff soonest. It's in everyone's interest. It would be best to keep our involvement from him, at least for now. The less folk in the loop, the better.'

I pointed to the one still in his hand. 'What about the rest?'

'This is evidence. We'll have it dusted for prints and so forth. We'll need a set of yours for elimination purposes.'

I almost said I needed it to write the article for Rosenberg. Subservient, brainwashed; Gilardino's *hooks* even deeper into me than I realised. 'What would you have me tell him? That he's been targeted for extortion but to pay it no mind?'

'Don't be flippant.'

'Flippant? I just watched a man get killed—' I closed my eyes, Lizzie standing right there, the line too explicit, wishing I could take it back. 'I'm asking how you want me to approach this.'

'In the first instance, he just needs to be informed. We've got twenty-four hours, maybe thirty-six, before time becomes a pressure – gives me a chance to run it up the chain of command and formulate a plan. And there's always the chance he chooses to pay.'

'What would that solve? It only serves to embolden them.'

'It buys us time, and ensconces you deeper in Siegel's outfit. It wouldn't be the worst outcome. It's not as if Kosoff would want for the money.'

'I can't believe—' I threw my hands up.

'Focus on the greater good, Yates. Keep it at the forefront of your mind. There may come a point where you have to publish the article they want.'

'What?'

'You've seen what the alternative is. I'm talking about the last resort.'

'You're facilitating his scheme. At what point are you going to take your damn handcuffs out and start arresting people?'

'When I have a case. We've been through this.'

I pointed to the envelope in his hand. 'You have a case.'

'I have a start. And, thanks to you, an opportunity.'

We stood there, staring at each other. Waiting for the other to blink. Then he held his hands up, palms out. 'Let's not meet trouble more than halfway. This is a pressured situation, take it an hour at a time. Inform Kosoff and leave it at that. It's not for you to advise him how to proceed.'

I stared at him a minute longer, then turned away. I reached for Lizzie's hand to help her to her feet. 'We need to talk alone a moment. Have you arranged somewhere for us to stay tonight?'

He nodded to Caxton, who picked up the telephone. 'We'll make a start on that now. Make yourself comfortable.'

We stepped back into the antechamber and I closed the door. Lizzie made to speak, but I moved her away from the frosted glass, my finger to my lips. Then I pointed to the staircase leading to the exit, mouthed, '*GO.*'

I kept hold of her hand, eased open the outer door and led her down to the street.

*

I fumbled for the ignition, looking at Lizzie. 'Check their window. Is Tanner watching?'

She twisted her neck to look out and up. 'The light's reflecting on the pane, I can't make it out.'

The engine caught and we took off with a jerk. I pointed through the windshield to the familiar sedan parked across the street. 'There. That's Bryce's car. Watch it as long as you can.'

She swivelled in her seat as we sped past it.

'Anything?'

'I can't see them.'

I pushed the car on and made a turn to get out of their line of sight, Lizzie having to brace herself against the swerve. Back on the straight, she righted herself in her seat.

'Are you okay?'

She nodded, looking stunned.

'It's best they don't know our whereabouts. For the time being.'

She said nothing, a loaded silence. I glanced over, saw her watching me, wheels turning behind her eyes.

'We can contact Tanner whenever we need. It's safer this way—'

'I think you did the right thing.'

I glanced again, her face taut. 'Then what's spooked you?' The question seemed ludicrous as soon as it left my mouth.

'Something Agent Caxton said. When he brought the coffee while you were gone. It seemed innocuous, but now I think about it . . .'

'Liz?'

'He asked if I had family in the city, or if you did.'

'To stay with?'

'He didn't say.' She turned to the road, her voice distant. 'Maybe I took it wrong.'

I checked the rearview again, everything behind us a blur.

It was dusk by the time we pulled up at the *Pacific Journal* building. A cool wind was blowing off the ocean, the sun taking the last of the day's warmth away with it.

We went straight to Acheson's office. His secretary had left for the day but he was inside, the door open. An oversized angle lamp illuminated his desk at point blank range, the only light in the room. The sky outside was dark enough that I could see my reflection in the window behind him; the image was dim and distorted in the black glass, rendering me insubstantial.

He got to his feet as soon as he saw us in the doorway, his eyes bright. He made his way over and pumped my hand, then took Lizzie by the shoulders, causing her to break into a smile. 'It's tough to surprise an old man like me, but this is a good one. Come in.' He waved us inside and closed the door. 'How are you?'

'Still walking and talking.'

'That's more than some of these hacks manage on a good day.' He said it with a humourless grin, leaning on the door handle for support. He looked from me to Lizzie and back, a note of hesitation in his manner. 'Don't take this the wrong way but . . . is it safe for you to be here?'

'As safe as anywhere else. Anyway, we'll be gone in no time.'

'That's not how I meant it.'

'I know.'

He held my stare a moment, then blinked. 'Good. Did you speak to Detective Belfour?'

I nodded, flopping down onto a chair. 'The name was a put-up. He's FBI.'

He bulged his cheek with his tongue. 'What in god's name are you wrapped up in?'

'It's better you don't know. We ducked out on him and his men, I'd guess they'll contact you at some point, so if you could see your way to forgetting you saw us . . .'

'You're on the run from them?'

'No. Trying to stay ahead of them.'

'Doesn't that amount to the same thing?' I started to reply but he waved me off. 'It's better if I don't know. I'm just glad to see you.' He looked at Lizzie. 'Both of you.'

'It's all Siegel, Buck.' I cradled my face in my hands and rubbed my eyes, fighting exhaustion. 'It all goes back to Siegel. Did you manage to track him down?'

He levered himself off the door handle and crossed back to his desk. He opened his top drawer and rustled through it, finding the paper he was looking for and placing it under the light. He stared at it for a moment and I wondered what he was thinking. Then he looked up at me. 'I don't mind telling you, I wrestled with whether to relay this or not.'

'He finds us wherever we go. You'd only be levelling the playing field.'

He brought the slip of paper over to me, favouring his right hip. 'It's not what you think.'

I got up to take it from him, waiting for him to finish.

'He's in Nevada. You've heard of Las Vegas?'

I nodded once, but didn't understand. I knew of the place – a railroad stop in the Mojave desert that had legalised gambling to scalp the Boulder Dam construction crews a decade back. 'What's his business out there?'

'Purportedly, building a hotel-casino.'

I looked at Lizzie, could sense the words had sparked the same thought as me: *Hot Springs*. 'Is it legitimate?'

'I couldn't say. He's a lifetime criminal; would that give him more or less incentive to try going straight?'

I shook my head and looked away, no answer to offer.

'Regardless, I spoke with Peter Brown at the *Las Vegas Sun* – do you know Peter?'

I shook my head.

'He says this "monstrosity" – his word – is due to open in a fortnight, so Siegel pays a visit to the site most days. If you really are minded to speak to him, that's your avenue.' He stepped back, pressing his knuckle to his lips. 'Charlie, at the risk of labouring the point, I would urge caution.'

I put the address in my pocket. 'What would you do in my shoes?'

'I don't know the ins and outs, I'm not best placed to comment. What I would say is that if you're running from the Bureau and towards Siegel, something seems very amiss to me.'

Out of the corner of my eye, I saw Lizzie look away from him and hang her head.

*

I stopped by my desk on the way out, to make use of the telephone. The newsroom was sparsely populated at that hour, but still a few friendly faces came over to exchange greetings. Buck was discreet, so I doubted he'd told them much, and there were unspoken questions in people's faces – but none came right out to ask where the hell we'd disappeared to for weeks on end.

Suited me that way – and Lizzie kept it all at bay with idle talk about our time upstate.

My desk was overflowing with newspapers, unopened mail and message slips, the telephone buried. I set about clearing it all away, but as I swept the messages to one side, the one at the top of the pile caught my eye:

Hector King, Los Angeles Times, telephoned to speak to you Wed Dec 15, 1250hrs (Working for the enemy now, Charlie??)

Earlier that day. A bolt fired through me, surprise that he'd bothered to follow up on my request, hope that one of his legmen had turned up something on the girls. I dialled the *Times*, twisting the cord around my finger, untwisting it again. The operator tried to connect me to King's extension, but came back saying there was no answer. I hung up, wheels spinning under me. I stuffed the message slip in my pocket, picked up the phone again and dialled a different number, distracted now – by Hector King at first, but then by thoughts of Las Vegas.

I could be there by morning. Tiredness weighed on me, the prospect of more hours behind the wheel, racing across the desert. And if I went, then what? Pull up at Siegel's joint and tell him to go straight to hell? I thought about his eyes in the back room at Ciglio's, and Rosenberg's warnings about how much Siegel wanted me dead. What was to stop him putting a bullet in me and Lizzie on the spot? Bury us in a hole in the desert where even the vultures wouldn't trouble to look. The futility of it all brought on a lunatic notion: set his hotel ablaze, watch it go up in flames. The ashes of his master plan scattered on the wind—

A voice answered, cutting off the madness. A bad line. 'Mr Kosoff's office.'

I was at a loss for words, realising I'd given no thought to what I would say. 'This is Charlie Yates from the *Los Angeles Times*, I'd like to speak to Mr Kosoff.'

'Mr Kosoff isn't taking unsolicited calls. Are you a reporter, Mr Yates?'

'Yes, but—'

'Switchboard can direct your enquiry to our press office. Hold, please.'

It went to a dial tone and then the operator answered. I hung up. I called his secretary's line again.

'Mr Kosoff's—'

'This is Charlie Yates calling on behalf of Benjamin Siegel. Please tell Mr Kosoff the matter is urgent.' I felt a pang of disgust at myself – using Siegel's name to open doors, as though I were a proud flunky.

'I'm sorry, sir, but Mr Kosoff is not available to journalists. I can pass a message?'

I looked up at Lizzie, talking to one of the clerical girls and feigning enthusiasm for her end of a conversation about Cary Grant's new flick.

'Sir?'

I looked at the paper in front of me, Kosoff's home address in Bel Air written underneath the telephone number I'd dialled. 'Tell Mr Kosoff I'll meet him at his office. What time will he be there until, please?'

'Sir, that won't be possible—'

'What time, please?'

'Mr Kosoff will be leaving in the next twenty minutes, he won't be receiving anyone this evening—'

I rang off. I could doorstep him if I made it to his pad in Bel Air before he did. I signalled Lizzie to wind up her chat and made my way over to the door, Las Vegas looming ever larger in my mind.

*

Kosoff's manse was hidden behind ten-foot hedgerows, a set of black iron gates across the driveway. It was as I'd hoped for – the best chance at getting an audience with him.

I parked two cars back from his place and checked my watch. Thirty-five minutes since the call to his secretary. Figure a half-hour for him to make it to Bel Air from the studio – if she'd been telling the truth about his movements. I climbed out and walked over to where I could peer up the drive, hoping his car wasn't already there. There was a double garage attached to the right side of the property, a chance it was stashed away and he was already home and out of reach.

I went back to the car and slid in next to Lizzie, brooding on how long to play wait and see.

'What are your thoughts?' she said.

Kosoff. Las Vegas. Nancy Hill and Julie Desjardins slipping ever further away. 'A mess.'

'What Mr Acheson said is on your mind, isn't it?'

I nodded, eyes forward, watching the quiet street.

'Are you giving serious consideration to it? Las Vegas?'

I took a silent breath. 'If I am?'

She twisted her fingers together. 'I know you want to confront this, but you'd risk forcing his hand in ways I can't bear to think about.'

'I know.'

'But you're thinking about it anyway.'

I propped my elbow against the window and shielded my eyes against the glare of the streetlight. Hiding.

'Charlie?'

'Right now they hold all the cards, and I refuse to believe there's no way to redress that.'

She put her hand on my forearm. 'Don't talk that way. Please. It sounds too much like you're saying you'd rather go down fighting.'

'That's not how I meant to come off.'

'I know. I'm just ... I don't see a way through this. I keep telling myself not to panic, but it's becoming impossible to convince myself.'

I put my hand on hers. 'I'll never let them touch you. Never.'

'I'm not just worried for me.'

A pair of headlamps cut through the night, rounding the corner at the end of the block and coming towards us. A Lincoln Town Car, the man behind the wheel in a driver's hat and getup. I reached for my door latch.

The Lincoln slowed, turning in to stop at the gate. The driver climbed out and made to open up and I was already on my feet and darting towards the car. Kosoff was in the backseat, and I was at his window before the driver even noticed me. Kosoff looked up sharply when he saw me, and I pressed the photograph of him and the black woman to the glass. 'We need to talk.'

'Hey—' The driver took a faltering step towards me, an older man, caught in two minds.

Kosoff looked at the image but his expression didn't change. Then he cracked the window. 'Who are you?'

The driver came over now, but Kosoff signalled for him to back off.

I took the photograph away. 'I need a moment of your time. Is there somewhere we can talk?'

He held my stare a moment, then frowned. 'Are you armed?'

'What? No, I'm a reporter—'

'Open your coat.'

Slowly, I flared my suit jacket.

'Get in.' He reached across to open the door on the other side.

The driver watched me go around the car, incredulous, his look how I felt. I pulled the door all the way open, lowered myself inside and closed it again. When I did, Kosoff raised a pistol.

I spun away, scrabbling for the door handle. 'Wait—'

He grabbed my coat and wrenched me back. 'Sit still, or this just might go off.' He snatched the photograph from my fingers. 'Where did you get this?'

I took a moment before turning back to him, shallow breaths to steady myself, hoping Lizzie couldn't see the gun in his hand. The piece was tiny – like a starter's pistol.

He was studying the photograph. 'Benjamin Siegel wants fifty thousand dollars from you or this goes public. You have until Saturday.'

He glanced up as I said it and then looked at the image again, slight movements in his jaw as if he were chewing the skin inside his mouth. Then he dropped it on the seat between us. 'She wasn't even a good lay.' He rested the revolver on his thigh, grasping it by the cylinder, on its side but still pointed in my direction. 'Since when did Bugsy send men without heaters?'

'It's the truth. Use your eyes, I'm not about to waste time trying to convince you.'

He planted his fist on the photograph, creasing and warping it as he shifted his weight to lean closer. 'Then you go back to him in your five-dollar suit and tell him he can kiss my ass. Word gets around, his troubles are an open secret.'

'What troubles?'

'The kind of trouble has him trying me with a waste of skin like you and a laughable threat like that. There's not a rag in this town would Judas me.' He took up the photograph and tore it, tore it again and again, tossed the pieces at my chest. 'And what else is, you can tell him there won't be anyone under an MGM contract showing up to launch his goddamn casino either. That bastard has a short memory. See who schleps to Nevada when there's only George fucking Raft to pal around with.'

I brushed the shredded pieces off my lap. 'Mr Kosoff, I don't work for Ben Siegel. Believe me when I say I'm here under duress, so if you could elaborate on his troubles . . .'

He stared at me, rubbing the revolver up and down his leg like a nervous tick. 'You have to be putting me on. Who are you?'

'My name's Yates, I'm a reporter.'

'Twenty-two years I been making movies, and I never heard of you.'

'I've been in New York City.' Another lifetime now. 'Please, if you've got something on Siegel, I'll take it.'

He was silent a moment, the air in the car cool and still; the smell of seat leather and his hair lacquer. 'There are more photographs?'

I nodded.

'Siegel has them?'

I thought of Colt Tanner and the envelope – a complication I couldn't admit to, still not convinced by the decision to keep silent on his behalf. 'Moe Rosenberg. Siegel's right—'

'I know Moe, shit-heel that he is.' He looked out of the front window, towards the house. 'And your game is to play both sides against each other, is that it? For a cut, or for a story?'

I shook my head, watching the gun on his leg – back and forth, back and forth, betraying the cracks in his front. 'The only thing I want is to get out from under Siegel's boot.' I followed his eye line, lights showing in the house at the top of the drive, got an inkling of what was worrying him – not public disgrace but private. 'If you want to get at Siegel, we're on the same side here. You won't find a better ally.'

'Than some two-bit hack no one ever heard of? What paper are you with anyway?'

'The *Pacific Journal*.'

He flicked his wrist, dismissing it. 'I'd find better help at the dime store.'

'Look, I have no intention of writing the story, but here's a tip: this isn't the first time they've run this gig and last time out, when the mark acted up, Siegel put a package in the man's mailbox, addressed to his wife.'

He tore his eyes away from the house as I told the lie, realising he'd given himself away and confirming what I thought.

'So my advice to you would be to whisk Mrs Kosoff away

to Palm Springs or someplace first thing in the morning. Have someone monitor your mail while you're gone. Hell, I'll do it if you want.'

'You got a nerve. Bringing my wife—'

'You're too smart for stage outrage and it's a little late to be playing the devoted husband.' I pointed to the ugly confetti on the floor. 'I'm willing to help you out. All I want is information in return.'

He breathed out through his nose, taking his time. 'Siegel owes markers all over town. He's been squeezing loans out of every talent dumb enough to entertain him, knowing they'll never have the stones to call them in.'

'He's a racketeer, that's another racket. So what?'

'So what, is the debts run to six figures according to what I hear – even allowing for the inevitable exaggeration – and he's burning bridges left, right and centre on account of it. He's gone to a lot of effort cultivating movie star types since he got out here, and now he's throwing it all away for a hundred grand? It doesn't take Einstein to see what's going on.'

Siegel hustling movie stars and extorting studio bosses. A hotel-casino in the desert, construction in the home straight. His resources were considerable – hard even to estimate – but maybe this was an overreach even for him. 'What do you hear about the casino?'

'What he puts out there. That the Flamingo's going to be the best hotel in the United States, that it's going to put Las Vegas on the national map, blah blah blah. It's the rebop Billy Wilkerson started up about before Bugsy muscled in on his stake. Except no one's buying it because it's sending him broke and it isn't anywhere close to finished yet. He can go to hell if he thinks I'm about to toss my money into the pit. Son of a bitch.'

I reached for the door, setting myself to leave.

'Slow down, we're not through yet. How many more are there?' He motioned to the remains of the photo.

'I didn't count. Ten or thereabouts.'

'You have a set of the prints?'

'That was all I had.'

'Tell me the truth.'

'That was all.'

'I want the negatives.' He was looking at the house again now, shaking his head, disbelieving. 'I want every copy. I've never claimed to be a saint but she doesn't deserve this.'

*

I drove us to a payphone and called Hector King at the *Times* again – this time getting one of the night shift, confirming he'd called it a day already. I talked the man into giving up King's home number, then cut the call and re-dialled. I tapped the side of the kiosk double-time, watching Lizzie in the car, her eyes glinting in the dark. A moonless night, the stars smothered by the clouds.

'King residence.'

'Hector, it's Charlie Yates.'

'Charlie, you got my message.'

'Yeah, thanks for following up.'

'I don't think it's news you'll want to hear.'

My chest went hollow. 'Tell me.'

'You see the story about the body they found?'

'No.'

He sighed, reluctant. 'A girl dumped on a stretch of waste ground, beaten and strangled according to the talk coming from the scene. County coroner's report is expected in the next couple days, that'll tell the tale.'

My chest collapsing, a memory rising – *Texarkana, a cavalcade of police lights racing past me.* 'When?'

'Yesterday. Tom Pence was out there trying to swing an interview with Senator McCarran when he picked up on it from the locals. A piece of luck, really—' He stopped himself. 'Sorry, poor choice of words.'

Dread filling me, memories I didn't want, living it again. *'Here, over here. We found another one.'* 'Is it ...?'

A pause, static on the line. I watched Lizzie watching me from the car, her eyes wide now, placing a pale hand on the dashboard. Sensing something was wrong.

'I don't know for sure, I don't have all the facts. But the locals have named her as Diana Desjardins. The name ... well, you see why I thought to call.'

'Did Pence get a look at her?'

'He said he thought she broadly matched the description you gave me ...'

I kicked the kiosk – once, twice, hearing the car door thrown open, Lizzie bursting out and running across to me. Not sure I could take any more. Surprised to hear my own voice: 'Where did they find her?'

'Las Vegas, Nevada. As I say, it's pure happenstance Tom was in town—'

CHAPTER FIFTEEN

We had nothing to prepare us for the cold.

The temperature had plummeted as soon as we left the valley, and the mercury kept falling all through the night. I hadn't noticed for a time, my hands locked on the wheel, eyes on the dead blacktop in front, driving into the darkness because it was the only thing left to do. As though I could still save her if I just got there fast enough. Denying my failure.

It was only when I saw Lizzie's breath fogging right in front of me that I realised. She'd been huddled close, for warmth, refusing to issue a word of complaint, the cold severe enough to keep her awake through her exhaustion. After that, I'd found an all-night diner in Barstow and stopped long enough to load up on coffee.

We approached Las Vegas shortly after sunup. The morning sky in the desert was a brilliant white-blue, so vivid I could barely look. The La Madre Range in the distance glowed red and ochre, the light catching every crease and fold in the rock. Lizzie was taken with the beauty of it, pressing her face to the window, and I was grateful for the moment's relief it granted from the wretched life she'd been dragged into on my account.

The road in took us past the construction site – a man-made oasis surrounded by barren desert. The sign said *Flamingo Hotel*, and it towered over a glass-fronted structure with an overhanging roof that took its inspiration from the architecture of Beverly Hills. I slowed some as we passed it by. Construction crews were arriving for the day, and I wondered if Siegel was there somewhere, overseeing the finishing touches. The thought of what had been done to facilitate its creation sickened me, making me think of an animal that devoured its own kind.

*

The route to the Clark County Sheriff's Department carried us through downtown Las Vegas – a small grid of streets packed solid with drinking clubs, hotels and gambling halls – often all in the same building. Neon signs danced in a blitz of colour, lit even in the daytime. If I'd expected a western version of Hot Springs, I was off; this was bigger and bolder – Broadway without the class, pried out of Manhattan and laid down in the desert.

'I can't believe what I'm seeing,' Lizzie said, her voice weary and fractured.

But the lightshow barely registered with me, my mind filled with thoughts of Desjardins – if it was her. Of how she could have ended up in this place and what had happened here. And of Nancy Hill, and whether the same fate had befallen her.

*

The Sheriff's Department passed me around for twenty minutes, two different officers in brown uniforms and western hats coming out to tell me someone else would be along shortly. The situation eating at me: another small town, dust coating my trouser hems, and cops with hard eyes; a glance at Lizzie, wondering how many times I could put her through this.

Finally, the sheriff himself came out to where I was waiting, and I took an involuntary half-step backwards, the look and feel of things too familiar by now. A tall man made taller by his white Stetson, I placed him somewhere in his middle fifties, grey hairs showing around his ears. He was lean more than slim and moved like an old athlete, with the build of a swimmer. He introduced himself as Robert Lang.

'Charlie Yates. I'm here about the young woman was found dead a couple days back.'

'What about her, Mr Yates?'

'Have you managed to identify the woman in question?'

'May I ask what your interest is, sir?' He made a point to look over my shoulder at Lizzie, sitting behind me on a chair near the door.

'I'm trying to trace two missing women and I've reason to suspect the lady in question may be one of them.'

'You're a private investigator?'

I shook my head. 'A reporter. The family have tasked me to help find her.'

'I see.' He straightened his shirtfront. 'Kindly tell me the name of the woman you're looking for?'

'Julie Desjardins. The woman you found went by Diana Desjardins, and she matches a description I gave to a colleague of mine.'

He looked around, signalled to the desk officer and then turned back to me. 'Mr Yates, would you step over here with me?'

He led me to a side room with four chairs positioned around two sides of a bare wooden table. He shut the door and gestured for me to sit. I stayed on my feet.

'Where're you from, sir?'

'Los Angeles.'

'How long have you been in Las Vegas?'

'I came in this morning, we just arrived.'

'Overnight? Hell of a drive to make in this weather.' He gestured to my clothes.

'I only got the tip-off last night. I came right away.'

'When was your last visit to Las Vegas?'

I narrowed my eyes. 'Never. First time.'

'What about to Clark County?'

'Never. What is—' I took a step back. 'Wait a second, I had nothing to do with her murder.'

He raised his eyebrows. 'I don't recall saying you did. What would compel you to say that?'

'I've worked crime beats for years, I know cops. I've never set foot in this town before today, quit reaching.'

'Let me see some identification, please.'

I took out my press credentials and passed them to him.

He opened his pocketbook and copied something down. 'Can anyone confirm your presence in Los Angeles the last day or two?'

'Buck Acheson, editor of the *Pacific Journal*. I was in his office last night.'

He wrote the name and looked up again. 'No photographs of the victim have been released to the press. Mind telling me how you square that with what you told me about a description?'

'Tom Pence from the *LA Times* alerted me to the story. He was in town on an unrelated matter. He told his editor the woman matched the description and his editor called me.' I planted my hands on the table. 'It was the name, that was the red flag. How many Desjardins crop up in this town?'

He scribbled something else down. 'Well then, how did this Pence know what the victim looked like?'

I looked at the ceiling and then back at him. 'Say he was at the scene.' He started to write. '*After* you found her,' I added.

Lang looked at me and tilted his head.

'Look, if you let me see the body, I can confirm whether she's the woman I know as Julie Desjardins.'

He kept looking at me, flicking his pocketbook slowly with his thumb. 'That's a duty for the dead woman's next of kin. You provide me with their particulars and I'll see to it they're reached.'

I thought about what to say, knowing I'd talked myself into a corner and deciding that truth was the safest course. 'I don't know her family. My working theory is that Desjardins was an assumed name.'

He got up and stood between me and the door. 'I think I'd like for you to take a seat.'

'You've no grounds to arrest me. Why would I call in here to—'

'Who said anything about arrest? That's the second strange comment you've made.' He pulled a chair out for me and locked his eyes on mine.

I took the seat and told him from the start. Nancy Hill and Julie Desjardins, the conversations with Hill's despairing mother, the fact that I knew nothing about Desjardins' identity or where she hailed from. The last sighting of them at Mrs Snyder's house. The appointment at TPK, no record of them ever making it. I finished up on the detail about Desjardins working at the movie theatre on Fairfax, under the name of Virginia Lake – watching his face as I said it to see if it jibed with an identification they might have made, unlikely as it was. But his expression didn't change and he never looked up from his notes.

When I finished, he wrote on a moment longer, then closed his pocketbook and placed the pen on top. 'Were you having relations with either or both of these women, Mr Yates?'

'What?' I pushed my seat back.

'That your wife outside?' He hooked his thumb towards the staging area.

'What the hell does that have to do with it?'

'Looked a little younger than you, is all.'

I stood up, shaking my head. 'I've heard enough.'

'Don't tell me you wouldn't ask the same question, you were sitting in my seat.'

That shut me up. I thought how it could look to anyone who didn't know me, didn't know about the lengths I'd go to numb my conscience. Thought about the man I was before Texarkana and realised it was exactly the question I'd have asked. 'I never even met them. I just wanted to prevent this. If Miss Hill is still alive somewhere, I'd mean to see her returned home safe.'

He pushed his hat back on his head. 'Hell of a story to walk in off the street with.'

'It's the truth, I swear to god. Why the hell else would I drive all the way out here at a moment's notice?'

'Hard to understand a lot of the things Los Angeles folk do.'

I planted my hands on the table and dipped my head. 'Please. I've been tearing up Los Angeles looking for these two women. It's killing me, I need to know. I need to help.'

'You still haven't told me why that's the case. Two girls you never met. Everything you're saying sounds like it comes from guilt.'

My mouth parted, tears forming in my eyes, keeping my head low so he wouldn't see. All of it crashing down on me now. All of it. About to say it was guilt – but not the way he meant—

He stood up. 'Have you arranged any place to stay?'

I shook my head.

'Wait here a moment. Let's see if your story checks out.'

Without looking up: 'My wife . . .'

'Best you stay here.'

I rested my head on my fists, guilt and failure suffocating me.

*

Lang posted an officer on the door while he was gone. When I'd tried to go to check on Lizzie, the new man blocked the way. 'Won't keep you but a moment.' When Lang returned twenty minutes later, the two men shared a hushed conversation before he dismissed him again.

Lang retook his seat. 'I spoke with Mr Acheson, he confirms what you told me to be the case. Even so, I'd like for you not to leave town for a day or two.'

'Can you get me a look at the body?'

'How is it you mean to identify a woman you never met?'

He was staring at me in a way that told me he knew the only possible answer. Slowly, I took the photograph from my pocket and placed it on the table in front of him. I put my finger on Julie Desjardins.

He took out a pair of eyeglasses and bent over the photograph. 'Where did you get this?'

'It was left at their boarding house. The owner of the property gave it to me. It's her, isn't it?'

He sat upright and took the eyeglasses off again, holding them by one arm under his chin. 'There's a resemblance. Strong resemblance.'

'What about the girl next to her?'

He glanced again and then shook his head, saying nothing.

'Who gave you the name Diana Desjardins?' I said. 'Maybe they . . .' Leaning over the table, imploring him.

'One of the local press men. I couldn't say who.'

'Did you find any identification on her?'

He shook his head again, staring past me, thinking something I couldn't decipher. 'She was found without a stitch on her.'

I closed my eyes, trying not to see it. Every fear I'd held for her, realised in deed. 'Where was she found?'

He stood up. 'Mr Yates, I'm very grateful for you coming forward with this information. I'd like to speak with you again. Kindly call in first thing tomorrow morning. If you need lodgings, you'll find plenty on Fremont Street – try the Hotel Apache. I'll let you see yourself out.'

He walked out, leaving the door open.

I saw Lizzie through the doorway the same time she saw me. She hurried over.

'What did he say?'

'It's her.'

'They took me into a room to ask me about where we've been and when we arrived. They can't think—'

I put my hands over my face. 'I should have expected it. From their perspective . . .'

She made me take my arms down and linked hers through mine to guide me outside.

I started to say something as we approached the car, but she silenced me with a look and watched as an officer passed out of the building and across the lot to his cruiser. Only when we'd climbed inside did she say, 'You ought to be mindful of how you're carrying yourself. What if they try to hang this on you? From the questions he was asking me – it's plain he had suspicions.'

I'd been thinking of my innocence as my ultimate protection, but I realised she was right; that to certain men it was an irrelevance.

I thought about his invitation to come back the next day. Enough time to trump up a charge, no matter how flimsy. Then I thought again. 'Why would they go to the trouble? They don't even know who she is, no one's clamouring for this case to be solved.'

'Are you willing to take that chance?'

'Nancy Hill is still missing. If she's here . . .'

'What about matters in Los Angeles?'

'I can't leave until I know.'

'And the consequences be damned?'

'The consequences of going back are worse. That's as good as leaving her for dead.'

'If we don't go back now, we can never go back. I can settle myself to that, but I want to be sure you can.'

'I can't have another on my conscience, Liz.'

We looked at each other – stalemate.

Or so I thought until she broke it.

'Dammit, Charlie, you couldn't have saved them.' Shutting her eyes, regretting raising her voice. She looked again, hands splayed in front of her. 'You couldn't have saved Alice, and I don't love you any less because of it. You can't hold yourself responsible for all the world's ills, we'll never put it behind us.'

I rubbed my eyes, grit and sand accumulated, more than a day since I'd last slept.

She closed her hands tight in frustration. 'I'm sorry.' She brought them to her mouth. 'I'm sorry, I don't mean to go off on you. I have this feeling as though we're skating along a knife edge, and not knowing when we're going to fall off is worse than anything else.'

I reached out to take her hand in mine. 'Siegel will kill me when this is through. I know you know that. Going back only hastens that.'

She held my gaze, red eyes bursting with anxiety.

'I don't trust Tanner,' I said, 'and we know he can't protect us anyway. So the only way out of this is to take it to Siegel. That hotel is his weak spot; that's where we hit him.'

*

I slotted the coins into the payphone and looked along Fremont Street as the operator made the connection. A row of neon signs: The Golden Nugget, The Boulder Club, The S.S.

Rex – the last seemingly named for Tony Cornero's cruise ships that sailed out of Los Angeles, floating casinos that carried players out three miles to international waters to gamble in quasi-legal peace. LA's tentacles reaching all the way across the desert, even before Siegel had set his sights. The promise of money lured them here; had to be the same for Julie Desjardins. That was where to start.

'*Sun*, Peter Brown speaking.'

'Mr Brown, this is Charlie Yates. Buck Acheson said you'd be expecting my call.'

'Mr Yates – yes. This is in regards to the young woman they found.'

'That's right, sir. I've been searching for this woman in Los Angeles a long time so I'd appreciate knowing anything you can tell me.'

'I understand that, Buck said as much, but I don't know how well placed I am to help. They know virtually nothing about her.'

'I heard she was named as Diana Desjardins – was it one of your men reported that?'

'Yes and no. He heard it from one of the *Telegraph-Register* men – but all that party will say is it came from a source.'

'Who he won't name?'

'Safe bet.'

'Why?'

'I suppose on principle? Why do we ever protect a source?'

He'd missed my point but it was my fault for jumping three questions ahead. 'Can you tell me the reporter's name at the *Telegraph-Register*?'

He let out a small laugh. 'Buck warned me you were direct.'

Not for the first time, I owed Buck a debt for smoothing my path. 'Look, I mean nothing by it. I'm already late to this, so I'm eager not to lose any more time.'

'Without being blunt, she's dead, Mr Yates, what more—'

'There were two of them – roommates. They disappeared at the same time.'

'I see.' He took a breath. 'Trip Newland. He used to work here before he went over to the *Telegraph-Register*. I've known him a number of years, he's a good hand.'

'Where can I find him?'

'Their offices are on Main but he might be on the street already, this time of morning.'

I thanked him and rang off, then placed a call to the *Telegraph-Register* and got my first break in what felt like for ever: Newland was at his desk and agreed to let me buy him breakfast. A diner across the street from him – fifteen minutes.

*

Newland walked in wearing a brown stingy brim fedora that looked out of place among all the western hats. He glanced around once and came over, sitting down without offering his hand. He signalled for a coffee, looking Lizzie up and down. Then he side-eyed me. 'First time in the desert?'

'Yes. Thank you for—'

'Clothes are all wrong. Always that way with Angelinos, none of you have a clue.' Still staring at Lizzie.

'We came at short notice. When I heard about the body.'

'Tom Pence got a fast mouth, don't he?' The waitress set his coffee down and he poured in some milk and stirred it with his index finger. He reached for the sugar and I took a grip on it.

'What's with the attitude?'

He let go. 'Los Angeles is always bad news for this town. Now we got bodies turning up on our doorstep.'

I slid the sugar to him across the tabletop. 'What does that mean?'

He caught it but put it to one side. 'Place is changing. You would've seen the hotel Benny Siegel's building out on the highway when you came in?'

'I know about it.'

'Isn't even open yet and look where we are. You're the second hack from LA I had to do this dance with this week.'

'Are you implying there's a connection between the two?'

'It's made us a magnet for bad sorts. The local owners are doing what they can to freeze him out, but they know they're on a losing tip. He's chartering airplanes to bring the hordes in for god's sake.'

I lifted my hand off the table to slow him down. 'About the girl – Desjardins.'

'Not her real name.'

'Figures. But the Sheriff's Department haven't come up with an identification yet.'

'They won't. Heck, how can they? Way she was.'

'Where was she found?'

'About a mile out of town, in a ditch twenty feet from the LA Highway. Bold as that.'

'She was strangled?'

'Yeah, by hand. The beating might've been the final cause though, we'll see.'

'Why would they choose to dump her there?'

'Could be they were disturbed in the process of burying the body – some cops sticking to that line of thinking. Ask me, I think they just didn't care. I mean, she's young and fetching, so someone's losing money on not putting her to work, but spilt milk is spilt milk. Why take a risk going to any more trouble than you need?'

'*Losing money?* She was selling her body?'

He nodded. 'Young. Pretty. Not from here. Always the same.'

I ran my hand over my face, a film of muck coating me. 'How did you source the name?'

'How does anyone? I asked around, someone answered.'

'I'd like to talk to that someone.' I glanced at Lizzie, hesitant to spill the rest, knowing I'd have to anyway. 'She was with a friend when she disappeared, and the woman in question is still unaccounted for. If there's a chance your source could lead me to her—' I stopped myself, realising I'd missed the obvious question. 'Your source – was it a young woman?'

He tangled his fingers together. 'Come on, I'm not about to give up my—'

'If it was her friend – the other girl . . .' I was gripping the edge of the table.

'Don't get a wrinkle in your pants, it wasn't a broad.'

Should have expected it wouldn't be that straightforward. 'What's his name?'

'Nice try.'

I shifted in my seat. 'You've got to give me something.'

'You speak to the sheriff's office?'

I nodded.

'Who'd you speak with? Lang?'

I nodded again. 'Didn't have much he could tell me.'

'Of course not. He's not about to say anything until he figures out which way he needs the cards to fall.'

I came forward in my seat. 'Meaning what?'

He slouched back, folding his arms. 'Would you look at me flapping my lips like a greenhorn . . .'

I drummed my fingers on the tabletop, realising he'd led me to the dinner table just to sell me a seat. 'If there's something you want, just come right out with it.'

'What's your pull with the *Times*?'

I squinted at him. '*Los Angeles*? None. I used to work there.'

'Tom Pence made a point of seeking me out to ask about this girl – that's a first. Right afterwards, you show up. You have some measure of clout.'

'News to me if I do. What of it?'

'This town is as good as dead. Siegel and the kikes will bleed it dry. I got no inclination to see out the last rites.'

'You're tapping me for a job?'

'In crude terms.'

I shook my head in disbelief, the mundanity of it. 'I'll walk you into the damn building myself if you give me what you've got on the victim.'

'Fine – but words cost nothing, and buy less.'

Lizzie set her hands on the table, just hard enough to jolt it. 'What exactly is it you're asking of Charlie, Mr Newland?'

Breaking her silence caught him off guard and he flicked his eyes between us, in the end settling on me again. 'Get me a gig at the *Times*. I'll settle for stringer work – somewhere on the west coast. Anyplace but here. Then we'll talk.'

He got up to go and I saw more wasted days, the last thread

to Nancy Hill fraying to nothing. I jumped up and put my hand on his arm. 'Sit down.' Before he could say anything, I shot over to the payphone and slipped a coin in the slot.

'*Journal.*'

'Buck, it's me. I need a favour.'

'Charlie? What goes on?'

'Can we take a man on as a stringer? Peter Brown will vouch for him.'

Silence came over the line. When he eventually spoke again, surprise had nudged his voice to a higher register. 'Even by your erratic standards, this is fresh.'

'He's one of the locals here, it's the only way he'll cut me in on his source. Please, Buck – I know I'm way in the red already . . .'

'I don't— He's willing to give up a source for personal gain?'

'It's just access to the source.' I looked around the diner, grasping for something to convince. 'Look, he can work for me, I'll be responsible for him. I'll post him to Sacramento, he'll quit after a month up there.'

'I don't appreciate being put on the spot this way, Charlie. What's his name even?'

'Trip Newland. You know him?'

'No. We don't have an opening—'

'I'll take a pay cut. If it'll help.'

More silence, faint background chatter on his end. Then: 'God knows I indulge you, Charlie, but this is . . .'

'I need this, Buck. Please.'

'You can't call me out of the blue and . . .' He let out a slow breath.

'I'll make it up to you, I swear.'

'This is bad business, Charlie.'

'I know it. Thanks, Buck.'

I hung up and beelined back to the table. 'Legman work at the *Pacific Journal*. My watch. Headquarters out on the beach – you'll forget this place in five minutes flat.'

'What?'

'Offer's good for the next thirty seconds.'

'Just like that?'

'No fooling. Twenty seconds.'

He glanced around, dazed, reaching for a line to buy a breath. 'It's not the *Times*.'

'You wanted a ticket out. My wife and I walk out of this diner and you come away with nothing.'

He stretched his neck. 'Same for you.'

'I can ask questions the same way you did. I'll get there. You're a shortcut, that's all.'

He searched my face, turning his head sideways.

'He's not bluffing, Mr Newland,' Lizzie said. 'I can promise you that.'

He looked at Lizzie, then started nodding, breaking into a smile. 'Some reason, when you speak I believe you, ma'am.'

He stuck his hand out and I shook it.

'How soon can you put me in contact with your source?'

He withdrew his hand slowly. 'I don't know how eager he'll be for that.'

'Then what would you propose?'

'Tell me what you want to know and I'll ask him.'

'I don't have time to go around the houses, there's a woman's life at stake. Coax him – get him to speak to me on the telephone if he won't meet in person.'

He cast his eyes down at his lap. 'It's not as simple as that. There are complexities.'

Lizzie straightened in her seat. 'He knew her from her work. Your source – he was a customer. That's it, isn't it?'

I put my hand over hers on the tabletop, taking her intuition one step further. 'Is your source a suspect?'

Newland hesitated before he shook his head.

'Is that in your estimation or the sheriff's?'

He blinked and looked away, moistening his lips before he spoke. 'To my knowledge, the authorities haven't talked with him yet.'

I swiped my hand across the table. 'Then how the hell can you know for sure?'

'Give me some credit. Why would he come forward?'

'Were you offering tip money?'

'A lousy ten bucks. No chance a killer steps into the spotlight for that.'

I clenched my jaw, wondering. 'I'll pay the same again if he'll talk to me.'

He nodded. 'I'll put that to him.'

I slumped back in my seat, afraid I was running down another dead end. 'What can you tell me about the girl – was she working the street or at a cathouse?'

'Neither. Appointment only – a high-class call girl.'

'Then I need to know who for and how to contact whoever's running the girls.' I held his stare.

'I see you eyeballing me but I don't know. I'll ask soon as I speak with him, and I'll tell him about your offer. But just be prepared that he might not want to talk to you – even through me.'

'Give me something for right now to get started on.'

He leaned forward over his arms. 'Such as?'

'Anything. I can't sit here waiting on you. How did you find your source? Where did he meet with her? Did he ever use another girl from the same outfit?'

He nodded his head. 'When the body turned up, I put the word out that I was paying for a name. After that, he found me. That's the only one I can answer off the top of my head.'

I reached into my pocket and pulled out some change, dashed it on the table. 'Go ahead and make the call to your man.' I tipped my head towards the payphone.

He took some dimes and walked across the diner.

Lizzie picked up a nickel and turned it in her fingers. 'Why would a man with money enough for that kind of service need tipster cash from a newspaperman?'

'You don't believe his story?'

She looked at me a moment, then gave a slight shake of the head. 'I don't think he's showing all his cards. Do you?'

'No, but I wouldn't expect him to.'

She put the coin back on the table, started stacking the rest into a pile on top of it. 'Were you serious about the job offer? What did Mr Acheson say?'

I rubbed my forehead, elbows on the table. 'I didn't give him much a of a choice. I'll smooth it over somehow – if it comes to pass.'

She looked about to say something more but saw Newland coming back over and kept silent.

He retook his seat. 'No answer.'

'At his home or place of business?'

'It's not like he's a buddy, I only have the one number for him.'

'Can you get a message to him?' Lizzie said.

He spread his hands. 'If I knew how . . .'

I screwed my eyes shut, gripped by frustration. Then I opened them again and stood up. 'Come on.'

'Where we going?'

'Take us to where they found her.'

*

We headed out of town and retraced our route down the Los Angeles Highway, speeding into the frigid desert. The sun hung in a clear sky, but the cold was just as severe, and so dry that the skin on my knuckles had started to crack.

We passed two large hotel-casinos adjacent to the highway, the El Rancho and the Last Frontier, and beyond them there was nothing to see for miles. Nothing until we came upon the Flamingo construction site for the second time that day. I couldn't tear my eyes from it, even as I felt Newland watching me with curiosity.

'It'll never make money.'

I glanced at it again as we passed. 'How can you be sure?'

'Won't even make the construction costs back.'

'You said the locals tried to stop him and even they couldn't.' I thought of Lyle Kosoff and his talk of blackballing the place around Hollywood.

'Couldn't stop him opening it, I meant.' He folded his arms tight across his chest against the cold. 'He'll fill it for the big launch, but who's gonna come out here to pay over the odds after that? Siegel doesn't understand this town – there's no one here calling for Beverly Hills in the desert. They want to come here to gamble and still have enough money left for a steak dinner and a decent room.'

We left the site behind, speeding onwards down the highway, me watching it still in the wing mirror as the dust in our wake obscured the view. Newland jolted me out of it, pointing through the windscreen. 'On the right. It's coming up.'

I guided the car onto the shoulder and brought us to a stop where he said. We climbed out and I felt the sun on my face, the barest trace of warmth. There were no other cars on the highway, an intense silence, broken by Newland's footfalls as he set out across the rocky ground.

I turned to Lizzie. 'You don't want to stay in the car?'

'It's as cold inside as out.'

'That's not what I meant.'

She flashed a sad smile. 'I know what you meant. I want to come – you don't have to do this alone.'

I looked away to one side. 'I can manage.'

She took my arm anyway and guided me after Newland.

He'd come to a stop a short distance ahead, next to a ditch that looked like a shallow ravine, and was glancing about as if to orient himself. 'Somewhere around here. Hard to be exact now.'

We picked our way across the terrain and came up to where he stood, Lizzie letting go of my arm to slip behind me as we slowed. I crouched down and ran my hand over the ground, my mind jumping back in time: Jimmy Robinson letting the dirt run through his fingers in a clearing outside Texarkana. The smell of rotting leaves came to me then, even there in the desert. 'Who found her?'

'Passing motorist. Stopped to relieve himself, if you can believe that.'

162

I stood up and looked back to the road, twenty yards away, wondering if I did. But my eye was drawn to the north, the incongruous palm trees and towering sign of the Flamingo visible on the horizon. 'Cops take a look at the man as a suspect?'

'Yeah, but he was never in the frame. Regular Joe on his way home to San Diego, wife never left his side the whole time he was in town.'

'His story stand up?'

'They let him go home, so I guess so. You'd have gotten a look at him, you'd know.'

A year ago I might have agreed with him, complacent in my belief in a newsman's instinct. Events since had stripped me of such misplaced arrogance. 'You said it's your feeling whoever killed her just dumped her here.'

'Yeah.'

'If it was one of her Johns, wouldn't they go to more trouble than that?'

'I don't follow.'

I pointed back to the highway. 'Big risk of being seen or the body being found, this close to the road.'

'Say he panicked. He kills her for whatever reason, carts her away in his trunk then ditches her in the first place out of town he can find.'

'But walk that back; the John arranged to meet Desjardins, so whoever's running these girls knows who he is and who killed her. They're not going to be happy about this – you said it yourself, someone's losing money. So wouldn't he be afraid of reprisals – leaving her out in the open like that?'

'Possibly. I go back to him panicking, though. What are you getting at?'

'Doesn't feel right, it's too flagrant for an amateur. I'm wondering if whoever she was working for left her out here.' Someone cold enough to ditch her like broken-down machinery.

He looked at his shoes, turning his mouth down. 'Can't understand that. Whoever's making money off of her is the last one in line with a motive to kill her.'

'I'm not saying they killed her, just that they were the ones dumped her. Either way, they'd have a line on who did kill her.'

He took a pack of cigarettes out and offered it to Lizzie and me. When we declined, he stuck one in his mouth.

'You know what I'm driving at,' I said. 'Who runs girls in Las Vegas?'

'You want to solve a murder or find her missing friend?'

'They're all tied up together, why are you ducking the question?'

'I already told you I don't know who she was working for.'

'Speak in general terms.'

He snatched the unlit cigarette from his mouth. 'You're asking for the telephone directory. It's a legal business here, various parties have a piece of the action. And they go to real trouble to keep their noses clean.'

'What about girls-by-appointment specifically?'

'I don't know.' His response made me throw my hands up, and he waved the cigarette in the air to placate me. 'I don't know. First time I came across that.'

'And you didn't think to ask your source who she was working for?'

'Sure I did, but he didn't want to say. I didn't press him because I wanted her name.'

I put my hands on my hips and turned away, faced myself

towards Lizzie. She was huddled against the cold, trying not to show she was shivering. Her face was stony, but I blanched at the thought of the things she'd had to hear in my company. I put my arm around her and pulled her close, started to make for the car again. Over my shoulder I called back to Newland. 'We need to find your source, right now.'

As we walked, the low rumble of diesel engines resounded across the desert, construction equipment at work. I found myself staring, again, towards the Flamingo.

*

We stopped at the first payphone back in town so Newland could try calling his man again. He climbed out and darted across the street, Lizzie and I watching from the car. When he dropped the coin in the slot, I scoped the businesses along the block and turned to Lizzie.

'I need you to do something. Head to the coffee shop just there and wait a few minutes. When he comes back I'll get him out of here – you stay out of sight until we're gone. Then I want you to call the operator from that telephone and see if you can't get the details of who he called. I'll take him to his office and be back for you in ten minutes.'

She glanced at Newland. He had the receiver to his ear but wasn't speaking. She looked away and then at me again. 'Is that ethical?'

My eyes flicked to Newland, who'd turned away from us. 'Please, Liz. Think about why we're doing this.'

Her eyes were locked on him, tension in my chest as the seconds ticked past.

'It's now or never. Please.'

She looked at me with an expression I couldn't read. Then she reached out and opened her door.

I watched as she walked into the coffee shop, looking back to Newland just as he hung up the phone. He crossed back over and slid in. 'Still no answer.'

'You have any idea how else to reach him?'

He shook his head. 'I spoke to the man twice in my life; let it lie a couple hours, he's got to show up some time. Where's your wife?'

'She hasn't eaten all day.' I tipped my head down the block to the eatery, layering a note of weariness to my voice. 'Come on, unless you have something else up your sleeve, I'll drop you at your office.'

'You don't want to go eat with your old lady?'

I pulled away from the kerb. 'I'll eat later. I want you to keep trying your source.'

He pointed ahead. 'Make a left here.'

I switched lanes. 'What you said earlier about Sheriff Lang – something about him working out how to make the cards fall. What were you implying?'

'Who is it pays his salary?'

'The county. I'm not interested in guessing games—'

'And where does Clark County get its revenue from?' He bobbed his head, indicating I should humour him.

'The hotel-casinos. So you're saying he works for the owners?'

'That's going too far, but he knows whose side he's on.'

'Who's the other side?' It came to me as I spoke the last word. 'Siegel.'

'Partial credit. Los Angeles is the other side – but Siegel's the lightning rod for that at the moment.'

'So what does that mean for the investigation?'

'I don't know, you'd have to ask him – but I can tell you he doesn't pull his pants on without giving thought to the consequences.' He tapped the dash and pointed. 'You can leave me right here.'

I pulled over and set the brake, trying to remember what I'd said to Lang about tracking the girls in Los Angeles, what inferences he might draw – and what he might do on account of them.

*

I stopped sharply outside the coffee shop and jumped out to look for Lizzie. I'd been gone twenty minutes and couldn't see her through the window or on the street. I looked over to the payphone, but there was no one there.

I crossed the sidewalk to the coffee shop's entrance and pulled the door. As I did, I heard Lizzie call my name. I turned and saw her hurrying towards me.

'Are you all right?'

'Yes, I'm fine.' She held up a small paper bag. 'I went to the drugstore to buy some aspirin.'

'Something the matter?'

'Just a headache. It's nothing.' She put the bag in her purse. 'I have a name for you.'

I took her elbow and guided her back to the car, opening the door for her to get in. When I climbed in the other side, she was holding a scrap of paper.

'Shoot.'

'Henry Booker.' She glanced down at it. '445 East Brady Avenue. I have directions from the man in the drugstore.'

'Good job.' Nervous excitement made me crack a smile – but she didn't return it. 'What did you have to say to the operator?'

She rubbed the back of her hand. 'I told her I was worried my husband was having an affair and I wanted to know if he was calling another woman.' She looked sheepish. 'I think she felt sorry for me.'

I put my hand on her shoulder. 'You've nothing to feel bad about. Every reporter that ever lived has done the same and worse. Much worse.'

'I'm not a reporter.'

I was turning the wheel to take off but stopped as she said it and looked over at her. 'But you take my point.'

She didn't reply, instead dipping into her bag for the aspirin and dry-swallowing a pill.

*

The address was a timber frame house on the last subdivision before the town gave way to the desert. With a lick of paint it could have looked homely, instead of isolated. The mailbox at the front of the property bore the name Booker in uneven lettering – hand-painted in what looked like a rushed effort.

I walked down the path to the front door and knocked. There was no car on the driveway, but the tracks in the dirt suggested it had been in use recently. No sound came from inside as I waited. When no one answered, I stepped back and off the small porch, glancing over at Lizzie in the car.

I skirted the edge of the building and poked my head to look around the side. I couldn't see anyone. I went a short way along the side of the house to get a view of the whole of the backyard, but it was empty so I doubled back to the street.

Lizzie lowered her window. 'Nobody home?'

I shook my head.

'The neighbour over there looked out when you knocked.'

I looked to where she pointed, the next house along separated by twenty feet of scrub yard, a tattered Stars and Stripes flying above the doorway. I nodded a thanks to her and cut across the patchy crabgrass, knocked on the door and waited again.

After a moment, an older man with thinning grey hair opened up. I introduced myself and asked after Booker's whereabouts.

'Couldn't tell you. I haven't seen him in a while.'

'Are you friendly with Mr Booker?'

'Only so far as to say good morning.'

I rubbed my mouth. 'Do you know what he does for work?'

He squinted. 'Seen him loading tools into his truck the mornings. I'm of a mind he works construction.'

The word made me glance back at Lizzie, wanting someone else to confirm the significance I took from it. I faced front again, chest tightening. 'But you wouldn't know where?'

He was already shaking his head. 'Sorry. But with that said, the biggest construction site in the state is right down the road . . .'

CHAPTER SIXTEEN

I couldn't put a name to the emotions buffeting me as we turned off the highway into the Flamingo. Fear was at the forefront, but it was tempered by the thought of finally confronting him again; no more time spent wondering.

The buzz of the construction site was a counterpoint to the foreboding that had filled me. A place of business, crawling with regular men – witnesses – didn't have the same hold over me as the back room at Ciglio's. I peeled off to one side of the site, stopping the car next to a swimming pool that stood empty.

The main building looked almost complete, but through the glass frontage, I could see it was a facade. Crews were swarming around the inside, and the sound of hammering and sawing rang out through the uncovered entranceways. Around the outside, palm trees had been planted in a grid pattern, but most of the grounds were still bare dirt, waiting to be landscaped.

Lizzie was surveying it the same as I was. 'It doesn't look even nearly finished.'

I stepped out and stuffed my hands in my pockets, looking around. No sign of him.

Lizzie slipped out and stood beside me. 'Don't think to say it. I'm coming with you.'

'I'd prefer it. I'd rather you not be out of my sight here.'

She squeezed my elbow and let it go. 'Likewise.'

A flatbed carrying lumber pulled off the highway and crawled to a stop. A foreman in an aluminium hardhat who'd been making his way towards us doubled back to meet it. We crossed close to where he stood giving directions to the trucker. Finished, he waved the driver on and stepped back as it pulled away, kicking up a swirl of dust. He turned around and waited for the engine noise to fade before he called out.

'You folks lost?'

'Name's Yates, I'm looking for Henry Booker. He one of your men?'

The foreman started to nod then stopped, looking at each of us in turn. 'Mind telling me your business here?'

'I owe him money,' I said.

The foreman half-smiled. 'That's a first.'

'I'm a reporter, he helped me out with a story.'

The foreman came over serious. 'About Mr Siegel?'

'Nothing like that.'

The man's face relaxed again. 'Good. Mr Siegel's got no time for you men, the things you write. The other owners must be all over you.'

He said it without looking around and I got an inkling Siegel wasn't there. 'Mr Siegel on the site today?' I asked.

'I thought you wanted Booker?'

'I'm star-spotting,' Lizzie said. 'I'd love to have a photograph with Benjamin Siegel.'

The man rolled his eyes. 'You're out of luck on both counts.'

The straps around my chest seemed to loosen a notch even as disappointment filtered through me. 'When's he expected back? Booker, I mean?'

'Your guess is as good as mine.'

'He quit showing up?'

'He's not here now, I know that much.'

'When's the last time you saw him?'

'Two days ago?'

I looked over at the tower bearing the hotel's name, the word Flamingo and an image of the bird displayed in unlit pink neon. 'Anyone talked to him?'

'Look, mister, I got to get on. You catch up with Henry, you tell him there's plenty other men can swing a hammer for a paycheck, he don't want it.'

'What about Siegel? When's he due here?' My voice withered at the end.

The foreman shrugged. 'You honestly think he runs his diary by me?' He turned and set off towards the main building.

Lizzie watched him go and then turned to me. 'I think we should get away from here.'

I nodded, distracted, and slowly started moving.

'What are you thinking?' she said.

I walked a few paces before I could voice an answer. 'It took us a matter of hours to turn up the name Henry Booker. If someone local was looking for him, it would've taken them no time at all.'

We carried on walking, Lizzie's brisker pace telling me she understood my meaning. 'If he knew more than he let on to Mr Newland . . .'

'I think it would be best if we find him first.'

If he was still for finding.

CHAPTER SEVENTEEN

Night seemed to come early in the desert. We took a room at the El Cortez, a low-rise mission-style hotel a little further out from the main drag and one that seemed big enough for us to pass in anonymity. Even out of the way as it was, it boasted the same oversized neon sign and a banner outside advertising cocktails, all the hotels seeming to craft their offering to the same appetites.

The casino dwarfed anything I'd seen in Hot Springs. It was full to bursting, with the loudest noises coming from an over-heated craps table near the middle of the room. I went to find a payphone in the lobby and called Newland at his desk.

'You manage to speak to your source?' I said, almost making the mistake of referring to Booker by name.

'No. I'm getting the feeling he's gone to ground.'

I closed my eyes, wondering if he had the same bad feeling about the situation I did. 'I'm desperate, Newland—'

'You already made yourself clear about that.'

'There must be someone else you can speak to. What about his workmates?'

He hesitated before answering and I wondered again if I'd given myself away. 'I'm doing what I can,' he said. 'Leave it with me.'

I screwed my eyes closed. 'All right. I'm at the El Cortez if you have news.'

I hung up and went back to our room.

Lizzie was sitting on the bed, leafing through my folder of notes on the missing girls. She stopped and looked up when I came in. 'I didn't think you'd mind.'

A sense of intrusion came over me, but faded just as fast. 'Of course not.'

'There's something I'm curious about.' She gestured with one of the sheets of paper. 'The first you heard of Colt Tanner was when you visited the girls' boarding house.'

I thought back, meeting with Angela Crawford, the other boarder at Mrs Snyder's, her telling me a cop had been asking about me. 'What of it?'

'I don't understand why he would've went there to ask after you. What was the relevance to his investigation?'

I looked at her and at the paper, my writing scrawled all over it, drawing a blank. 'I don't know. I suppose he wanted to know what I was doing.'

'How would he know to go there – independently of you, I mean?'

'He was following me.'

'As far back as your first visit there?'

'What are you suggesting?'

'I don't know.' She shook her head and set the paper down, frustration showing. 'I don't know. It just ...' She closed her eyes and reclined onto the bed, rubbing her face. 'It just seems a strange way to go about matters.'

I cast my mind back, thinking about Tanner and when he'd first approached me, what he'd told me and how much I believed of his story. Then the discrepancy I'd filed came back to me – him not knowing about my first beating in the back room at Ciglio's, almost a week after I'd first visited Mrs Snyder's. Had he stopped tailing me by that point? And then resumed later?

Lizzie's breathing had deepened and slowed, and I realised she was drifting off, tiredness finally overcoming her. I waited a few minutes until she was fully asleep, then lifted her legs onto the bed and covered her with the comforter. I switched off the light and waited, thinking. I could hear the sounds of the casino – the crunch of the arms on the slots and applause coming from the tables. Weary as I felt, my mind was still racing – no chance at sleep.

I cracked the door open, waited a moment to ensure Lizzie didn't stir, then slipped out.

*

I started with the cigarette girls and cocktail waitresses, working my way around the casino floor and asking variations of the same questions over and over: Did you hear about the dead girl they found in the desert? Do you know anything about her? Anyone that knew her? Is the name Henry Booker familiar to you?

I struck out on the last, and got nothing new on the rest. Most had heard about the victim and it seemed common knowledge – or at least assumption – that she was selling her body, but not one person could tell me more than that.

I moved on to the dealers and bellhops, another go round on the same questions, with a new one added in: Do you know anything about a girls-by-appointment service?

It was no surprise to be offered a line on all manner of ways to spend money for female company, but again the trail stopped dead at girls-to-order. One nugget turned up on Henry Booker: he was a regular casinogoer with a reputation for showing up on payday to blow his earnings on drink and blackjack. But according to the same dealer, he hadn't pulled that routine at the El Cortez in a while.

I sat across the otherwise empty card table, running out of questions and out of steam. I'd changed five bucks to chips to buy time to grill the man further and still had two left; I set one down in front of me and watched him deal the cards. Thinking to get my money's worth, I threw out one more question. 'You know where I can find Ben Siegel?'

The man didn't look up. 'What you want him for?'

I took a sip of my drink, bourbon making my head woolly. 'Settle a debt.'

He held the deck in his hands, waiting for my instruction. I tapped the felt for another card. 'You'll have to get in line,' he said.

'Behind who?'

'Just about everyone.'

I asked for another card and he turned up the two of diamonds, my hand now eighteen. 'On account of the Flamingo?'

'What else?' He flicked his eyes up, glancing around the casino floor, then looked down again. 'They tell us we're supposed to warn folks not to go there because it's run by mobsters, but I can't see what they're worried about – it'll never be finished. Everyone knows he's being robbed except him.'

I tapped the felt again, not concentrating, a seven turning up.

'Bust.' He showed his hand and then used it to sweep up my cards.

I set down my last chip. 'In what way?'

'He's being charged two, three times the going rate. No one has a problem with it because he seems to be at the top of the building needs list for anything he wants. The VFW and the Elks can't lay their hands on materials that Siegel's got coming in by the truckload. It was in the papers, they're holding protest meetings against the place and it's not even finished.'

'If everyone's set against him, how's he manipulating the needs lists?'

The dealer turned his mouth down slightly. 'Beats me – but someone must be making out from it. More money out of his pocket.'

My hand showed twenty and I waved to stay. The dealer turned his blind card over – eleven. He hit to sixteen, had to hit again and turned up a king, making him bust. He matched my chip with another.

'Keep it,' I said, standing up from the table.

I went back to the room and slipped inside so as not to wake Lizzie. She'd shifted position but was sound asleep. I sat down on the end of the bed and tried to bring order to my thoughts, but two drinks had dulled me enough to let tiredness take over.

I lay back on the bed and tried not to think where Nancy Hill might be right at that moment.

*

The ringing telephone woke me with a start, Lizzie too. I was disoriented, both by the unfamiliar room and the daylight, and through the haze my first thought was that it was Tanner calling to tell me Lyle Kosoff had been killed.

I shot up and snatched the phone from its cradle. 'Yes.'

'Yates, it's Trip Newland.'

Lizzie looked at me, worried, mouthed, *'Who is it?'*

If my mind had been up to speed I could have guessed it would be him – the only person knew we were there. 'What's the news?'

'All bad. Cops just found Henry Booker's corpse, and I want out of this town today . . .'

CHAPTER EIGHTEEN

Clark County Sheriff's Department were at the scene when we arrived – a service road between the backs of a saloon and a sawdust gambling hall called Club 21. I saw Robert Lang talking with a deputy at the head of the alley, a sheriff's car parked across it to hinder access. A third officer was just in view further down, bent over and examining something on the ground.

Lizzie was staring out the passenger window at the officers.

'Will you stay in the car? This isn't something you'll want to see.' I blanched as the words left my lips – forgetting she'd been there at Alice's murder scene; the image of her holding her dead sister in a final embrace one that would pain me for ever.

She looked at me sideways. 'It's fine, you're right, I don't want to see.'

I nodded and climbed out, holding the car door across me, cautious, watching Lang. He was fifteen yards from where I stood, hadn't spotted me. I was still weighing my options when Trip Newland appeared from nowhere, looking like he'd been up all night. He was breathless when he spoke. 'This is out of hand.'

'What happened?'

'Someone put a bullet in him.'

Lang turned now, breaking off his conversation to look at Newland and me. His gaze lingered a moment and then he resumed what he'd been saying.

'Had you spoken with him?'

He shook his head. 'Friendly dispatcher at the sheriff's tips us off to any serious call-outs. I made it here just before I telephoned you.'

I took a look around, a sudden fear that the perpetrator could still be close by. 'You get anything out of them yet?' I nodded in Lang's direction.

'Only about him being shot. And that it's recent. Early hours, looks like.' He checked the cops were still talking and then crowded into me, turning his face away from them. 'You rustled up his name and now he's dead. How short of a line should I draw between those two things?' His voice was an angry hiss.

'Are you accusing me of something? You're way out of—'

'Not of killing him. But of getting him killed? Sure looks that way to me.'

A cold flush ran through me. From the corner of my eye I saw Lang look over at us again.

'You had no goddamn right to do that,' he said. 'My source, my story.'

'You're getting ahead of yourself.'

He was shaking his head. 'Don't make me out for an idiot. Whoever killed your girl killed him.' He jammed his thumb into his chest. 'And who the hell do you think they'll be looking for next?'

'Will you get a goddamn hold of yourself?'

Lang broke away from his colleague and started towards us. Newland saw him and clammed up, turning away to brace himself on the car roof. For my part, my thoughts jumped to Booker's house, wondering if it might hold a clue as to how he was able to identify Desjardins – and maybe a lead to Nancy Hill. How soon would the cops show up at his address?

Lang walked with ease, but ramrod straight. He touched the brim of his Stetson as he neared. 'Mr Yates, Mr Newland. I didn't know you two were acquainted.' He glanced towards the alley then focused on me. 'Eventful start to the morning. Mind telling me your interest in this here?'

I waited for Newland to say something, cycling through a list of lies I could tell, wondering if the truth would serve me better.

Newland kept his silence and Lang kept his eyes on me even as I looked away.

'Nothing to say. Let's see, Mr Yates shows up in town on account of a young woman was murdered, and wants to know who put a name to the girl. Mr Newland, I believe that was you. So that's A to B, and the poor gentleman in that alleyway is point C; what's the connection? Was he involved with the late Miss Desjardins?'

I looked at Newland, wondering if he did know more than he'd told me.

He ignored both our stares, keeping his eyes locked on the car.

'Do I need to go around you, Mr Newland? My department has always been a friend to your newspaper . . .'

'He was a source.'

'I'd arrived at that already.'

'He gave me her name.'

Lang nodded, what he'd expected to hear. 'Which takes me back to my first question – was he involved with her in some way? A customer maybe?'

I kept watching him, waiting to see if he'd lied to me.

'I don't know. We spoke on the telephone, he gave me the name.'

'C'mon, Trip. I respect your right to protect your source, but in the circumstance . . .'

He turned around now, slouching back against the car in defeat. 'I think so.'

'Did the deceased have anything on his person?' I said, thinking about an address book.

'We're still cataloguing his effects. Why do you ask?'

'The other missing woman. From the photograph.'

Lang nodded. 'Tell me her name again.'

'Nancy Hill.'

'I'll keep it in mind.'

I wanted more, but held back. 'Who's behind this, Sheriff?'

'You?'

I flinched as he said it, tried to hold onto my composure. 'Don't talk crazy.'

'Maybe you arrived at the thought he killed the young lady you came all this way for. Do you own a gun, Mr Yates?'

I felt my neck go hot, remembering Lizzie's fears about them pinning something on me. 'I never set eyes on him before.'

'That so?' He took out his notebook, scrutinising something on the page. 'A man matching your description, with a car much like this one and what I'd guess was the same firecracker sat inside it—' He glanced at Lizzie, watching on intently. '—visited his house yesterday. Did you perhaps catch up with Mr Booker later on?'

Newland shot me a dirty look but I could only stare at Lang, my vision tunnelling. 'You know why I was looking for him, the same damn reason I came to you yesterday. Nancy Hill.'

'Every time you say that name you sound a little bit angrier.'

I wanted to protest more, but realised that was to walk further along the blind alley he was leading me down.

'I'd like for you to come back to the department with me. Both of you.'

'Are you arresting me?' I fought to keep my voice level, bluffing he couldn't rattle me.

'Second time you asked me that in the day I known you.'

'You can't arrest me because you know this is garbage, so if I'm not under arrest, I'll go about my business.'

He took a deep breath, drawing it out. 'Your business is to be at my office anyhow, the way I instructed you to yesterday. I have some questions about your movements; if you don't want to discuss them voluntarily that's your choice, but it wouldn't reflect well. Now, I insist you allow me to give you a ride.'

I gritted my teeth, hating myself for making it easy for him. That same unending loop of murder and lies and guilt trampling me. The feeling that I was being railroaded to fit Lang's agenda and that if he put me behind bars, Nancy Hill was gone for ever. 'I need a moment with my wife.' Before he could say anything more, I walked around the car and opened the door to lean in.

Lizzie spoke first. 'This is a trap, Charlie, you can't go with him—'

'I have no choice.'

'Charlie—'

'Call Colt Tanner. Tell him where I am and get him to pull some strings to make them back off. Don't let on where you're staying. Stay out of sight – everyone's.'

Lang tapped the car's hood. 'Mr Yates . . .'

She looked at me a moment and nodded, her eyes hard but resolute – enough to shame me at how acclimated she'd become.

I mouthed, '*Be safe*,' and stepped back, closing the door as she slid over to the driver's seat.

Lang put a hand on the windscreen. 'Don't stray far, Mrs Yates. I may want to speak with you as well.'

I followed him to his car, hearing Lizzie take off behind me.

*

Coming in from the fresh air, Lang's office was stifling. He motioned for me to take a seat along the wall then left again without explanation, leaving the door open. His latest move in whatever game he was playing. Another officer had led Newland to a different room when we arrived and I hadn't seen him since.

There was a window across from me, slick with condensation. It looked out towards the Union Pacific depot in the distance, a new building in the Moderne style that was so prominent in LA. Had to be a recent replacement for the original. A railroad town trying to reinvent itself; it made me question Newland's certainty that the Flamingo had no place in its future.

Lang returned and took a seat behind his desk, started searching for something in his paper tray.

'I took a room at the El Cortez last night. I was in the casino until around midnight – ask any dealer or waitress and they'll confirm it. After that I was in my room sleeping until Trip Newland called me there at seven this morning.'

He looked up. 'The El Cortez?'

I nodded.

'"El" means "The" so you're saying it twice. It's just "El Cortez".'

I picked at the chipped armrest. 'Did you bring me here with the intention of wasting my time?'

He set a piece of paper down and put on his eyeglasses. 'El Cortez is an interesting choice of lodging. All the hotels available to you and you went ahead and picked that one.'

I shook my head, shooting him a questioning look that said I didn't know what he was talking about.

'It was owned until shortly ago by, among others, Mr Benjamin Siegel of Los Angeles, California. Of course, you knew that already.'

I glanced away, mind racing – Lizzie left on her own there. I flicked back to him again. 'I did not.'

He lifted his chin. 'Mr Siegel and his backers sold it in the middle of this year – not twelve months after they bought it. To the same man they bought it from. At a profit.'

I stilled my hand on the armrest. 'So what?'

'That seem like a normal business arrangement to you?'

'I don't know anything about the hotel business.'

'Normal for Mr Siegel, though, correct?' He sat back in his chair, eyes locked on mine. 'You think maybe he sold it back soon as he'd had it long enough to staff with people loyal to him?'

'Why am I here, Sheriff? You know I didn't shoot Henry Booker.'

'I don't know that at all.'

'I had more interest in keeping him alive than anyone—'

He held his hand up to stop me. 'What's your association with Benjamin Siegel, Mr Yates?'

I kept looking at him, fighting to show calm even as he wrong-footed me every time he spoke. 'I have none.'

'If I may, I find that hard to swallow. You arrive here from Los Angeles at short notice, claiming your story about a missing woman – now dead. You waltz onto Mr Siegel's construction site with apparent impunity, take a room at one of his properties – forgive me, *former* properties – and go to the home of a man who turns up dead no time later. A man was working on building Mr Siegel's Flamingo and who, turns out, was mixed up in the death of the aforementioned young woman. What am I missing?'

I was rocked that he knew I'd been at the Flamingo. I tried to find clarity in my head. 'If you thought it amounted to anything, you'd arrest me.'

'I might yet.' He stood up. 'Did Mr Booker cross Ben Siegel in some way?'

'I don't know.'

'Did Siegel have a tryst with the dead woman?'

'What?'

'Were he and Booker rivals for her affection? Was it jealousy?'

'No.'

'No? Something else then. Siegel only cares for money or women, and I can't see where Booker and money intersect.'

'I don't know.'

'You said "no" first time, implying you do know something. Did Siegel send you here?'

'What? No, I have nothing to do with—' I stopped dead.

He was one move ahead of me every time and I suddenly wondered if he was aware of Siegel's shakedown scam. My role as point man – and how bad that would look. Impossible as it seemed, I wondered if he knew the names Trent Bayless and Lyle Kosoff.

'Speak free, don't hold your tongue.'

I took a shallow breath, let it out. 'Siegel didn't send me here and I don't know why they're dead.'

He stood looking at me, saying nothing, working his left thumb with his other hand.

I closed my eyes and opened them again. 'My only care is finding Nancy Hill.'

Someone knocked on the office door, breaking the silence.

He kept looking at me as he rounded the table and crossed over to it. He placed his hand on the door handle. 'But not finding out who killed Miss Desjardins?'

He whipped it open before I could issue a rebuttal.

I closed my eyes and sank into the chair. I was seated on the other side of the open door and couldn't see who Lang was talking to. The man outside said something I didn't catch before Lang said, 'Show him up.'

He ducked back around the door. 'On your feet. This appointment can't wait but we'll talk again directly. Wait here, please.' He pointed to a row of chairs outside his office door and signalled to another officer. 'Get him a glass of water, would you?'

I thought about Lizzie at El Cortez again. 'I need to make a telephone call.'

'To ask the boss for an attorney?'

'I need to speak to my wife.'

'We'll see if we can fix that up.' He left me standing there and went inside again.

I took a seat and lolled my head against the wood panelling behind me. There was no one else in the waiting area, and the door to the outer office was open, affording a view of the exit leading to the stairwell. It seemed as if he was testing me, daring me to run. To what end, I didn't know – but it gave rise to dark possibilities. I'd come in willingly, convinced he didn't have me as suspect, but I hadn't taken the care to look at the sequence of events from his perspective. There were holes in his theory, and he knew it, but it sounded compelling the way he laid it out – which might be all he wanted. It was enough to make me certain I needed Tanner's help.

A civilian came through the outer door and led a heavyset man through the waiting area and into the office, depositing him with Lang and closing the door on them. I reached to grab his sleeve. 'I need to make a telephone call.'

'That's up to the sheriff.' He turned and went.

The office wall I sat against was only a partition and I could hear the men start talking inside.

'*He came around again, Bob. That goddamn Hebe only takes his hand out of my pocket long enough to put it in the other one.*'

'Hebe' caught my ear – Siegel?

'*You know you're not alone, Harry.*' It was Lang talking now. '*Wheels are in motion.*'

'*And what the good goddamn does that mean? You have a tendency to talk vague when I—*'

'*It's not a problem can be fixed overnight.*'

'*Which implies it can be fixed in time – but I'm seeing no signs.*'

I'm sick of paying the Jews and Italians back East only to pay another goddamn Hebe down the street.'

'Down the street' – had to be Siegel.

'*I know it,*' Lang said. '*I know it. Will you be in attendance this evening?*'

'*The Flamingo?*'

A pause – Lang nodding an affirmative to the man's question, perhaps. Then the heavyset man carried on. '*You bet your ass I will. He's gonna take my money, I'm sure as hell gonna make sure he sees me drink his liquor and eat his food. I'm paying for it, god's sake.*'

'*All due respect, it's not the moment to kick up a fuss.*'

'*We're in your office, but don't overstep your mark, Bob.*' There was silence a moment, uncomfortable. Then the man again: '*What about the girl?*'

'*Go on.*'

'*Can you pin it on him?*'

At that everything else tuned out. 'The girl' – Desjardins?

'*I'm not comfortable with that choice of words,*' Lang said.

'*Well, I'm not comfortable with his hand up my ass, and I'm sure as hell not comfortable that nothing's getting done about it. What is it until the elections, fifteen months?*'

'*It's in hand, Harry. Stay with me, the others are.*'

A loud sigh, followed by the sound of shuffled footsteps. My brain was freewheeling. Pinning Desjardins' murder on Siegel: because it was a weapon to use against him – or because they suspected he was involved but couldn't prove it? I thought back to standing in the desert where they found her, his grand plan rising in the distance.

A loud back-and-forth kicked up in the squadroom outside, making it hard to hear what they were saying behind me. I whipped over to the outer door and closed it, went back to the partition to listen again.

The heavyset man was speaking. '. . . *the dead man's part in it? He worked for him, correct?*'

'*Correct.*'

'*Well, isn't that enough?*'

'*It's a start. There's another party I'm interested in too, he may be the link.*'

There was silence and then a grunt – as if Lang had gestured to where I sat. Odds on: referring to me.

I heard footsteps moving towards the partition I was pressed against and I tore myself away. I saw the heavyset man's silhouette through the frosted panel in the door, then he spoke again, clearer now he was close. '*You say the others are with you but that's not what they say in private. I'm the only one will tell it to your face.*'

He wrenched the handle and the door swung open. He marched across the outer office, stopping briefly to peer at me, and then he let himself out the other door.

Lang stood in his doorway and watched him go. Then he went back inside, beckoning me to follow.

I lifted myself out of the chair and did as he indicated. 'Who was that?'

He ignored me, skirting the edge of his desk as I came inside. His face was creased in a different way than before, as if he'd had a bad night's sleep in the fifteen minutes since we'd been interrupted.

He retook his seat. 'When we first spoke you told me you were in Los Angeles right before you arrived here. Your man Acheson confirmed your presence there the night before, but what about prior to that?' He was glancing at the sheet of paper on his desk again; I tried to get a look but he saw what I was doing and picked it up to hold it out of view.

'Is that the coroner's report on Desjardins?'

He slammed his fist onto the desk. 'I asked you a damn question.'

I sat straight, chastened and trying not to betray it. I tried to remember my movements in Los Angeles, seeming so distant now even at a couple days' remove. The timeline came clear then – before Acheson, I'd been with Moe Rosenberg when he and Gilardino killed Bayless. And before that, at Ciglio's. Benjamin Siegel's fingerprints all over my life. I stared hard at Lang, stilling gut tremors, wondering if he knew.

'Well?'

The answer, again, was Tanner. I'd spent the whole afternoon in his presence, after Trent Bayless' murder, and I'd been with him the night before that. I wondered whether to volunteer it – whether Lizzie would be able to contact him and, if so, whether he'd be willing to speak up for me. I'd run out on him and his operation; his comeback could be to leave me swinging. And without his confirmation, my story about the FBI as my alibi sounded too ludicrous to carry any water.

'I have a man can confirm my whereabouts.'

'Name?'

'My wife is trying to contact him now. I need to speak with her first.'

'Give me his name.'

'I have to speak with my wife.'

He hung his head, bristling. 'You talk as though withholding your alibi gives you some credibility.'

He got up and moved to the door, went out. When he came back, he had a deputy with him. 'Take him downstairs. See how long you want to keep playing games with me.'

*

The cell was one of a row of six, only two of the others occupied. To my right, a man slept on a bare bunk, facing the wall, his shoes still on his feet. To my left, a man was on his haunches smoking, huddling against himself for warmth. I stood holding the cold bars, peering along the corridor, waiting for Lang or someone else to appear.

Coming on noon. I'd been there more than three hours. The deputy had ignored my protests for a telephone call when he locked me up, and when I'd asked to call an attorney, his response had been, 'What for? You're not under arrest.'

I let go of the bars and stuffed my hands under my armpits, lack of food making the cold that much more penetrating. The cinderblock wall opposite was unpainted and it felt as though the air from outside flowed right through its pores.

A door opened at the end of the cellblock. The sleeping man didn't stir, but the man smoking got up and went to the bars to look, same as me.

Footsteps – two pairs coming towards me. A deputy came into view and then so did the man behind him. Special Agent Colt Tanner.

The smoking man sloped back to his bunk. I checked my watch, wondering if I'd miscalculated how long I'd been there.

The deputy hung back. Tanner stopped in front of me,

folded his arms with his thumbs under his armpits. 'Safer here than on the street, I'll grant you that.'

'My wife spoke to you?'

He nodded. 'What you did in Los Angeles was foolish and reckless.'

I stepped back from the bars. 'Where's Kosoff? Is he . . .'

He bulged his cheeks, blowing out a breath. 'What the hell possessed you?'

I shook my head, looking away.

'You think that'll suffice? Hold your tongue and shrug?'

'I was scared for my wife.'

His eyes flared. 'So you brought her here? I mean, why not lay up in Siegel's house instead? Don't run that noble husband number on me.'

'What about Kosoff?'

He turned and walked a few paces, looking at the sleeping man and then the empty cell at the end. 'He's alive. According to MGM he's unavailable due to a family emergency. We know that he's holed up at the Toluca Lake Country Club, with a man on the door day and night.'

'They haven't moved on him yet?'

'It's a little late for guilt, wouldn't you say?' He walked back to where I stood, watching me, but I didn't know what for. 'There's every chance they've issued a contract on him.'

I gripped the bars again and met his stare. 'I need you to get me out of here. They're trying to hang something on me I had nothing to do with and—'

'I helped you before and you ran out on your end of the deal.'

'This is my life, Tanner, you can't play games.'

He kept staring at me, no response.

I shifted my weight. 'What do you want?'

He pointed at me. 'You know damn well already.'

I looked from Tanner to the deputy along the corridor. The man was standing stock-still, hand on his keychain, watching us. Something wasn't right with the scene.

'Why did you come here, Yates? The truth now.'

I looked at the deputy, then the man in the cell next to me, wondering about those listening on. 'Not here. Get me out of this cell and we'll talk.'

He looked at the deputy and nodded, and I got it then. 'You already told them, didn't you?'

The deputy came over and unlocked the door, swinging it open for me.

Tanner stepped inside to block the way. 'I do not appreciate having to stick my neck out like this. Are we on the same page?'

I nodded, waiting, antsy.

He backed away to let me out, then indicated for me to follow the deputy along the corridor.

We passed through the doors and I tapped the deputy on the shoulder. 'Where's Newland?'

'He's with the sheriff.'

'He had nothing to do with—' I stopped mid-sentence. I was about to plead his case when I realised I couldn't say anything about him for certain.

'Who's Newland?' Tanner asked.

'Nobody. A local hack.'

His silent acceptance was uncharacteristic.

The deputy led us up the staircase and through the station to a back exit, saying nothing, walking a little way ahead of me. I looked around for Lang as we went, wondering what his reaction would've been to the FBI speaking for me. But there was no sign.

Tanner's ride was parked along the block. We passed a payphone on the way and I slowed. 'I need to call my wife.'

'We talk first.'

I stopped and picked up the receiver, reached for a nickel. He put his hand on my forearm to halt me.

'She's at a hotel Siegel owned,' I said. 'I had no idea.'

'El Cortez?'

'You know of it?'

'I've done my homework. We'll go get her, it'll be quicker.'

I looked at him, remembering Rosenberg's photograph of Lizzie at the Breakers, doubts still lingering.

He set the telephone gently back in its cradle. 'Come on.'

*

He'd barely hit the ignition when he started in on me. 'What's the deal with the dead man? Why are you here?'

'It's unrelated to your investigation.'

'Everything in this town relates to Siegel. Besides which, you've involved me now.'

I looked at my hands, recalling the conversation I'd overheard outside Lang's office; turning it all over in my head.

'He worked for him,' Tanner said. 'The dead man. From what I understand.'

'The sheriff tell you that?'

He nodded, watching the road.

'It's a coincidence. It pertains to an old story I was working in LA.'

He raised his eyebrows. 'Important enough to make you drop everything and clear out to come here.'

I waved a hand, nonchalant. Change the subject. 'Siegel is desperate for cash. The Flamingo is sending him broke, he's making enemies all over LA and Las Vegas because of it. That's what the shakedowns are in aid of.'

'That tallies with what we're seeing. How does it help me?'

'The pressure is making him careless. You stay tight and he'll do something stupid soon enough.'

'He's no use to me dead,' he said.

'I'm not saying dead. But I'm worried others will get caught in the blowback.'

'Is that a reference to the man that died this morning or yourself?'

I shot him a sidelong look, giving no answer. The name Nancy Hill on my lips, doubt like a lump in my throat, stopping me from saying it.

*

We pulled into El Cortez and I jumped out of the car, leaving Tanner behind. I took the steps two at a time and came up to our room, rapping on the door and calling Lizzie's name until it opened.

'Charlie, thank god.' She took my hands and I pulled her to me.

I held her silently until a sound made me look up and I saw Tanner coming along the corridor.

'You'll forgive me for intruding, but after last time . . .'

Lizzie pulled back as he approached. 'Special Agent Tanner, thank you for your help.'

'It's your husband should be thanking me. But you're welcome.'

I stepped past Lizzie and into the room to get the bags. She turned to look. 'Are we leaving?'

I nodded. 'Right now. I'll explain when we're out.'

'Where are we going?' She looked at Tanner and it bugged me – his show again now.

'Do you have a field office here?' I asked.

'We'll have to improvise.'

*

Tanner paced back and forth in front of the window, reading from his pocketbook. 'You said Moe Rosenberg gave you three days for Lyle Kosoff to raise the money. That's tomorrow.'

I nodded.

'But you're telling me he demanded to see your smear today?'

I looked past him and out the window, nodding again. Tanner had led us to a motor court a short way out of town, on the highway headed north. The view was an expanse of desert that looked grey under gloomy skies, even the peaks in the distance appearing dulled by the grinding cold.

Tanner knocked on the wall to get my attention. 'What's your best estimation of their next move?'

'Are you kidding me? After what they did before?' I looked at Lizzie, sitting on the second bed, then back at him. 'You know the answer to that.'

He held his pocketbook by his side. 'It won't be easy to get to Kosoff.'

'Can you protect him? You have men watching him, surely?'

'We're doing what we can. But we're spread thin, as you know.' He shot me a look, a note of accusation about it. Enough to compel me into a peace offering.

'There's something going down at the Flamingo tonight, a reception. I think Siegel's going to be there.'

'Wouldn't be a surprise, my information has it that he's in town. That's why you came here, isn't it?'

'Does it matter any more?'

'The man who was killed – do you believe Siegel was involved?'

'I don't know.'

'You don't know? I can't think of any other reason you'd be wrapped up in it.'

'You'd need to speak to the cops.'

'I already did, if you recall.' He was pointing at me but he lowered his finger when he realised it. 'Look, a dead construction hand may be trivial by comparison to what else he's done, but you never know what's going to break a case open. Think about Capone.'

I could feel Lizzie looking at me, and I wondered if she was about to spill about Hill and Desjardins. At the same time wondering if Tanner had already put it together and was just trying to trap me.

'You made good time, Special Agent Tanner,' she said. 'To get here so fast.'

He paused, the line seeming to back him off. 'I flew. A necessity of the situation.'

He looked away, taking no account of her, and back to me. Lizzie kept staring at him.

'This function tonight – what's the purpose?' Tanner said.

'I don't know, I need to ask around.' In my head, thinking to track down the heavyset man from Lang's office. *Harry.*

'Who's on the invite list?'

'Why do you care?'

'Because it's an unguarded moment.' He went to the window and drew the curtain back to reveal more of the grey vista. 'Because if certain parties were to be in attendance, it could present an opportunity.'

Lizzie stabbed her finger into her palm. 'No.'

Tanner whipped around. 'No, what?'

'I see what you're about to propose, Special Agent, and the answer is no. There is no cause for Charlie to be there.'

Tanner let go of the curtain, shadow flittering across the bedstead. 'With respect, Mrs Yates, Bureau business is not a matter you're qualified to make pronouncements on.'

I watched the exchange without speaking. Caught between wanting to defend my wife and the truth I hadn't spoken – that I'd been intending to go from the moment I heard about it.

But as Lizzie looked at me, I could tell my silence had given me away.

She took a step backwards, shaking her head. 'No. Charlie, no . . .'

'Just hear him out.'

'No—'

'Liz—'

'NO. I stood by and watched you walk out the door in Venice Beach and felt sure you'd never come back. I'll be damned if I'm going to do that again. We've pushed and pushed and pushed and—'

'Mrs Yates—'

'With respect, Special Agent, allow me to speak. You've had your say and I mean to have mine.' Tanner folded his arms, one eye narrowing. 'I will not have my husband used as a pawn any longer. You have eyewitness testimony of a murder and of conspiracy to blackmail, what more can you possibly gain by sending Charlie into the lion's den again?'

He was silent long enough to see if she was finished, then turned to me. 'You have anything to say for yourself, Yates?'

Lizzie stamped her foot. 'How dare you dismiss me?' She marched to the door and opened it. 'I mean to speak to my husband alone, I'll thank you to leave.'

He put his hands on his hips, his tongue in his cheek. 'You've a short memory, Mrs Yates.'

'So do you, Special Agent.'

Tanner came over to me, watching Lizzie. 'Get your wife under control, then come find me. And if you think to cut out on me again, I won't be there to save your ass next time. Whoever it is catches up with you first.'

He carried on to the door, touching the brim of his hat as he passed Lizzie without looking her way.

She slammed it shut and marched to the bathroom.

'Liz—'

I heard the faucet come on, the sound of running water. I went to follow her, but she came out again right away, her finger to her lips. She crept lightly over to the front door and looked through the spy hole.

She straightened up and beckoned me to follow her to the bathroom again.

I did as she indicated. Inside, I reached to turn the faucet off, but she grabbed my hand.

'Mind telling me what the hell is going on?' I said.

'I couldn't think how else to get rid of him.'

I looked at her, stunned. An incredulous smile split my face.

'I don't trust that man, Charlie.'

I glanced to the side, seeing her in profile in the dirty mirror, wondering what I'd ever done to deserve her. 'Neither do I, but he came through this time . . .'

'How did he get here so fast? Answer me that.'

'He said he caught a flight.'

'It can't have been three hours from when I called to when he sprung you. Even if the FBI used their own airplane, does that sound right to you?'

'I don't know. Where was he when you spoke to him?'

'That's just it, I didn't speak to him. I called the number in Los Angeles and spoke to Agent Bryce who agreed to contact him.' She looked down as if only just realising she was still holding my arm. 'Do you think it's possible he was already here?'

The sound of running water intruded on my thoughts again. 'What's with the faucet? You think he's listening at the door?'

She closed her eyes and put her hand to her mouth. Then she shut the water off. 'Am I being paranoid? I feel as if this situation is making me crazy.'

I closed the bathroom door, shutting us in.

Lizzie leaned on the sink, her head bowed. 'I just keep thinking about your notes. How he was on your trail so long before he made contact with you – the boarding house. Then he pops up here the second we call for him – even after . . .'

I put my hand on her back. 'You're not crazy. There is nothing normal about this situation.'

She looked up. 'What if his interest is in you?'

I stood motionless, watching the top of her head in the mirror.

'What if he sent you into Ciglio's with the hope something bad would happen?' Her voice was as quiet as a gliding bird. 'What if he's doing the same now?'

'That's . . .' I thought back to the crack I'd made when he warned me there'd be no cavalry when I went back to Ciglio's – *'You'd have your case at least.'* 'That can't be right.'

'You don't sound convinced.'

We watched each other in the mirror, feeling as though each was daring the other to speak next.

'You were meaning to go to the Flamingo tonight, weren't you?'

I took a moment to gather my thoughts. 'I want to speak to the man I heard talking about it. There's resentment to Siegel here and that man was browbeating the sheriff as if it were nothing. If I can marshal that . . .'

She watched me a moment longer, then looked away as she pushed her hair off her shoulders.

'If his focus is diverted, he can't go on doing what he's doing,' I said. 'And if that hotel goes belly-up, maybe it takes him with it.'

'He could . . . He—' She stopped herself. I waited for her to finish, but she ran her fingers slowly through her hair, tightening her grip until she was pulling at the roots. I reached out for her, but as I did, she screamed and swiped her hand across the shelf over the sink, clearing it of bottles. They ricocheted off the walls, crashing to the floor.

She turned around to face me, pushing me off as I tried to embrace her. 'I was going to say he could kill you for interfering,

202

but that's already how it is. One goddamn door after another is closing in our faces.'

I ran my hand over my head then reached out to her. 'Siegel's got the FBI and the locals ranged against him, and he's flat broke. He's teetering, we just need to give him the last push.'

She withdrew her hand and looked up at me. From her words, I expected to see tears, but all I saw was cold acceptance. 'I'm sick of feeling hopeless, Charlie. I can't remember feeling any other way and it makes me want to just march in there tonight and stick it to him. There must be ... He doesn't know about the FBI. Why don't we just tell him they'll arrest him if he doesn't leave us alone?'

I was struggling for words to reassure her and before I could get anything out, she spoke again. 'I know, I know ... it's more complicated than that. But— It's just that he hides away and sends men after us and this is the one time we know where he'll be. I want so badly to feel as though we're on the front foot.'

The notion horrified me as much as it buoyed me. The prospect of coming face to face with him again, Lizzie there to witness whatever humiliation he could inflict next. Delivering her into his clutches. Side by side with the dream of bringing an end to this – however unlikely.

I opened the bathroom door. 'Let me take care of Tanner.'

*

Tanner was sitting in his car in the parking lot, his door open so he could face sideways towards our room. He got up as I came over, his coat slung over one arm. 'You work it out with your old lady?'

'Don't talk that way to my wife again. Consider the situation she's in.'

'I'm well aware; she's the one needs to face up to it, then maybe she'll realise she ought to be listening to me.' He took his coat from his arm, dangled it from his finger.

'Why would you have me go to the Flamingo tonight?' I said. 'The truth.'

'Are you in any position to demand the truth out of me?'

I looked away sharply. A saloon cruised into the lot, stopping outside the office and disgorging a family. 'Eventually you'll have to forget about what I did before.'

He smoothed his necktie, tucking it inside his jacket, watching mom and pop hustle the kids inside. 'Let me tell you the truth, Yates: you came to Las Vegas for the very reason of confronting Siegel. You crave a showdown because you think it'll bring an end to your problems. You were intending to go there tonight long before I suggested it; that's why you didn't take your wife's part back there, and why you've spent the last ten minutes trying to make it up to her.'

I let his words settle before I spoke. 'Doesn't answer my question.'

'What?'

'Why do you want me there? Are you sending me as a sacrificial lamb?'

He waved the suggestion off, looking sour. 'Ridiculous.'

'You think I'll go in there and get myself killed and then you'll have him. That it?'

He drew up to his full height, a half-head taller than me.

'I ought to knock you on your ass. I've spent my adult life upholding the law and you have the nerve to say that? You ungrateful son of a bitch.'

The pop looked over at us from inside the office, averting his gaze again when he got the measure of the atmosphere between us. 'Then tell me what you'd have me do there.'

He held his free arm out. 'Use your eyes. Listen. See who's there and who he talks to. Same as before, you might not recognise what has value to us, so store it all.'

'*Same as before*' – a trip to Ciglio's that ended with the murder of an innocent man. The lingering feeling that he was hoping my presence would provoke as unpredictable an outcome this time – whatever his denials. But something in his face said he was holding back. 'That's not all of it, is it?'

He hooked his coat over his shoulder from his forefinger. 'I want you to tell him you'll write the piece on Kosoff.'

I screwed my eyes shut, about to speak, but he cut me off.

'You're just buying us some time, that's all. Come up with a reason for why it'll take a couple extra days. I'm not saying you have to go through with it.'

I emptied my lungs. 'And what does a couple extra days do for us exactly?'

'Leave that to me. I see the look on your face but consider it this way: could be you're saving Kosoff's life. Remember what happened to Trent Bayless.'

My mouth fell ajar, the absurdity of it – as if I needed reminding. But through it came a hardening certainty: that I would go anyway, for my own purposes. To look Siegel in the eye and plead with him to tell me anything he knew about the murder of Julie Desjardins. Whatever that cost me.

CHAPTER NINETEEN

Discovering the identity of the man Lang had called 'Harry' proved no great task. The forename and a description were enough for the duty manager at the motor court to come up with a likely candidate – Harry Heller, owner of the Pioneer Club.

Finding him proved harder. A frantic run to his office at the Pioneer was a bust – one of the deskmen said he hadn't been seen that day, and that daytime wasn't the time to catch him there. But the trip wasn't a total waste. Through the small window in Heller's office door, I could see the walls were adorned with a number of framed newspaper cuttings; the man I'd seen with Lang appeared in most of them.

I called the sheriff's office from the Pioneer, and a desk sergeant confirmed Trip Newland had been released. I drove with Lizzie straight to the *Telegraph-Register*, but that proved to be a bust too; Newland hadn't been in yet. But his colleague kicked loose his address, and we tore across town. When we drew up, Newland was on the driveway wrestling a box into the trunk of his car. It escaped his grip when he looked up and recognised me, scattering shoes and books on the cracked concrete.

I left the car on the street and went over.

'They let you go,' I said.

He stepped out from behind the trunk lid, watching me approach. He didn't reply.

I stopped a few paces short of him. 'What happened with you and Lang?'

He bent down to right the box, staying crouched. 'Nothing happened with Lang. He knows I don't know zip.'

'Then why—'

'It's tit-for-tat. A swipe at me because he thought I'd given up Booker's name to you when I'd been holding out on them.'

'Sorry he took that impression.' I lifted my hand to my face, taking in the row of small cacti that lined the front of the yard. 'How did you know I'd found Booker?'

He looked up at me. 'The cops were talking about it when I got there, their hot lead – some reporter that'd been asking around the Flamingo about Booker. Lang called you "*That LA jackass*".' He stood up and toed a shoe back towards the box. 'They let you go so figure you didn't do it?'

'Don't be a jerk.' I pointed to the trunk, a duffel bag and another box visible inside. 'You're leaving town?'

'I got a new job, remember?'

'I was questioning the timing.'

'After what's happened? You should be questioning why I'm still here.'

'What has happened? If you're ducking out, at least tell me what you know.'

'I'm not ducking out of anything.' He reached up to place his hand on the trunk lid, resting it there. 'Look, it's beyond me. Swear to god.'

'You don't know anything about Booker's connection to the Desjardins girl?'

'Everything I told you is the truth.'

An answer to a different question than the one I'd asked. I

let it go, shuffling on the spot, the cold penetrating again. 'Do you know Harry Heller?'

He squinted at me. 'Sure. Not personally.' The non sequitur made him want to ask, but he looked down to stop himself.

'I overheard him talking to Lang. He wanted to look at Siegel for the Desjardins murder. Any idea why that would be?'

He scoffed. 'Sounds a little like desperation.'

'You don't think it's possible?'

He looked at me like I was simple. 'It's a play to stop him getting his gaming licence. The County Commissioner has denied him twice already, but he's got Senator McCarran in his corner so it's still on the table. Money he's spent, I'd have said he's a cert – unless they can make this stick.'

'He's a killer – how's a trumped-up murder beef supposed to make the difference?'

'That's his California rep. This is local, something the commission can get their teeth into.'

'And if he doesn't get his licence?'

'No casino. An expensive hotel with no guests.'

Dragged under by his own dream. Something to use against him – but the prospect of a sickening decision lumbering into view.

'Don't leave town yet,' I said. 'Booker wasn't the end of this. You can help.'

He stuffed the last shoe back in the box and closed the lid, hefting it into the trunk. 'I wouldn't even be talking to you now, wasn't for how bad I want out. So thanks, but I'll see you in California.'

*

The car was shut tight against the cold, our breath coating the windscreen with a sheen of condensation that blurred and dissipated the pink neon of the Flamingo sign.

We were waiting on the shoulder of the highway. Cars pulled off into the Flamingo lot at regular intervals, the purpose of the night coming clear after the conversation with Newland – Siegel greasing the local great and good to firm up support for his gaming licence. With time running out until opening night, he had to be getting desperate. Enough at least to let me air my proposal.

Lizzie turned to say something and it was only then I realised we'd been silent a stretch. 'What would you have him say? If you had the choice.'

A cloud moved from in front of the moon, bathing the desert in a cold light. 'I don't know.'

'He can't admit to his involvement,' she said. 'He'll have to deny it. Where will that leave you?'

'With leverage. If he wasn't involved in her murder, he's going to need someone to be searching for the real culprit. Lang won't be looking for any other suspects if the owners are railroading him.'

'And would you be able to go through with it?'

'Yes.'

'You'd be prepared to help Siegel.'

'Yes. If it keeps us safe and finds her killer, yes.'

'What about Special Agent Tanner?'

'It's not his concern.'

'Don't be obtuse, Charlie.'

I looked at the moon, trying to keep ahead of my own thoughts. 'Tanner wants to play a waiting game, this way serves to give him more time. The worst shame for him would be Clark County Sheriff's being the ones to finally take down Siegel.'

She looked forward again, the dancing pink light playing on her face.

'Would you do differently?' I asked.

She shook her head slowly, taking my hand but somehow more distant for it. 'I'm glad it's not my choice to make.'

*

From the inside, it was obvious the Flamingo was in worse shape than it appeared. Hosts in tuxedos ushered guests through to a casino area that sparkled and smelled of wood polish and new leather – but once we were there, the glitz couldn't distract from the drop cloths cordoning off other sections of the property on all sides. Although styled to look like decorative drapes, there was no disguising their purpose. One had come unpinned in a high corner, revealing plywood boarding behind it and hinting at the level of disorder that lay beyond.

White-gloved waiters moved through the crowd handing out champagne flutes, and a good level of noise rose from the bar, but it wasn't the easy chatter of enjoyment; there was a halting feel to proceedings, as if no one quite understood their purpose in being there. I'd worried that our getup – me in a wrinkled suit and Lizzie in a three-day-old dress – would give away the fact we had no business being in attendance. But in the event, the crowd was a mix of men in Stetsons with western shirts and bolo ties, local pols in lounge suits, and sullen Hollywood cats in black tie; enough of a hotchpotch that no one looked our way for long.

Siegel was nowhere to be seen, his absence only adding to the jittery anticipation in the room. Lizzie and I moved through the crowd, passing between two roulette tables attended by cigarette girls dishing free casino chips. I thought back to Heller's words in Lang's office and wondered at how Siegel had the front to shake men down and then invite them to a reception for his own benefit; the thug mentality that a spin of the wheel on house money made everything copacetic.

I took a glass of champagne and handed it to Lizzie. She held it but didn't drink any, carrying it with her like a spent match. We were tracing a loop around the room, waiting for him to show. We rounded a bank of slots, but I stopped us dead when I saw Sheriff Lang at the other end of the row. He was in conversation with three other men, but our movement was abrupt enough to catch his attention. He looked over and tagged me with a nod, without breaking his verbal stride. I backed Lizzie up and led us away from his position.

'What's he doing here?' she said.

I looked back to see if he'd come after us. 'Being seen.'

'By who? Siegel?'

'Not sure. Maybe letting all sides know he's keeping tabs.'

'He bothers me. He's got the same look about him as the others.'

'Because he's bought and paid for, same as them. Put him out of your head for now.'

I was facing her as I said it and when I looked forward again, Harry Heller was standing alone at a blackjack table five yards in front of us.

'That's Heller.' I nodded in his direction. We were already drifting towards him, as if moved by convection.

He was holding a large tumbler of drink, his back to the dealer and the table. He'd loosened his necktie and was resting his fist on the stool next to him, taking in something across the crowd with a hard look. Following his eyes gave no clue as to what.

He snapped out of it as we drew up, glancing at me before turning his gaze to Lizzie.

'Mr Heller, my name's Charlie Yates, I'm a reporter from Los Angeles.'

He turned back to me when I offered my hand, ignoring it. 'I'm surprised to see you have your liberty again.'

I hadn't expected he'd recognise me. 'A misunderstanding on Sheriff Lang's part.'

'This must be your wife,' he said, taking a bite out of her with his eyes.

'Elizabeth.' She held her hand out and he made a show of kissing the back of it. She looked at me as he did, unsure what to make of the formality.

'This doesn't have the feel of a chance encounter, Mr Yates.'

'In a way. I'd like to talk to you about a shared interest.'

'Would that happen to be our fair host?'

'You're a perceptive man, Mr Heller.'

'Informed. There's a difference.' He winked at me. 'The sheriff has the notion you might be in the employ of our kosher friend.'

I was shaking my head before he'd finished speaking. 'Nothing could be further from the truth.' The image of Trent Bayless' corpse popped into my head and made my neck flush as I said it.

'And yet here you are at his party . . .'

'The same as you . . .'

His face darkened. 'I know why I'm here. He's already

picking my pockets clean and now he wants to have me say uncle while he does it.' He took the lapel of my suit coat and rubbed it between his thumb and forefinger. 'Appearances can deceive, but I don't think he has you here for your green.'

'He doesn't know I'm here at all.'

He looked off to one side, a nod of the head to acquiesce. 'Cut to the chase, then.' He glanced at Lizzie when he said it, checking he'd impressed with his command. She blinked and checked her watch.

'You're aware of the young woman that was killed?' I said. 'Named in these parts as Diana Desjardins.'

He nodded once. 'When you put that out there that way – am I supposed to ask you for her real name?'

'No. I want to know if you have reason to believe Ben Siegel was involved in her murder.'

He lowered himself backwards to sit on the stool he'd been hovering over, cracking a rictus grin. 'That sounds like a question could get me in trouble. If the sheriff was right about you and your associations.'

I dipped my head, working through what to say. 'You've dealt with Siegel and his men. You really think he'd send the likes of me to put a squeeze on you for talking out of turn?'

He swirled his drink, rattling the ice cubes. 'You'd be a bad choice, I'll warrant.'

'Look, I think you know I overheard you talking to Lang, so my cause for asking is no mystery. What set you on that tack?'

He sucked in a breath, filling his lungs, then let it out as he spoke. 'That question is below anyone with a half a brain. He's a stone killer – and I'll risk saying that to you because if he's the man I take him for, he'd consider it a compliment.'

I felt my hope for quick answers sliding away. It was what it sounded from the start – a power play, no basis in evidence. 'That's an empty answer.'

He snapped his eyes to something behind me, following it across the room with his gaze. Lizzie caught it and turned just before me. When I did, I saw Moe Rosenberg in a slack tux, glad-handing his way through the crowd as though he'd just arrived. Even expecting he'd be there, the sight of him woke the butterflies in my stomach.

'You know who that is?' Heller said, still watching.

'Yes.'

'Of course you do.'

I ignored the barb, no conviction behind it. 'How far will you go to get Siegel?'

'Look at him.' He motioned with his head to Rosenberg. 'He's like a trained gorilla, makes me sick. His keeper won't be far behind.'

I pressed him, aware of the irony that the more spurious the case against Siegel's involvement, the greater my leverage with him. 'Because it strikes me you'll need more than bogus charges to worry him.'

But he wasn't listening to me, still scorching Rosenberg with his stare. 'You know what Siegel said to me? He comes into my office out of the blue and tells me I need new slots, he'll front them, but I gotta cut him in on the business. '*It's my way, all the way, and twenty-five percent.*' In my own damn office. I found out later he used the same line on all of us.' He broke the look and rubbed his eyes with his thumb and a knuckle. 'I'm not a rube, I know who he represents in New York, what else am I supposed to do? But then he comes back a month ago and he wants ten more on top. I know where that's going – right into this place. I might as well pour the cash in with the concrete.'

A murmur went through the crowd, and then a commotion kicked up on the far side of the room. The noise level jumped and every head turned, the gas pumping at last on the evening. Through the bodies, I caught a glimpse of a white dinner jacket, a red carnation on the lapel; looked like fresh blood from my distance. Then a sightline opened up and I saw the rest: Ben Siegel shaking hands left and right, a smile plastered on his face that looked like it cost him.

Heller got to his feet, as though to step to him, but didn't advance. I put my hand on his chest anyway, a sop for his ego.

'Tell me about the casino licence,' I said. 'That's your move against him, isn't it?'

That got his attention and he looked at me. 'Every question you ask sounds like it came out of Bugsy's mouth.'

I glanced at Lizzie to buy myself a beat. She gave a slight shake of the head, as if to say Heller's usefulness was played out, and I wondered if her nerve was faltering with the new arrival.

I turned back. 'I've got more reason to hate Siegel than all of you put together. If money was all he'd taken from me, I'd be thankful.'

'And yet you doubt he's a killer.'

'Not for a second. But if you're going to *pin* the girl on him, you need more than thin air.'

'Thin air? Maybe there's a little more to it than you know.'

I wanted to look over to Siegel again, but the way Heller said it made me zero in on him. I waited, a breath trapped in my throat.

'You should have your wife take a powder,' he said.

Lizzie had moved tight to me now, sensing the change, all eyes on Heller. 'I'm fine, but thank you for your concern.'

Hard eyes on Heller.

He shot her a half-smile. 'As you will, darlin.' He flicked his gaze to me again. 'The one that died, she was a working girl. You knew that.'

I nodded.

'She was also an actress – trying to be.'

I inched closer to him. 'How did you come by that?' Knowing he could only have got it from me – via Lang.

'Sheriff has his sources.' He winked at me again and twisted at the waist to set his tumbler down on the card table behind him. 'Last few weeks, Siegel's been touting girls to certain types – money men exclusive. He's billing them as starlets, chartered in direct from Hollywood . . .'

I looked over my shoulder, searching. I felt Lizzie grab my forearm. The room, the noise, the lights, they all dimmed. Siegel the only thing I could see.

'. . . so now you heard that, you tell me again that son of a bitch isn't involved somehow.'

I felt Lizzie's grip tighten. But I was already turning, pulling away from her. I twisted my arm free and started moving towards him across the floor.

'Charlie—' Lizzie's voice behind me. A thousand miles away and fading.

Muscling through the crowd, a straight line to him.

Rosenberg seeing me first when I came close, only his eyes giving away his surprise. Collecting himself enough to alert Siegel. One hand slipping inside his jacket – and holding there.

Then Ben Siegel ten feet in front of me, turning to look, his face rippling with hate; the opposite of Rosenberg, no attempt to hide it.

I pointed a finger at him. 'Diana Desjardins. Your office right now, or we talk here.'

I felt a hand clawing at my back, heard Lizzie's voice; words I didn't catch through the roar in my head.

Rosenberg stepped in front of Siegel and moved to grab me, Gilardino appearing from nowhere with the assist. They locked my arms to my sides. Siegel was already futzing with his tie, trying to laugh it off in front of the shocked onlookers, mimicking I was a drunk.

I got my right arm free and used it to pry a gap between the men wrestling me away. 'Tell me what happened to her—' Gilardino stuffed his hand over my mouth but it wasn't enough. 'Tell me, goddammit—'

They were dragging me backwards, my feet scraping the carpet. Lizzie was tearing at Gilardino's arm, shouting, being pulled along as she tried to stop him. I called for Siegel again, but the crowd had already swallowed him up. I was struggling, kicking out. I connected and Rosenberg stumbled, all of us crashing to the floor, Lizzie too. One of them punched me in the gut, driving the wind out of me, and Lizzie screamed. I tried to tell her to run, but the words wouldn't form. Rosenberg was in my ear: 'You stupid fucking cocksucker.'

They pulled me to my feet and bundled me the rest of the way across the room, then parted a drop cloth and took me through the gap. From the bright casino into the gloom, my eyes not adjusting at first, then making out the bare walls of a corridor under construction. To my right, a plyboard partition with a bank of empty spaces at regular intervals, waiting for the elevators that would fill them. I kicked out again, but they had momentum now.

Then we burst through an exit to the outside. Cold air hitting me like a wall. Before Gilardino had even let go, Rosenberg punched me in the face, sending me sprawling. Rocks and gravel beneath me, shredding the skin on my cheek. I heard another scream, realised Lizzie had come out with us. I croaked for her to run, but they were on me then, kicking and stomping. I pulled tight into a ball, taking kicks to my ribs, my back. One of them stamped on my head and I nearly blacked out. Another scream, knowing she was seeing it the worst part. Starbursts behind my eyes, nothing I could do.

Then they stopped. Lizzie was sobbing, calling my name. I didn't dare look, expecting them to catch their breath and start in again. Or shoot me. But then there was another voice.

'That'll do it, fellas. I'll take it from here.'

I felt a weight pressing down on my torso, smelled Lizzie's perfume and realised she'd moved to drape herself on top of me. She screamed at them. 'You animals. You animals—'

Rosenberg spoke, addressing someone else. 'You must've saw what he did, he's stewed.'

The new party spoke again. 'Might be best for you to go back inside, miss.' I placed the voice just as I opened my eyes. Sheriff Robert Lang. He was looking at Rosenberg. 'Yeah, I saw what went on. Best if I handle it.' He reached for his handcuffs.

Lizzie was holding my face, calling my name. Lang reached down and shook me gently by the shoulder. 'Can you stand, Yates?'

'He needs a doctor, what are you doing? He hasn't done a damn thing wrong.'

'He can stand, we'll get him seen to at the department.' He raised his voice, spoke slow. 'Yates – can you walk?'

Lizzie eased herself off me and helped as I scrambled onto all fours. My head was pounding and there was blood on my hands and sleeves. I looked up; Rosenberg and Gilardino were gone. Lang stood over me, Lizzie on her knees by my side.

'Go arrest them,' she said, stabbing the air. 'You saw the whole thing.'

I coughed my throat clear. 'The girl . . .'

'What's he saying?'

'Nancy,' I said. 'Siegel knows.'

'Forget that for now,' Lizzie said.

I struggled to my feet, unsteady, trying not to let Lizzie take my weight. 'They'll kill her—'

Lang came forward with the cuffs and locked them on my wrists over Lizzie's protests.

'Miss, you'll thank me for this.'

'Like hell.'

Lang put his arm under mine and manoeuvred me back inside before I had wits enough to resist. We retraced our steps down the corridor, the sound of music and chatter rising as we approached the drop cloth they'd bundled me through.

'Do you mean to humiliate us as well?' Lizzie said.

Lang didn't answer before he swept the makeshift curtain aside and led me through it. A hush came over the crowd when we appeared, rippling out from our corner of the room. I'd had my head down from the pain, but I looked up then, blinking against the too-bright chandelier light.

'SIEGEL.' I couldn't see him, called out again. 'Siegel, tell me where she is.' The room felt cavernous in the quiet, my voice like a jagged thunderclap.

Lang pulled at the cuff chain, shooting me a stern look. 'No. C'mon.'

'Siegel, you lay a finger on her and I'll be on you for ever.'

'Go sleep it off, friend, you'll feel better.' His voice. I turned, saw him playing host at a crowded craps table.

'I know what you did,' I said.

'Is that so?' He spread his arms, magnanimous. 'You gotta take more water with it, folks, it's the desert air.' He glanced side to side, soaking up the polite laughter. His mouth was ajar in a shape the crowd might mistake for a smile.

Lang took us out through reception, Lizzie flushed red with anger and shame, dipping her head to hide her face. Her hair was out of place, a small detail that tore at me until I realised that wasn't the worst of it; as I stumbled across the lot to Lang's car, I saw a slashing welt on her cheek where she'd been struck.

With his hand on my head, Lang guided me into the backseat. Lizzie was on the other side and I couldn't bring myself to look at her. The Flamingo filled my window, all I could see until Siegel appeared at the entranceway; watching as we took off, his eyes were two black bullets.

CHAPTER TWENTY

Lang surprised me when we got to his office, taking the cuffs off me before I could even ask. 'You want to see a medic?'

I shook my head, wincing as it intensified the pounding in my brain, and gestured to Lizzie. 'Someone to take a look at my wife.'

Her hand shot up to the welt on her cheek, hiding it more than favouring it. 'I'm fine.'

Lang looked at me as he folded his handcuffs away, deliberate movements as if he was thinking, then switched his gaze to her. 'Even so, we should get you fixed up. Wait there a minute.'

He looked at me again as he stepped outside, and I got the impression he was giving us a moment's privacy.

'Are you in pain?'

She shook her head, turning to put it out of view. 'It's fine, Charlie, thank you.'

I went over and crouched beside her, cradling the back of her head. 'They hit you.'

'Nothing like they did to you.'

The guilt made me feel ill. 'Which one was it?'

She shied away again. 'Why does it matter?'

Because I'll kill them. 'I suppose it doesn't right now.'

Lang walked back in, carrying a first aid kit. I backed off, knowing that she blamed me. Knowing she was right to. He set the kit on the desk and opened it up. 'Would you tilt your head to the light, ma'am?' He wiped the wound clean, displaying a gentle touch I wouldn't have expected of the man. Then he reached for a tube of salve. 'This might sting.' Lizzie was stock-still as he applied it, a distant 'Thank you' when he finished.

Lang beckoned to someone outside the office and a woman in civilian clothes came in.

'Ma'am, this is Mrs Hampton, I'm gonna go ahead and ask you to go with her a minute. She'll get you taken care of.'

Lizzie looked at me, hesitant. 'I'm not leaving Charlie.'

'You'll be right across the way there, I promise you're in good hands.'

It felt like he wanted to spare her whatever was coming next. I nodded to Lizzie, signalling for her to go, mouthing, '*Tanner.*'

She frowned, a slight shake of the head.

I shot her a questioning look. '*I'll handle him.*'

Her frown turned to annoyance and she looked at the floor before she stood up and turned to Lang. 'I'd like to make a telephone call.'

'That can be arranged.' He faced the woman. 'Mrs Hampton'll see to it.'

She smiled and gestured to lead Lizzie out.

When they were gone, he held up the salve and said, 'What about you?'

'You have an aspirin in that bag?'

He fetched a pill bottle and handed it to me. 'Could've got yourself in real trouble back there.'

I shrugged. 'Siegel's running girls he's billing as starlets. Exclusive clientele. Odds on he's linked to the Desjardins murder and that means Nancy Hill might still be in reach. I need to know everything about—'

'Hold on, cowboy, where'd you get that from? Harry Heller?'

'Yeah.'

He nodded, as if mentally putting a file back in its drawer.

'Wait a minute, did you know?'

He ran his tongue around the inside of his mouth. 'No.'

'No?'

'No. I did not.'

'The sheriff of Las Vegas didn't know Ben Siegel was running—'

'Settle down, son.'

'Heller was in your office, telling you to look at Siegel, and you're saying you knew nothing?'

A second stretched by in silence. 'I had suspicions.'

'This is . . .' My brain was whirling, trying pieces for a fit, the scene flipping on me as I thought about it. 'The clientele is money men only. Men like Heller?'

Lang said nothing, his jaw set hard.

'. . . but he wouldn't be about to admit to you he was consorting with girls Siegel's peddling, even while he's trying to run him out of town.'

Still silent.

Me recalling the conversation I'd eavesdropped, at the time thinking I was being smart, but maybe— 'You meant for me to hear that conversation. In here. You wanted me to go after Heller tonight.'

Still silent – but a look of satisfaction on his face as good as a yes.

I felt dumb, used. But the sense that I'd got Lang all wrong eclipsed it.

He sniffed and leaned against his desk, folding his arms. 'This other girl, Hill, if she's still alive, we have to assume she's in danger.'

I sat down and stood right up again, my head spinning. Thinking you're a step ahead and finding you're two behind. 'We find her, tonight. Now. Where does he operate out of?'

'I don't know. To my knowledge he's not been involved in the trade up to now.'

'Heller, then. He knows how to contact them.'

He nodded. 'He won't talk to me, though.'

I was at the door. 'He wants to stop Siegel, this is it. This is the way.'

'Still. There's pride at stake; reputation. He let slip to you, though, makes me hopeful.'

'Put me in a room with him again then.'

'You sure you're up to it?' He tapped the side of his head with his knuckle.

After all of it, still a chance at finding Nancy Hill; a surge of adrenaline that took the pain away faster than morphine. 'I'm up to it.'

*

I asked for thirty seconds with Lizzie before we left. I felt bad running out on her that way, but couldn't see anything else for it.

'Did you manage to reach Tanner?' I couldn't take my eyes off the welt on her face.

She shook her head. 'He's not at the motor court. I'll try to get a message to him via the office in Los Angeles.'

I thought about Tanner's instruction to tell Siegel I'd write the smear piece on Lyle Kosoff, blown out of the water. I justified it, telling myself I was the target of his anger now. As if he hadn't enough for two. 'Do that. Tell him he needs to warn Kosoff.'

'Do you think . . .'

'I think all bets are off now.'

'What should I say to him about where you are?'

'Nothing. Tell him to meet us at the motor court.' I squeezed her hand and turned to go.

'When?' She didn't let go and I turned back. There was a desperation in her eyes, the question double-edged.

'Tonight. Tell him to wait for us there. I'll come back here and pick you up as soon as I can.'

'Are we free to go?'

'Yes. I was wrong about Lang, I think he's on our side. But stay here until I get back – you'll be safest that way.'

'Promise me you won't do anything reckless.'

'I can put an end to this, I swear.'

*

Lang sped away from the department in the direction of Fremont Street, briefing me as he drove.

'This has to be done with a gentle hand,' he said. 'You can't tell him about my involvement.'

'Where are we going?'

'The Pioneer Club. He keeps a suite above his office, but he'll most probably wind up in the bar when he's back from the Flamingo. He favours a late dinner.'

I looked at my watch: ninety minutes since we'd left Siegel's joint. 'What's the next move if he's not there?'

'Wait.'

'There isn't time for that. How long you think that girl has?'

'I've made some calls, there are men on the street asking questions, but unless that turns something up . . .'

I rubbed my forehead, eventually nodding. 'He ought to have said something sooner. For a man claims he wants rid of Siegel—'

'He may not have put it together that the dead girl was Siegel's.'

I looked over. 'Until?'

'Until he heard Desjardins was an aspiring actress too. Up to that point, all he knew was she was a dead working girl.'

'You let on to him after I told you.'

He flicked his blinker to make a turn. 'I put a few items out there. I didn't know what might be significant.'

'But you suspected he knew something?'

'Hoped. Harry's public reputation and his private one are not in step, if you understand me. He thinks it's his guilty secret, but it's not as secret as he'd like. He's got a lot of clout, though, so it's not like anyone's ever going to bring it up to his face.' He side-eyed me. 'Not anyone from around here, anyway.'

'Why not just ask for my help?'

He bristled a touch and I realised I'd overreached. 'Don't talk like you're a deputy. We have common cause, nothing more.' He shot me a look, softening the reprimand. 'It's only to-night I'm certain you're not part of Siegel's outfit.'

We passed every shade of bar and hotel and gambling den,

each seeming to get gaudier as we approached downtown. 'What did you mean throwing me in jail?'

He steered around a pickup. 'See who came for you. FBI was a surprise.'

'You thought it'd be one of Siegel's lawyers?'

'It's always the same one, Victor Curzon. I had it fifty-fifty he'd show up for you.' He looked over. 'Some time soon, we gonna talk about why the Federals did come for you. Let's find the girl first.'

We came to a stop at the corner of Fremont and Second, and Lang pointed to the giant vertical sign spelling *Pioneer* down the block. The neon lightshow was a sight to behold at night, raucous colours vivid against the black sky. 'I'll be waiting here.'

I opened the door and got out, then ducked through the doorway to speak to him. 'If I get a lead on the girl, I mean to go get her.'

He had one hand on the wheel. 'I have no doubt about that.'

'Thank you. For getting me out of there tonight.'

He looked down at the buttons on his shirt.

'How much did you see?' I asked.

'Enough. Why's it matter – you worried about a charge?'

'No.'

'Then?'

'Who hit my wife?'

He set his eyes on the windscreen, his chest inflating with a deep breath. 'Rosenberg. He backhanded her when she tried to get in his way.'

I nodded once, then tapped the roof of the car and set off.

*

The Pioneer was in full swing; every table in the casino was seeing action, with a crowd of spectators two or three deep around the centrepiece roulette wheels. There was music coming from somewhere – a crooner in a showroom I couldn't see, a song I didn't recognise. People swirled around me, very few looking twice at the blood and dust on my suit, everyone holding a drink but not holding their drink. A sea of faces happy to lose themselves in a place I'd come to hate.

Heller was at the bar tearing into a T-bone bigger than his plate. He saw me coming towards him and stopped with a fork halfway to his mouth.

He set it down as I drew up. 'Twice in one night. Quite the capacity to surprise.'

I dropped onto the stool next to his. 'How did you know about Siegel and the girls?'

He gestured to the casino floor. 'You own a casino, you hear things. Sometimes unsavoury.'

I was shaking my head. 'A high-class service, that's what you said. I don't buy casino chatter.'

He picked up his fork again and put the chunk of meat in his mouth. He spoke as he chewed. 'Don't think I don't hear the accusation in your voice. You come here looking for someone to blame—'

'I don't need anyone to blame, I know where that sits well enough. I want the rest of it so I can put Siegel down.'

He sputtered, reaching for his drink to clear his throat. 'Hell, I'm no advocate for the man, but last I saw, wasn't Bugsy on the floor.'

'Tell me how I reach them. Girls-to-order. Give me a way in.'

He took another swig, coughed and spoke again. 'Look, you put on a good show tonight, but this is for us to take care of now.'

'Then why did you tell me what you did?'

He shrugged, twirling his fork. 'Your arrogance was wearing.'

I reached into my inside pocket and pulled the photograph of Desjardins and Hill, slapped it on the counter next to his plate. He wasn't sure where to leave his eyes, flitting back and forth between the picture and my face, until recognition dawned.

'They disappeared from Los Angeles together,' I said. 'They were both trying to crack Hollywood. One of them is dead, the other one might just still be alive. I don't care what you did or how you know, but every second you waste is a grain of sand on her grave.'

He put his fork down and squared it next to his knife. 'No one wants young women turning up dead, and that's a fact. But this is a delicate matter that's got to be handled right.'

'I understand that. Think about what she could have to offer. Her testimony could blow Siegel out of the water.'

'A runaway with a story?' He said it out of the side of his mouth.

'A girl from the heartlands. Picture that on the stand.'

He tapped her image. 'A child. Even if she knew something, who's going to take her part over him?'

'You're . . . are you afraid of him?'

He feigned a yawn. 'This isn't kindergarten.'

'It's a woman's life.'

He got off his stool. 'I've told you what I know.'

I stood up, a hand on his chest to stop him. 'I've dragged myself and my wife through hell to try and save that young woman. I've come this far and there is no goddamn way I'm about to stop now. So tell me what I want to know, because if you let her die, I swear to god I'll be back for you.'

I shocked myself with the words. Not what I'd meant to say, anger spilling out of me. He tried a tight smile, brushing it off, but down low he was beckoning someone frantically with his hand.

'Give me a name, a number, anything,' I said, my face in his.

He moved to look over my shoulder, desperation growing, waving openly now.

'No one will know it came from you.'

'Mr Heller?'

A voice behind me. I turned to look. A cowboy in a plaid shirt, hovering.

I turned back. 'No one. On my life . . .'

He pursed his lips, grease in the corner of his mouth. He looked at the photograph again, lingering over it. 'She's a fine-looking woman.' He backed up and stepped around me. 'Wait here.'

He walked off, curling his finger for the cowboy to follow him.

I thought about going after them, but the last working logic wire in my head said to stay put. That if he wanted to have me kicked out or beaten down, he would have done. That walking off wasn't his style.

The music droned in my ears, the sound of laughter and empty chatter. The cowboy reappeared. He zipped across the casino, came to where I stood and handed me a slip of paper. It had a telephone number scrawled on it, nothing more.

'Ask for DiSalvo,' he said. 'Mr Heller sends his regards.'

I nodded and took it. Then I ran for the exit.

CHAPTER TWENTY-ONE

I hit the street and stopped, my brain catching up with my feet.

I stared at the number on the paper. If I gave it to Lang, would he freeze me out? If I was just his front man to let Heller keep his public face intact, my usefulness was shot.

I looked up too late. Lang cruised up to the kerb and called for me to get in. I hesitated a second, grasping for an alternative – make a run for it, dial the number and take my chances. I recognised the selfish thought for what it was. Finding Nancy Hill was what counted; running from Lang would only prolong matters.

He was already out of the car, propping open his door. 'You have something?' Eyes on the slip in my hand.

I bolted across the sidewalk and climbed in.

He did the same and took the scrap of paper from me before I could protest. He glanced at it. 'You tried calling it yet?'

I shook my head. 'No.'

'That's good.' He stared at the number on the paper. 'We can use the line in there.' He was pointing at the S.S. Rex Casino down the block. He pulled a U-turn and swerved across the street to park around the corner, and I had the feeling of being swept away by events.

I followed him into the S.S. Rex. Another gambling den full of flushed faces, chasing the night. A woman shrieked as she hit a slot jackpot, nearing giddy as the coins slammed into the payout tray. A square John patted a cigarette girl on the behind as she passed by, slopping his drink and drawing a squeal from her and a chorus of yuks from his buddies. By the roulette tables, a skinny kid was going spot-to-spot, skimming stacks and pocketing chips while the players were distracted watching the wheels. For all the money Siegel had spent buying into Las Vegas, I wouldn't have given you a nickel for it.

Lang badged one of the deskmen to get use of a telephone. He dialled the operator and read out the number, getting the corresponding address back from her. He didn't write it down. He hung up without another word.

'It's a brothel on the Boulder Highway.' He said it quiet, hesitant, and I knew why.

'Then we go take a look. Now. You're not leaving me behind.'

He shook his head. 'You're turned all around. I know the place, it's legit.'

'All the more reason for them to talk to us.'

'It's not as straightforward as that. There are folk in the ownership have seats at the right tables. I can't waltz in there without due process.'

'Just to talk? Take a look around?'

'I'm the sheriff, I can't dress it up as a social call. Their lawyers would be calling the mayor before I had my hat off.'

'Let them call. We'll be out of there before they can stop us.'

'Easy for you to say when what comes next doesn't fall on your head. Besides which, we don't even know the girl's there.'

I twisted on the spot, hands on my hips, the pain in the back of my skull reigniting. 'It's still the best place to start looking.' I turned back to face him. 'I'll go. What's the address?'

He stared at me a beat too long. 'I think that would be un-wise.'

'I'm a private citizen, that solves your problem.'

He flipped the torn pocket of my suit coat. 'Are you fooling yourself about what he'll do to you?'

'He's tied up at the Flamingo.'

'Goddamn but you're a hard-head. Maybe he is, maybe not. Maybe your little drama spooked him and he made a call. Maybe—'

'If he did, and if the girl's in reach, what do you think happens to her next?'

We stared at each other until he broke it, a cheer from the casino floor drawing his empty gaze, acceptance creeping across his face.

'Still, you should think this through before you go charging,' he said.

'What choice do I have?'

'Every choice under the sun. If I was in your shoes, I don't know I wouldn't be taking that young lady back at my office and getting as far away from Siegel as I could.'

I shifted so I was in his sightline. 'I don't believe you.'

'Come again?'

'You've strayed a mile out of your lane already. The Flamingo, Heller, now this. You want to see her safe as bad as me. Can you give me a ride?'

He shook his head. 'There's nothing around there. You can't roll up in a department car and you can't say you walked in off the street.'

'My car's at the Flamingo.'

He scratched his throat, me counting the seconds. 'I'll drop you at a cab stand. Rings truer that way anyhow. I'll follow and wait a half-mile down the road, you come find me soon as you're out.'

I nodded and offered my hand. 'Thanks.'

He pinched the corners of his mouth between his fingers, watching me, then he shook it. 'Good luck.'

CHAPTER TWENTY-TWO

The cab ride on the Boulder Highway took a half-hour – a straight shot into the desert in the direction of the Dam. It was time I didn't want. Too much of it. I couldn't see Lang behind us, but I had to think he was out there. I sat alone in the darkness of the backseat, thinking, planning, regretting. All the lies I'd told, all the people that suffered, all the guilt I earned. All the truths I'd betrayed, except one – that I'd never give up on finding her.

And the knowledge that it was all for naught if she was gone already.

I clung to the belief that Siegel wouldn't be there, nor any of his men that would recognise my face – and yet as we drew close, it was that fear that rose in me. He might have had me killed at the Flamingo if Lang hadn't shown up; the desolate location of the brothel gave him licence to do anything he liked. I felt stupid going there without a gun. I thought about the calls I could have made before I set out: Tanner, a plea for help. Lizzie, save her from wondering. But to say what? A final admission that finding Nancy Hill mattered more to me than my own life?

The property came into view. It had the shape of an extended barn, looked like a converted roadhouse. Constructed of a dark wood and almost windowless, it was hard to make out its form against the night sky. There were two small squares of light on its huge flank, the only thing to suggest it wasn't derelict. A hand-painted sign in white letters above the door announced it as the Kitten Litter.

The cab driver dropped me out front and asked if I would need a ride back later. I shook my head, earning a conspiratorial grin from him as he got my meaning all wrong. 'You watch yourself, them girls'll eat a man up.' I walked away before he could say anything more.

I pulled the door open and went in holding my breath. From the doorway, I scanned the room: no Siegel, no Rosenberg. A woman greeted me inside the entrance. She wore a cowgirl outfit that showed too much skin and a smile that didn't wash. 'Well, howdy there. Looking for some company?'

The interior didn't feel as cavernous as the structure led me to believe. A wooden partition wall hid more than half the space inside, a small closed door in one corner of it. There was a bar to one side, four women in varying states of undress sitting on stools along it – none of them Nancy Hill. A few tables dotted the floor between them and where I stood – the suggestion that this was just like any other lounge in Las Vegas. Metal lamps hung from the ceiling on long cords, lighting the space like a pool hall. If there were any other customers in the place, I couldn't see them. 'Sure.'

'Come and have a drink with us.' She took my hand and made for the bar. 'Have you joined us here at the Litter before?'

'No. My first time in town.'

'Well, we'll look after you real nice. Have yourself a seat.' She patted a barstool.

The bartender nodded a greeting, but he held his station just along the counter from where she set me, and I had the idea that was the spot he kept a weapon stashed.

The working girls sat in a cluster at one end, talking in low tones among themselves but making a point of flashing smiles my way. The cowgirl caught me looking and winked. 'See anything you like?'

'I was hoping . . . are there any others?' I felt as if ants were swarming up my back.

The women looked away in unison, smiles in place but lower-wattage now. 'Well, you couldn't want for a more beautiful set of girls, but . . . what did you have in mind?'

'Petite, brunette.' The best description of Nancy Hill I could give.

She glanced at the women – two bottle blondes, a natural and a redhead – looking for a new pitch. 'If that's your usual thing, maybe you ought to mix it up a little.'

I had the urge to walk across the room and bust open the doorway in the wall. The bartender was watching me, hands together on the counter now.

'I'm particular.' I made a point of looking to the back. 'You have any more you could bring out?'

Her tongue was in the corner of her mouth. Then she smiled, shook her head. 'Whatever your choice, I can promise you a good time.'

I looked along the liquor bottles behind the bar, labels of every colour – somewhere to put my eyes while I regrouped. 'I'll take a bourbon.' I held up two fingers for a double measure.

The bartender turned away to fix the drink.

I faced the cowgirl. 'I was looking for DiSalvo.'

She looked puzzled. 'I'm sorry, handsome, I don't know who that is.'

The bartender had stopped pouring.

'You're sure?'

'Quite sure.' She swivelled away from me and I couldn't see if she gave the barman a look as he came over with my drink. 'Mr Landell, can you help?'

He set it down in front of me. 'The young ladies here aren't to the gentleman's taste, I think perhaps he ought to try somewhere else.' He held his arm out to the door, not so much the choice he made it out to be.

My heartbeat accelerated. I looked over at the women again. 'It's a long way out here, how about I buy the ladies a drink first?' I feigned giving the redhead another look.

I could feel the bartender's indecision. Out of the corner of my eye I saw the cowgirl looking at him for direction. My intuition: he knew the significance of the name DiSalvo, she didn't.

I circled my finger in the air, signifying another round. 'Whatever they want.'

He stared at me and I had no clue what he was thinking. Then he moved over to the shelves and took a bottle down. He carried it to the counter and set it right above the spot where he'd first been standing. 'Where'd you hear the name DiSalvo, friend?'

His hands dipped out of sight.

I slipped off my seat and inched towards him. I leaned over, as if to offer a confidence. Then I tossed my liquor in his face.

I dived onto the bar top, reaching under the counter. One of the women screamed. He staggered back a step, wiping at his eyes. I scrabbled blind with my hand, feet off the floor. He got his vision back and lunged as my fingers touched metal. I snatched the object up just as he grabbed for it, pushing myself back off the bar. I steadied myself, righting the pistol in my hand, aimed it at him. The cowgirl was on the floor, looking up at me, a dropped glass to her right. No one moved.

'Nancy Hill. Petite, brunette. DiSalvo. Where is she?' Breathing hard.

'Give me back the gun.'

Eyes on him. 'DiSalvo, tell me. It's not too late.'

He glanced over at the partition wall – fleeting but enough.

I started backing away towards it, the women on the stools silent, staring at me bug-eyed. Halfway there I turned and sped up, glancing back to keep the gun trained towards the bar. I called out to him. 'Stay where you are.'

'Worst mistake you ever made.'

I glanced at the small door, twenty feet away, and back. The cowgirl staring at it now. I kept moving. Another glance, her still looking past me. I turned back, a snap—

I dived to the side as the door flew open. Behind it, a man holding a shotgun – the backup they'd been expecting. I fired twice in panic, wild shots aimed at the wall, enough to make the gunman retreat into the darkness beyond the doorway.

I scrambled to my feet and threw myself against the partition. There were shouts and screams, the four women running for the main door. The cowgirl ducked around the bar to cover out of sight with the bartender.

'I only came for the girl,' I shouted, my voice wavering but holding. 'Nancy Hill. Give up the girl and we all walk.'

I could hear movement behind the partition, but I was side-on to the doorway, flattening myself as much as I could, no view of what lay beyond it.

A voice came back from the other side. 'Lay down the piece and we'll make a deal.' It sounded distant. I gave no response.

Wisps of gunsmoke swirled, dissipating into the gloom of the rafters. A rush of thoughts screamed through my head, nothing sticking. I inched closer to the doorway, the gun held out in front of me, thinking frantically. A back way out? If so, maybe another gunman circling around right now, about to pin me in a crossfire. My arm shook holding the pistol, and it spread through my chest and up my throat.

But the fear set off my anger. I hammered the gun butt against the wood. 'I'll shoot every damn one of you to get that girl. Tell me where she is.' I ducked low, hoping he wouldn't have adjusted for it if he took a pot-shot.

No answer came. There were sounds of movement behind the wall, but from far off – footfalls on a staircase, more than one set. My pulse was strong enough that I could feel it in my fingers, pounding against the grip.

Then the wall exploded along from me. The blast knocked me sideways. The retort was dizzying, wood splinters showering me.

I staggered onto my haunches, ears ringing. Smoke leaked out of the hole – a pot-shot, but not how I'd expected. It was right where I'd been standing a minute before. I heard a shotgun being cocked.

Panic descended. No way in, no way out. Empty desert for miles around, even if I did make it outside. No getaway car, Lang a half-mile away.

I waited a second more, the one way to salvage something coming clear. I took off across the floor.

I was halfway there when another shot came. My eyes screwed shut, braced, but I kept running. I opened them again just before I reached the bar, diving behind it.

The cowgirl screamed as I slid into sight on my side, crashing into a shelf of highball glasses. She was taking cover with the barman at the other end of the bar. I got my feet under me and stole a look over the counter but the gunman was out of sight. I stayed low and scuttled along behind the bar.

'Take off,' I said to the cowgirl.

'What?'

'Get clear of here. Go.'

She stared a second, then nodded a half-dozen times. She got up, woozy, and ran along the bar in a crouch. Coming into the open, she threw her hands up and sprinted, screaming.

The barman, Landell, was three feet away. I turned to him. 'Is she here?'

'You're out of your goddamn—'

I pointed the gun. 'Is she here?'

He eyeballed me.

'Make me ask again, I'll put a bullet in you.'

He looked down the gun barrel. He shook his head, rapid.

I held my breath, listening. A burst of footsteps in the main room and then silence. Moving closer with caution, station-to-station.

I poked the gun over the bar and fired once, whipped it back down.

'Where's your car?' I said.

'Forget it.'

'On your feet.'

He hesitated so I snatched a handful of his shirt and put the gun to his temple. 'Up.'

He rose slowly. He called out to the room. 'It's me, don't shoot.'

I waited a second to be sure they wouldn't plug him, and then I stood up behind him and locked my arm around his throat. 'WE'RE COMING OUT. BACK THE HELL OFF.'

I dragged him along the bar and out across the main room, moving slow, clumsy, him saying nothing, me too damn scared to think. All the while searching the room.

Crossing to the main entrance, I spotted the barrel of a shotgun poking out from behind a pillar. Couldn't see anything of the man holding it.

We backed up until we reached the door, and I kicked it open with my heel.

'We'll find you.' The shooter's voice echoed across the room.

We burst out into the darkness. 'Car. Where's the car?'

'Far side.' His voice was a rasp, my arm tight on his neck.

I whirled us around and pushed him a distance in front of me. 'Run.'

He broke into a loping sprint, me trailing behind.

We bombed around to the far side of the property, thinking he could be leading me into a trap just as three parked cars came into view. He arrowed for the middle one, an old Chrysler.

He threw the door open and got in. I dived into the backseat and jammed the pistol into the base of his skull. 'Drive, drive—'

He threw it in reverse and backed out with my door still swinging. He braked hard, momentum slamming it shut, and shifted into first. The wheels spun and then we lurched forward, careening over the jagged ground until we made the blacktop. I looked out the back window, saw a crack of light widen as the doorway came open, and then we were gone.

CHAPTER TWENTY-THREE

I checked the highway behind in the wing mirror, saw no sign of anyone following. I guided him north, to Lang's rendezvous point.

'Nancy Hill, where is she?' I said, still panting.

He didn't answer, eyes glued to the road.

'She was friends with Diana Desjardins. You don't need me to tell you who that is.'

'They'll kill you.'

'If that girl dies tonight, I'll kill all of you.'

His mouth was a thin line in the mirror. 'Where're we going?'

I strained to see in the dark ahead, looking for a glimpse of Lang's car along the highway shoulder. I switched the gun to my other hand to wipe my palm on my trouser leg. 'You panicked hearing DiSalvo. You know what I'm talking about, tell me if Hill was part of it.'

Back to silence. I searched the road ahead, still no sign of Lang. Old doubts about him rearing up again. One of Winfield Callaway's lines coming back to me out of the blue: '*Somebody's using you.*' A taunt from a dead man.

'Slow down.'

I shifted across the seat so I could monitor the rearview. No lights behind. Eyes front again. 'Dammit, Lang . . .'

I was sure we'd gone more than a half-mile. I was reeling,

a voice in my head saying over and over that I needed a new plan—

A red light appeared in the night. On the shoulder, swirling around once, twice, then extinguished again.

'There. Pull over.'

He peeled off the highway and came to a stop twenty yards in front of the other vehicle.

It prowled up behind us, its headlamps on now, lighting us up like floodlights. It came to a halt behind us and no one moved.

I went to get out but stopped myself. It felt wrong. The beams were dazzling, I couldn't make out the driver beyond a silhouette. Why the hell wasn't he getting out?

'You mean to just sit there?' Landell said. Another smart mouth bastard taunting me.

I flexed my right hand, working out the cramp, then wrapped it around the gun again. I cracked my door and called back. 'Lang?'

The sound of the other car's motor filled my ears.

Then, 'Yates?'

I cracked my door wider. 'It's me.'

Lang emerged from the other car. His right hand was hidden behind his open door. 'Who you got in there with you?'

There was an edge to his voice. The situation turning on me. The drumbeat of my heart, wondering now what his intentions were. 'What's in your hand?'

'A gun. Who's in there?'

I glanced around, as if I might find an escape route. 'The bartender from that joint.'

He stepped out from behind his door and started towards

us, a silhouette in the rearview. He stopped when he came level with our trunk, ducking to inspect us.

'You holding a weapon, Yates?'

It was bathed in the headlamp beams, so bright in the dark. 'Yes.'

'Go on and set it down.'

I lowered it to the seat.

'Turn your face, driver.'

Landell complied, sullen. 'Howdy, Sheriff.'

'Hell.' Lang took a step closer and popped my door. 'Get out.'

I still had the gun in my hand and he snatched it from me as I exited, the movement so fast I had no time to react.

'He didn't come with you voluntarily,' he said, pointing.

'No.'

'Talk fast.'

I glanced at the highway, seeing a headlamp beam in the distance moving towards us. 'We need to get out of here. He knows something about Desjardins and Hill—'

'How do you know that?'

The lights kept approaching.

'I mean it, we should go. Someone else was there. Those lights—' I nodded in their direction.

He looked over his shoulder down the highway, the sound of the other car coming in waves across the night.

He went back over to his cruiser and reached inside to switch the red globe on.

The headlamps in the distance slowed and then stopped thirty yards short of where we were. The other car idled a long moment – five seconds, ten. Lang stuffed the pistol he'd relieved me of in his belt to take a two-handed grip on his own.

Then the car turned around, its beams lighting up the desert in an arc as it went, bringing the blackness to life for a fleeting second and leaving a glare on the eye like the trace of a bullet. It accelerated sharply, heading back the way it'd come.

He faced me again. 'Where'd you get the gun?'

'He was about to pull it on me.'

'What for?'

'For asking about DiSalvo. He flipped his lid when I said the name.'

I heard the passenger door open. 'That's a damn lie, Sheriff—' Landell was climbing out of the car.

Lang raised his weapon, stopping him dead. 'You armed?'

'No.'

'Sit your ass back down.'

'This man took me hostage, Sheriff. Stole a gun, threatened me and the girls—'

'I said sit down.'

Landell stayed on his feet and slammed his door shut. 'You know who my boss is. We're all paid up.'

Lang holstered his weapon and marched around the car. He stopped in front of him and reached for his handcuffs. 'Put your hands on the roof.'

'You arresting me, Boss? What charge?'

'That's two instructions you disobeyed. On the roof.'

Landell looked away in disgust. He faced around and put his hands on the roof to be patted down.

But Lang switched his grip on the cuffs, holding them like a set of brass knucks. Then he raised them up and slammed them down onto the back of Landell's hand.

The empty car underneath magnified the sound of the blow,

a hollow thud that was immediately drowned out by Landell's scream.

Shock rooted me to the spot. Lang held the cuffs by his side, watching him writhe. Then he did it again.

I winced. Landell's scream split the desert. I couldn't bear to look.

I tried to go over but my legs wouldn't work. I fought to get any words out. 'Lang, wait—'

'Tell me about the starlets.' Lang's mouth was an inch from his ear.

Landell slumped against the car, his hand covered in blood, torn skin flapping loose. His legs buckled but he managed to stay standing. 'Goddamn, this ain't right. You can't do this to—'

Lang gripped a handful of his hair to hold him up and smashed the handcuffs into the roof, an inch from the mangled hand, the sound like bullets hitting the bodywork. 'Don't you ever talk to me that way, you pissant. Your boss's money is all's keeping you breathing right now. Be grateful for anything more.' He slammed the cuffs into the roof again, two, three, four times, ramping himself up. 'Flap your gums at me like you can't be touched. Piss on you.' He shifted his grip to Landell's wrist and raised the cuffs in the air. I flinched as he brought them down on his hand once more.

Landell's legs gave this time and he collapsed down the car, vomiting as he went. 'Lang, that's enough.' My feet were moving and I rounded the car in a daze, too late to do anything.

Lang held his arm out to back me off, eyes blazing. 'You want to find her or don't you?'

He turned away and crouched next to Landell. 'Starlets. Talk.'

Landell was clutching his hand between his thighs, whimpering. 'Siegel. Mr Siegel. He came down heavy on Joe, made him do it. It's just a telephone number, we don't see a dime.'

'Have you seen the girl this man asked you about?'

He nodded, rolling side to side in the dirt.

'Nancy Hill. Yes?'

More nods.

I dropped to my knees, leaning over him. 'Where is she?'

Praying he wouldn't say *dead*.

'Don't make me say. Please, Boss.'

Lang reached for the injured hand.

He jerked away. 'NO.'

'Answer the question.'

'Ranch. A ranch. It's on the road to Red Rock. They keep girls there.'

'Is she still alive?' I said.

'How would I know? This is nothing to do with me, I swear. We take the calls, we pass it on.'

Lang stabbed a finger in his chest. 'What about the other one, Desjardins? Was she a part of it?'

'Yes.'

'Who killed her?' he said.

'Don't know. I swear it.'

I got to my feet, my hands trembling, unable to stop gawping at Lang. He looked up from Landell and stared back down the highway towards where the chase car had been. My brain broke through the sludge and I cottoned what he was thinking. 'Lang, if his crew go back and sound the alarm . . .'

He nodded in agreement and grabbed a handful of Landell's shirt. 'On your feet.'

*

It was a frantic race back down the highway to the Kitten Litter, Landell cuffed and slumped in the backseat. My nerves were raw at what I'd seen, but all I could keep in my head was how many minutes had passed since the other car had turned back; whether they'd have had enough time to call and warn whoever was holding Nancy Hill at the ranch. She was surely dead if so.

The brakes squealed when we skidded to a stop in the parking lot. Another car was parked there. Lang jumped out and pulled his gun, checking around for signs of life before he moved to the entrance. I slipped over to the other car and placed my hand on the hood.

I signalled to Lang. 'It's warm.'

The place was still.

I ran back over to the entrance, keeping my footfalls light. Lang tried the door but it was locked. He ducked his head back into the car. 'How many men inside?'

Landell looked catatonic, gave no response. Lang shook him hard.

He opened his eyes with a start, pain shooting across his face as his senses awoke again.

'I asked how many.'

'One . . . just one.'

'Name.'

'Bader. Verne Bader.'

Lang went to the door and hammered on it. 'Bader, open the damn door before I kick it in.'

The silence was total and oppressive.

Then a voice came from inside. 'I'm opening the damn door – put your gun down.'

The lock sounded and then it opened a fraction.

'Step out here where I can see you,' Lang said. 'I see a weapon in your hands, I'm not waiting to ask questions.'

The door opened wider. 'I ain't holding. Tell that to the damn maniac by your side.'

The man stepped from the shadows, hesitant. He flashed his hands – empty. As he did, Lang snatched his wrist, jerked him forward and slugged him on the skull with his gun butt.

The man hit the deck. Lang stood over him. 'Did you make a call to warn the others?'

Bader's eyes were rolling in his head. He stammered trying to say, 'No.'

'I go to check with the operator on your line, they about to tell me the same thing?'

He said nothing, clutching his head.

Lang kicked his foot. 'Answer me.'

Bader rolled away. 'Oh shit, oh shit, oh shit . . .'

'You stupid, goddamn . . .' Lang straightened up and shot me a look, his eyes wide. 'Goddammit.'

My stomach dipped. 'How long to get out there?'

'Too long.' He flung the driver's door open and stuck his finger in Landell's face. 'I want directions right now.'

*

We sped west out of town in Lang's cruiser, the Red Rock Cliffs just visible as a dark outline in the distance.

I hadn't spoken a word to him since we left, still trying to

251

come to terms with his sudden outburst of violence. I saw him in a darker light, the distance between him and the men I'd encountered before now much smaller. He may not have been a killer like Horace Bailey of Texarkana, but the abuse of power was out of the same playbook – regardless of whether lowlifes like Landell and Bader deserved what they got. What troubled me most was that I was riding with him regardless, the beneficiary of his vicious streak – willing to grant tacit approval to those methods when it was to my advantage.

Among it all I was bargaining with a god I'd never given credence to, cutting deals to spare Nancy Hill's life. I couldn't face the thought of finding her corpse waiting for us, and I tried to quiet my conscience that way by telling myself the end justified Lang's means. It didn't detract an ounce from my hypocrisy.

He broke the silence. 'When we get to the ranch, I want you to stay in the car. You hear?'

I was mindful there'd been no time to call for backup. 'You don't know what's waiting out there.'

'Exactly why it needs to go down my way.'

'They'll be expecting you.'

'I know that.' He glanced at Landell in the rearview. He'd sworn under threat of another beating that he didn't know how many men were based there. 'They're not about to start a shooting war.'

'You can't know that. If it's them killed Desjardins, there's no telling what they'll do if they're cornered.'

'You meaning to talk me out of this?'

'No. I want you to give me that gun back.' I nodded to the stolen pistol in his waistband. I kept my face even, trying not to let my fear show.

He looked over at me and away again, saying nothing.

We turned off the state road onto an unpaved track, the cruiser's headlamps piercing a darkness that was otherwise complete. The route took us up a slight incline. The rutted ground slowed our pace, desperation making me think to get out and run.

It felt like we covered miles. Then we crested the ridge and I saw lights less than a quarter-mile distant. Lang tapped the brakes but kept us moving. It was a ranch house, all the windows lit. There were two cars parked at an angle outside, their headlamps crossing, lighting up the front of the building. Exhaust gas drifted across the beams like smoke on a battlefield.

It was a hive of movement. Two shapes fleeted past an upstairs window in silhouette. A man ran from one side of the property to the other, carrying a box. Another came out of the front door, dragging a second by the arm. They passed through the beams, and I saw the second form was a woman.

'They're clearing out,' I said.

'We'll wait and take them in the cars.' He killed the lights and hit the brakes.

'What? No, you have to keep— They could be dead by then.'

'We go now, they'll scatter.'

I smacked the dash. 'They'll be alive. Go.'

'For how long? They run and there's no way we find them.'

My legs were twitching – adrenaline and fear. 'Give me the gun.' I held my hand out, beckoning him.

'What?'

I cracked my door. 'Give me the gun, dammit.'

A faint cry from ahead drew our eyes. The man leading the

woman by the arm had opened the trunk of his car and was wrestling her inside.

Lang shot his hand out, absently, as if it could stop what he was seeing. 'Hell . . .'

The woman caught the man in the face, a scratch or slap, enough to stagger him and make him back up a pace. He got his feet under him again, then reared back and belted her in the head. The blow sent her sprawling against the open trunk and he bundled her the rest of the way inside and slammed the lid. He reached to favour his face. As he tried to catch his breath, his eyes strayed to the horizon.

The hand on his face went still. He was looking right in our direction. He gazed a minute, motionless, not sure what he was seeing. Everything froze. I could hear Landell breathing in the back.

Then the man broke for the house, hollering to alert the others.

'GO, GO—'

Lang stamped on the accelerator. He hit the lights and sirens, the noise screaming through the desert. Rocks and cacti flickered in a red wash.

'You see your girl?' He was shouting above the roar.

'No.' My face pressed almost to the windscreen.

He ripped the stolen gun from his waistband and passed it to me without looking. 'I just deputised you. Don't use it unless you have to. Bring back anyone tries to make off with a woman.'

I gripped it tight to my thigh, straining to make out faces as we closed.

A hundred yards out, the scene descended into chaos.

The front door flew open and a half-dozen bodies spilled out

– men and women. They criss-crossed and stumbled, the women running in all directions. The two men made for the cars.

Then a gunshot rang out, the muzzle flash dead ahead. I ducked on reflex, heard a second. I stole a look over the dashboard, no clue how close the bullets came.

We hit the hardscrabble turnaround at the end of the track and Lang slammed the brakes, swerving to leave us side on and partially blocking the way out. His window faced the ranch; he stuck his gun out and fired twice at the porch then threw his door open.

I kicked mine open and jumped out. There were shouts and screams in every direction. I glanced all about, trying to track the runners. I heard an engine turn over and the car with the woman in the trunk started backing up. Lang ran towards it with his gun up, firing.

There was a shout right behind me. I looked around, saw Landell prone on the backseat, hysterical. I darted back there in a crouch and yanked his door. I heard more gunfire.

He snapped his head up. 'Get me out, get me out—'

I grabbed his shirt and dragged him off the seat into the footwell. 'Stay low.' I slammed the door and hunkered down for cover, looking around again to follow the women's paths. The car in motion was freewheeling backwards slowly, its driver collapsed against the steering column, the side window blown away. I couldn't see Lang. The car rolled into a boulder and stopped.

Two of the women had taken off behind the house and were out of sight. Another was breaking for the desert to the left of the ranch, almost at the furthest reach of the light field it gave off. She had on a black dress and her hair was pinned – so out of place it would have been absurd another time. I looked around, couldn't see the fourth.

I broke cover and ran in a crouch after the one I could see. Another burst of gunfire came from the porch and was returned. In my peripheral vision I saw Lang circling around towards the Pontiac still parked out front, snapping a shot off.

I ran full pelt. The woman had a fifty yard start on me. I called out to her but my voice was lost in the commotion. But she was moving slowly and I realised she'd kicked her heels off and was barefoot. It took me no time to close her down. Coming near, I called out again; she glanced around, flashing me the snapshot of a terrified face, and darted right.

I caught her up and reached for her arm. She screamed and whirled around to slap at me. I wrapped her arms up and eased her slowly to the ground. She looked nothing like Nancy Hill.

'You're safe. I'm with the sheriff, I'm here to help.'

Her eyes were two harsh spotlights and she was shaking her head like crazy.

'Ma'am, listen to me.' I let her go. 'I'm with the sheriff, we came to help.'

She stared at me in shock. There was a small rocky outcrop to our left. I pointed to it. 'I want you to hide behind there until it's safe. I'll come get you, I swear.' I got to my knees. 'Do you know Nancy Hill?'

Her head went still but she said nothing. I realised she was staring at the gun in my hand. I swiped it away behind my back. 'Ma'am? Nancy Hill?'

She said nothing, still staring. I planted my hand on the floor and pushed myself to my feet. I glanced back to the ranch. Lang was on one knee taking cover behind the Pontiac, pinned down by the gunman on the porch he was preventing from getting to it.

I pointed to the rocks again. 'Ma'am, please, listen to me, I have to go. Wait there, I'll be back for you.' Then I took off towards the ranch.

I was coming at it from the side. As I ran, a column of light erupted from the rear of the building, illuminating another car stashed there. Two figures emerged from the house, one manhandling the other. He was heavyset, suited. Familiar—

Moe Rosenberg.

I raised my gun but didn't fire, the second shape a woman. The light slid away again with a clap – a sprung door snapping shut. Rosenberg opened the car and tossed the woman inside.

I angled towards them, the welt on Lizzie's cheek burning in my mind.

Out front, a man came haring off the far side of the porch, sprinting across the turnaround towards Lang's cruiser. He turned his face in my direction, spraying shots at Lang as he ran. I got a glimpse and saw it was Vincent Gilardino.

Lang took aim and fired. Gilardino spun and crashed to the ground. Lang didn't see the other gunman had shifted position to get an angle on him.

'LANG—'

I was too far away. The man fired and Lang slumped forward.

I whipped my gun up and fired twice. The gunman glanced at me over his shoulder and ducked around the Pontiac, firing behind himself without looking.

The lights on Rosenberg's car came on. I was twenty yards distant. He gunned the engine and took off, wheeling around the side of the house.

Lang was prostrate, motionless.

Rosenberg's car trundled across the ground towards the front of the ranch, passing between my position and where Lang was lying. I started running again, chasing it, checking for the gunman by the Pontiac as I went. I couldn't see him.

I closed the gap until Rosenberg made it to the turnaround, the flattened ground allowing him to speed up. He steered for the road out. I got my gun up and fired at his back wheels, squeezing the trigger again and again.

The back half of Lang's cruiser was blocking the narrow track. Rosenberg had no option; he tried to swerve around it but lost control because of the banking and veered off the roadway. His car careened into the scrub, bouncing over the rocks and dirt until it crashed into a dip. The impact left the car upended, the rear wheels hanging in the air, still turning.

I kept running towards him, glancing back to check for the other gunman but seeing no sign. I slowed to a jog as I came close, cutting around to the driver's side on rubber legs. The motor was still running.

I walked slowly in a diagonal, gun trained on the car. In a year, from never having fired one out of uniform to this. There was a creak and a scratching sound from inside. I stopped, waited. I heard a door open on the other side and darted around the back end to see.

The woman was scrambling out of the car feet first. I stopped on the edge of the dip and the rest of her came into view as she lowered herself gently to the ground. She looked up, saw me and froze. It was dark and she had blood on her face but I recognised her anyway.

'Miss Hill—' I scrambled down the bank of the hollow, losing my footing and slipping. 'Nancy—'

She was sliding along the side of the car, moving away, but she stopped when she heard her name.

'Nancy . . .' I walked up to her slowly and just looked. The right side of her face was marked with blood, a wound I couldn't see.

She was trembling. 'Please— Please . . .'

I held my hands up to show I meant no harm, a lightness filling my chest. 'I'm not here to hurt you, I swear it.'

She pressed herself back against the car.

'I'm from Los Angeles, I've been looking for you. I've come to take you home.'

She lifted one arm to keep me back. Inside the wreck, Moe Rosenberg was draped over the steering wheel, pitched there by the impact, his forehead against the shattered windscreen. He was stirring and he let out a rough moan.

I could see the noise spooked her. She turned to look and then barged into me trying to get away from the car. I held her just long enough to check no one was on the bank above and then let her get clear. She stopped and turned around after a few paces, uncertain. There was a sound in the distance, back towards the ranch, another car crunching over the dirt. She heard it too and froze.

'Wait there,' I said.

I clawed my way up the side and looked over the top. I got there in time to see the Pontiac smash into the back of Lang's cruiser, shunting it out of the way before carrying on up the track, the remaining gunman making his getaway. I watched to make sure he didn't stop or double back, but he had the only things he wanted – an escape route and a chance to distance himself from the night's wreckage.

I slid down again, hit bottom and held my palms out again to show I wasn't coming any closer. 'Nancy, how many men were in the ranch?'

Her gaze shifted from me to the upturned car and back again. 'Four. I only saw four.'

Three cars for four men. Could be, could be there were more, still haunting the shadows.

I offered my hand to help her up the slope.

She tensed but made no movement towards or away from me. 'Who are you?'

'My name's Charlie Yates, I'm a reporter. I know how strange this must be, but I've spoken to your mother, she's desperate to see you. Please, I came here with the sheriff.'

She fixed me with a look. 'You can't make me go home.'

I didn't know what to say to that. A movement inside the ruined car drew my attention and I ducked low to see. Rosenberg had righted himself and was trying to pick his way over to the open passenger door, his hand and one knee planted on the dashboard. Nancy Hill skittered back when she saw he was in motion.

I set myself in the doorway and aimed at his head. He flicked his eyes up to look at me, his necktie dangling.

'Gilardino's shot. So's the wheelman. Your last gun just took off. Only you left now.'

Blood was dripping from a gash on his forehead. 'You certain of that?'

But the face he showed wasn't riding the same rails as his words; defiance out of habit. I had the feeling Nancy Hill's numbers were right. 'Who killed Diana Desjardins?'

He moved his lips, but Nancy spoke first from behind me. 'What did you say?'

'Diana Desjardins. Julie. Who killed her?'

'He did.' She pointed, her voice hollow. 'He did. He . . .'

I looked back at him. 'Why?'

He jerked his hand forward to shift his weight, still coming. 'Let me out of here.'

I shook my head. 'You son of a bitch.'

He closed his eyes and when he opened them again, he moistened his lips, gingerly. 'I can give you Ben. Let me out.'

I stared at him a second, a spasm in my chest as anger and adrenaline went to work on me. 'Make peace with yourself before I get back.' I stepped away and closed the misshapen door as far as it would go.

'Come on.' I started up the bank and waved for Nancy Hill to come too.

'Where're you going? You can't leave him—'

'He'll keep, I need to go to the sheriff.'

I pulled myself up the slope, pausing a split second at the top to check the scene. The ranch dominated its scrap of desert, its lights glaring out into the night like an abandoned ship on the ocean. Gilardino lay where he'd fallen. So did Lang.

Nancy was following. I reached down to help her over the lip of the bank and then set off towards Lang at a run, pulling her along with me, not wanting to expose her to any more horror but not wanting to let her out of my sight either.

When we were ten yards short of Lang, I stopped and told her to hold back. She was staring at him, no expression on her face. I stripped off my battered suit jacket and draped it around her shoulders. 'Stay low, keep your eyes open, holler if you see anything at all.'

I left her there and covered the rest of the ground to Lang. He was face down, the collar of his shirt soaked with blood on one side. I put a hand to his neck and felt a weak pulse. 'Lang? Lang, can you hear me?'

He was unconscious. I called back to Nancy Hill. 'Where's the telephone?'

She shook her head, shivering violently now as cold and shock took hold.

'Nancy?'

But before she could reply I picked up on another sound. A quiet rumbling; distant but getting louder. It seemed to come not from one point but from the whole length of the horizon. I looked towards the crest of the incline we'd come over, saw the shadow of a dust cloud obscuring the stars as it drifted into the sky. A car barrelling towards us.

Scratch that – looking hard, I could make out two. The gunman coming back. With reinforcements. *Should've run when you had the chance—*

I looked over to Lang's cruiser, sitting on the side of the track at a drunken angle. It offered no obstacle to the incoming cars now. I weighed if I could get to it in time. A snap take – no way of knowing what damage it might have sustained. A bum axle would leave me stranded out there.

I whirled around in desperation, saw the car with the woman trapped in its trunk, nestled snug against the boulder it'd rolled into. I turned again, remembering the fleeing woman I'd told to hide. I could make out the rocky outcrop but not what lay beyond it, no sign of her from my vantage point. My mind was crumbling.

I stuffed the pistol into the back of my pants and grabbed Lang under the armpits. I started dragging him towards the cruiser, panic making me doubt my own judgement from just seconds before, but the cars were coming too fast so I switched direction and made for the main door of the ranch. Nancy Hill looked on, unblinking, unmoving.

I lost my grip and tumbled backwards, landing on my rear end. I hauled myself up, cursing under my breath, in my head railing at the bullshit injustice of it.

I started again, but after a few paces I lost my hold on him once more, my hands stinging in the cold. I cursed, loud this time, the light from the house so bright it hurt, Nancy Hill rushing over now, grasping his right arm and trying to help, then pulling at my shirt when she couldn't shift him and telling me we had to get inside. Clawing at me, begging me to move. Me glancing at the outcrop, the hurtling cars, the locked trunk, indecision killing me.

Rosenberg. A one-word thought crashing through all the others.

I looked down, saw Lang's gun in the dirt, a short way from the start of the drag marks his boots had made. I scooped it up and pressed it into Nancy's hand. 'Go inside, call for help. Tell them the sheriff's down, they'll come quicker. Whatever happens, stay hidden until they arrive. Tell them about the other girls when they do.'

'What about—'

'Go. Just go.'

I took off towards Rosenberg, old pains in my legs rising up in protest. I made it to the ditch and hurled myself down the side as the lead car sped onto the turnaround. Rosenberg had worked his way out of the wreck. He was a short distance from it, crawling like a bug that needed putting out of its misery.

I put the gun to his skull. 'Get up.'

He stopped still but said nothing.

'The only way you leave here tonight is if I do,' I said.

'Same for you.'

I heard the second car tear past us and pull up outside the ranch.

'UP.'

'Get me out and I'll give you Ben.'

'You played that card already.'

'He's your enemy, not me. Use your brain.' His voice was laboured, whittled thin. Trying the same line as Gilardino after he'd shot Trent Bayless – *Just a pawn.*

I locked my arm around his throat and forced him upright to his knees.

He struggled, clawing at my face. 'There's things you don't know—'

I arched my back to apply more pressure, silencing him, wanting him to feel an ounce of the suffering he'd inflicted. He gurgled, popping spit. I held a moment longer.

Then I let go. 'Stand up.'

He stayed on his knees, coughing. When he caught his breath, he buried his face in his shoulder, wiping his mouth on his suit coat. Then he looked around at me. 'I'm gonna cut your old lady apart an inch at a time.'

I almost kicked him in the head. The sound of voices from in front of the house made me remain still, the occupants of one car shouting to the next. I couldn't make out what they were saying. I slipped the magazine out of the pistol, a Colt semi-auto, saw there was one bullet left. I pushed it back into place. An urge to put it in Rosenberg, to have that certainty to take with me wherever I wound up next.

Knowing I never could. A line I'd drawn back in Hot Springs.

I crawled up the bank and poised on all fours to peer over. Two cars, four men I could see.

Something off: neither of them the Pontiac. Two of the men were talking, then the taller one broke off and shouted something towards the house, the wrong direction, words lost in the night. But then he turned and shouted again. 'YATES?'

I put my arm on the lip to haul myself over it, seeing the man's face now.

'YATES?'

My blood racing, spreading relief and apprehension around my body in equal measure. My finger on the trigger. The words coming even as I was still weighing speaking them. 'Here. I'm over here.'

Colt Tanner spotted me and came over at a jog.

I held the gun by my side and just waited.

He waved to the others and yelled for them to follow him. I recognised Bryce and Hendricks, a third agent I didn't know.

Tanner made it first. He clasped my shoulder. 'Are you hurt?'

I shook my head and waved for the others to go back. 'By the house, the sheriff is shot but alive. Help him.'

Tanner motioned over his shoulder for the others to double back as I'd said. There was urgency in his orders.

I gestured with the gun. 'Rosenberg's down there. He's says he'll give up Siegel.'

Tanner's eyes narrowed. He slipped past me and stopped at the bank, resting his hand on the fender of the upturned car. He shook his head and came back, pointing to the gun in my hand. 'You have that in his face at the time?'

'No reason you couldn't do the same. Who would know?'

He ran his hand over his mouth. 'You're some piece of work.'

I rubbed the back of my neck. 'How did you find me?'

He glanced past me, to where the agents were kneeling to attend to Lang now. 'You leave a trail like a buffalo herd.'

*

The scene was little less chaotic for the end of the shooting. Hendricks and the unknown agent worked on Lang, so I gave Bryce everything I could on the man who'd pulled the trigger – five-nine, dark hair, dark suit cut long, slim build, driving a dark green Pontiac. I hadn't got the plate. We both knew it didn't matter; chances were the man was halfway to the state line by now, home free if he could make it to Los Angeles. The Sheriff's Department would drag the county regardless, so better to get the details down now.

Tanner went straight for Rosenberg, slipping into the ditch and out of sight. Something was turning behind his eyes from the minute he'd shown up, but I didn't care – I wanted to find the women who'd spilled from the house. I told Bryce about the one hiding behind the outcrop and pleaded with him to go look for her. He agreed and set off, and I ran inside to find Nancy Hill.

She didn't respond to my calls from the entryway of the ranch. In the end I went room to room, locating her in a closet in one of the bedrooms upstairs. There were four single beds crammed inside the room, one at an angle across two others, forming a rough triangle to allow the door to be opened, the last against the wall beside me. There were no personal possessions on display. The closet door had a latch for a padlock on the outside, but the lock was missing. Opening it, I found it filled with cocktail dresses and ball gowns, like a child's dress-up box. Nancy was sitting on the floor, sequinned trains and sparkly hems parted around her shoulders. She looked up but didn't say anything, turning her eyes back to Lang's gun in her lap.

It took me several minutes to coax her out, eventually doing so by pleading for her help to bring the other women back. She refused to give up the gun and I didn't press it.

We went outside and to the coupe first. Its trunk had been bent out of shape in hitting the boulder, and it needed a crowbar from Tanner's trunk to get the job done. The screech of metal on metal prompted a new round of screams from the woman locked inside, even Nancy's reassurances not enough to calm her. When I bust the lid open, Nancy helped the woman as she scrambled out; she was hyperventilating, overcome with relief at taking fresh air into her lungs again.

I stepped back, giving the two women some space. As I did, on the far side of the property I saw Bryce walking back from the direction of the outcrop, carrying the woman I'd chased down. She was draped across his arms as though lifeless. I ran to them.

'She's alive.'

I already had my finger on her neck, found a pulse. Her skin was freezing cold. 'Get her in the car.'

*

Clark County Sheriff's arrived in force. Three cruisers came racing down the track, sirens and spotter beams blazing up top, an ambulance car trailing a distance behind. I was searching the land behind the house for the two women I'd seen take off in that direction. Nancy Hill was with me and had supplied names – Ramona and Bea. I'd called for them until I was hoarse, but heard only the echo of my own voice. Rooting about in the dark, finding no sign to keep hope alive, it felt as if the desert beyond was boundless.

I came back around the house just as the first of the sheriff's cars skidded to a stop out front. The men piled out looking angry and scared, one with his gun drawn. An argument kicked up right away, Lang lain across the backseat of Hendricks' car, ready to roll, the lead deputy demanding he be transferred to the ambulance. I looked around for Tanner, expecting him to intercede, but he was gone, his car too.

It raged for thirty seconds. Hendricks emphasised what he'd learned the hard way in the Pacific – moving shot men did them no favours. But the sheriff's boys were itching to take their anger out on someone and, at seeing a second gun being eased from its holster, Hendricks wised up and let them have the day.

I waited until Lang was inside the ambulance and then tried to buttonhole two of the deputies to join the search behind the ranch. The shorter of the two instead slapped a pair of cuffs on me.

*

They kept me alone in the back of one of the cruisers. I saw them arrest Nancy Hill and stash her in one of the other cars, along with the woman from the trunk and the one who'd hidden out behind the outcrop, now revived and talking. I kicked and yelled for the deputies' attention, and when one finally came over, I begged him to look for the two women I'd seen tear off into the desert. Ditto the third I'd seen come from the house and lost sight of right away. He said he'd do what he could and to shut the hell up.

I managed to get Bryce's attention and he made a protestation on my behalf, but the sheriff's boys were angry as hell and determined that everyone there was to be taken back to the department and put through the grinder. The different ways this could unfold started to pan out before me; if the sheriff didn't pull through, the rule book went out of the window.

*

It was past first light when they finally took me back to town. A crew from the county coroner's office had taken over the scene, accompanied by fresh men from the sheriff's day shift. It was one of them had found the barman, Landell, in the footwell of Lang's cruiser, beaten up but alive.

Bryce and the other agents had left sometime during the night. I'd seen them haul out, the sheriff's men watching them go with hands on hips and hard looks. Bryce had shot me a glance that seemed almost apologetic as they went.

As the cruiser carrying me climbed the incline on the way out, I looked back at the ranch and the desert beyond. I couldn't see anyone searching. The rising sun laid bare the vast desolation of the landscape.

CHAPTER TWENTY-FOUR

No one was waiting for us when we arrived back at the Sheriff's Department. It was a surprise and it wasn't; I'd half-expected to find Colt Tanner there, wanting every detail, and reprimanding me for going off without involving him.

There was no sign of Lizzie either. I figured she must have gone back to the motor court to keep the meet with Tanner when I hadn't come back. I had no desire for her to see me in cuffs, but I badly wanted her to see Nancy Hill in the flesh, so she'd know that all her sacrifices had been worth it.

They took Nancy out first, leading her across the parking lot as I looked on. She was still wearing my suit coat. It dwarfed her, making her appear smaller, younger, nothing at all like the woman I'd found hours before. They hadn't bothered with cuffs, but her shoulders were tensed and rigid, and her eyes were wide, as though she'd never risk shutting them again.

I realised then I was thinking of her as a trophy, something to be held up as a sign of validation – not as a young woman who'd passed a night seeing things no one should have to witness. And god knew what in the weeks before. Not that any of it felt like a triumph; with Lang in the emergency room and three women still missing in the desert, the word that kept coming back to me was *botched*.

*

Emotions were running high inside the department – you could sense it, just walking the hallways. I was marched to an empty room, pushed onto a wooden chair and peppered with questions by a new deputy. I lost track of how long for, the same ones coming around again. He shifted between threats and conciliation, the strain showing as he smoked butt-to-tip throughout the interrogation.

I gave him the same lowdown on the gunman I'd given to Bryce. I told him I'd been deputised. I skirted the specifics of what had led to us being at the ranch, saying only that I'd been helping Lang with his investigation.

After my third description of the shooter revealed no further details, he ran out of steam. The questions came at a slower clip until they petered out all together. There were gaps as wide as a canyon in my story, but he skimmed over anything didn't pertain directly to the trigger man and his movements – identifying and locating him their only focus for now. Satisfied he couldn't glean anything further from me on that score, he kicked me back to a holding area next to the booking desk.

From there I was ignored. It felt as though they didn't know what to do with me now, all their attention elsewhere. I saw Nancy Hill and one of the other women being taken from one room to another and I resisted the urge to call out to her. After an hour, I asked a passing officer when I could go and was told only to sit down.

As I retook my seat, a commotion flared at the booking desk. A man was jamming his finger into the tabletop, demanding to be taken to his client. His suit was too well cut to be local – LA or New York, maybe – and his act smacked of courtroom theatrics. The duty officer was working hard at keeping a lid on his temper, and it confirmed my thought the attorney had to be a heavy hitter to garner that measure of leeway in a tinderbox situation. I heard the sergeant direct the man to calm down, calling him Mr Curzon as he did. The name rang a bell – the lawyer Lang had told me always showed up to spring Siegel's men. The sergeant was insistent: 'We don't have him, Vic. I'm telling you we don't have him.'

Curzon threatened to inspect the cells himself, but was already heading for the parking lot. He hadn't put a name to his client, but it had to be Rosenberg he was there for, and a picture started to emerge. The last I'd seen Rosenberg he was sitting in Tanner's car; Tanner slipped away before the sheriff's men turned up; now even Rosenberg's own attorney didn't know where he was at. Putting it together, it seemed plain Tanner had decided Rosenberg was too big a prize to give up to the locals.

I turned that over some more. Tanner had been insistent about keeping his operation a secret from Siegel and his men. Taking Rosenberg brought an end to all of that – meaning he had to feel he was close to his end game. His plan was always to break Siegel's outfit open from the inside – and there was no one better placed to do so than Rosenberg. Keeping him out of the hands of a Sheriff's Department bent on exacting revenge might be leverage enough. The logic felt solid, even if it represented a change of tack for Tanner. It made me sick to think Rosenberg would be the man to catch a break when the hammer came down.

I watched the room. Some of the night shift from the ranch were hanging around, dusty and dead on their feet but waiting for word from the hospital. Scuttlebutt held that the rest were out with the day shift hunting for the green Pontiac carrying the shooter – that part of my story being accepted as fact, it seemed. Figure they were trying to corroborate it with the others they'd swept up. I thought back over how it'd all gone down, Nancy Hill still behind the house when Lang got shot. I'd heard nothing in the chatter to suggest Lang was awake, so either they believed my story, or someone else was talking.

I asked to use a telephone to call my wife. The expected denial never came, reinforcing my sense that the prevailing state among the men was exhausted confusion. I was taken to a desk and a clerk stood over me as I dialled. I made a show of fumbling the receiver and asked him to remove the cuffs. He went off through the crowd and then returned with a key, looking over his shoulder as he came back, distracted by something in the adjoining room.

The operator connected me to the motor court but there was no answer from our room. I had the call re-routed to the office, asking the man that picked up if he'd seen Lizzie, but he told me he'd just come on shift for the day and had no idea if she'd been back there. The clerk waiting with me was fully diverted now, so I pretended to carry on the conversation while I cut the call and dialled Colt Tanner's office in Los Angeles – but the line just rang out. I couldn't stop remembering Rosenberg's threat about Lizzie, and the only thing that gave me hope was that if I couldn't find her, neither could anyone he might send after her.

I was still holding the receiver when the first cheer went up. It started in the adjoining room, the one the clerk was looking towards, and quickly spread into the holding area where I stood. The place was filled with the sounds of clapping and whooping, and it had to be that good news had come in from the hospital. Two bottles of bonded appeared from nowhere and were passed around the sheriff's men, riding on a wave of back-slaps and handshakes.

A deputy came through from the inner office and met with a hail of questions. He flipped a box to stand on it and started recounting the details of the call – Lang was awake and talking, the doctors saying he was out of the woods.

Every head in the room was turned towards him. The clerk watching me pressed into the back of the crowd, trying to hear better. No one was paying me any mind. There was a corridor a short way along from me. I hugged the wall and inched towards it. The deputy reeled off his victory line – 'Sheriff's wife says the docs want him to stay there as long as he can 'cause you're all so damn ugly the sight of you could kill him!' When the laughter kicked up, I slipped around the corner and into the hallway.

I jogged along it, trying to get my bearings. I passed an empty muster room and two closed doorways, then the corridor turned ninety degrees and passed a staircase that I recognised as the one I'd been led up from the cell block. I carried on, almost running now. I went through a set of double doors and then there were rooms on either side of me, the doors shut. I went from one to the next, pinballing along the corridor and peeping through the small windows, seeing one office after another.

Then – jackpot: Nancy Hill sitting alone on a gurney. I opened the door and curled my arm. 'Let's go.'

She startled, trying to look past me as if it were a trick.

'We've got ten seconds to get out of here. Come on.'

'Go where?'

I opened the door wider. 'Home. Anywhere you say. It's now or never.'

She slipped off the bed and stopped.

'Please.' I glanced behind me, checking the corridor. 'Please.'

She started then – across the room in two steps, then out into the corridor. I closed the door behind us, overtook her and grabbed her wrist. We ran a few paces back past the staircase, made a right and burst out the back exit.

*

I flagged a cab a block from the department and gave him directions to the motor court. I sat in the back, along from Nancy Hill, both of us breathing hard.

'I don't understand what's happening,' she said, looking at me and then out the back window.

'I had to get you out. It's my fault you were there in the first place.'

'You said . . . you told me you were with the sheriff.'

'I was – but he's the only one can vouch for me. I don't have time to wait for him to recuperate and tell it.'

She looked at me again, her mouth ajar but saying nothing, as if too many questions were coming to her at once. Finally, she said, 'My mother, you spoke to her.'

I nodded. 'She's worried sick.'

'What did she say?' She feathered the skin along her collarbone. 'What did you tell her?'

'I didn't know anything to tell her, except that I was looking for you.'

She studied me a long moment. 'Why were you looking for me? Have we met?'

I looked away sharply, shaking my head. 'It's a long story.'

She watched me, waiting to see if I'd offer any more. We turned into the motor court and the cab pulled around to a stop. I fished a bill out of my pocket and held it out for the driver. Nancy said, 'When can I see Ben?'

*

The man from the motor court's office watched us through his window as I opened the door of our room. It was unlocked but Lizzie wasn't inside. Our bags were on one of the beds and I tried to remember if that was how we'd left them the day before. Looking for a clue to Lizzie's whereabouts where there was none.

There was no couch in the room so I dragged over one of the wooden chairs and held it for Nancy to sit. She flattened the back of her skirt with two hands as she did so. 'You didn't answer my question.'

'Which one?'

'About Ben.'

I was scouting around the room, checking if Lizzie had left a note for me. I stopped and looked at her. 'Meaning Ben Siegel?'

'Yes.'

I straightened slowly, the fondness in the way she spoke his name like a cockroach in my ear. 'What do you want him for?'

'He'll be concerned.'

I could feel despair creeping over me at her words. I perched on the edge of the bed and a standing mirror opposite confronted me with my own reflection. The cuts Rosenberg left on my face were matted with dust and sand, almost black; my cheekbone was bruised and swollen; my white shirt was now a shade of grey, torn in several places.

I looked away, trawling my mind to think where to start looking for Lizzie. That I couldn't think of a single safe place she might run to served as an indictment of the life I'd made for us.

I was thinking what the hell to say to Nancy next when I heard a car pulling up outside. She heard it too and snapped her head around to look. I snuck across the room with my finger to my lips and stood behind the drape. I expected to see a sheriff's cruiser. Instead, I saw Colt Tanner.

I whipped around. 'Go hide in the bathroom. Keep the door shut.'

She was already on her feet. 'Who is it?'

'I'll explain after. Go.'

'Is it the police?'

'Yes. Go.' I squared it as a white lie.

She crossed the room on her toes and shut herself inside without making a sound.

Tanner knocked on the door. I took a breath and opened up. 'Is Lizzie with you?'

He frowned, shaking his head and stepping around me to come inside. 'They let you out fast.'

I saw the man in the office peering over at us and got wise. 'You have the manager keeping watch for me?'

He frowned, as if I were fussing. 'I didn't know when you'd get out.'

I stared, unblinking, wondering if the man had mentioned

Nancy Hill being with me. It felt like I'd been silent a beat too long; I blurted the first thing came to mind. 'My wife's missing, do you know where she is?'

He arched his eyebrows. 'No.'

'She hasn't tried to contact you?'

'Not today.'

'The Los Angeles number? Is anyone manning the—'

'Charlie, I haven't heard from her. I'd tell you.'

I slammed the door closed. 'Rosenberg threatened to kill her. At the ranch, if I didn't let him go.'

He nodded, his face grave. 'He was cornered, I wouldn't pay it undue heed.'

'Clark County Sheriff's don't have him.'

He kept his face empty.

We eyed each other like card players, except we both knew I didn't have a hand.

Finally, I said, 'Did you let him make any calls?'

He remained impassive. 'I don't know what you're talking about.'

'Goddammit, Colt, quit with the bullshit. I don't care what you did with him, just tell me you didn't let him make any calls.'

He looked at me dead on. 'I'm not about to admit to knowing anything about Mr Rosenberg's whereabouts.'

'I brought you this far and you're hanging me out to dry now?'

He stuck his thumb in his chest. 'Me? You've played me for a fool every step of the way.'

My face flushed. 'If you came here to dress me down—'

'Dress you down? I could arrest you. How about obstruction of a Federal investigation? Hell, I don't even need to bother with that – I can just take you back to the sheriff's office and let them take turns bouncing your head off the floor.'

I was stunned, my comeback lodged in my throat.

'How'd you do it?' he said. 'Just waltz right out the door?'

I flattened the hair on the back of my head. 'Lang pulled through, he'll smooth it over.'

'Still, a hell of a risk to take, them all riled up that way.'

'So's snatching Rosenberg from under their noses.'

He opened his hand. 'Who's to say he was ever there? You? The girl?'

I felt as if he could see through walls.

He pushed his suit coat aside to put his hands on his hips. He stared at me that way for a long moment. Then he walked to the wooden chair and toed it like he understood the significance of it sitting in the middle of the room, all by itself. He sat down. 'Why didn't you clue me in to what you were doing?'

'What?' I could feel my neck twitching.

'The ranch, the girls.'

I held a breath. 'I never had a chance. By the time I had the address, they'd sent up a warning to Siegel's men. I thought they'd kill her.'

'I understand that but I mean before, the whole thing; why didn't you tell me what you were doing back in Los Angeles?'

'It wasn't pertinent. At least at the start. Not for a long time.'

He watched me, his look as good as telling me I was lying. It riled me enough to fire back. 'Besides, you knew already. You were at their guest house asking after me.'

He leaned forward, elbows on his knees, eventually nodding once to concede the point. 'I didn't understand the relevance then. But you did as soon as you came here; you were wrong not to say something at that point.'

'It unravelled fast. Would it have made a difference?'

He looked away, interlinking his fingers as if he was praying for patience. He got to his feet and went to the mirror, rubbing at one of the smudges as he looked into it. 'As it happens, I didn't come here to chew you out.' He turned around.

I waited, saying nothing.

'Look, the fact is, whatever your intentions and your cack-handed methods, you've had an effect.' He put his hands in his pockets. 'Siegel is gone.'

I took a step towards him. 'What?'

'My information is that after your actions last night, he went to the airport and hopped a flight to Mexico on a one-way ticket. Our working theory is that there's no way he'll get his licence now, which, apart from deep-sixing his plans, is an embarrassment to the money men back East, so he's gone to ground. If we're right, it ought to stay a one-way deal.'

I was lightheaded – Siegel gone. After everything he'd put us through. I wasn't sure what to feel; relief, anger, a spool of emotion uncoiling inside of me. But just that – no violent lurch of feeling. 'You can't be satisfied with that.'

'If I'm wrong and the door's open for him to come back, then I won't be. But that's not my read on the situation.'

I knocked on the table with my knuckles, working up a rage thinking about the injustice. 'What about your grand plans? What happened to blowing his organisation apart from the in-side?' I suddenly remembered Nancy in the other room and lowered my voice. 'You never said anything about him getting off scot-free to sit on a Mexican beach.'

'That's not how I'd characterise the situation. You ever heard of a *Federale* wouldn't off a gringo for a sawbuck? Think about it: every minute of every day, looking over his shoulder.'

'He's not another gringo, he has connections—'

'Not if he's running from them. They'll cut him off faster than you can sneeze.'

I righted myself, eyeing him. 'You've changed your tune because you've got Rosenberg on ice. You mean to make him sing instead of Siegel.'

He returned my look without speaking.

'What deal are you offering him?'

He sighed, shaking his head as if there was nothing more to say.

I came around the table to stand in front of him. 'Rosenberg killed Julie Desjardins, the girl they found in the desert. Did you know that?'

'According to whom?'

'Someone who'd know. Makes him the prime suspect for Henry Booker as well. To add to the list that includes Trent Bayless. Real swell guy to pick up a sweetheart deal from the Bureau.'

'You don't know what you're talking about.' I went to say something more but he had his two forefingers up, motioning for me to let him speak. 'Look, you've had one hell of a night and you're lashing out, I realise that. But I came here as an ally. There's something you deserve to hear.'

I cocked my head, waiting.

'Siegel issued a contract on you, before he left. We picked up on some chatter from a source in LA.'

My skin prickled. 'What about Lizzie?'

He closed his eyes too long, and I knew even before he nodded.

I heard the faraway sound of another car pulling up outside, my senses overloaded by the scream inside my head. I drifted to the window to look, my eyes refusing to focus, my spine rigid but weak, like a stick of chalk. Tanner said something else but it was white noise to my ears.

I expected to see Siegel out there, even though it made no sense. Through the haze I saw a flash of red bounce out of the car. My car – the one I'd had to abandon at the Flamingo. She looked over and her eyes met mine. Seeing me, Lizzie darted the short distance the rest of the way across the lot.

I threw the door open and she crashed herself into my arms. She smacked me on the chest with the flat of her hand. 'You swore you wouldn't do that to me again.'

She must have seen Tanner over my shoulder because she drew back to compose herself, reddening.

'Mrs Yates.'

'Special Agent Tanner.'

I glanced at the car. 'How did you ... Did you go back to the Flamingo?'

She nodded. 'That man has taken enough from us already. It was either that or stay here and . . .' She looked at Tanner. 'Well, anyway. You know.'

'But what if . . .' I looked at her in disbelief.

'He wouldn't be there at this hour, not after last night.'

I had to stop myself from saying how wrong she was.

She looked at me and then at Tanner. 'Have I interrupted something?'

He broke the stare, swivelling away to lean on the wall. She turned to me. 'Charlie?'

I took a breath, Lizzie watching me, stock-still.

'Siegel's gone,' I said.

She waited, then said, 'There's something else. You're as white as a sheet.'

I closed my eyes and told her.

Her gaze slid to the window behind me and she twisted her hands across her chest.

'Who did he give the contract to?' I asked Tanner.

He drew closer. 'I don't have that information. It might be open season – whoever wants to claim it.' He glanced downward, holding a hand up in apology. 'I didn't mean for that to sound flippant.'

The room fell silent, the implications sinking in.

Lizzie was the first to speak. 'What of it?'

We both looked at her.

She let her arms unfurl and fall to her sides. 'That was his intention all along, so it needn't change anything. We already knew we couldn't go back to Los Angeles.'

Tanner was tapping his finger against his palm. 'I don't want to alarm you but the threat is more serious than that, Mrs Yates.'

'I'm well aware how serious it is, Special Agent.'

He turned to me. 'I can arrange some form of protection for you, if you'd stand for it this time.'

'For how long? Indefinitely?'

He cleared his throat, giving no answer. I could feel Lizzie's discomfort at the idea.

'That's what it would amount to, isn't it? As long as Siegel's on the lam,' I said.

'Let's not get ahead of ourselves. Will you give it consideration at least?'

I nodded, relieved he was shaping up to go.

'I wouldn't take too long thinking about it. It's my strongest counsel that you remove yourselves from Las Vegas today – with or without my help.' He stepped over to the door and stopped. 'Did you have a chance to speak with the girl?'

My face drained again.

Lizzie laid her hand on my wrist. 'Nancy Hill? You found her?'

I nodded and turned back to Tanner. 'There wasn't time. She was helping me search for the others and then they arrested us and kept us in separate cars.'

Lizzie screwed her face up. 'Arrested?'

Tanner ignored her. 'What about at the department?' His eyes moved from mine to someplace behind me and it took all my restraint not to look around to the bathroom door.

'No. Why do you ask?'

'I mean to have a talk with her once the sheriff's men have cooled down. With all of the women, but her in particular – seeing as how she came to be here from Los Angeles. If Siegel's outfit transported her to Nevada for immoral purposes, it's a violation of the Mann Act. The courts go wild for anything looks like white slavery – gives us a real chance to make something stick.' He flicked his eyes behind me one more time and back again. 'I'd like to make that plain to her.'

He opened the front door and held it. 'Meantime, give my offer serious thought. I'll have a man here in an hour to keep watch, but that's strictly an interim measure.' He went out and was gone.

Lizzie came over to me. 'What was the meaning of that? What was he driving at?'

I planted my hands against the wall, seeing his angle as clear as day. 'He wants me to deliver a message.'

'To who?'

I waited until the sound of Tanner's tyres on the gravel had faded and then crossed to the bathroom door.

'Charlie?'

It was opened from inside before I could do it, and Nancy Hill came out. Faltering, uncertain steps.

'Lizzie, this is Nancy.'

*

I sat on the bed watching Lizzie rifle through her bag for something Nancy could wear. She was two inches taller, and broader in the shoulders than Lizzie, but they agreed anything had to be better than a dress dotted with blood.

I'd already thrown my trousers and shirt in the trash and changed into fresh threads. It felt like the first step into a new life. Colt Tanner's words were clear in my mind, his motives less so. I thought for sure he'd known Nancy Hill was stashed in the bathroom and he wanted me to convince her to tell the story the way he'd laid out. It made me furious that he gave no care to knowing what had really happened to her.

The girls settled on a patterned green shirtwaist number and Nancy went into the bathroom to change. Lizzie watched until she shut the door, then came over to me, putting her hand on my cheek. 'How are you feeling?'

I offered a thin smile, nodding my head. 'She's in shock.'

She nodded. 'I think she's coping as best she can.'

I laid my hand over hers, savouring her touch. 'She asked me when she could see Siegel.'

She glanced at the bathroom door. 'She what?' Her stare lingered as if she couldn't believe my words. Slowly, she turned to me again. 'You don't think . . .'

I nodded, Lang's take echoing in my ears – *Siegel only cares for money or women*. 'He has a reputation as a charmer.'

She pulled a face in disgust. 'But after what he's done to her. How can she think that way?'

'She's young, maybe he seemed glamorous. A misplaced crush.'

She brushed her mouth with her fingertips. 'That man is sickening.'

'I don't think she has a grasp on what's happened to her. It could take a long time.'

I'd closed the drapes as soon as Tanner left. I went to the window and parted them to look out, counting it as the third time I'd done so in a half-hour. The other wings of the motor court were on either side of us, forming a U-shape, the parking lot spread in front, only our car and two others in view. The sky stretched above, a thin gauze of white cloud hardening the blue. 'We need to get her away from here.'

Lizzie came over and took the drape from my fingers, smoothing it closed. 'Charlie, what about us? What are we going to do?'

The bathroom door opened and I snapped around to look, whispering, 'Disappear.'

Nancy Hill stepped out. It was jarring to see another woman in my wife's dress.

I stood by the closed drapes, a glow from the daylight behind them, thinking how strange the situation must have seemed. Lizzie moved a little towards her, holding her hand out. 'You must have a lot of questions.'

Nancy positioned herself on the far side of one of the beds. A barrier. 'What that man said about Ben going – is he telling the truth?'

I looked at Lizzie, choosing my words. 'I don't know.'

'You said he was with the police but you called him Special Agent.' Her tone was flat.

'Look, what's important right now is that we get out of here. Will you let me take you home to Iowa?'

She shook her head. 'You can't make me go back there. I told you.'

I could feel Lizzie reach for my hand before she spoke. 'Nancy, would you mind if Charlie and I stepped outside a moment?'

She didn't wait for an answer, leading me to the door. I cracked it a fraction to check outside before opening it the rest of the way. We came out squinting in the bright daylight, the cold still like sandpaper on the skin. Lizzie went to speak but I glanced at the highway across the parking lot, the other rooms all around overlooking us. 'We shouldn't be out in the open.' I took her arm and guided her to the car to sit inside.

When the doors were shut, she said, 'Did you mean what you said back there? Iowa?'

'It's as good of a place to disappear as any.'

She frowned. 'She said she doesn't want to go.'

I rested my hand on top of the steering wheel. 'Her mother's worried sick. Nancy just needs time to adjust, it's the best place for her.'

She looked thoughtful, her eyes distant. Then she focused on me again. 'Shouldn't we take her to the authorities?'

'They arrested her, Liz. She's the victim here but all they see is another whore. They'll chew her up and she'll either end up in a cell or back on the street.'

She tilted her head back, shaking it in resignation. 'So no one pays. Again.'

I gripped my hands together. 'I'll make sure they do.'

'In Iowa?'

I let out a long breath. 'One day at a time. We play the long game. I promised you we could run as soon as we found her.'

She closed her eyes, interlinking her fingers and resting her chin on them. 'I know.'

'What's the matter?' The question sounded ridiculous spoken aloud. I was dangling a life on the run as a reward.

'Perhaps I never believed the day would actually come.'

She looked away from me then, as if it was an admission of doubt in me. I couldn't deny feeling the same.

A big rig strapped with lumber rumbled past on the highway, loud, even at a distance. I wondered if it was headed to the Flamingo. When the noise died, she said. 'What about Colt Tanner?'

'What of him?'

'I worried you might be tempted by his offer of protection.'

I ran my hand over my mouth, buying a moment to confirm my own feelings about his offer still held. 'I couldn't face it – a life under guard. You?'

She shook her head. 'Are you going to ask Nancy to speak

to him before we take off? If she's soft on Siegel I can't imagine her telling it how he wants.'

I rubbed my temples, a throbbing pulse building in my head. 'Liz, what did you say to Tanner after I left you at the Sheriff's Department last night?'

She kept her eyes forward.

I waited a moment but she didn't speak. 'What?'

She slipped her mouth behind her fingers. 'Charlie ... I didn't try to contact him. Please don't be mad at me.'

I felt the same nervous rush as when he'd showed up at the ranch.

'I'm sorry,' she said. 'There were just so many questions in my mind, I didn't think he could be trusted. When you didn't come back, I felt so awful. That's why I went to the Flamingo again, I thought if I could at least retrieve the car that would be something. And we'd be able to get away when you came back.'

In my mind I was already running through the chain of events. The last time I'd seen him before the ranch was in this same parking lot, almost twenty-four hours previous, when he'd told me to go to the gala at the Flamingo. That was long before I'd tracked down Harry Heller and followed the trail from the Kitten Litter to Siegel's ranch. So how the hell did he find me there so fast? Or was that asking the wrong question?

'Charlie, say something.'

I blinked, returning to the moment. I heard a distant echo of my own voice and then realised I was speaking. 'I think you made the right decision.'

*

We cleared out in a rush. I was determined to get gone before Tanner's man showed up.

Nancy was adamant she wouldn't go back to Iowa. Lizzie made a hurried effort to talk her round, but she dug her heels in – enough to make me question whether we were doing the right thing by her. But it came clear her reticence wasn't born out of a desire to speak to the law – local or Federal; all she wanted was to see Siegel. I tore through a half-dozen ploys trying to get us out of the room, out of the motor court, out of Las Vegas.

In the end, it was a promise to head upstate to Reno that did the trick. It was close enough to the California line to tempt her. She made mention of holing up at a divorce ranch until he surfaced again, and it broke my heart to hear the fantasy she was living in. More so to play on it.

Reno meant heading west not east, but the old Lincoln Highway routed right through the town, before running all the way to New York City – and passing through Iowa on its way. It was a compromise I could work with.

The motor court was on the Reno Highway, so as soon as the bags were in the car, I sped out of there and put Las Vegas a dozen miles behind us before I even took a breath. Sheriff's cruisers, Siegel's men, maybe Tanner's men – it felt like almost any car behind us could be a tail. Lizzie sat up front with me, Nancy in the back. I angled the rearview to be able to see her. I wanted to ask her so many things, but from experience of dealing with victims, I knew she'd speak only in her own time.

*

A hundred miles in, there was uninterrupted desert on all sides. The road was a two-lane, a solitary car visible behind us. It'd been back there less than ten miles. I felt sure no one had followed us, and somehow that made me more alert – as if some sleight of hand was at play that I had no way to detect.

Nancy Hill had only spoken once – to speculate on Siegel's whereabouts, questioning whether he really would have gone to Mexico.

We stopped for gas and food in a busted mining town called Tonopah. I was checking the road as the attendant started the pump when I noticed Nancy gazing at an abandoned shaft headframe in the distance. She looked away when she saw me watching.

I asked if there was a payphone in town and the man said no, but I could use his line for a dollar. I made it up with coins and forked it over. I opened the back door of the car and ducked inside.

'I'm going to make a call to your mother, you want to come with me?'

She shook her head. 'You can tell her I'm doing fine.'

Lizzie looked at me, asking with her eyes if she should say something. I signalled to let it pass. 'I'll tell her you're safe.' I crouched down, hesitating. 'There's something else. About Julie – I should alert her family. Do you know how I can reach them?'

She looked over, at a loss. She shook her head.

'What was her real name? Can you tell me?'

'I don't know.'

I kept my gaze on her.

'Really, I don't know.'

'She's not from the same town as you?'

She shook again. 'We met on the bus. In California.'

'She never told you her name? Her hometown? Anything?'

'She didn't want to talk about it. That's how Hollywood is, no one cares who you were before.'

The prospect of a family somewhere never knowing their daughter's fate opened up a new fissure inside me.

*

There were black fingerprints all over the telephone's housing. I lifted the receiver and dialled and it took a time for the operators to make the connections before they finally announced my name to Nancy's mother. When she spoke, it was with a mix of hope and fear in her voice. 'Mr Yates?'

'Mrs Hill, I have your daughter with me. She's safe.'

'Oh—' The line went quiet. There were muffled whimpers, as if she had her hand over her mouth.

'We're heading in your direction, but it'll take a few days. Mrs Hill, did you hear me?'

'Yes, I heard you. Blessed Jesus, oh, Mr Yates, you have no idea— I'm so relieved, I'm in your debt. I'm in your debt.'

'I'll call you again in a day or two to let you know our progress.'

'Thank you. Mr Yates, thank you so much.'

I rang off, guilt tugging at me because I didn't know if I could make good on my words.

*

It was another hundred miles and late into the afternoon when Nancy said, 'It wasn't how you think.'

She said it soft enough that I glanced at Lizzie to make sure I hadn't imagined it.

I waited to let her speak again, but she offered nothing more. 'What wasn't?'

'Ben loves me. He told me as much.'

Her eyes were wide as full moons in the rearview – imploring, certain.

'Sometimes a man will tell a lady what he thinks she wants to hear.'

'Don't you think I know that? He had others, too, I'm not stupid. But I know what's in his heart.'

Lizzie swivelled in her seat to face her. 'Have you considered how he could make you do the things he did if that were true?'

'No one made me.'

I saw her staring hard at Lizzie. In a murmur, she added, 'At the start, anyway.'

'But you can't have . . . it wasn't by choice.'

'You can say that because you don't know the alternative. We were flat broke. I had sixty cents to my name my last morning in Los Angeles.'

I was burning to ask her about Julie Desjardins, but feared she'd clam up if I was too direct. 'Nancy, what happened when you went to the TPK lot?'

She took a sidelong look out her window. 'We thought we knew what to expect.'

She was tiptoeing towards it. I watched her in the mirror. 'How do you mean?'

Her mouth moved but she didn't say anything at first, as if

rehearsing how she'd tell it. 'Nick Maskill approached us at a call we went to. He's this big wheel at TPK. He said he could get us a private acting gig that paid well and said we should come down to his studio. Julie rolled her eyes when he called it that – she'd auditioned for him before, so she knew all about him. But he swore it wasn't how it sounded, to come along and he'd explain. He promised us ten bucks just for showing up.'

'When we went there that day, he treated us like we were already in pictures. He had one of his girls fix our hair and makeup, he took us to Wardrobe to pick out dresses for us, he gave us a script to read and had us do a screen test; it was fun. When he was happy with that, he asked all kinds of questions about where we came from and where we lived and things of that kind. Then when he was through, he told us we could keep the dresses and suggested we all go out to eat.'

There was control in her voice as she spoke, and a precision to her words that made me think she'd been practising this account for some time.

'He drove us to Ciglio's, this Italian joint on Hollywood Boulevard, and he bought us some wine and that's when I met Ben – he came and joined us at our table and I recognised who he was right away. I could tell he liked me because he told me I looked beautiful. He stayed a little while and had a drink with us, and then when he left he winked at me and said maybe he'd see me again someplace else.

'After that, Nick took us back to his house and I figured that's when he'd want to get fresh. Julie said not to worry about it because she thought he was cute anyway. He opened champagne for us all and then he kissed Julie, but he was just kinda fooling around and she didn't have any objections anyhow.

Then sometime later he said we could live this way every day and earn a lot of money for doing it, if we'd just go to Las Vegas and keep some wealthy men company. He took two hundred-dollar bills out of his billfold and put them on the table and said they were ours to keep if we agreed.'

'I was tipsy so I didn't know what to think. I blurted out that we'd have nowhere to stay, but Julie laughed at me and Nick said all of that would be taken care of. He made out like if we did it for a month, he'd bring us back and maybe have a part for us – kind of like we were in training. He told us everyone we'd ever heard of had done the same when they were breaking in.

'Nick went off to make a call and next thing I knew, a car showed up and he said we should go right then. I was in two minds but Julie was insistent, she kept saying she couldn't make the rent and Mrs Snyder would kick us out on the street. I was so tired by then I thought, *why not?* and went along with it. I was tipsy, it didn't sound so bad. We were in Las Vegas the next morning.'

Listening to her tell it, it was clear she was still trying to make sense of the situation she'd got caught up in; maybe even explain her own actions to herself. The defiance, the insistence that no one had made her at the start – it was a trait I'd en-countered in victims time and again; an underlying illusion of control, created by reassuring herself that even though she'd made bad choices, they'd been her choices to make. It worried me because it was the start of blaming herself for what had happened.

The other part that came through was guilt over what had happened to Julie. Taking pains to note Julie's enthusiasm at every stage was Nancy's way of signalling she couldn't be blamed for her death – a sign of what she really felt.

'You told me Rosenberg was responsible for Julie's death.'

She nodded. 'He was always a swine.'

Lizzie looked numb at all of it. She glanced at me and then turned back to Nancy. 'How did you find out?'

'He told us. He said he'd do the same to anyone else tried to steal from him the way she did.'

Beaten, strangled and stripped, left in the desert to be found. A warning to the others. 'What did she steal?'

She faltered for the first time, her voice cracking. 'The money. The hundred dollars.'

I saw it right away but Lizzie frowned in confusion. 'The money they gave you in Los Angeles?'

'He told us— The first night he came to the house, he told us the money was an advance and we all had to work it off. She . . .' She moistened her lips but couldn't finish.

'Julie tried to run away,' I said.

She covered her eyes and nodded.

Lizzie swivelled around fully to take her hand.

She sobbed in silence and I imagined her stuck in that ranch house having to do the same, too afraid to even make a sound.

We travelled that way for a long minute, the engine a relentless purr that sounded cold in its indifference to the young woman in the back.

Then she said, 'It was because she'd tried it once before.'

'Running away?' Lizzie said.

She closed her eyes and nodded. 'The first time, when that pig caught her, he brought her back and made us watch while he put a pillow over her face. I only figured out later it was because he didn't want to leave a mark. He pressed it down while she was kicking and bucking, and no one even dared to scream. I thought he was going to kill her for sure. When he took it off her, he said if any of us tried it again, he wouldn't be so gentle the next time.'

I could see the image in my mind. I glanced at Lizzie's face, the welt he'd put there, and shook at the memory of his promise of what he'd do to her. Having no doubt he would, if given the chance. And now, instead of rotting in jail, he was sitting pretty under Colt Tanner's wing.

*

We made Reno at dusk. An arch spanned the road on the edge of downtown; it read, '*Reno The Biggest Little City In The World.*'

We found a motel close to the Truckee River and holed up for the night. The proprietor took Nancy to be our daughter and we let him keep that notion.

Nancy asked to take a bath so I went outside to give her some privacy. I walked across the parking lot and stood on the edge of the highway, the river beyond it burbling in the darkness. I looked back down the road, following the line of the blacktop to where it met the night.

Lizzie came up behind me, a blanket wrapped around her shoulders. She stopped next to me and followed my gaze, the road empty. 'Sometimes I wonder if there's good in this world at all. That poor girl.'

'I never imagined . . .' I shuffled my feet, scraping them in the gravel. 'Her story's so much worse than I thought.'

'You looked faraway. What are you thinking about?'

'All of it.'

'Siegel? And Rosenberg?'

I nodded. But there was more.

'Do you think we did the right thing?' She inclined her head towards the room.

'Do you?'

She lingered, taking a breath. 'I change my mind once an hour.' She slipped her arm through mine. 'I want so badly for those men to pay, that's the part I have a hard time with. It feels as if they're getting off lightly and I wonder if we've let that happen.'

'She wouldn't have spoken against Siegel.'

She looked at the ground, nodding. 'I can't understand how she can still have a care for him.'

'She's lost. There's an avalanche of guilt and anger and blame waiting to hit her and the only thing holding it back is her infatuation for him. So she's clinging to it.'

Something unspoken passed between us, and I wondered if I'd skated too close to our own circumstances in the wake of Alice's murder. The chance it was still unfolding.

'What will you do if she keeps refusing to go home?' she said.

'I'm hoping she'll see sense when we get closer.'

'What did her mother say on the telephone?'

'Her emotions got the better of her. *Thank you* was about as much as she could manage.'

'After everything and she still won't speak to her.' She shook her head. 'They must have had some falling out.'

I turned to look at her then, surprised I hadn't seen it myself.

'What is it?' she said.

'I never thought of it that way.' My wife's capacity for insight was startling; even in this, my own obsession, she saw things I'd missed. 'I always assumed she was running to Hollywood. I never considered she'd be running from something.'

She kissed me on the cheek. 'Don't be hard on yourself.' Her breath fogged in the air.

I felt her shiver and pulled her close. 'Don't get cold. You should go inside.'

'What about you?'

'I'll be along in a minute.'

She kept her eyes on me, reading me as plain as day. 'Is there something else on your mind?'

I gazed back down the road.

'What is it?'

I was about to say *nothing*; old habits die hard. But I stopped myself, knowing she deserved better. 'Tanner.'

She circled around in front of me now, looking me full in the face.

'We ran from him in Los Angeles and he never forgot it. Then he catches up with us this morning, says he wants Nancy, then gives us a window to ditch out on him again.'

Her eyes flicked between mine.

'If he meant to have a man guard our room, why didn't he bring one with him?' I said.

She took my sleeve. 'What're you suggesting?'

'He's shown up at the drop of a hat time and again, but today needs an hour's notice to summon one of his men. In a town as small as Las Vegas.'

She looked away over her shoulder. A pool of light came

from the motel's office, the road melting into the black shortly beyond it. The feeling of eyes lurking just out of sight.

'Are you saying he knew we'd run?'

*

The cold snap broke the next morning and although the air was still crisp, there was real warmth in the sun.

None of us had slept much. We gathered our few things and loaded them into the car in near silence. I offered to fetch some breakfast, but neither Lizzie nor Nancy showed any enthusiasm for food.

Before she would get in the car, Nancy asked where we were headed.

'We have to keep moving,' I said.

'That doesn't answer the question. I wasn't fooling when I said I'd wait here for him.'

I laid my hands on the hood. 'Clark County Sheriff's won't just forget about us. They can get here just as fast as we did.'

'Women come here all the time on their own. I can blend in.'

'The Reno Cure' – loose divorce rules that drew runaway wives from all over the country. 'You have no money.'

'I can earn.'

'You'd sooner that than go home to your family?'

She looked away.

'What caused you to leave, Nancy?'

She didn't respond.

Lizzie had already sat herself in the car but now she stepped out again. 'Whatever it was, there's nothing can't be patched up.'

'You don't know the half of it.'

'I know your mother would give anything to see you,' I said. 'She's been a wreck while you were missing.'

She looked over as if deciding whether to believe me.

'I haven't told her a word about what happened to you,' I said. 'As far as she knows, you were in Los Angeles. There's no shame in what you've been through, but it's nobody's business but yours to say anything more.'

The silence stretched. I could hear a car passing along the highway in the distance, the flow of the Truckee a murmur underneath it.

I was about to try again when she opened the door and slipped into the backseat.

*

It took three days to reach Iowa. Nancy hailed from a company town name of Enterprise, some twenty miles north of Des Moines in the centre of the state. The route from Reno took us across northern Utah, into southern Wyoming and through Nebraska, the terrain shifting colour as we passed from the red-brown of the desert to the blistering white of the snow-covered prairie. The only constant was the sky above, blue and cloudless most all the time, and seemingly limitless.

We drove from sunup to dusk every day, staying at whatever motel was closest when I reached the limit of my endurance. I watched the road behind compulsively, but saw nothing to suggest we'd attracted a tail. We were the only car in sight for hours at a time, and after enough stretches on those straight, empty roads, it became easier to believe what my eyes were telling me

– that we were an anonymous speck, crossing the continent unnoticed.

We passed long periods without speaking, but the silence was never easy. I sensed Nancy struggling to come to terms with what'd happened, the beginnings of a reckoning that would last long beyond our journey. I wanted to say something to offer her solace, but I didn't know where to begin. On occasion I'd return from the restroom to find Lizzie in quiet conversation with her, and I was hopeful my wife would be able to impart something that would help. With the resilience she'd shown in the face of everything she'd endured, there was no better person to try.

Nancy gave up intermittent snatches of what had gone on. At different times, she told of how Siegel would visit with her at the ranch to shower her with gifts and promises; of his talk of bringing her back to Los Angeles and making her a movie star; of taking her to Europe with him to see Paris and Rome and London; of living in mansions and riding in limousines. All of it there to be had, if she could just wait a little longer while he finished his business in Las Vegas. It didn't need to be said what he'd expected of her in return, and it seemed she'd never questioned it in the depths of proceedings. His horseshit sounded so fantastical as she recounted it that there were moments she seemed incredulous at her own words; it was those moments gave me hope she'd see it all clearly one day. The one thing I wanted her to understand was the illusion she'd been free to leave; if she could see that, she could scotch the notion that she was somehow to blame.

For my part, when the silence returned it allowed Siegel and Rosenberg to fill my thoughts. And Colt Tanner. At a gas station near Cheyenne, I slipped away to the telephone kiosk to call his office in Los Angeles. I hadn't arrived at what I would say to him, but it didn't matter; I dialled twice, but no one answered.

In Nebraska, on the last day before we reached Iowa, we passed a sign for the town of Broken Bow and the name jarred. The significance came to me a short way down the road – the same name as the town in Oklahoma where I'd ditched Sheriff Bailey's car the morning I fled Texarkana. I remembered how I felt that day, thinking if I could stay ahead of the law long enough to reach Los Angeles, I'd be safe. Never imagining that almost a year later, even that refuge would be lost. That I'd still be running, no end in sight.

*

Nancy Hill lived in a tall, grey clapboard house that sat on a wide clearing of grass on the edge of a bare cornfield. A stand of birch trees separated the two, the only things taller than a barn for miles around. The land was flat to the horizon in every direction.

A short dirt track ran from the highway to the side of the house, barely visible under the snow. I turned onto it and stopped the car, glancing back at Nancy. She was fiddling with the collar of her blouse, refusing to look at me or at the property. A dog started barking inside the house.

A minute after we arrived, a woman opened the front door and stepped out onto the small porch, not much wider than the doorway. The resemblance was unmistakable. She was wrapped in a large shawl, the hem of a grey skirt hanging to her ankles.

She squinted, looking in our direction, shielding her eyes from the dazzling reflection coming off the snow. She came forward, standing on the top step of three that led off the deck.

I got out of the car and went to open Nancy's door, but she'd climbed out by the time I reached her. Her footfalls were muffled in the snow. A weathervane on the roof turned in the breeze, squeaking as it made each lazy rotation.

Mrs Hill took her hand away, her face falling at seeing Nancy standing there. She glanced at me, her eyes moist, and then back at her daughter. She gathered her skirt up and took the last two steps down, then ran across the snow.

Nancy hadn't moved. Mrs Hill rushed to her daughter and threw her arms around her. She gripped her close, burying her face in her hair. One of them whispered, 'I'm sorry'; I wasn't sure which. All of it was conducted in a silence soft enough to hear the branches swaying behind the house.

CHAPTER TWENTY-FIVE

We stayed at the Hill place through Christmas. I'd intended for us to leave that same day, thinking to get us out of the way so the two women could start piecing their lives back together. But Luanne Hill was insistent, showing us to the small guest house a short way behind the main building. It was basic, little more than a bed and an old stove by way of comforts, but she was on the verge of pleading when she led us inside, and I didn't have the heart to turn her down. A glance at Lizzie told me she was of the same mind.

*

Three days later, Lizzie woke me in the dark and bare room with a kiss on the cheek. The stove was lit, but I could see her shivering. She wished me Merry Christmas and handed me a candy bar wrapped in newspaper and tied with a green ribbon. I took it, faltering, feeling like an ass for having nothing to give her in return, not even realising the date. Then I looked down and read the message she'd written on it. '*Our First Together.*' It was meant sincerely, but it served only to underline to me how badly I'd failed my wife.

*

Somehow, the longer we stayed, the harder it became to leave. The hole left by Mr Hill's absence became more apparent with every day that passed, and I did my best to plug it – turning my hand to whatever needed doing around the farm. It was hard work, but liberating with it – leaving me cold and exhausted enough at the end of each day that thoughts of what waited for us in the world beyond were pushed out by the most basic demands my body placed on me: food, warmth and sleep.

Over time, a bond grew between Nancy and Lizzie, one forged on the common ground of the traumas they'd survived. It happened slowly, Nancy lowering her guard inches at a time rather than yards, but Lizzie was patient and open with her. It was a month after we arrived that I first saw Nancy laugh – Lizzie whispering something to her as I trudged through the snow in front of the house and drawing a snigger.

At nights, Lizzie and I would lie in bed and talk, trying to thrash out a plan. We went through cycles of being upbeat and downcast; one day it would be me telling her that the heat would die down soon enough and we'd be able to go on with our lives – only for her to have to pick up the same mantle and try to reassure me a few days later. Neither of us stayed convinced for long, because at root we knew that holing up in that place was just another form of running away.

That uncertainty was what wore us down. You could put the fear to the back of your mind for stretches because the country was so remote, it seemed impossible we'd run into anyone looking to collect on Siegel's contract – and as time passed, the possibility someone had followed us from Las Vegas dwindled to nothing. But the void left by fear was filled instead by questions, the kind that had me awake at night long past the point where exhaustion should have seized me – and the kind I had no answers for. Where do we go next? How long can we run for? When will we be safe?

*

We waited out the winter in Enterprise. The house was the only one for miles around, and you could see two miles along the highway in either direction. Every day I watched the road, a kernel of fear sprouting each time a car I didn't recognise came along it. Nancy still went cold at any mention of Ben Siegel, so I never could elicit from her if she'd told his men about her hometown; it was the glaring hole in my sense that we were safe there – the knowledge that I'd been able to trace her back to a speck of a town in Iowa, so others might too. I wondered how rich Siegel's price on our heads was.

I started writing as a way to calm myself and bring order to my thoughts. I called Buck Acheson once, to let him know we were alive but not where we were. He'd got wind of the contract and agreed it was best he didn't know anyway. He agreed to keep our jobs open as long as he could, but I admitted to him I didn't know when we'd be able to return; we left that part of the conversation unfinished. After that, I wrote a little every day. It started out as an exposé on the links between organised crime, Los Angeles and Las Vegas, but each time I picked up a pen it contorted into something different.

I wrote down all the things that I'd been through – Texarkana, Hot Springs, even back to my army days and the jeep crash that spared me going to war. I'd tear the pages up, and a few days later write the same part again. I couldn't settle on what to commit to ink, so it went on that way – writing some, destroying some, until, finally, I wrote it all. Everything that had passed, everything I'd seen and learned. I didn't know what I'd do with it in the end, but just the act of writing fortified me.

Spring was showing its hand by the time I'd got it all down, and it was no coincidence the decision to move on came with the convergence of those two things. We took our leave on a bright Friday morning, turning down Mrs Hill's invitation to stay longer. Nancy took it hard – her eyes were wet saying her farewells to Lizzie and she made her swear to come visit again. But we all knew it couldn't go on that way for ever. Before I left, I made Nancy a promise: *I'll make them pay for what they did*. Her comeback line cut me even as it showed how far she'd come: 'Go easy on Ben.'

*

Every time I'd studied the map, the country looked smaller. Two states south was Arkansas – Texarkana and Hot Springs looming. East was Chicago, with all its links to Siegel. Minnesota lay to the north, the Canadian border beyond it. The last of those held appeal for a time, and Lizzie and I talked through the notion as we drove. But our hearts were never in it, recognising another bolthole for what it was. So it was we turned west, into South Dakota, taking a scattergun route towards the Rockies while I tried to get a grip on what waited for us beyond.

We were in Sioux Falls when I made the first call to California. If Trip Newland was surprised to hear from me, he didn't show it.

'I'm glad you called, Yates – what's this jive about posting me to Sacramento?'

'That's not important now, we'll talk about it when I'm back.'

'*Back?* It's been months, don't soap me. You think I don't know about the deal with you and Siegel? I already talked to Buck A. about slotting into your spot. He's listening, too, let me tell you—'

'Shut your mouth a damn minute.'

He went quiet and I took a breath to tamp down my temper.

'Hey, look, I didn't mean to come off a jerk,' he said. 'Talk is you went back to New York or Texas or someplace for keeps, that's all.'

'Forget it. But you can scotch that talk right now.'

'Oh yeah? Where are you?'

The question was a natural one, but still managed to put me on edge. 'Never mind. I want you to do something for me.'

'You still owe me a make-good for Henry Booker. I guess you didn't hear about him?'

'Hear what?'

'The slug they pulled out of his face matched a .38 Special they recovered from that ranch house you shot up.'

'I didn't shoot—' I grunted, frustrated – a night in hell turned into a quip. Let it pass. 'Whose gun was it?'

'Character name of Gilardino – he died there. They pegged him as an associate of our friend Siegel. You wanna give me the dope on that night and we'll call it even?'

No surprise – Siegel's outfit behind Booker's murder. In the old days, finking to the press might earn you a beating; since the war, it seemed as if every life was cheap. 'So you're still talking to people in Las Vegas.'

'Sure, what else am I gonna do? There's not many here will talk to me – yet. I'm getting a handle on it, but—'

'I want to know where Siegel is.'

For the second time, he was silenced.

'Last report I had on him he was in Mexico,' I said.

'He was back in Las Vegas for the big opening.' He offered it fast.

'The Flamingo?' I said.

'Mmm. The whole thing was a disaster. Almost none of the Hollywood set showed their faces and the house took a hit on the tables to the tune of fifty grand. The place was still covered in drop cloths.'

The memory of being dragged out of the casino lit bright in my mind. Gilardino and Rosenberg beating me on the ground. But the part that burned was the one I hadn't seen: Rosenberg raising his hand to Lizzie. Even with one of them dead and the other in Federal custody, it felt nothing at all like justice had been served. 'How did he get his licence?'

'His pal McCarran came through. A fat campaign contribution, I guess.'

'Is he still there? Siegel?'

He coughed. 'Nope. Joint shut its doors a month later. It opened again a few weeks back, but it's no secret the place is running bankrupt. He cropped up in LA a while ago – figure to raise some more dough. But then he dropped out of sight.'

I glanced away from the receiver, thinking. 'What about Moe Rosenberg?'

'Unknown. Someone who knows things in Las Vegas told me Siegel must've offed him because he's been a ghost. Guess they had a falling out.'

That surprised me – Rosenberg still on ice and out of sight. I wondered what Tanner's plans were for him, amazed that the Bureau had the discipline to pass up the chance of making a splash in the press. It occurred to me that if he could get his hands on Siegel, Rosenberg's value dropped to nothing. 'Talk to whoever you need to, LA, Las Vegas, anyplace you can think of; get me a line on Siegel's whereabouts.'

He exhaled, drawing it out. 'I mean . . . what for? You know there's a contract, right? That's what I was talking about earlier when—'

'I know. I want to talk some sense into him.'

He made a guttural sound as if he couldn't get his words out. 'But the man can't be reasoned with. You'll get yourself killed – and god knows who else.'

'Can you do it or can't you?'

The connection fritzed. When it cleared again, I could hear him muttering. 'They told me you were a crazy.' He sighed. 'All right, leave me a number to reach you at.'

That same antenna perked again. 'I'll be in touch.'

I hung up and hesitated a beat in the kiosk, hovering over the telephone. Then I went back to the room.

*

I let two days pass before calling again. When he answered this time, Newland was subdued.

'I couldn't get a good answer outta anyone. Consensus of opinion is Bugsy oughta be headed for Venus after what happened.'

I turned around in frustration, the cord wrapping around

my body. 'Trip, I want you to go back to Las Vegas. I need to know where he's—'

'Not a chance.'

'I'm giving you an assignment.'

'I'm already putting myself in harm's way for you. Word gets out we're talking, the wrong people are gonna come sniffing around, and I can't spare the pound of flesh and more it'll take to convince them I don't know where you are.'

'I need a man with the contacts to get the job done.'

'No, nix, *nein*. I'll do my utmost from here, but that's you in my pocket for the rest of time, okay?'

I took a deep breath, knowing what he was saying was right. We were at a lodge overlooking Lake Whitewood, the waterway still frozen in places. I gazed out across the patchwork of blues and whites and greys. In the far distance, bare trees lined the opposite shore, as small as toy soldiers; in front of me, a tumbledown wooden pier jutted out from the bank, on the verge of collapse. 'Just do what you can, don't put yourself in danger. Okay?'

I cut the call but held onto the receiver. I dialled again, another Los Angeles number. It rang twice before I changed my mind and hung up. I lingered there in the booth, thinking about the one person with the means to help me, a bridge I'd burned twice already. Wondering what the price of Tanner's help would be now, even knowing I didn't trust him. Hot on its heels, the damning estimation that it'd be the same as before: Nancy Hill's testimony, bent to suit his needs. My needs.

Unless I could give him Siegel myself.

*

I called Newland every day after that, at the same time angling us back towards Nevada. I reasoned Siegel wouldn't let the Flamingo go down without a fight, so chances were he'd show up there again at some point. Nancy Hill and Colt Tanner were a constant presence on the edge of my thoughts; a crack had formed in my certainty that I'd do anything to avoid involving her again, and it only hardened my resolve to locate Siegel.

I was honest with Lizzie about my conversations with Newland – the time for any misplaced idea of protecting her by keeping her in the dark long passed. But I kept one name out of what I reported back to her, and it became apparent she'd seen through me when she asked, 'What will you do if you find him?'

When I didn't answer right away, she said, 'Please do not say *Colt Tanner.*'

I looked out of the window. We'd crossed back into northern Utah, caustic white salt deposits gleaming in the flats and basins around us. 'He has the means to end this.'

She laid her hand on the dash. 'I thought we agreed he couldn't be trusted?'

'He can't. But we can keep ourselves at a remove this time. All we need do is find Siegel and give him up.'

'As simple as that.' She clicked her fingers. 'He could have had him before and he didn't want him, what's different now?'

'He's had Rosenberg for months. He'll have the means to put him away now.'

'Charlie, he has the resources of the FBI at his disposal – if he wanted to find him, he would have, and without your help.'

'Maybe Rosenberg's not talking.' I opened my hand on the wheel, looking over. 'If he's smart, he's saying enough to negotiate a deal for himself but keeping the meaty parts back. If I put Siegel on a plate for Tanner, it'll get his attention – he can play them off against each other. And it means Rosenberg's leverage with the Bureau goes up in smoke – so he takes the fall he deserves.'

She ran the flat of her hand across the bench seat, thinking. 'What if that means Siegel getting a favourable deal instead?'

My eyes flicked to her cheek, the laceration healed but not forgotten. 'They both deserve to fall. Right now one of them is walking free and the other is on easy street. My way means they both lose everything.'

She turned her head, closing her eyes. 'Do you really think it could work?'

'It's the best shot I've got.'

'What if you can't find Siegel?'

The two-lane in front of us was razor-straight all the way to its vanishing point in the far distance. 'I'll find him.'

*

We sat tight in western Utah, close to the Nevada line, changing motels every few days. I called Trip Newland each morning, but sightings of Siegel were sporadic, and always came well after the fact.

Days turned into weeks. Frustration tore me up. Newland fed me reports of Siegel sightings in Cleveland, in Chicago and in New York. '*And those are just the credible ones.*' But he must have been thinking the same as me because all the places he did mention had links to organised crime, and a picture began to emerge – Siegel making the rounds, pleading to raise enough money to keep the Flamingo going. The reports kept coming – Miami, Kansas City. Always too late.

There was one city missing from the list and its omission was glaring. Instinct told me that was where we needed to be, and I decided to move us west, as close to it as I dared.

Three days later, my hunch paid off. When I called Newland that morning, the first words he said to me were, 'He's in Los Angeles.'

CHAPTER TWENTY-SIX

From our holding point in Riverside, we made it to LA in two hours. Siegel had been spotted dining at a restaurant in Hollywood the night before, but Newland hadn't picked up on it until morning and couldn't pin down his whereabouts beyond that. I raced through the heat of the midday sun, drinking coffee like water and praying he wouldn't move on again. Lizzie was alongside me. She'd been holding the ignition key in her hand when I came back from speaking to Newland that morning; she must have sensed something in my urgency because the first words out of her mouth were, 'I'm coming with you.'

I didn't tell Newland or anyone else we were on our way.

The sun was at its apex when we arrived, the palm trees along the Boulevard casting almost no shadow. The streets were bathed in sunlight and the bustle of vehicles and streetcars and people reassured me we'd have cover to hide in plain sight.

We drove to West Hollywood and parked across the street from Empoli's, the eatery Siegel was rumoured to have graced the night before. Lizzie laid on her thickest drawl and went inside clutching a nickel tourist guidebook, asking for a hint when she might star-spot a handful of notables – Benjamin Siegel chief among them. The act got us no closer; the maitre d' confirmed Siegel had been there, but that he wasn't expected there again that night; an infrequent guest was how he referred to him.

From there, I made a run through Beverly Hills, bracing low-risk types only – hotel doormen and bellhops, strictly those who wouldn't know my face. The tactic proved fruitless, so I doubled-down by calling Hector King at the *Times*. He drew a blank, but suggested asking some of his legmen, giving me the names of two bars around City Hall I could try. Talking to other hacks was a last-ditch ploy because once word I was in town hit the street, there was no controlling whose ears it might reach. But any way I looked at it, the window of time I could be in the city was short.

I drove to Lacey's on East Second Street, spoke with three of King's men in there, then crossed to the Banbury. One man after another gave me the same retread as what Newland had already told me, and none of them could come up with a location for Siegel. But just as I was about to give up, one of Hector's men dropped a nugget about 'some Hollywood guy, been rattling the can around town for Bugsy'.

He couldn't put a name on the man, but I thought I could, and I realised I'd been wasting my time at the wrong end of the ladder.

*

It was past seven when we rolled up to the security hut at the main gate of TPK Studios. I was hoping Joseph Bersinger would've been on shift, but I struck out on that too. I lowered my window and waited as the guard stepped out with his clipboard.

'Your name, sir?'

'Miss French for Mr Maskill.' I inclined my head to Lizzie.

She had on a pair of dime store black sunglasses and kept her gaze straight ahead.

He looked down his list. 'I don't see that name on here . . .'

I winked at him. 'It's more like a delivery.'

He reddened. 'I don't . . . I'll have to make a call.'

'You think that's wise? He wanted to be asked about it, he wouldn't have made the appointment out of hours.'

The man hesitated.

'Look, you do what you want to do, but I got instructions from Mr Siegel to see this dame to the door, so how about you hurry it up?'

The man glanced at his clipboard again. He took a step towards the hut and stopped, then turned and lifted the bar across the road. 'Make it fast.'

I drove past the hut and inside the complex, parking near the main entrance. I put my hand on Lizzie's leg, felt it trembling. 'You did good.'

She took the glasses off and tossed them on the dash. 'Let's get this over with.'

*

Nick Maskill kept an office on the fourth floor, overlooking Gower Gulch. I'd called ahead of time from a payphone around the corner to confirm he was still at his desk, posing as a stringer for the *Hollywood Reporter*; the switchboard lady ran me off the line, but not before she'd let slip what I needed to know.

We rode the elevator and came out into a corridor carpeted with inch-deep pile. I walked along the row of doors, reading nameplates until we came to Maskill's. I tried the handle and it swung open.

Maskill was at his desk writing and snapped his head up to look. He was wearing a light blue seersucker suit with a grey necktie. He had the build of a man used to lunching on someone else's check, but his face was youthful, with strong features and an aquiline nose. I stepped inside, Lizzie trailing close behind, and shut the door.

'Who—' Maskill stopped abruptly and reached for the telephone.

I darted over, ripped it off the desk and dashed it behind me, the cord flying out of its socket.

Maskill snatched his hand away like he'd touched a griddle.

I pointed at him. 'You pimp girls for Ben Siegel.'

He stood up. 'That is—'

I went around the desk and pushed him back into his chair. 'Now you're trying to help him raise money, correct?'

'Who in god's name are you?'

'I'm a friend to two young women you plied with liquor until they thought going to Las Vegas to sell their bodies was a good idea. One of them is dead now, but you probably don't want to hear about that.'

He'd paled to the point it looked like he could vomit.

'Yeah, I know the full story. And you know what else?' I dropped my press card in front of him. 'I can tell it and name your name because I haven't got a damn thing to lose.'

He tilted his chin to stretch his throat and fumbled a cigarette from his jacket pocket. He put the smoke in his mouth and I swiped it away. 'Where do I find Siegel?'

He stared at me, his eyes flaring. 'I don't— I don't—'

'Yes you do, Maskill. You thought it was all fun and games playing gangster and palling around with Siegel; well, this is the other shoe dropping.' I rabbit-punched him in the face.

I heard Lizzie gasp and saw her put her hand over her mouth. I'd surprised myself just as much, not even realising what I was doing until my knuckle met his cheek.

I took a breath, shaking, a combination of shock and rage, trying to bring it all under control again. 'The story's written and ready to print, Nick. I walk out of here empty-handed and it hits the street tomorrow.'

He was holding his face, a mark already rising under his right eye. 'Please, it's not how you think . . .'

My fist was still cocked, but I lowered it a little.

'He has certain materials,' he said. 'Photographs I never knew . . .' He dipped his head and rubbed his eyes with the heel of his hand. 'Oh, god . . .'

I took a step back, looking for somewhere to put my eyes. Another blackmail scam, something I should have reckoned on.

Lizzie drew up beside me. 'Mr Maskill, Benjamin Siegel has a hold over lots of people, but not all of them fold like a house of cards.' She glanced at me, then fixed him with a look. 'Now it's time to do the right thing.'

He didn't look up.

I took the pen he'd been writing with and held it out to him. 'I can make Siegel go away, but only if I know where he is.'

He glanced at Lizzie, at me, at the pen.

'How many other girls did you recruit for him?'

'You owe every last one of them a debt,' Lizzie said.

He shook his head. 'You keep the pen, write this down.' He

dictated an address in Beverly Hills. 'Keep my name out of it, please? I've got two daughters—' He pointed to a framed photograph of two adolescent girls on the wall to his left. 'Please...'

It gave me the opening I needed. 'Then for their sake, you need to go the rest of the way. You'll testify against Siegel when the time comes. Talk to a lawyer now, you'll be able to command a reasonable deal for your co-operation.'

I took the paper and bolted, feeling more disgust than sympathy.

*

I stopped at a payphone on the run to Beverly Hills and called Tanner's office again. No answer. I counted off thirty seconds, called once more, still no answer. I jammed the receiver back in its cradle, the place apparently abandoned. Then I picked it up again, dialled the Bureau's LA field office, routing through switchboard to a voice that didn't give his name.

'Charlie Yates calling for Special Agent Tanner.'

'Hold on a minute.'

I drummed my hand on the top of the payphone's housing.

'Sir, Special Agent Tanner is unavailable.'

'I'll hold. Tell him it's urgent.'

'That won't be possible.'

'What do you mean? Is he there?'

The voice was flat. 'It means he's unavailable, sir.'

I slapped the side of the booth, the picture coming clear: Tanner freezing me out.

'Tell him I'm about to gift wrap Benjamin Siegel for him, so he better take the damn call.'

'I'll pass along the message.'

'No, it's not a message—'

The line was dead.

*

The property was a Spanish-style whitewashed mansion, two wings extending from a central turret-like section, with tall, arched window openings and terracotta-tiled roofs. Dark-coloured drapes were drawn across all the windows and no lights were showing. A statue of a lion stood guard at the top of the driveway, the house number shown at the bottom of its plinth.

I cruised past the place once and carried on to the end of the block, parking on the other side of the street. I turned the engine off and sat in the dark, the feeling that my plan was coming apart.

'Looks empty. How long do we wait?' Lizzie said.

I leaned on the bench seat and twisted around to look at the house.

'What is it?' Lizzie said.

'I'm going to take a look.' I opened the door before I lost my nerve.

'Charlie, wait—' She groped for my hand. 'You could walk right into him.'

'Then I'd have my answer.'

I stepped out then turned around and reached back inside to hand her the ignition key. 'Keep hold of this. Just in case.'

'In case of what? You're not here to confront him, Charlie. Don't lose sight of what we came to do.'

'I'm not. It's a precaution.'

She tossed the key back to me. 'Then you take it. The only way you can be sure I'm safe is if you come back.'

'Liz—'

'No, I mean it. I've seen that look in your eyes before.'

I could tell what she was referring to. I gestured to the big houses along the street. 'This isn't Texarkana and I'm not carrying a gun.'

'It's what's in your head that worries me.'

'I'll be careful.' I made a show of putting the key in my inside pocket. 'I love you.'

*

I crossed the lawn at the front, coming to a balustrade at the top of the gentle slope. It fronted an expansive terrace running along the length of the house. I ducked down and looked along the dark windows, seeing no sign of occupation. A line of trees and bushes in front of the balustrade shielded the terrace from the street; I backed away and used them as cover to move towards the side of the house.

A small carport at the top of the drive led through to the rear of the property. I walked under it but stopped at the far edge when I saw a glow from a window towards the back of the house. I pressed myself against the wall and peered around to see.

I saw it was actually a row of five narrow windows next to each other under an arch. The glow was faint because a drape was partially drawn, but not all the way. I couldn't see inside from my vantage point. I waited, listening, but could hear nothing from inside. Katydids chirruped in bursts, jangling my nerves.

I crossed to the opposite wall of the carport, moving on my

toes. I craned my neck but still couldn't see inside. Concerned that I was more exposed at that angle, I retreated into the shadows.

The windows ran almost to ground level, nixing the thought of crawling over to them to look in. Besides that, anyone inside that room would be able to see me before I got close. Ditto anyone in the neighbouring mansion, one of its windows directly overlooking the lit room.

I stood there, breathing hard but silent. I knew I should go back to the car. I wished I hadn't seen the light, but I couldn't leave there not knowing.

Opposite me there was a side door in the wall adjoining the house. I tried the knob; it turned silently and the door cracked open. I held for two heartbeats that stretched for ever, hearing Lizzie's words and Tanner's silence, then slipped inside.

I was in a large foyer. In the gloom, I could see five doorways leading off of it, the front door to my right and a staircase across from me. Only one of the doors was open, to my left, leading into the room where the light shone. I could just see inside, an ornate reading lamp on a mahogany side table casting a glow that ended well short of my feet.

I took a step forward, expanding my view. A grand piano dominated one corner, flanked by various busts and carvings, the walls adorned with portraits of men I didn't know. From my angle I could only see one half of the room, the far end from where the windows were.

I looked around. From behind the staircase, I'd have a view of the opposite side of the room. I went the long way around, skirting the walls and passing the front door until I was on the far side of the foyer.

As soon as I got there, I could tell there was someone inside. I couldn't see, but I could sense him – that primal instinct that kicks in to alert us to the presence of another. It heightened everything – the smell of fresh-cut flowers and cigar smoke overpowering, the thud of my heartbeat like a war drum.

A floral-pattern sofa ran perpendicular to the windows and I could see one end of it. The man was sitting on the other end, I was sure of it, my view of him blocked by the open door. I stretched my neck as far as I dared, caught a glimpse of the edge of a newspaper being held up. The sound of rustling pages as he straightened it.

I was risking everything to keep myself and my wife alive, and the son of a bitch was reading the *LA Times*.

I moved to the doorway. He must have heard my footsteps and he lowered the paper just as I got sight of him.

Siegel startled, when he saw me. 'Jesus fucking Christ. You?'

He still had the newspaper occupying both hands. Through my rage, I had wherewithal enough to know I was safe only as long as I could see them.

'Me.'

'You must be out of your mind.' He laid the paper on his lap, as calm as if I'd offered to fix him a drink. He was wearing a light brown suit and I couldn't see the telltale bulge of a weapon anywhere.

I knew I should make a run for the car but I couldn't tear myself away. His eyes were almost doleful, his eyebrows naturally sloping downwards from his forehead, but his mouth was a slit.

'You've cost me,' I said.

He raised a hand and I flinched, drawing a smile from him. 'Should've kept your nose out of my business, shouldn't you.'

'I wanted no part of your business. You came for me.'

'How's that, you cocksucker? I'm sitting right here on my sofa.'

'Go to hell.'

He squinted. 'I would've credited you with being in Patagonia by now. What the hell are you doing here?'

The truth was on my lips, but I only realised what it was as I spoke it. 'I wanted to look you in the eye.'

'Knock yourself out.' He raised his other hand, presenting himself. 'I'll piss in yours when you're through.'

I wanted to hit him but couldn't tell if it would raise or lower my chances of staying alive.

'So what now, Ace? You done gazing, gonna ask me to dance?' He uncrossed his legs.

'What now is I walk out. You're finished and you know it. You wouldn't be hiding here in the dark otherwise.'

'Is that a fact?' Before I could move, he reached into the left pocket of his jacket and pulled a snub nose.

He pointed it at my face. 'You saved me paying out on the contract, so I'll do you quick as a favour.'

There was a gunshot and I shut my eyes, hearing a second and third.

I felt no impact. I realised I was still standing. I opened my eyes again and heard another shot, Siegel's face punctured and bleeding. I threw myself to the floor just as another two rang out, each one causing him to jerk.

The room fell silent again but the sound was still reverberating through my head. Siegel was limp on the sofa, his head flopped to one side, blood leaking from his left eye and his mouth. His copy of the *Times* had fallen to the floor, now soaked red.

I checked myself but was unmarked. My whole body was trembling. I looked up and saw the window panes laced with bullet holes. I staggered to my feet, gawping at Siegel. Even if I'd had time, there was no call to check for a pulse.

I took a step towards the doorway, then realised going out through the side door was to run towards the gunman. I froze, glancing over at the window again, wondering if he'd seen me. The open door to the reading room might have concealed me from his view. Staying put my best chance—

I heard the side door being pushed open. Footsteps coming towards me across the foyer.

I glanced at Siegel – the snub nose still in his hand. I ran to the end of the sofa and pried it from his warm fingers. I got it up and trained on the doorway just as Colt Tanner stepped through it.

'Shit—' He dodged backwards, taking cover outside the room. 'Yates, it's me. Put it down.'

My throat rattled in my neck. 'What is—'

He peered around the door. He was holding a rifle across his chest. 'Charlie, put it down. It's over.'

I kept the gun locked on the doorway. 'You killed him.'

He said nothing, making a show of putting his weapon down and standing it against the doorjamb. 'I want to come inside, will you put it away?'

I couldn't feel my arm, could barely speak.

'Charlie, if I meant to shoot you, I would've done. We don't have all night.'

He was right on both counts. I strained to listen for sirens – nothing yet, but surely coming. I brought the gun to my side.

Tanner waited until I'd pointed it to the floor and stepped

inside. 'You did good, Charlie.' He turned his eyes to Siegel, not examining his handiwork so much as surveying the damage.

'What the hell did you do that for?'

He wiped his hand on his trouser leg. 'I thought you'd be the last man to ask me that.'

'I've tracked him down so— You were supposed to arrest him.'

He pointed at Siegel's corpse. 'This is the best way. This is justice.'

I followed the line of his finger, blood running in channels from Siegel's face across his shirt and jacket and onto the sofa, staining everything it touched crimson. 'For who?'

'Don't go weak sister on me now. Come on, I came to get you away from here.'

My pulse surged. 'I'm not going anywhere with you.'

'You want to stay here and wait for the cops?' He gestured to the pistol in my hand.

'You could have taken him, goddammit—'

'Enough. You don't know a fraction of what he's done, but what you do know should tell you this was the only answer. This is why you went to Las Vegas and it's why you came back to LA. This is why you called my offices all those times.'

I tilted my head, wondering how he always knew. 'Why didn't you take my call?'

He closed his eyes and moistened his lips and I knew a lie was coming. The real reason came to me before he could start. 'Deniability,' I said. 'You could claim to know nothing when . . .' I trailed off, seeing the blood and remembering the message I'd left at his office on the way. A message that shattered his deniability – and just as much so if my corpse was found in the same room. *I came to get you away from here.*

I snapped the gun up level with his chest.

He thrust his palms out. 'What the hell is wrong with you?'

'I'm leaving. Get over there in the corner.'

He glanced where I pointed. 'You've lost your mind. That man had a contract on you and your wife, now he's dead. I don't understand your reaction.'

He didn't move, my path to the doorway blocked. Lizzie's voice in my head. 'Trust,' I said.

'Trust?' He looked at me again and scoffed. 'Charlie, how is it you think you killed Winfield Callaway and just walked away?'

The room started spinning at the mention of the name. Winfield Callaway: where it'd all started, back in Texarkana. The man who'd ordered the killing of Lizzie's sister, Alice, to protect his murderous son. The death that had thrown us together.

The man I'd wished dead but hadn't killed.

Tanner tilted his head forward. 'I can't take credit for all that happened there in the aftermath, and I won't claim it was done purely for your benefit – but benefit you did, and I never saw a need to upturn that.'

He was talking about events almost a year before we met. It was nonsensical, improbable; I wanted him to shut up for just a second, just a second so I could think. Words came unbidden from my mouth. 'There was a cover-up . . . it wasn't—'

'Justice was done, Charlie. I know all about Callaway, you don't need to explain. All I ask is for you to keep this close the same way I have for you.'

It would've been so easy to do as he said. Siegel gone, the contract on our lives dead with him. A real chance to start over in LA, if we could just walk away one more time. But everything about his pitch felt wrong. 'I'm leaving, right now. I won't tell a damn person what you did here tonight, all I want is for you to leave me and my wife alone. And for you to get out of my way.'

He lowered his hands to his sides. 'Then we want the same thing. No one's going to miss this son of a bitch.' He circled around in front of me, stationing himself next to the piano. He lifted the lid and tinkled the keys, three high notes. 'I wish you'd rethink my offer, though. Tell me you have a car nearby at least?'

I moved to the doorway, turning as I went to keep the gun on him. 'I can look after myself.' I pulled my jacket sleeve over my hand and snatched up his rifle.

'Charlie, I can't let you have that.'

I backed across the foyer, only turning forward again when he was no longer in sight. I threw the side door open and took off for the car, tossing the rifle onto the lawn as I ran. The first sirens in the air.

CHAPTER TWENTY-SEVEN

Sepulveda Pass took us out of the city. The San Fernando Valley stretched before us, a sprawl of dim pinpricks of light.

I spouted all of it to Lizzie – out of sequence, out of control, her questions bouncing off in my rush to tell it. The part about snatching Siegel's snub nose brought me to a halt – the gun still in my coat pocket. I thought about ditching it, but figured I might need it before the night was out. I handed it to Lizzie and asked her to wipe it clean, eliminating any link from it to Siegel. She tried using the hem of her skirt until she switched to a rag she found in the glove compartment.

At first I planned to just drive. Until news of Siegel's death reached the street, the contract on our heads was still good as far as anyone looking to collect knew. I pushed on north, waiting for the adrenaline to burn off so I could think straight. But as the rush started to wane, I regained clarity of thought enough to realise that if Siegel's neighbours could place our car at the scene, the cops would have a radio alert out for our plate. Getting off the road took priority then.

*

The motel room was eight paces at its widest point. I went back and forth enough times to know. I checked the rear window on each return, overlooking the spot where I'd stashed the car. It was hidden from the highway at the back of the building and halfway obscured by a live oak.

Lizzie sat on the bed hugging her knees to her chest as I went through it again. I was calmer but not calm, searching for answers in my own account.

'I don't understand how he would've gotten involved in Texarkana,' she said.

I was standing against the wall and I rested my head back. 'Maybe one of the local agencies called in the Bureau. God knows.'

'Tell me again what he said about it.'

I rubbed my forehead, verbatim recall eluding me. 'He implied he'd orchestrated the cover-up. That he'd been protecting me since.'

'That cannot ... Do you believe that?'

'No. I don't know. He said—' This memory came to me complete. 'He asked how I thought I'd walked away from killing Winfield Callaway.'

She stared at me in silence. 'But it wasn't you, why ...?'

'William Tindall said the same to me.' Tindall – Siegel's lieutenant in Hot Springs; the man I'd helped to bring down, inadvertently sparking Siegel's vendetta against me. 'Join the dots – Tindall to Siegel to Tanner. How can that be a coincidence?'

She buried her face deeper in her knees.

'How does he always know our movements?' I said. 'At every step he knew ...'

'You're certain you didn't speak Siegel's address when you called his office?'

I shook my head. 'Certain.'

An edgy silence fell, each of us lost in our own thoughts.

At length Lizzie said, 'I can't believe he's dead. I never ima-gined feeling this way.'

'What way?'

Her voice was muffled. 'I thought I'd be relieved, if it ever came to pass.' She looked up at me again. 'Is there any chance Tanner's good to his word?'

'That he's looking out for us?'

She nodded but turned away.

'You saw through him first, Liz. Way before me.'

I dragged a wooden chair from the desk and collapsed onto it. I looked at my wife and wondered how many more nights like this she could endure.

'What I don't understand is if he really wanted you dead, why did he stop Siegel from shooting you?' She covered her mouth when she said it, shocked at speculating on my killing. 'Charlie, I'm sorry—'

'It's okay.' I gave her a grim smile. 'I hadn't thought about that.' I planted my elbows on my knees to lean on them. 'I think it's the message I left with his colleague. If the cops found me there dead, it would incriminate him in Siegel's killing. Or at least link him to it. Without me there, it most probably gets written up as a gangland hit. Same reason he didn't shoot me himself.'

She let out a breath, thinking. 'It seems so tenuous a link. That supposes he meant to take you away after and . . .' She swallowed. 'Surely it would've been easier to kill you both and deny your message ever reached him? In fact, less than that; you never left the address, so he could claim your message was irrel-evant. And even that is only if anyone ever thought to suspect him in the first place – and why would they?'

I started to rebut it but realised there was sense in what she said.

'The risk in killing you after the fact is huge compared to something so easily dismissed.'

It dangled the prospect I'd got it wrong. Which meant he'd kept me alive for some other purpose.

CHAPTER TWENTY-EIGHT

A few hours alone with my thoughts brought questions.

At some point we'd exhausted all talk, and Lizzie had passed out in her clothes on top of the covers. I sat on the bed next to her, a pencil and scrap of paper in my hand, writing them all down by moonlight, ideas beginning to coalesce into answers.

*

When the clock reached eight the next morning, I ran to the motel payphone and called Trip Newland.

'You gotta be walking tall this morning,' he said.

I gripped the receiver tighter. 'What?'

'Ben Siegel got whacked last night. It's all over the wires. Turn the radio on.'

'Yeah—' I breathed again. 'Yeah, I heard it.'

'You don't sound so happy.'

'I need to know something. Who gave you the tip that Siegel was back in LA?'

'I don't— Why's it matter?'

'Humour me.'

'I don't remember, it was just talk—'

'You told me before no one was talking to you.'

'It was a figure of speech.'

'Newland—'

'Hold on, the last time you got hold of one of my sources he didn't last five minutes.'

'Whitey Lufkins,' I said. 'That's who told you, isn't it?' The same man who'd sold me out to Siegel, and a natural first stop for a legman finding his feet in a new town.

'How did you—'

'Get hold of him and set up a meeting.' I glanced at my watch. 'Midday. Don't breathe a word about this call, if he hears my name he won't show. Front up whatever cash it takes to make it happen.'

'What the hell is going on? You sound like a crazy man.'

'Something else: I need to know where Henry Booker called you from when he gave you Diana Desjardins' name.'

'No clue.'

'I don't believe you. You were holding something back when we first met and I know what it was.'

'He called me, he gave me his home number, we talked one more time before you got him killed.'

'It wasn't me got him killed, but I have an idea who did. He gave you his home number but that's not where he called you from, was it?'

He went quiet.

'Trip, an anonymous source calls you with a tip like that, the first thing you'd have done is called the operator and get a fix on where the call originated.'

Still silent.

'He called you from the house phone at the Flamingo, right?'

All the colour had drained from his voice. 'I'm not saying another word until you tell me what's going on.'

'Make the meeting. I'll call you back in two hours for a location.'

CHAPTER TWENTY-NINE

For the second time in my life, I stepped into Wilt's diner to meet Lufkins.

I wondered why he'd chosen the same venue, whether he thought he had some stroke there because of what he'd done to me, affiliating himself to Siegel's outfit in the process. Or whether he was just a sucker for low-rent joints.

He clocked me just as I came up to his booth.

'Oh, shit—'

He shot out of his seat. I took a five spot from my pocket and planted it on his chest, holding him in place. 'Keep quiet and sit down. I'm going to ask you two questions and then we both walk out of here for keeps.'

He was in a half-crouch, folded around the table, only his eyes moving to look down at the money. 'Newland said fifty.'

'How about we call it five and you keep the use of your legs?'

'Not your style, Yates.' I could feel him trembling. His breath smelled raw, black coffee on top of liquor.

'You sold me out to Siegel's outfit when I came asking about those missing girls months ago. Start there.'

He glanced around. The counterman was looking over, wiping a plate on his apron.

'Sit down,' I said. 'Make nice.'

He lowered himself into the seat. The counterman looked away.

'I swear to god, Whitey, I've got bigger problems than a grudge against you. Answer my questions and I'm gone.'

He took the note from me and flattened it in front of him. 'There was talk ... Ben sent the word out that if anyone came asking about those two broads, to call his men immediately. I had no idea what was ... I figured it was some dame he was sweet on.'

Siegel knowing about my search way back then; no one apart from Lizzie knew I was looking for them at that stage – or so I'd thought. Now I knew there'd been another: Tanner; the name I kept coming back to. The explanation shattering, impossible—

'Second question: who tipped you off about Siegel being back in LA two days ago?'

The muscles in his throat contracted. He was shaking his head.

'Answer me.'

He kept shaking it.

I picked up a fork, gripped it like a dagger, horizontal just above the table. 'I swear to Christ I'll put this through your hand—'

He pressed himself as far back into the seat as he could, as if he wanted to dissolve. He was staring at me like he didn't dare look away. 'What the hell has gotten into you?'

'One name and I walk.'

He stared, his eyes wide, unblinking. 'I don't know the guy.'

'Name.'

'Yates, please—'

'NAME.' I reached for his wrist.

'Belfour. He's a cop.'

My jaw locked up. I dropped the fork and looked away from him, seeing the walls crawling. 'No, he's not. Take my advice and disappear.'

CHAPTER THIRTY

I tore back to the motel to pick up Lizzie, the picture almost clear to me but still not believing it. The outline terrifying enough.

I parked at the back, Lizzie watching for me from the window. I signalled for her to come to the car while I went to the payphone.

I was out of breath when I shoved the nickel into the slot. Newland picked up right away.

'What are you hearing about Siegel's murder?' I said. The radio newscast in the car was speculating about an assassination by rival mobsters – but that was always the first story the cops would've put out.

'Did you get to Lufkins?' he said.

'Yes. Tell me about Siegel.'

'No way. You sound like you just watched your own funeral. Something's going on with you and I want in.'

'Believe me, you don't.'

'Siegel's dead. Moe Rosenberg's back from the dead. And you turned into a mind reader—'

'Say that again.'

'Yeah, I wondered if you'd heard about Rosenberg.'

The missing piece. 'Tell me.'

'You go first.'

I couldn't even think where to start. Unproven, unassailable, no part of it I could break off to divert him with. 'If I'm right, you're in as much danger as me. Unless I know all of it, I can't protect you.'

The line fuzzed as he exhaled hard.

'Whatever it is I'll find out soon enough,' I said. 'The best way to protect yourself is give me this head start. This goes way beyond a damn story, but if there's any of us left alive at the end of it, you can have it all.'

The line was silent. I looked at the highway, expecting cars to come screeching off it any second.

Then he said, 'Moe Rosenberg walked into the Flamingo this morning and took control.'

CHAPTER THIRTY-ONE

It was a short run to Lockheed Air Terminal, just north of Burbank. As hard as I was driving, my mind was moving faster, seeing all the ways I'd been used. An unwitting accomplice to the grand plan; why I'd been chosen still murky, but the result plain to see. Lizzie barely spoke after I laid my theory out, her face gaunt and pale.

We made one stop en route to the airfield, clearing out our checking account to ensure she'd have funds to travel. The rest of the way, we thrashed out the details of what came next. Her part of the plan was as important as mine, and carried almost as much risk. But there was a calm determination in her voice as we spoke.

At the terminal, we purchased a one-way ticket on the next departure – an American Airlines nonstop to Chicago Midway. From there she'd be able to connect to New York. 'I'll call Sal to let him know to expect you.' Sal Pecorino – the man who'd saved my job at the *Examiner*.

She wrapped her arms around me. When she let go, I passed her my papers – everything I'd written in Iowa and since; my life for the last year and a half. 'I'll join you as soon as I can – three or four days.'

She wrapped her fingers around one end but didn't take their weight. 'I can't believe we're still in this. Even with him dead . . .'

'We're almost there.'

She closed her eyes and nodded. She placed the papers in her bag, then she took my tie and kissed me on the lips. 'Three days.'

CHAPTER THIRTY-TWO

I drove out of Lockheed and straight to Las Vegas. Took me six hours with two stops: one to fill up on gas, the other to test fire Siegel's revolver. A barren stretch of desert provided the opportunity; the weapon worked fine, the retort echoing off the broiling highway.

The closer I came, the more doubts surfaced in my mind. Knowing Lizzie was on her way to the other side of the country gave me strength. If things went bad and I didn't make it out, my papers would give Sal enough to carry out his own investigations. There was nothing close to proof in them, but they'd leave him with dozens of avenues to pursue. The names were all there; it'd take him years, but he'd find a way to tell the story – my story: a coast-to-coast web of organised crime groups, working in concert; collusion between those groups and law enforcement agencies at all levels; racketeering proceeds funding developments in Las Vegas; cover-ups, kickbacks, murders. We'd worked together long enough at the *Examiner* that I trusted him to do what he could – and to do right by Lizzie with any money that came of it.

But with that realisation came certainty of my own responsibility.

*

The parking lot of the Flamingo was half-full. I parked on the kerb just along from the entrance and stepped out. The desert couldn't have been more different to how I'd experienced it before; the sun was beating down, the reflection off the other cars' chromework blinding. I shielded my eyes and put my other hand in my jacket pocket to triple-check the snub nose was there.

Going inside, the place was transformed. The drop cloths were gone, replaced by patterned walls and plush fittings. As hot as it was outside, air conditioning made it cool almost to the point of being cold. The lobby buzzed with guests, a queue of people ten-deep at the check-in line. All the chairs had been upholstered in hot pink, even the barstools topped with the same.

I moved through to the casino, the one part that had been operational on my first visit there. I watched for Moe Rosenberg, needing him not to see me before I made the call. There were enough bodies milling around to hide my presence.

There was a house telephone on a wall near the front of the room. I went to it and examined the casing – two small dents showing and a pen mark next to the dial. A telephone that'd been in use longer than most in there – maybe as far back as last winter, when Henry Booker was helping to build the joint. It didn't matter too much if I used the exact same one he had; the line I would be calling was the key, but if it was the same, there'd be a certain elegance to the symmetry.

I lifted the handset and asked for Mr Rosenberg's office. 'Tell him it's Charlie Yates calling.'

There was a pause, and then his voice. 'You have to be ribbing me.'

'Nice deal you worked out for yourself, Moe. Keys to the kingdom.'

'You're on the casino line? Stay where you are.'

'Sure. But one thing: you'll want to come see me for yourself.'

'It'll be a pleasure.'

'Not when you hear what I have to tell. Special Agent Colt Tanner has your telephones tapped. All of them. He's listening to every damn word you say.'

I hung up and steadied myself against the wall, my heart coming out of my chest.

I walked to the middle of the casino, craps and blackjack tables around me, at least fifty people within twenty feet – as close to safe as I could get. I waited for him to show.

It wasn't long before I saw him bustle through the crowd. As he drew up to me, he hollowed his cheeks sucking on his cigar, three hard puffs in succession.

'He played you, Rosenberg. He played all of us.'

'You're the dumbest cocksucker I ever knew, coming here.'

I was shaking my head. 'You had Gilardino execute Henry Booker for blabbing to the press and putting a name on the girl you killed – Diana Desjardins. Think about how you came to learn that was him, and so fast, too.'

'That the best you got?'

'You didn't even know it came from Tanner, did you? Ask whoever it was brought you Booker's name, I bet the trail leads back to Tanner – or a cop named Belfour. Even his cut out might not know his real identity.'

He deadpanned it, but the lack of comeback was its own response.

I stole a breath. 'Booker's mistake was to call in his tip from here. Maybe he did it on his break. Tanner was listening so he made sure you found out. A little favour, something to cash in later, perhaps.' I kept my hands in plain sight, fighting the urge to brush against the pocket holding the gun. 'Another man might've got off with a beating, but someone on the payroll talking out of turn that way? You couldn't let that slide. The poor bastard probably had no idea it was your toes he'd stepped on.'

He came closer to me. 'How's Mrs Yates?'

I held my ground. 'She's on vacation.'

He lifted his chin. 'Hope she travels safe. Let's go to my office.'

'How long have you been working with Tanner?'

He stared at me, the muscles in his cheeks pulsing, glancing over his shoulder as if to check who was close enough to hear.

'What did you have to offer him to help you knock off Siegel?' I held my arms out to gesture at a room dripping with money. 'An off the books share in this place? A promise you'd snitch the bosses?'

He tossed his cigar into a standing ashtray, anger coming off him like a furnace. 'Come with me.' He took my arm but I snapped it away.

'You still don't see it, do you? You thought you were using Tanner, and all the while he's using you. You didn't know about the wiretaps, and now you do, so that leaves you a decision to make: do you go after Tanner for double-crossing you, or do you tell your bosses in New York what he's been doing and try to limit the damage? Not a comfortable set of choices. And don't forget, there's someone else who's wondering what you're going to do next.'

His face gave nothing away, but I could see a sheen of sweat at his hairline.

I pointed to the telephone I'd called his office from, and he glanced back to look. When he turned to me again I said, 'Colt Tanner just heard me tell you about his precious bugs. I think his ambitions go way beyond you, Moe, all the way East. How long do you think he'll chance leaving you alive?'

His whole head was shaking. 'I'll outlive you, I know that.' He said it so soft, it was like he was already dying.

'He has a knack of turning up real fast when he needs to,' I said. 'Better get moving.'

I patted him on the shoulder and started to move off, and as he raised his hand to stop me, I tightened my grip and smashed my knee into his balls. I held onto him as he doubled over and whispered in his ear, 'From my wife.'

I let go of him and he collapsed to all fours, and I was already running when the first gasp went up at the sight of him hitting the floor. My hand was wrapped around the gun in my pocket. I couldn't even feel my legs; through the casino, through the lobby, out into the parking lot. I threw myself into the car, gunned the engine and left the Flamingo in my dust.

CHAPTER THIRTY-THREE

I kept my promise and made it to New York in three days, sleeping in the car and stopping only for gas, food and coffee.

I drove straight to Sal's apartment block and ran up the steps. I'd called ahead before I crossed into Manhattan, letting them know to expect me, so I'd barely pressed the buzzer before the door flew open and Lizzie shouted my name. Sal stood behind her, beaming, a little heavier in the face a year and a half on. 'It's good to see you, Chuck.'

*

News of Moe Rosenberg's death emerged a day after I arrived. According to the reports that made the papers, an unidentified gunman had opened fire on his car as he arrived at a bank in Las Vegas, hitting him in four places and killing him instantly. Analysis of bullets recovered from the scene suggested an M1 carbine had been employed in the murder, the same weapon as used in the recent slaying of Benjamin 'Bugsy' Siegel. Some of the reports made mention of speculation by police sources that Rosenberg's assassination was linked to, or perhaps even in retaliation for, that of Siegel – citing an underworld rumour that the two men had recently had a falling out.

Clark County Sheriff Robert Lang, heading up the investigation, was quoted in one piece as saying, 'The machinations of racketeers being as they are, we may never know the true motivations of the men who carried out this attack. But my department will explore every avenue to see justice served.' The story went on to note that no suspects had so far been identified.

I imagined the case file in his top drawer, the spine barely creased.

*

I spent two days taking Lizzie on a grand tour of New York City. We moved as if in a daze, two people trying to make like any other sightseers, the morning after having a death sentence lifted. She took in Liberty, the Empire State Building and the Brooklyn Bridge with empty eyes; the contrast was so jarring, it was if we'd stepped through the looking glass into someone else's life. I wondered if we could ever go back to being the people we'd been before.

On the second day, we were on the deck of the Staten Island Ferry with Manhattan floating slowly away from us, when she turned to me and said, 'You didn't really send me here for the reason you told me, did you?'

My pitch to her back in LA – that she should travel to New York and if she didn't hear from me inside of twenty-four hours, to tell Sal about Tanner's wiretapping, so he could get a tell-all message to Rosenberg's bosses. 'What makes you say that?'

'You meant to have me out of harm's way.'

I scratched my top lip. 'It served two purposes. It was an insurance policy.'

She stared at me without saying anything. She laid her hand

on my arm and faced the railing again, turning her eyes to a sail-boat jutting through the whitecaps in the harbour.

I saw no call to mention that I'd briefed Sal to do no such thing.

*

For my part, I thought obsessively about what was coming. One last hurdle to clear – but maybe the biggest. My instinct told me I'd walk out of it alive, and it worried me more that the cost of doing so would be too great to bear.

Because at the same time I'd called Lizzie and Sal to let them know of my arrival, I'd placed a call to the FBI office in Los Angeles and left a message for Colt Tanner – telling him I'd be in Times Square at noon three days hence.

*

I stood with my back to the too-bright Pepsi-Cola sign and watched the lights blink and dance all around me. I'd chosen the location because it was so public, but the resemblance to Las Vegas became apparent now, and I wondered if that'd been in the back of my mind somewhere.

It was three minutes after twelve. I had no idea if he would turn up – but if he didn't, it'd give me an answer of sorts about my future safety. Anything was better than being left wondering; back in the same situation as when Siegel was gunning for us, just a different tormentor now.

I couldn't pinpoint why I was certain he wouldn't kill me on sight. It had something to do with Lizzie's reasoning about his choice to keep me alive on the night he shot Siegel. Afforded three days' driving time to think about it, I couldn't shake the sense that he'd showed himself, when he could've just ditched out unseen, because he wanted me to know what he was capable of.

At ten past, I settled on giving him another five minutes. I lived each one of them a dozen times over.

He never showed.

CHAPTER THIRTY-FOUR

It was too hot in the desert to drag matters out. But it needed to be done.

Lizzie was holding the flowers, a small bunch we'd picked up coming through town. The creased photograph of Julie Desjardins and Nancy Hill that had been with me from the start was in my hands.

We made the same short walk from the highway that we'd taken before, to the patch of stony ground where Julie Desjardins' body had been discovered. There was nothing to mark the spot, no way to even know exactly where it was. The county coroner may have arranged to have her buried somewhere, if they hadn't cremated her, but I didn't want to leave my remembrance on an anonymous grave. Somehow this seemed closer to her memory.

We came to a stop. Lizzie crouched to set the flowers down.

I placed the photograph on the ground next to them and put a rock on top to keep it from blowing away. Never knowing who she really was. A family shorn of a daughter, left to always wonder. The kind of hell my wife spoke of.

I stayed crouched. 'I'm sorry.'

Lizzie put her hand on my shoulder.

After a moment I stood up again, seeing the Flamingo in the distance. A cruel monument to her passing. The parking lot was full.

I looked away, a brilliant blue sky stretching forever above us, thinking about all the secrets I was keeping and the men I protected with my silence. All the dead looking to me for retribution, for my failures and otherwise. A debt that could never be paid – but I'd go to my grave trying.

I took Lizzie's hand and started retracing our steps. Los Angeles was still hours away.

Another car pulled in behind ours, a rising cloud of dust in its wake. A grey Dodge—

'Charlie . . .'

I moved in front of her and stopped.

The driver's door opened and Colt Tanner got out. He laid his arm on the roof, squinting at us.

I glanced at the Flamingo, weighing if she could make a break for it.

Tanner started towards us, something in his right hand. Not a gun.

I reached for the snub nose in my pocket, keeping it just out of sight.

When he was ten yards away, he called out. 'I'm not armed, Charlie, and you're not about to draw on a Federal agent. Let's start there.'

He kept coming, and I saw it was an envelope he was holding.

I studied him, feeling my neck flush as he closed. 'Is that what you are?'

'Don't come at me like you have a grievance.'

I pointed my finger in his face. 'You were in league with them the whole time. You gave us up to them when we were at the Breakers Motel. You gave them Trent Bayless. You gave them Henry Booker—'

'Christ, you want to hang the Lindbergh Baby on me as well? Listen to yourself.'

I swiped my hand away. 'I saw through you, too. Soon as I saw that photo of us at the Breakers, I knew you were rotten and I talked myself out of it—'

'When I showed up to bust your ass out of jail? Or when I showed up to save your ass at the ranch?'

'Go to hell. You came to that ranch for Rosenberg, he called you there – that's the only way to make sense of it. That was how you cemented your pact. You're a mobster with a badge—'

'You're not possessed of all the facts, Charlie, and you're fitting them to a narrative that doesn't work. Henry Booker was a degenerate with statutory rape jackets going back years. Bayless was a queer, you knew that. However they came to meet their ends, if you asked me to trade their lives for Ben Siegel and Moe Rosenberg? I'd do it and sleep like a baby.'

I was gritting my teeth hard enough to crack. 'Don't pretend this was all some grand plan. Don't insult—'

'It's a war, Charlie. You take casualties.'

'Like Julie Desjardins?'

He'd started to say something but stopped with his mouth ajar.

'She'd be alive but for you,' I said.

He closed his eyes and took a breath. 'That was unfortunate.'

I waited, stole a glance at Lizzie, standing beside me now.

When he kept his silence, I said, 'That's all you've got to say? You must've known where they were all along.'

'My operation was barely aware of that aspect of Siegel's dealings. It wasn't a high priority, I had no idea lives were at risk. And you're wrong, I didn't know where they were keeping them.'

'You lying son of a bitch.'

He waved his hand as if he was swatting away a fly. 'Siegel and Rosenberg are dead. I thought I'd find you in better spirits.'

'You were expecting gratitude?'

'No, but I didn't expect to find you mourning them either. I think you're coming to realise something about yourself, Charlie.' He looked out across the desert.

'I didn't call you to have my head shrunk.'

He turned to me again. 'They both of them deserved to die, and you can't be at peace with it because now you're empty. You live for the chase, Charlie: you could've bargained for my help in finding those girls when we first talked in LA. You chose not to, so don't delude yourself you gave a damn about them. I bet you'd have preferred to never find them so you'd always have your doomed search – someplace to put all that guilt you carry. The same with Siegel and Rosenberg.'

I shook my head, trying not to show hesitation. 'Must've stung to have to off your business partner that way.'

He narrowed his eyes. 'Now we get to it. That's why you called me, isn't it? You wanted to know if my feelings are hurt.'

'That's not how I'd put it—'

'But it's right.' A thin smile crossed his face, looking as if it was something he was trying for the first time. 'You didn't sing to any of the bosses in New York—'

'You don't—'

'You didn't, I'd know. That's good. Smart move going there – make sure you had my attention.'

I looked him dead in the eye. 'I've lived under the sword

long enough. If you're coming for me, now's your chance. Otherwise you walk away and leave me and my wife the hell alone.'

The smile disappeared and he held my stare. 'Tell me one thing: how did you figure out about the bugs?'

I wondered if that was all he really wanted to know. The truth was, his mistaken belief that I'd killed Winfield Callaway was what sparked the notion; a rumour that'd spread through the criminal fraternity that he'd picked up on – but how? Seemed unlikely someone would tell him direct, so it had to be he was overhearing their chatter. Once I'd tested the thought, it made sense of his ability to show up out of the blue. Lizzie's suspicion that he was already in Las Vegas when she called him to bust me out of jail was almost certainly right; my guess was the foreman at the Flamingo made a call on one of the house lines to warn someone in Siegel's outfit I'd shown up at the site – and Tanner was listening.

I stayed silent while I thought about all this, and wondered if he'd try to force it out of me.

Instead, he patted me on the shoulder. 'No matter. You played a bum hand well. The way you compromised Rosenberg was ingenious, and it got you what you wanted.'

'What did he buy you off with, Tanner?'

'Buy me? Not even close.'

'You manoeuvred him into Siegel's seat.'

He took a deep breath and sighed. 'Let me ask you this: you know how you win a fight against two grizzlies?'

I stared at him, silent again.

'You don't,' he said. 'You make them fight each other and you pick off the survivor.'

I threw my hand up. 'I can't listen to this horseshit—'

'It worked, didn't it? You played your part, be proud.'

'Why?' I grabbed his lapel. 'Why me?'

'You got yourself into this, I just—'

'No, don't lie to my goddamn face. You were the only one knew I was looking for those girls, you set me up for Siegel to find.'

He looked down, feigning chagrin. 'You were the perfect vessel to stir the pot. Siegel wanted you dead so bad but Moe kept counselling against it, knowing what a pain in the ass you'd be if he could keep running you into him. He just didn't figure on you outmanoeuvring him as well. Like I said, I'm impressed – and that's why you have nothing to fear from me. I knew you'd be useful all the way back in Texarkana.'

'I don't want a goddamn thing to do with you.'

He tapped the envelope against the flat of his hand. 'That's not how these things work, Charlie. You're in the life, now, it's where you belong.' He passed it to me. 'Go back to Los Angeles. Cool your head in the ocean, we'll talk when the time's right. My only condition is you don't disclose my methods to anyone else. That would necessitate a swift end to our agreement.' He pointed to the envelope by way of an explanation and walked away whistling 'Yankee Doodle'.

I waited till he was in his car and then tore it open. Inside was a single photograph.

It showed two women talking on the small porch of a snow-covered house in Iowa, Lizzie and I just visible on the edge of the shot.

ACKNOWLEDGEMENTS

My sincere thanks to everyone who has contributed to the creation of this book, and in particular: Angus Cargill, my exceptional editor, whose suggestions and encouragement never fail to improve the manuscript. Jane Gregory, and all the team at Gregory & Co., for taking me under your wing. Lauren Nicoll, for endless enthusiasm and tireless dedication in getting my books into readers' hands. Mark Burborough, Oliver Wheatley, Jon O'Donnell, James White, Tim Caira, Emma Callaghan and Tarun Naipaul, for your incredible generosity and support.

All the bloggers, readers and reviewers who have championed Charlie Yates with such amazing passion – in particular Liz Barnsley, Victoria Goldman, Joy Kluver, Gordon Mcghie, Christine Elizabeth, Susan Heads, Kate Moloney, Pete Savage, Anne Cater, Janet Emson, David Odeen, Andrew Durston, Dave Graham, Andrew Hill and Linda Boa (with apologies to anyone I've forgotten to mention.) All the crew at CS: you know who you are, and why you're here. Katherine Armstrong and Karen Sullivan for your amazing friendship and advice.

And most of all, my family, for letting me do something that I love.